BLOCK PARTY
5K1

BLOCK PARTY

5K1

DIPLOMATIC IMMUNITY

BOOK TWO

AL-SAADIQ BANKS

True 2 Life Publications Presents:
Block Party 5k1

Author: Al-Saadiq Banks
Contact Information
True 2 Life Publications
P. O. Box 8722
Newark NJ 07108

Email: alsaadiqbanks@aol.com
Twitter: @alsaadiq
Instagram: @alsaadiqbanks

www.True2LifeProductions.com

THE NEXT DAY

SMOKE STANDS IN the Wendy's parking lot here on West Market Street. His eyes scan the lot, very alert. Inside his pocket he grips his gun, aimed at the man who is walking toward him. They've met here as a result of the man's phone call to Smoke.

Smoke has known this man for years but he wouldn't necessarily call him a friend. They're both from the same slimeball circuit which means Smoke would never trust him. They've made a few petty dollars together in the past as well as done some dirty business together. One thing Smoke knows about him is he won't bust a grape in a fruit fight. Although he won't do anything with his own hands his danger is altogether different.

He's sneaky and crafty which is why Smoke keeps one eye on him and the other on the parking lot. Smoke will never allow him in his car and he will never get into a car with him. This man is famous for connecting the dots and pulling the strings that have caused many men their lives. He weaves the perfect situations and everybody gets away without a trace. Not even the streets have a clue of the murders that are a result of his work. He's quite paranoid so he keeps his business to himself so it never comes back to haunt him.

The man looks around sneaky like as he walks toward Smoke. Smoke aims his gun at the man's chest inside his pocket. Smoke is prepared to fire at the first sign of anything peculiar. He peeks around wondering where the man has parked and sees not a trace of the car that he's gotten out of. That's more of a reason not to trust him or this meeting. He finally stands before Smoke. He extends his hand. As Smoke reaches to reciprocate the handshake he peeks around cautiously.

This man is referred to as 'Super Blood' to those that know him. His pride in being Blood can be sensed from many miles away. In 2015 he's still stuck in the old ways of gang banging. The red Yankee hat on his head, his jeans with the red stitching and the red bandana hanging from his back pocket displays one of two things; either he's a wanna-be Blood or a Blood stuck in a time capsule.

Smoke grips his hand. "What's popping, Blood," the man says very animated-like as he begins to do their signature handshake. Smoke grips his hand tightly, interrupting the handshake.

Agitation covers Smoke's face. "Ain't no need for all that, bruh. Keep that shit tucked. We supposed to be on the low," Smoke says as he looks around to see who could be possibly be watching them. "What's the deal though?"

Super Blood looks around before speaking like what he's about to say is top secret. "I got something for you," he says speaking out of the side of his mouth. "You know the streets talk and I keep my ears wide open. I heard about the war between y'all and the broad, Mother Nature."

Smoke stands in somewhat of amazement. He wonders how he knows this. He also wonders who else may know this. "What war?" he asks trying to throw him off.

"Word on the street is the war has been balled on," he says purposely avoiding the c in called. He's so old school Blood that he doesn't use words with the letter C in them. "Some information that I'm sure you ban use bame through my ears."

"What's that?" Smoke asks curiously.

"Dig this, my uncle some old school stickup nigga. Bame home a few years ago and left the streets alone. He drive a bab but his ears stay to the ground, you know? He be putting me on mad little stings. Motherfuckers think he just a regular bab driver, not knowing his eyes be open to everything. He told me he drive this same nigga home every night and they got type tight. He was just asking me about dude to see if I heard of him. Bum to find out it's the nigga, Wesson."

Smoke is dizzy from trying to understand his language. Wesson is the one word that sticks out. "Wesson?"

"Yeah, Mother Nature's lil pup. He don't trust nobody to drive him home at night but he trust my uncle because they built a little rapport. When I heard that I thought of you. I figured you ban use that information to your advantage and bapitalize off that."

Smoke stands quietly just observing the man. He wonders if he can trust him on this or if this is one of his capers. "Why though? What made you think of me?" he asks bluntly.

"Just on the strength of me and you. We always been alright and if it was the other way around I would hope you would put me on," he says staring Smoke directly in the eyes. "Ain't nothing in it for me. Give me the word and I will get all the details of where he live and everything."

Smoke thinks it over and although he realizes this is a risk he's willing to give it a shot anyway. Smoke nods his head up and down. "Blood, you know I fucks with you, right? You know if this go anyway other than what you're telling me shit gone get crazy, right?"

"Bruh, come one. Have I ever steered you wrong? I'm surprised that you think I would be on some grease-ball shit with you. We go too far back. I respect you to the fullest and think the respect is mutual."

"Of course it is. I'm just letting you know. You know I don't bite my tongue."

"And that's what I respect about you the most, Blood. I'm gone hit you as soon as I put it all together," he says as he reaches for Smoke's hand. They lock hands and he attempts to go through the whole handshake. Smoke snatches away with agitation.

Super Blood steps away without another word. Smoke makes his way toward his car. He keeps his eye on Super Blood. Just as he reaches his car he looks over his shoulder and Super Blood has disappeared like a ghost.

Smoke gets into his car and analyzes the situation before pulling off. Pulling this off will put him ahead of the game. To knock off one of Mother Nature's strongest pups will leave her at a huge disadvantage. Without her right hand she will be an easier target. This victory will leave him in good standing with Manson and that's the ultimate goal.

70

DAYS LATER

MANSON LAYS BACK in the passenger's seat of Pebbles' truck suffering from jet-lag while Hamza sits comfortably in the backseat. Steam can be felt coming from the driver's seat. Her attitude stems from the fact that she didn't even know that Manson left the country until he called her to pick them up. She's sat quietly for twenty minutes fighting the urge to chew him out

"Motherfuckers taking trips outta the country," she mumbles under her breath just loud enough for Manson to hear her. "Life must be good," she snickers with sarcasm. Manson pretends to not hear her at all. "Wish I could take trips out the country but I got a son fighting for his freedom and been spending every dime I make to help him," she says a little more audible.

She doesn't look his way once. "Do 15 years by a nigga side, you would think the first trip he takes would be with her. Since when men start taking trips out the country together anyway. That's some type weirdo shit if you ask me."

Manson looks up for the first time. "Nobody asked you though," he says rather sternly. Hamza sits back staring out of the window, pretending to not hear a thing but his discomfort is evident.

Before she can offer a rebuttal, Manson sits on the edge of his seat. The look in his eyes says it all yet he backs it with words. "You see company in that backseat?" She sees the severity in his eyes yet the rebel in her won't allow her to submit. She continues on but only mumbling wherein he can't hear her.

Pebbles pulls in front of Hamza's store and hits the power locks without even putting the truck into park. Hamza gets right out, feeling as if he's

worn out his welcome. As he makes his way to the back of the truck Manson gets out as well. They shuffle the luggage around in the hatch until he has all of his belongings.

"I apologize for her," Manson says with sincerity.

Hamza flashes a smile. "No need to. No worries at all. Well, not exactly. The only worries we have is executing the plans we made overseas and putting them into effect," he says with a wink of an eye. "That's my only worry."

"Don't worry about that because I'm not," Manson says as he reaches for Hamza's handshake." "We are gonna take over the world."

Hamza makes his way to the store and Manson gets back into the passenger's seat. Pebbles doesn't give him the time to even sit down before she starts back at him. "You spending money going out of the country and shit, I hope you got the rest of that money for your son."

"Don't you ever for the rest of your life disrespect me in front of company," he says sternly.

Pebbles doesn't offer a rebuttal. She just mashes the gas pedal speeding recklessly through the airport. They ride in silence for minutes before she speaks again. "And that lawyer you got for him, I don't know about him. I been calling him for days with no answer. Finally he got back to my yesterday with barely any news."

"Listen, stop calling him, aggravating him and shit. Let him do what he have to do. The money has been paid and now it's all on him. Let him work."

"You're so fucking nonchalant like your fucking son's life ain't on the line!"

"Listen, I have total faith in him. That man got the lethal injection and all that time overturned for me. I have no choice but to believe in him. Leave him alone and let him work."

"I'm gonna leave him alone but if our son don't get out of this mess, I'm blaming you!"

ONE HOUR LATER

Manson and Pebbles steamy argument led to an even more fiery one. Her disrespect and finger pointing in his face almost led to violence but Manson figured out a better way to handle her. He hasn't been intimate with her since he's been home and realized that is exactly what she needs to calm her emotions and suppress her anger toward him.

Manson had to dig deep in his bag of tricks to find the cure to her anger and rage. Pebbles is so used to being in control and dominating every situation that she's grown accustomed to it and deep in her heart she feels as if she's the boss of every situation. Manson had to take that power and sense of dominance from her.

This very moment Pebbles lays sprawled across the bed bonded by straight jacket. This old straightjacket Manson used to use for torture during his robberies many years ago is now being used for pleasure. With restricted movement of her arms, she sways her head from side to side as she grips him tightly in between her thighs. The deeper he strokes her the tighter she squeezes him in attempt to prevent him from going any deeper.

The long deep strokes are not strokes of pain. It's all pleasure but it's the lack of control that frustrates her gravely. His stroking evolves into pounding. He power-drives her with deep concentration. Long and deep strokes fill her up in entirety.

He shortens the strokes and drops the jackhammer on her. She cries tears of joy as he pounds away. Pebbles opens her legs wide giving him free range to please her in totality and he does. The more inviting her legs become the slower he goes.

His wrath causes her to heave a euphoric sigh. The tempo switches and with short impactful thrusts he bangs away all of her frustration. She growls like a ferocious lion but underneath the loud roar the purring of her kitty can be heard faintly.

At her height, Manson pulls himself out of her. All motion stops leaving her yearning for more. She stares into his eyes pleading for him. He takes a peek in between her legs and can see the kitty breathing and panting for more. It's now that he takes all sense of control from her.

"Give it to me, please," she begs as her kitty pulsates begging for more of his abuse.

"You don't deserve me," he says with a look of seductiveness in his eyes.

"I do baby, I do," she whines. "I been waiting for this for 15 years. Please give it to me?" she begs. Unbeknown to her until now, the begging and lack of control is a huge turn on for her. "Please," she begs again just for her own pleasure.

With precision he drives himself into her, deep enough to touch her stone cold heart. Her kitten moistens enough to melt the cold wall that has taken all of her life to build around her heart. Before he fully extracts himself, he teases her opening, twirling himself around and around, using only the tip of his manhood. She locks the door of her opening by contracting the mouth of the kitty, gripping him tightly. The contractions get tighter and tighter giving him the desire to stay inside but he can't give in. He draws himself out of her.

"Stop teasing me, please, Daddy?"

Manson ignores her pleading and stands there staring into her eyes. "Tell me why you deserve me?"

"Manson, please stop and give it to me?"

"Tell me," he demands.

Submission takes her over. "Because I have dedicated my whole life to you," she mumbles. "Now please give it to me."

With unexpected quickness he inserts himself into her again. He pounds her with four deep and meaningful strokes. He stops short still inside of her. He flexes himself inside of her, filling her up. He begins slow stroking her, teasing her by painting her walls with the tip of his brush.

"Apologize for disrespecting me earlier," he whispers into her ear.

"I apologize, baby, I do," she whispers. "Now give me all of it, please."

Manson can sense that she has totally submitted to him but still his work isn't done. He pulls himself out of her and drops to his knees. He kisses the kitty dead center in the mouth, Muuuaahhh, before tongue kissing the hole. He tongue fucks the hole with a stiff tongue.

She grips his head tight by wrapping her legs around the back of his neck. She force feeds him the pussy, pumping his mouth as fast as she can. He snatches his head back to come up for air. The eye of the kitty trembles right before his eyes.

As much as he desires the taste of her inner juices, her love button is calling his name. He dives in face first and wraps his lips around the button. He flicks the button with his tongue briskly. She's on fire and the heat from within is enough to burn his mouth.

He blows circles around the button to cool it off. Once reaching his desired temperature, with puckered lips he grips the button and begins sucking. Pebbles loses herself in his attack. An orgasm is bubbling from deep within. Her body tightens up and the more it does the harder he sucks.

She puts up a fight because she's not ready for it all to end. Her fight is a defeated one and the orgasm erupts with no warning. Her body contracts uncontrollably causing her to react like one who has a violent demon inside of them. She growls viciously as she calls his name out in a demonic voice. "Manson, Manson!" she roars before going flatline.

Manson stands up with satisfaction on his face. With no orgasm of his own yet he's still satisfied. His satisfaction comes from knowing that he's not only pleased her but he's dominated her. He realizes that completing himself now would only give her sense of control back and even the scales so he'd rather not.

Pebbles lays back in a comatose state. Manson finds great pride in knowing that he's sucked the soul out of her.

ASHTON CIGAR LOUNGE/PHILADELPHIA

THE HUGE, ARTSY looking cigar lounge is packed from front to back. Brick walls, brass trimming and huge mirrors make up the entire room. Important people of all walks of life are in the building. The sense of power cries out based on the ambiance of the room.

Clusters of men indulge in their own conversation, segregated from the rest of the patrons. The many groups of people conversing makes the loud chitter chatter almost unbearable to anyone standing on the outside of the clusters. A huge bar sits in the center of the room, with a wall filled with the finest liquor. The menu is filled with the most prestigious and most exclusive alcohol known to any connoisseur.

In the back of the room, lounging on a couch there sits one of the most debonair men in the building. Attorney, Tony Austin sits back cool and calm. Although he's dressed simply casual his swagger alone makes him outshine the rest. His foot on the table rudely, gives the patrons clear view of his caramel suede Saint Laurent sneakers. His matching belt peeks from underneath his fitted long sleeved T-shirt.

The average person would charge him off as a young hood in here out of his league. Those in the room who don't know him probably have charged him as that. Anyone with a trained eye for prestige and class would know differently once they laid eyes on his watch. The black rubber band watch appears to be no different from an ordinary sport-swatch to the naked eye but a trained eye would recognize it as the Solo Bang by Hublot Tourbillion which values at 125 grand. The two Caucasian men sitting across from him are dressed in business suits but have nowhere near the class and prestige he has, even dressed casually.

Tony takes a a huge and quite disrespectful swig of the 25 year Old McCallan Whiskey as if it didn't cost him 200 bucks a glass. He chases the smooth whiskey down with a hefty drag from his cigar. He lays his head back, appreciating the flavor before blowing smoke rings into the air.

He grooves to the sound of the beautiful instruments of Musician Dizzy Gillespie's song, 'Dishwater' playing faintly in the background.

He's already two glasses deep. He got here early so he's a glass ahead of the rest of his party. Not even an hour in and a thousand dollars in alcohol and cigars sits on the table. That's nothing compared to the money that's piled into the Louis Vuitton briefcase that sits at his feet.

This meeting is so dangerous that they had to take their show on the road just to prevent anyone from possibly seeing them. For these three men to be seen together all of their careers would be on the line. In front of Tony to his left there sits a good friend of his, The Honorable Judge Bennett who he's known for years. To his right there sits The Honorable Judge Dewars who is nowhere near a friend to Tony.

Judge Dewars blows a few smoke rings into the air before staring through them looking at Tony. The look in his eyes shows the hatred that he holds for Tony. "Let's not sit here and pretend that we really want to be in each other's company. You know I don't necessarily care for you and I know you don't necessarily care for me," he says with piercing eyes.

Tony smiles charmingly, not showing his true feelings. "We don't have to care for each other to do business with each other. Money has no emotion so when dealing with money our emotions should be nowhere in the equation."

"Well, let's get on with the business."

Tony takes a drag of his cigar as he looks around on the sneak tip. He sneakily slides the Louis Vuitton Bag over to Judge Dewars with his foot. He nods his head at the bag. "That's the fifty large you requested."

"What about the prosecutor? You know he can be quite a dick. I don't need him going against the grain in there."

"Don't worry about him. He's already been taken care of. He's gonna lay down on the case. Everything on all ends have been secured."

"Uhmm, uhmm," the man sitting next to the judge coughs to get Tony's attention.

"Oh, how can I forget you? Without you, none of this would be possible." Tony says charmingly. Tony quickly slides the matching Louis Vuitton satchel case across the table. "And your fifteen grand."

The man snatches it quickly with a head nod.

"And Judge by the way, my client has never ever admitted any guilt to me pertaining to this matter. I just want you to know that so you can sleep at night, knowing that."

"I've been doing this job for 40 years. In my career I've given away seventy-five hundred years of prison time," he says with arctic eyes. "I will sleep at night either way. Their fate will never keep me awake not for an extra second. When I take that robe off and go home, work is over."

With no further hesitation Judge Dewars lays his cigar in the ashtray, takes a huge gulp of the Scotch and grabs hold of the briefcase.

Just as he's about to get up Tony interrupts. "No, please. As you've stated neither one of us wants to be in each other's company. I will leave. Y'all stay and enjoy yourselves," Tony says as he gets up.

The pretty waitress makes her way over to the table quickly. "Mr. Austin is everything okay?"

"Yes, everything is lovely. I will be leaving but these two gentlemen will be staying. Put everything they drink on my tab. Please, whatever they want from my locker, leave it open to them," Tony says as he counts through a few bills and leaves her a hefty tip.

"Thanks, Mr. Austin, will do."

Tony backpedals away from the table. "Oh, and the briefcase and satchel, don't worry about it. A gift from me to y'all as a token of my appreciation. Have a great evening gentlemen."

"Oh, one thing," Judge Dewars interrupts. "Please don't come into my courtroom looking like a rockstar," he says as he looks Tony up and down. Show me and yourself some respect and put on a suit."

Tony flashes a smile. "I will see if I can scrape up a few pennies and buy myself a cheap one. Unless of course you would like to buy me one," he says pointing to the briefcase. The judge looks away with rage. "Good evening, gentlemen. See you at the show," he says followed by a wink of the eye. Tony makes his exit as the judge watches him with hatred.

IN NEWARK

A LL THE WINDOWS of the cab are rolled up tightly, sealing in the pungent smell of the marijuana. The cab driver is high out of his mind without taking a single puff. The smoke coupled with the extremely loud volume of Bobby Shmurda's 'Bobby Bitch' ripping through the speakers has his mind somewhere else far away from here.

Wesson sits in the back seat of the cab, eyes closed, head tilted back just enjoying his high. All of a sudden he gets very hype and starts singing with the song. "Bobby Bitch, make that body flip. You know I don't know karate bitch... We dropping bodies bitch! They say shooting is my hobby bitch! And I'm down to catch a body bitch! If I hit you with the shottie bitch," he says as he pretends his holding a shot gun. "I bet that body flip. Caught him with them zombie tips and made his body flip," he says as he falls out into pieces as if he's being shot up. He sits back eyes closed, playing dead for seconds.

He peeks through one eye as the cab is being turned onto his block. He sits up, preparing for his exit. He snatches his shopping bag filled with Chinese food from the seat and puts it onto his lap. He then digs into his pocket a pulls out a sloppy wad of money. He quickly skims through the bills and separates twenty, single dollar bills.

The driver lowers the volume of the radio and peeks into the backseat at Wesson. "Another day down, lil bruh."

"Say that," Wesson replies.

"One thing for certain, everyday that you make it home is a blessing. Out there on them streets, you can't take a second for granted. The next minute ain't promised to none of us," the driver says as he slows down the vehicle. He eases his foot onto the brake directly in front of the raggedy three family house.

Wesson grabs the handle and forces the door open. Before he steps a foot out, he looks up at the driver. "Next day," he says as he steps out. He slams the door shut behind him and the cab cruises off.

Wesson drags along to his house, exhausted and quite fatigued from the mini Bobby Shmurda concert he just put on. He fumbles with the keys in his hand looking for the right one. He looks up before stepping onto the stoop. The element of surprise gets the best of him when he's greeted by an image dressed in all black.

The sight of the chrome handgun takes his breath away. He drops his bag and takes a step back. His reflexes lead him to reach for his gun but it's already way too late. BLOCKA! His face goes numb shortly after the bullet rips through the flesh of his cheek. He stumbles backwards blindly.

He's blinded by colorful spots. BLOCKA! BLOCKA! Wesson's body falls limply and collapses onto the concrete. The gunman aims at his head and dumps three more shots into it with the precision of a skilled sharpshooter. BLOCKA! BLOCKA! BLOCKA! He doesn't waste a single second before taking off.

The man gets into the backseat of the getaway car. Ooo Wee speeds off immediately. Super Blood sits in the passenger's seat on eggshells, not uttering a word. Smoke pulls his mask off his head and drops it on the seat next to him.

Ooo Wee peeks into the rearview mirror and he and Smoke lock eyes. He grips his gun in his left hand, just waiting for the command to reach over and off Super Blood. Smoke shakes his head no and Ooo Wee looks at him with surprise. Ooo Wee tucks the gun into his pocket and continues driving.

"Told you I had you," Super Blood says from the passenger's seat. Super Blood has no clue how close he was to losing his life. Smoke and Ooo Wee were both fully prepared for this to go another way. Smoke was so desperate to get this done that he took the chance. If by chance it went differently, no one would have walked away from the scene. Luckily for Super Blood that he was a man of his word and because of that he will live another day.

73

THE NEXT DAY

TODAY IS THE day that Manson has been eagerly anticipating. He feels like a kid on Christmas morning as he unloads the truck that's parked at the curb. In all the months that he's worked here he's never unpacked a truck with so much enthusiasm. He's unloaded more than a third of the truck singlehandedly without a complaint. The boxes that he used to view as work that he didn't want to do, he now views as work he can't wait to do.

Minutes pass and he unloads the last seven boxes onto the cart. He pushes the cart inside the store, straight to the back room where Hamza is busy at work, stacking the containers against the wall and jotting down the inventory. As he unloads the cart he watches Hamza closely. Hamza gets up and closes the door shut. "Here, take a look," he says to Manson.

Manson walks over with his full attention locked onto Hamza. He hands Manson a container of the Shea Butter. "See the green writing on the label?" he asks. Manson locks in on the label and nods his head yes. Hamza hands him another container. "Now see the orange writing?" Manson nods his head again.

"The green writing is the money," he says flashing a smile. "The orange is just plain old Shea Butter." Hamza stacks each container on opposite sides of the wall. Manson's eyes follow the money container without blinking. The pile Hamza stacks the regular She Butter onto is stacked twenty containers high and spread across the wall fifty containers wide. The targeted container is stacked twenty containers high and five containers wide.

Manson no longer sees the containers as Shea Butter. He views it as what it really is. He quickly multiplies the containers in his head and a spark brightens up his eyes as they set on one hundred kilos of raw heroin. He's no mathematician but he quickly figures at seventy grand a kilo, there is seven million dollars worth of pure heroin in this tiny room. He gets the bubble guts just thinking of it.

HOURS LATER

Manson works the counter alongside of Hamza bagging up. Customers have been pouring into the store by the second. Now that Manson knows exactly what's going on he watches the customers with a different eye. Hamza handles the containers nonchalantly as if they're worth a mere ten dollars instead the true value of seventy grand.

Manson is amazed at the appearance of some of the customers who he now knows are buying heroin. Some appear to be paupers, dressed in shabby clothing. Others are dressed in the finest Muslim attire. Manson has no choice but to wonder if the men dressed in garb are really Muslim or are they just playing the same game that Hamza is playing.

The store clears out, giving them a chance to breathe. Manson has kept count as best he could and the last container sold made a total of thirty sold in a few hours. "Damn, in all my years of living I never knew money to flow that fast," he says to Hamza. "Can't believe you make this much money in a couple of hours and paying me minimum wage," he says with a smile.

He smiles back at Manson. "Not exactly. You must understand the operation. Most of those customers you won't see again for a month or two months." His bright smile widens. "But then there are some that you will see again next week."

"I'm not trying to get into your business. I never count another man's money. I just want to make sure you got me to the side and not forget about me."

"Even if I don't have you to the side you have no worries. As you saw for yourself, the well never dries," he says in a cocky manner. "I am the well and it keeps flowing and flowing and flowing."

74

SUPER **B**LOOD **SITS** in the passenger's seat of the luxurious Mercedes CL Coupe. The driver counts through a crisp stack of hundreds, that look like they've come straight from the Federal Reserve. Super Blood's mouth runs a mile a minute. "I told you that would be easy. All these niggas easy, real rap."

The driver finishes counting and hands the money over to Super Blood. "That's the five racks. Good looking, my nigga," he says as he extends his hand for a handshake.

The five thousand dollars is payment for the murder of Wesson. Wesson violated this man a couple of weeks ago and he refused to let it go down like that. He hired Super Blood for the job, putting the bounty on Wesson's head. Super Blood dug into his bag of crafty tricks and weaved the perfect situation together. Knowing of the beef between Smoke and Mother Nature made it all perfect. He's managed to make it work in his favor by getting Smoke to murder Wesson and him reap the benefits of it. In the end everybody is happy and in no way should anyone know where the hit has come from. His hands are clean as usual.

"You already," Super Blood says as he grips the man's hand firmly. "Anything else you need... I'm out here."

MEANWHILE

It's a sad day for Mother Nature and her squad. The housing complex is swarming with gang members from all over the city, young and old. They're celebrating Wesson's life as best they know how and that's drinking, smoking and pill popping. The air is so tense back here that anybody can get it.

"On Blood," Smith shouts as he paces around in circles. He's high out of his mind right now. Somebody spilled my fucking blood! Ain't no way in the world this shit going like this!" he says as the tears drip down his face. "Bruh ain't here no more and we back here mourning? Fuck mourning! Let's move!"

Mother Nature leans against her truck just listening and observing. She hasn't said a word since they received the news. She feels there's nothing to talk about. From this point on, it's all about action.

"Move on who though, Blood?" a young man asks with tears in his eyes as well.

"On whoever! Anybody we ever had a problem with! Tonight, Blood, niggas gotta pay for this. We gonna tear the city up until we get answers."

Mother Nature stands up and intervenes. "The answer is right before our eyes. This a hit from Smoke and Manson. It's obvious. I was trying to avoid the wide open battlefield shit but they spilled blood. They struck now it's time for us to retaliate.

Get everybody rounded up right now and let's ride out. We gonna show them why you should never go against the wrath of Mother Nature. Let's mob!"

75

SMOKE STICKS HIS key in the door and steps into Samirah's apartment. Tasha who is laid out on the couch looks up at him upon entrance. This is the first they've been face to face here since the kidnapping. She lowers her gaze to hide the black eye and the swelling of her face.

Smoke walks past her, staring at her with a smart aleck smirk on his face. "You been sleeping on the couch the past few days. What happened? Did the important dick find out that you was just a piece of unimportant ass hoe pussy?" he asks before busting out laughing.

Tasha doesn't have a word of defense. She places the pillow over her head and hides in embarrassment. These last few days have been the worse days of her life. She feels like such a fool. She had it all.

In her eyes she had made it. To blow it all by creeping around with Omar. She thinks about it every second of the day. If only she had never got back in contact with Samirah she wouldn't even be in this situation. What she doesn't realize is the fact that she didn't get in contact with Samirah. Samirah got in contact with her. Through all the madness, her guilt has her totally blinded and naive to the fact.

Smoke walks into the bedroom still wearing a smirk. Samirah sits at the foot of the bed with piles and piles of money scattered across the bed. Like a skilled bank teller, she has all the bills separated and in thousand dollar piles in rubber bands. Smoke immediately starts counting the piles.

"That's seventy-two racks and here is eight hundred and fifty," she says as she hands him the loose bills.

Smoke quickly counts out five hundred dollars and hands it to her. He places the left over bills into his pocket. She quickly counts through the money as he starts dumping the piles of money into the duffle bag.

"What's this? Hell no, bruh! You said you got me this go round! Fuck that! I got shit I got to do!"

"Yo, chill yo! I got you," he claims. "Let me just get this bread to bruh and all the profit after that coming in is mine. Me and you gone eat together, you already."

Samirah pouts like a baby as Smoke zips the bag up and exits the room. Tasha is still on the couch with the pillow over her head when Smoke creeps up on her. He unzips the bag before snatching the pillow from her face. He holds the bag up to her face and grabs the back of her head, damn near shoving it inside. "You see that," he boasts.

"Stop, Smoke!" Samirah says as she comes to her defense.

Smoke lets her head go and backpedals away from her. "When your ribs start touching and your mouth dry from starvation, hit me up," he says as he grabs a handful of his crotch. "I might let you get some of this un-important dick for a few dollars so you can feed your fucking self. Fucking whore!" he chuckles.

Smoke makes his exit, leaving Tasha sulking in embarrassment. At this moment her life can't get any worse. As hurtful as the words he said to her are, she's completely numb.

76

DAYS LATER

MOTHER **N**ATURE **PARKS** in front of Wesson's house and walks up the steps. Her heart pounds with nervousness. She really hates to face his mother but she feels like it's the right thing to do being that she loves Wesson so much. She had all plans on getting over here but seeking revenge has gotten in the way.

She had no choice but to stop everything and make her way over after what she saw online while scrolling through her social media sites. A picture of Wesson attached to a GoFundMe account is floating all over the web. Her heart s saddened that his family has to beg for money to bury him. She also looks at it as a mockery to her. With all the work that he's put in for her she would never be able to live with herself knowing that her family had to beg to bury him. She's sure she's the laughing stock of the city right now.

Mother Nature rings the first floor doorbell and as she awaits an answer her eyes are attracted to the yellow police tape laying on the curb. A foot or so away from the tape is a huge blood stain on the concrete. Her heart sinks just looking at it and realizing that is where he died. Her eyes are stuck on the bloodstain.

The door opens and breaks Mother Nature's trance. She turns around where she finds his mother peeking through a small crack in the door. The chain lock holds it together. She's quite familiar with Mother Nature but right now she doesn't trust anyone. Everyday since his murder she's been calling Homicide Detectives and still they have not found a suspect for his murder. Right now everyone is suspect.

Huge bags hang underneath her eyes indicating that she hasn't slept in days. "Yes," she says with a look of suspicion in her eyes that she can't conceal.

"Miss Barnes, this is me," Mother Nature says with a warm smile. She addresses her as Miss out of respect when in fact they are about the same age. Wesson's mother being 33 years old had him when she was just 14 years old. At 14 she knew very little about being a mother and just learned as she went along. So close in age their relationship was more of a brother and sister relationship more than it was mother and son.

"I know who you are."

"Can I come in so I can talk to you?"

"I'm afraid not. We can talk from here." Mother Nature spots two small children step up behind their mother. Wesson's younger sister can be seen in the hallway as well.

"I understand," Mother Nature says with sincerity in her smile. "You do know Mall was like a little brother to me, right?"

The woman nods her head up and down. "Just want you to know that we will get to the bottom of this. No way will this go down like that. But that ain't what I came here for." The woman's eyes widen. "Came to find out how much money you need for the funeral?"

A look of sorrow fills her eyes. "I talked to the people at the funeral home and they want eight thousand," she says with despair.

"So how much you need?"

The woman looks away with shame. I don't get paid until next week. And even then I will only have about five hundred. I'm trying to see if I can borrow money from my credit union but I just took out a loan to buy that car," she says pointing to the fairly new car parked on front of the house. Really I don't know what to do. I can't afford life insurance on myself and four children," she says sadly. "I put up a GoFundMe account and I check it every hour on the hour and in three days all we collected is about two hundred dollars," she says with tears building up in her eyes. "All the friends he was supposed to have, where they at when you need them?"

"Don't worry about the rest of his friends. You don't need them. You got me. Give me a couple of days and I will have the eight grand for you."

The woman's eyes light up. "Really"? I thank you so much," she says as she snatches the chain off the door. She jumps into Mother Nature's arms and hugs her tight. The tears drip from her eyes and soak onto Mother Nature's shoulder. She lets herself go with no shame and sobs away. "My baby," she cries. "They took my baby. My first love," she sobs.

Mother Nature's woman side starts to kick in and makes her quite weak. She maintains a straight face, covering any traces of her wanting to cry herself. She pulls away from the woman and avoids looking her in the eyes. She maintains her cold aura. "Let me get out and get answers as well as the money you need," she says as she spins off and walks away. A few tears drips down her face once her back is turned.

She wipes her eyes quickly and turns to look over her shoulder at the woman. "Please take that GoFundMe page down," she says thinking of her reputation being at stake. "Ain't no need for that. I got this."

77

THE NEXT MORNING/8:15 A.M.

MANSON AND SMOKE sit side by side on the stools In Dunkin Donuts. They both keep their eyes on the busy Pathmark parking lot. "Big Bruh, I told you once we get that right work sky is the limit," he says very animated like. He feels great as if he's accomplished a huge achievement. He just hopes that Manson sees it the same way.

"I got seventy-five racks in the car for you. All I owe you is like seven and some change. I say we get with the plug right now before we sell out. This shit about consistency Big Bruh. I learned that from Bruh. The way he took over is because he never go a second without work. He was always loaded," Smoke says awaiting Manson's response. Instead he continues to sit in silence.

"The last lil bit of the work is out on the street right now. If we get with them now, there won't be no gap."

Manson looks over to Smoke slowly. "I just created a major situation," he says without blinking. "We don't need to get with the Dominicans because I just landed a situation that goes over their heads."

"Word?" Smoke says in complete awe.

"Yeah, unlimited dope. Ain't no brakes on this shit. No money outta pocket. The faster we move it the faster we get more."

This is music to Smoke's ears. "Get the fuck outta here."

"Like this on some Big Bruh shit. Like he might not even had a plug like this," Manson claims. "I been sitting back thinking. We can't bullshit with this. This plug way too heavy to be playing with it. I gave dude my word that I could produce. I need to produce," he says flexing his temples.

"I got you, bruh. You see how fast I went through that."

"I need faster than that though. This dude so heavy that lil shit you just did won't impress him at all. This the Heroin Cartel, bruh. This dude got factories of this shit. Fuck a few little ass bricks. I'm talking whole bricks, kilos of this shit."

"Raw dope?" Smoke asks in amazement. Manson nods his head up and down. "Awww man, Big Bruh. If we got that raw dope we can kill the city. No doubt about it."

"You know how to cut raw dope?"

"Hell yeah! That's nothing, Big Bruh."

Manson nods his head up and down. "Good. Now, in order to make this shit work, I'm gonna need the whole city to the neck."

"Like a takeover?"

"Exactly a takeover."

"Say no more, Big Bruh. I wish bruh was here to tell you," he says with a spark in his eyes. "I cleaned up the whole city in a month when we first got together. He couldn't even believe it," he says with boastful eyes.

"Well, we gone need to do that again. You're my eyes. I'm following your lead. Whoever can possibly be in our way, we must remove them as of right now."

"Big bruh, that's gone be easy. It's only a handful of niggas that can really get in our way. It's like this Big bruh, most the dope in the city is coming from the Dominicans from New York. Like nobody don't go over there no more. Dried up, Big Bruh. So they all done moved over here and opened up businesses.

But it's all a front, Big Bruh. They moving the work through their little stores and shit. That's why it's so hard out here for a motherfucker to eat because they got so much of that shit they selling it for dirt cheap."

Manson listens closely to the details while putting a plan together in his head. "Sounds easy enough. Let's get out here and shut the city down so we can open up the plug the right way."

"Say no more, Big Bruh."

MEANWHILE AT THE TOWNHOUSES

Dope fiends pour into the back of the townhouses through an alley, in twos, threes and fours at a time. This area has never seen this much drug activity in all the years the complex has been up here. It's nonstop action, dope sale after dope sale with barely a few minutes in between.

Right past the alley there stands two smooth-faced Caucasian young men around the age of 18-20, almost obstructing the entrance. Both are dressed in black slacks with a white shirt and tie on. The backpacks on their back are filled with religious literature. These men are Mormons from the Church of Latter Day Saints. They stand in the middle of the action-packed drug scene, not just here but all over the city. Despite all that goes around them on a daily basis they move around carefree, walking through war zones just spreading the word of the God that they worship.

They both stand there with pamphlets in each hand, attempting to pass them out to the dope-fiends. Some take the pamphlets and others walk right pass them, paying them no attention at all. "Jesus loves you," the young man says as he hands the raggedy dope-fiend a pamphlet.

The man takes the pamphlet. "I love Jesus, too," he says in a mocking manner. "Just not more than I love the dope," he says as he looks around entertaining the crowd of people around him. He stops short and pretends that he's caught the Holy Ghost. "Whew, thank you Jesus!" he says as he dances around with his hands high in the air.

The crowd of people laughs at his performance. He laughs in the face of the Mormons before flying the pamphlet in the air like a Frisbee. He continues on with his journey to get the dope that he needs to keep his spirits lifted.

The middle of the court is clear while all the action surrounds one house. Three of Smoke's soldiers hold it down as the dope money pours in abundantly. As fast as the customers pour in the three young men serve them and send them on their way. Some customers walk away briskly and others bust the bag open and scoff it down right there.

In the alley near the action there stands Mother Nature's prize pup, the other half to the Smith and Wesson duo, Smith. He scales the wall with a hood on his head and a bandana covering his mouth. Another young man follows his lead tailing on his heels. Smith has a gun in each hand while the other man grips one tightly in both hands like law enforcement.

Smith peeks around the building and waits for the perfect time. Just as all three of the young men have a group of customers in front of them, Smith dashes out into the courts, both guns already blazing. BOC! BOC! BOC! BOC! He aims at the crowd and it opens up, people scattering in every direction. Smith keeps his eyes on the three dealers who all have taken flight, fleeing in a group.

Smith chases behind them firing the whole time. BOC! BOC! BOC! BOC! His man aids in gunfire, the sound overshadows the sound of both of Smith's guns together. BLOCKA! BLOCKA! BLOCKA! One of the young men topples over, falling face first. Smith aims at his head as he's approaching and dumps two in the back of the young man's head, while still aiming at the two running men. BOC! BOC!

The young man's body bounces high off of the asphalt and before he can land Smith's helper is there to dump two more into the man's head. BLOCKA! BLOCKA! BOC! BOC! Smith fires, sending another to the ground. Smith stops short and dumps one into the man's face BOC! The other man dashes off and cuts into the first alley, making a clean getaway.

Smith looks around and finds the entire area empty except for the two dead men. "Let's go!" he shouts to his man. They sprint through the courts and dash through the alley they entered through. In seconds they're both in the Honda Accord and it's speeding up the block into the perfect getaway.

The young man who managed to get away untouched stands at the edge of the building breathing heavy and panting with nervousness. He watches the car speed up the block before making a wild right turn at the intersection. He makes his way to the courts where he finds his two friends lying in cold blood. "Damn," he sighs.

The sound of police sirens in the air gives him no time at all to mourn. He flips his hood over his head and takes off in flight, grateful to be running away and not laying face down dead. The two Mormons come stepping out of the alley from hiding. They're shocked to see the area empty and deserted looking. They peek around and the first thing they see are the two casualties of war. They run over with the quickness, one has his phone in hand dialing while the other grips his Bible tightly. All the praying in the world couldn't bring them back to life but that doesn't stop the young men from praying anyway.

ONE HOUR LATER

S MOKE GOT THE call and rushed right over to the spot where he found Homicide Detectives everywhere. He met up with the homie and got all the details. The very next call he made was to Manson. Right now him and Manson are back at the original meeting place that they just left not even an hour and a half ago. They stand in the far end of the parking lot at the back of the Ghost. Ooo Wee stands a few feet away, hand on his gun in his pocket and eyes on everything moving and sitting still.

"It was a hit from the bitch, Mother Nature," Smoke advises. "The lil homie saw the Honda leaving the spot."

Manson is amazed. "Bitch really do got some balls, huh?" he smirks. "She struck first."

"Nah bruh, that was retaliation. I struck the other night and knocked her lil pup Wesson shit off. I did my homework and caught him slipping at his crib."

Manson's gets more enraged the more he hears. "You take it upon yourself to make a move like that without telling me?"

"Nah, Big Bruh, it wasn't like that. It was so easy I had to go. I just wanted to knock them off one at a time. I wasn't gone tell you nothing until I brought that bitch head on a plate for you, bruh bruh. This shit be going on long enough."

Manson nods his head up and down. "Understood."

"This is what I was trying to avoid but ain't no turning back now. Shit about to go full throttle from here. They took two of ours. It's showtime now. Ain't no money gone be made now. The spot blowed up, homicide everywhere. We might as well go all the way out from here. Give me the command to press the button and the whole city goes under siege from this second on."

Manson thinks of the kilos of raw dope just sitting and waiting to be moved and sadness covers his face. Smoke can read the disappointment on Manson's face. "I know you just landed that fire plug and you ready to get to the money but... Shit, don't nobody wanna make no money more than me. I been starving for years now. But one thing I learned from bruh was you can't mix the two.

Before he put that dope on the street he made sure I cleaned up everything. Trust me on it, bruh. I will have this war done and over in no time or my gangster ain't what you known it to be. Big Bruh, I know I fucked up but one thing I'm sure of is if you didn't have trust in my gangster we wouldn't be standing here having this conversation. Just give me the go, so I can make you proud of me again." For the first time since Manson has been home Smoke notices a spark of joy in Manson's eyes. That spark fires him up even more.

"Like you just said, I want her head on a plate. Also while you at it, I want anything that could possibly get in our way destroyed."

"Got you, Big Bruh! Just lay low and watch my work."

"Lay low?" Manson asks feeling quite disrespected. "I built my reputation putting motherfuckers down, not laying low in times of war."

"Bruh, that was back then. It's different now. Whole new game."

Manson feels more disrespected as Smoke continues. He's sure that Smoke respects his reach, meaning the power that he has and the ability to get one touched. Something tells him that Smoke may be doubting his hands-on gangster though. He also realizes once your soldiers lose faith in you and believe that you won't get your hands dirty they're liable to lose respect for you as a leader.

"As a leader I will never send my soldiers out on front line to do something that I wouldn't do. So with that being said, let's get out here and destroy this city and rebuild it our way. City under siege."

79

TWO HOURS LATER

SMOKE CRUISES THROUGH the quiet back block behind Checkers. Up ahead his attention is captured by a cheaply painted red, raggedy Cadillac STS parked in the middle of the block. As he passes the Cadillac to no surprise he sees Super Blood sitting in the driver's seat. Smoke takes one long glance just to make sure Super Blood is alone.

Super Blood gets out of the car as Smoke is parking. Smoke parks, gets out and makes his way over to Super Blood. They meet at the curb. They shake hands and as usual Super Blood overdoes it. He locks and loads their signature handshake going through all the motions. "What's popping, Blood?" he asks as he finishes the handshake.

Smoke grips his hand tight so he can't get away. Smoke draws his gun and aims at Super Blood's face. "My 40 cal, that's what's popping." BLOC-KA! The slug to the face snaps Super Blood's whole body.

He stumbles backwards blindly. Smoke, still holding his hand is the only reason he hasn't fallen. Super Blood tries to snatch his hand away from Smoke. The bright glare from the gunfire still has him blinded. BLOCKA! BLOCKA! His body falls limply and lands on the ground dead with no motion. Smoke fires again, BLOCKA! He takes off in flight, dives into the driver's seat of his car and speeds off.

Smoke isn't sure of what Super Blood gained from the death of Wesson. He doesn't know if maybe they had a beef of their own or not. A part of him believes that he was used in some type of way but he can't prove it. What he does know is that Mother Nature retaliated with the quickness. For her to find out so fast he's sure that Super Blood must have gotten the word back to her. Smoke was taught the best way to handle a traitor is to kill him where you find him and he did.

MEANWHILE

Jada notices Manson's evident rage and it makes her quite nervous. She hasn't seen him this mad since before he went away to jail. She watches as he snatches the closet door open. Sneakily she backs away from him so she can be out of arm's reach. Although the days of him putting his hands on her are long gone, she still remembers them like they were yesterday. You can say she's like a shell-shocked war veteran who is haunted by the memories. Whenever she sees him in rage she gets far away from him.

Manson comes walking over to the bed, carrying a duffle bag. He drops the bag onto the bed and pulls his shirt off. He stands there bare chested as he digs through the duffle bag. He retrieves a bulletproof vest that he throws over his head and straps tightly around his torso. He feels Jada looking at him and turns away from her just to avoid looking in her eyes.

He puts his shirt back on, along with his jacket. He digs into the bag again and pulls out an Uzi. He grabs the extended clip from the bag and jams it into the butt. He tucks it into the front of his waistband before he grabs hold of a Mac 11 that he tucks down the back of his waistband. He puts on an oversized black hooded sweater and pulls it low to conceal the guns.

He storms out of the room without saying a word to Jada. She wants to ask him what's going on but has learned to never question him. She's witnessed first hand in the past that if she questions him she takes the chance of his taking out his anger on her. Her concern for the matter really has very little to do with him.

She doesn't move until she hears the door slam. She runs to the window and watches him get into the Ghost. No soon as the car pulls off she gets to dialing numbers on her phone. She waits impatiently as the phone rings.

Finally Smoke picks up. "Yo?"

"Everything alright?" she asks quite hastily.

"Why you ask that?"

"Just seen him buckling up and just wanted to make sure you're okay."

"I'm good," he says rather confidently. "I will hit you in a couple of hours."

She holds the phone in silence. She's more than nervous for him. She can sense in his voice that this is severe. "Be safe out there."

"I'm always safe."

"Love you," she says.

"Love you too," he says before ending the call.

She gets caught up in her own thoughts and can't believe this. The fact that her heart goes out to Smoke more than it goes out to Manson is still quite unbelievable. Sadly, she couldn't care less if Manson makes it back home. In fact, if he doesn't it would make her life better.

80

HOURS LATER

RIGHT NOW THE West Ward of the city of Newark is deserted and seems to be somewhat of a ghost town. Not a soul is walking the streets or even posted up anywhere outside. The word of the war has spread like a wildfire. The innocent and the neutral have cleared the streets to stay out of the way of what is about to take place. The rivals are packed into cars four and five deep mobbing through the city with their eyes wide open, looking for anything linked to the enemy.

As quiet as the city may appear to be, traffic is at an all time high. Over sixty percent of the cars that are on the street at this hour are of the two teams that are at war. Mother Nature has a total of approximately twenty cars on the road while Smoke and Manson have a few cars less. Mother Nature is at somewhat of an advantage because most of their cars are either stolen or rented which means no one will know what they're coming in. Smoke's soldiers are moving around in their everyday cars which can be spotted many miles away.

In the cars the young bangers are equipped with everything from handguns to machine guns that they can't properly use. That combination makes for quite a messy situation. These men drive around with no destination, just looking for their enemy. At any given moment at just the wrong left turn the rival gangs can collide and an all out war will open up right at the traffic light.

Smoke slams the door behind him as he exits Samirah's apartment. He tucks the 9 millimeter down his waistband as he steps through the hallway toward the door. He quickly slides the safety lever of the .40 caliber before placing it in his pocket. He steps onto the porch and just as he does he sees an image of a man at the bottom of the stoop.

Quite startled, Smoke takes a step back as he quickly slides his hand into his pocket. He quickly identifies the man as Big Show. Big Show stops in his tracks with evident fear on his face. Smoke leans back, gun held secretly on his side. He's gathered his composure and ready to go. "Peace!" Big Show greets with a look of fear in his eyes.

Smoke looks him up and down trying to play it cool.

"Is Tasha in there?" Big Show asks.

Smoke looks him up and down with venom in his eyes. "I don't fucking know," he says as he steps around Big Show.

Big Show watches Smoke closely as he steps down the stairs. Smoke has a good mind to blow his brains out right here right. He doesn't want the heat at Samirah's front door so he just keeps his gun in hand by his thigh as he keeps his eyes on Big Show who is now making his way up the stairs. As Smoke is walking to his car he peeks around and quickly spots the Impala that he's sure Big Show has gotten out of it. He also notices that no one is in the car.

Smoke gets into his rental and sits there eyes on the porch, both guns in hand. He watches as Tasha comes onto the porch and she and Big Show begin talking. "Sucker for love ass nigga," he says aloud.

A couple of thoughts creep into Smoke's mind and both of them have to do with murder. Although he doubts if anyone will ever find out that he was behind the kidnapping he still can't take the chance. Just seeing Big Show here at the doorstep was a close enough call for him. He will not live with this haunting him. The other thought he has right now is kidnapping Big Show and making him take him to the money they should've already had their hands on then murdering him.

He weighs his options and realizes that the Mother Nature beef is more important at this very time. He decides to put Big Show on the back burner and save it for later. He blew his first chance but he's sure next time it will be more than well worth it.

81

MOTHER NATURE'S WRANGLER pulls up and is parked on the quiet side block. Smith gets out of the passenger's seat and stands at the door with it wide open. "I'm rolling," the young man says from the backseat as he puts his hoodie on over his head.

"Nah, I'm going dolo," Smith says as he grabs an Izar(muslim garb) from the passenger's floor. He quickly ties it around his waist over his jeans. He then grabs a kufi from the dashboard and places it on the crown of his head. He bends over and rolls his pants up over his ankles. To the naked eye he looks like a righteous Muslim.

The look flows so natural for him because he was raised as a Muslim. To the gangster population he's known as Smith, half of Smith and the now deceased Wesson. But to the his family and on government paper he's known as Ibn Mu-Mitt which means the Son of Mu-Mitt. Religion is the one thing that his deceased father Mu-Mitt instilled in him and his siblings. That is when he was home and not away in prison for years at a time. In his short stays out of prison he made sure that his kids practiced the religion diligently, prayed five times a day and spent most of their days in the masjid learning and studying.

For a brief time they were even home schooled. Although their father was quite a crook he wanted better for his children and if he could have stayed out of prison he could probably have done better for them, but he couldn't. He did the best he could do with his diseased and hardened heart.

One would think with all the religion that was instilled in Smith aka Ibn Mu-Mitt he would've turned out to be an obedient servant but he didn't. He hasn't practiced the religion since his father got murdered several years ago. He never loved the religion and only practiced it out of force from his father so it never sank in his heart. He and his siblings hate the religion with a passion for they always saw it as a form of punishment.

A great percentage of the young men terrorizing the city were born Muslim. They are the offspring to some who may have been sinful Muslims. Their sins being the cause that they continuously revisit the jailhouse and prison system. In their absence, the religion is just in the backdrop of their children's lives.

In today's society religion is secondary and choosing a color to rep is more important. On the Day of Judgment one may believe that he will be charged for his religion but the youth can't see that far. What they see today is the peers being charged for the color that they represent. It all boils down to red or blue.

Just like so many other young men in the city with the same story, if you ask what their religion is indeed they will answer Muslim but the only thing in their hearts is the Blood gang that they live and die for. In most case Blood rules over everything, religion, and even family. Because Blood rules over everything, they can pray with you by day and slaughter you at night.

Smith tucks the Desert Eagle 9 millimeter down the waistband of his Izar and pulls his T-shirt over it to cover it. "Be right back," he says as he slams the door shut.

"Yo!" Mother Nature calls out as he crosses in front of the vehicle. Smith stops at the window awaiting her command. "You know that G you been asking me for?"

Smith's eyes light up with joy. "Yeah, it's all riding on how you perform. It's showtime," she says putting a battery into his back.

She knows how bad he wants G status. He feels like he's been a 5 star General for way too long and it's time for him to move up the ladder. Truthfully she knows he deserves the G but she waves it over his head to keep him hungry. She's seen it so many times before wherein dudes get the G and get lazy and comfortable which is why she has been using this tactic on him and Wesson and it's always worked. She's sure promising him the G will make him soar to new levels.

"Say that," he says as he walks off. Her words incite more bop into his step.

"And don't forget to take that tape afterwards. No trace."

"For sure," he sings.

In seconds he bends the corner and takes a few steps peeking around casually. He steps into the store and in a few steps he blends right on in with the rest of the Muslim patrons. He looks around in search of Manson who is nowhere in sight. Hamza looks up at him at his entrance and quickly goes back to ringing up his customer at the cash register.

Smith makes his way around the store as if he's really looking to make a purchase. He disappears into the middle aisle where he stands at a bookshelf while making a complete assessment of the store. He sees another employee standing at the end of the aisle but still no sight of Manson.

Many would take the safe route and start from the bottom ranking and work their way on up to the top ranking. That way they could get a gauge of their opponent. Smith, on the other hand, would rather start at the top and not even waste his time with the underlings unless they happen to get in the way. Mother Nature wanted to start from the bottom as well but after hearing Smith's logic she rolled with him. They've agreed to knock Manson and Smoke off first then destroy everybody else under that set thereafter.

Smith pretends to be reading from a book as he sees Hamza making his way toward him. Smith looks up from the book and pastes a fake grin onto his face. "As Salaamu Alaikum Wa Rahmatuallah Wa Barakatu," he says in his most eloquent recitation.

Hamza quickly notices a shiftiness in Smith's eyes but still he returns the greeting reciprocating a smile of his own. He furthers on with, "Kaifa haloka?" He asks how he's doing.

"Ana bekhair, shokran! Wa ant?" Smith replies I'm fine, thanks and you?

"Jayed, alhamdullilah?" Hamza replies saying good, thank God!

Smith's Arabic gives Hamza a sense of comfort despite the sneaky look in his eyes. Smith senses the comfort and continues on with a few sentences just to ease him further. He's finally found use in all of all the Arabic classes he was forced to take as a child.

"Can I help you?" Hamza asks.

"Yes, I'm looking for a book on introducing a woman to the deen. I'm thinking about taking on a wife."

Hamza smiles graciously. "Alhamdullilah! Right this way," he says as he leads Smith to the next aisle.

As he stops he notices Smith peeking around more suspiciously. Smith bumps into Hamza by mistake and when he does a loud bumping sounds off. When Hamza looks to the floor he notices Smith's gun laying there. He falls back three steps, not knowing what to do.

Smith fumbles for the gun clumsily. He grabs it from the floor and tucks it back into his waistband. "Pardon me, Ak," he says with a cheesy look on his face. "Allah says trust in him but still tie your camel," he says with a smile that he hopes will smooth it all out.

"No problem," Hamza says with evident fear. "Here's all the books we have on the subject," he says nervously. Hamza is stuck not knowing what to do. He looks around for help that isn't there. The whole store is now empty except for him, Smith and his employee.

Smith grabs the first book he can grab and without reading it he says, "Okay, I will take this one." He makes his way to the register where Hamza rings him up. He gives the salaams and disappears.

Hamza stands there still in fear. He doesn't know what exactly is going on but it doesn't feel right. He's not sure if he should call the police or call Manson. He stands there debating the two before he makes his decision. He picks up his phone and starts dialing.

82

A FEW HOURS LATER

SMOKE SPEEDS THROUGH the narrow street with the expertise of a race car driver. He's in hot pursuit of the car that Smith was seen leaving the scene of the murder in the other day. Just on a humbug Smoke spotted the car cruising along a main block. He jumped on the car at that very moment. Right now he's been tailing the car for the past five minutes as the driver of the Honda does everything in his power to shake Smoke.

The Honda has already caused a few accidents as well as crashed into about six parked cars trying to get away. Smoke has managed to miss every accident and has not touched a single car. He sits in his seat quite calm for the car to be zooming at 80 miles an hour. He grips the steering wheel tight with both hands, eyes on the car in front of him.

In the passenger's seat sits Dirt and in the back is Ooo Wee. Dirt invited his own self into the car. They've been in a few wars together over the years and he has total trust in Smoke. Not many will he put his life in the hands of, but Smoke is one of the few that he would.

Smoke on the other hand lost all the trust that he once had in him. He buried the fact that Dirt was willing to make the call for him in the back of his head. He's sure one day he will cash in on what Dirt owes him but for right now he plans to use him for all he's worth. The trust is no longer there though and that's why Dirt can never ride in the backseat behind him ever again. The distrust is the reason that Ooo Wee is in the backseat and Dirt is in the front but he believes his gangster is what earned him the front seat.

Dirt sits in silence. He grips his gun tightly as he's in deep thought. This is how Smoke knows him to be in war. He and Smoke are the same when it comes to this. They will sit in silence for hours just mapping out their strategy and staying focused, no music playing just deep thinking.

The Honda dashes out into the intersection, most likely without the driver even looking both ways. Smoke's eyes shift from side to side as he approaches the intersection. He slows down slightly and once he sees the coast is clear he mashes the pedal even harder. The Honda busts a wild right turn at the corner and loses control. It smacks into a parked car and slows them down but it doesn't stop.

The driver makes a few unexpected turns but Smoke is still within three car lengths behind him. Just as he closes the distance between them the back window of the Honda shatters outward. The sound of gunfire stuns Smoke as he flinches and slams on the gas pedal. A man in the backseat of the Honda squeezes with vengeance. BOC! BOC! BOC! BOC!

"Oh shit," Dirt says. He lifts up in his seat immediately and hangs his torso out of the window and tries to get a clean shot. As soon as his head is spotted the gunman in the backseat of the Honda fires at it. BOC! BOC! BOC! Dirt fires a series of shots of his own. BLOC! BLOC! BLOC! The man ducks his head low as the Honda swerves uncontrollably but continues on down the block at even more speed.

Ooo Wee is on the phone in the backseat. "Coming down 16th Avenue," he shouts into the phone. "And 17th," he adds.

Dirt positions himself securely, sitting on the ledge. He takes a few aimed shots at the driver's head through the back window. BLOC! BLOC! BLOC! The continuous driving tells him that he's not hit his mark.

"Coming onto 12th now!" Ooo Wee shouts. "Yeah right now!"

The Honda blows through the intersection and quickly approaches the next. Just as the Honda is nearing 11th Street the nose of a familiar car can be seen peeking out. As the Honda gets closer to the corner the car darts out of the intersection. In a matter of seconds both cars collide like a scene from a movie.

The impact of the steel banging can be heard for many miles. The Honda is forced sideways before flipping in mid air. It bounces on it's top twice before landing in the wide open lot. Smoke drives straight toward it with his car bouncing onto the sidewalk.

Two men struggle to crawl out of the car through the windows but it's too late. They're already surrounded by Smoke's men. The men in Smoke's car don't even get the chance to get out due to the men from the other car beating them to it. The gunfire sounds off from at least four different guns. They stand on both sides of the car firing away until the two men are no longer moving.

The sound of sirens can be heard coming from every direction causing all the men to get into their cars and speed off. The two men lay dead with only half of their bodies hanging from the windows.

"Damn, I wanted some of that," Ooo Wee says with excitement as he peeks out of the window at the trail of cars that are following them.

"Don't worry," Smoke says. "This is just the beginning. There are hundreds more for you to get."

83

A GROUP OF young men crowd a porch. One man stands at the edge of the stairs serving a few customers that have formed on the stoop. The other men are all focused on the young man who is bent over about to throw the dice. Just as the young man serves the very last customer another runs across the street with his fingers high in the air. "Two!"

The man digs down his pants, under his testicles and retrieves the plastic bag filled with bottles of crack. He digs into the plastic and grabs hold of the two vials. He hands them to the customer who hands him the money. He counts through the bills quickly as the customer dashes across the street.

The dice are slammed against the house. "Damn!" the man says as he realizes he crapped out.

"Damn, my ass!", another man says. "Gimme my money!"

BLOCKA! BLOCKA! BLOCKA! BLOCKA! Gunfire sounds off, taking all the men by surprise. They all duck low not knowing exactly where the gunfire is coming from. One man is struck and his howling pierces the airwaves. A second man grunts as he's struck in the gut. He tumbles down the stairs uncontrollably.

In the darkness Smith stands at the corner of the porch in the alley. He fires a series of shots aiming randomly. One man runs across the porch and gallops over the banister like an Olympic Hurdler. Smith aims at the moving target and fires, hitting him mid air. He screams as the hollow tip bullet rips through his flesh and sets his insides on fire. Smith fires two more just to keep everyone at bay before he dashes through the alley that he came through. He disappears into the darkness.

Smith is well aware that the men he just attacked are meaningless pawns on the board. His only reason for coming here is because it was an easy hit and it would keep up the momentum. Mother Nature has explained to him the busier they are the more off balanced their opponents will be. Knowing that, he plans to stay busy and never let them think clearly or even put together a solid plan. He figures as long as they are steadily striking Smoke and Manson will always be on the defense and never have the opportunity to think offensively. What he doesn't know is that his opponents have the same mindset and right this moment they are somewhere on the offense.

ACROSS TOWN

Total silence occupies the interior of the Ghost. The air is tense and everybody is in their own zone. Helter drives of course, while Skelter rides shotgun. Arson sits behind her and Manson behind Helter.

Their guns are not on their laps but gripped tightly in their hands, fully loaded and ready to go on sight. All are unfamiliar with who exactly their prey is throughout the city so, anything that looks like it can be against them, they assume are. Manson has no time to play so he decided to go right to the source of the action.

Manson is in a state of mind that he hasn't been in years. Not even a half hour ago he got the news from Hamza that a young man with a gun had come to the store. Although he always considered the fact that the young generation would eventually test his gangster, his ego sort of made him not really believe it. He truly thought that his reputation was enough to make them never cross that line. Now that he sees that his reputation means nothing these days he's prepared to rebuild another one, a more treacherous and mature one that will last for another 30 years. The things he plans to do in this war, he's sure will leave a strong legacy that no one will ever forget.

The adrenaline races through all of their veins as they approach the block of Mother Nature's set. Their necks are on swivel at high alert. The closer they get to the complex the harder their hearts pound. The pounding has nothing to do with fear but everything to do with anxiousness.

They approach the entrance and Helter slows down waiting for the command. They peek inside and get a clear view of the area. It's as crowded as it was the day they drove through. Helter stops short at the entrance before turning inside. Manson thinks it over quickly realizing the danger they will be putting themselves in by going inside.

"You know what?" he says. "Pull around the other side and let's hit them from the blindside." Helter pulls off with no hesitation.

On the inside a young man has spotted the Ghost lurking in front of the entrance. He shouts out a code and everyone adheres to it. He jumps up and down with anxiety as he points to the entrance, and snatches his gun from his waist. He watches through the alley as the car passes by them. He races toward the back exit and three other young men follow.

Manson and the crew pay attention to a small group of men who crowd the exit in a small huddle. They all appear to be off point in deep conversation. "Fuck making it hard for ourselves. Let's take what's in front of us. It all counts," he says as he raises the Uzi in the air and hits the power window button. Arson and Skelter both hit the window button as well.

Suddenly the attention of the men is captured by the approaching Ghost. They all stand like deers in headlights, not knowing which way to go. Manson pops up out of the back passenger's window, gun already aimed at the crowd. He fires at the center of the crowd.

The sound of the Uzi ripping consecutively echoes for blocks. The sound of the Uzi is overshadowed by the sound of the AK47 that Arson fires. The sound of Skelter's 9 millimeter can be heard faintly in the backdrop. One man falls flat onto his stomach and one falls onto his back.

Three other men flee in opposite directions. Manson braces himself as he continues to fire at the fleeing man he has designated as his target. The man's body jolts before tripping over his feet. Skelter fires at her target which is clearly getting away from her.

BLOCKA! BLOCKA! BLOCKA! Sounds off from an unfamiliar gun and in seconds the back window of the Ghost caves in. They all look around to see where the gunfire has come from.

"They behind us!" Helter says as she spots five men racing out of the exit guns in hand. She mashes on the gas pedal and Manson holds onto the roof for safety. He aims at the string of men who are all firing recklessly at them. The Uzi backs them up, stopping them in their tracks yet they continue to fire away.

BLOCKA! BLOC! BOC! BLOCKA! POP! POP! Bbbdddd! A few bullets bang into the body of the car, lighting it slightly. Bbbbbbdddddd! POP! BLOC! Bbbbddd! POP! BLOCKA! BLOC! BOC! POP! Bbbbd-dddd! Halfway down the block and totally away from danger the sound of gunfire still rips in the air. Bbbbbbdddddd! Bbbbddd! BLOCKA! BLOC! BOC! POP! Bbbbddddd!

Manson drops into his seat panting heavy with his adrenaline fully charged. "Everybody alright?" They all examine themselves quickly as Helter busts the quick right and zips down the block. "All good," they all say with gratitude. A satanic grin covers Manon's face. "This war right here! I love this shit!"

84

SMOKE PARKS HIS rental at the far corner of the block just in case someone from the other side happens to come by here looking for him. He gets out and walks toward Samirah's house. His hand is gripped around the gun in his jacket pocket as he watches every approaching car. He stares into every car because each one has the potential of being the enemy.

Two blocks away the chrome grill of a luxurious automobile can be spotted. Smoke can identify the grill of a Bentley miles away. The closer it gets he recognizes it as Big Show's car. The Bentley stops short and double parks across from Samirah's house. The flashers come on instantly.

Smoke stops and keeps his eyes locked on the car in which he spots Tasha getting out of the backseat. Another man is sitting in the front passenger's seat. Smoke decides to just lay back in the cut until he pulls off. Tasha gets out of the car and Big Show pulls off, leaving her standing in the middle of the street. Smoke sits on the step of the porch behind him, careful not to be seen. He watches the car as it passes by him.

Seeing Big Show riding like he doesn't have a care in the world pisses Smoke off. The jealousy and envy takes over him. As he thinks of how close he was to the money and blew it he becomes enraged as he always does. No way in the world does he plan to let that money get pass him. He worked too hard for it.

Once it's passed he gets up and makes his way toward the house. Tasha stands there pressing the doorbell. She peeks over her shoulder and sees Smoke coming behind her. An irritated look plasters her face at the sight of him. Just as he steps onto the porch, key in hand, the door is opened.

Samirah steps to the side as Tasha steps inside. Smoke steps in behind her, grabbing her from behind. He holds her tight as she attempts to wiggle from his grip. He gets an instant erection from his manhood rubbing against her butt. The sheer leggings she has on makes it feel as if they have nothing in between them.

His rock hard erection slides right in between her cheeks with no sign of panties to shield her. He grinds away with perversion. Indeed he's doing it to piss her off but truly he's enjoying it. The bulge she feels pisses her off gravely.

He plants his lips against her earlobes. "When you gone give me some more of that pussy?" he whispers in her ear.

She squirms with rage. "Get the fuck off me."

He holds her tighter. "You see that important dick don't give a fuck about you no more. Dropped yo ass off in the middle of the street, didn't give a fuck if you got in the house or even got hit by a fucking truck," he laughs as he lets her go. "Got you riding in the backseat like the help now," he teases as she walks away from him. He palm grips her butt. "Gimme some of that big ass butt," he says mockingly.

"Disrespectful ass," Tasha says as she stomps into the house behind him.

Smoke dashes right into Samirah's room leaving the two of them in the living-room. He quickly grabs a gun from the closet shelf and loads a clip into the butt of it. "Mirah!" he shouts.

Samirah walks into the room and closes the door behind her. "What's up?" she asks.

"Like, what's up?" he asks as he changes his jacket. "Like this nigga still coming through like shit sweet," he whispers. "I mean, we was right there at the money and we just gone let it go like that? I ain't trying to hear that." A thought enters Smoke's mind. "Oh and whatever happened to that massage parlor shit? You be dropping the ball yo."

"Bruh, that massage parlor shit ain't for me," she says brushing it off rather quickly. "I thought it over and changed my mind," she lies. "But as far as that other shit go, I did everything I was supposed to do. Y'all dropped the ball. Y'all had it right there and blew it bruh."

"Yo, shit happens but that don't mean we just stop. We gotta get right back on it."

"What you need me to do, though?"

"The nigga coming through real heavy, I see. He can't leave that hoe bitch alone. He love that bitch."

"They swear Omar was behind the kidnapping. They just trying to figure out who was with him on it. You know me I be throwing hints at anybody that could take their attention off us. We in the clear like a motherfucker," she says with a smile.

"Good, now all I need is an exact time and I can take it from there. If I got the heads up I can set it up, feel me?"

Samirah nods her head up and down. "I got you. Let me just see what I can put together. It's gone be tough though because he don't barely fuck with her like that since that shit. They be fucking in hotels and in the car. He don't even let her in the crib no more. He said he don't trust her."

Smoke smiles. "But he still fucking her though. Sucker ass nigga. He just playing hard to get so he don't look like no sucker in front of his sucker ass boys. He gone be moving that bitch in sooner than we think. Mark my word." His eyes go cold. "I ain't got time to wait for him to play this little game he playing. We need to put this together like yesterday."

Smoke zooms in close to her face, staring into her eyes. "You need money, don't you?"

"You already know," she says staring back into his eyes without blinking.

"Well, you got the megamillion right in the palm of your hands and you playing with it," he barks. He backs away still staring into her eyes.

"I got you," she says. "Gimme a few days and I will have something for you."

"Fuck a few days!" he says as she makes his way toward the door. "I need to know something by tomorrow."

85

THE NEXT DAY

MANSON AND THE crew cruise the city inside of the triple black Lincoln MKT. The long, sleek sharp nosed SUV with the dark tinted windows looks more like a futuristic hearse which carries dead bodies in it. They may not be carrying dead bodies in it but they surely plan to use it to leave plenty of dead bodies behind. When Manson saw the vehicle at Enterprise it was love at first sight.

He hated to get rid of the Ghost but now he has a new love and he's named it the Grim Reaper. The SUV is spacious enough for them all to ride in comfort, including Smoke who has been brought along for the ride. Manson decided it's best to have him with them instead of wandering throughout the city blindly. The gunfire exchange yesterday was a close call and as bad as he wants to go inside he realizes that he has to work his way toward that goal slowly but surely.

The situation yesterday set off a string of events. Smoke got the word that Manson's attack critically injured three and murdered two. That attack led Mother Nature and her crew to retaliate murdering one and injuring more than five. Back to back shootings have been taking place all over like the Vietnam War.

Manson didn't hesitate to admit to Smoke that he didn't expect this from Mother Nature. He's impressed with her persistent attacks. He's somewhat impressed with her heart. It's just beginning and the heat hasn't even begun and he wonders if she will be as courageous once it all turns up. The back to back random attacks are cool but he rather focus on the major players at this time. With Smoke now riding with them, Manson figures it should be able to identify and track down the enemy.

The chemistry in the vehicle is quite unbalanced and tension can be detected. Smoke feels totally uncomfortable in the vehicle with them. Right next to him is Skelter who has her face glued to the dark tinted windows in a world of her very own. Manson sits up in the passenger's seat in front of him laying low with his feet on the dashboard.

Heat can be felt on the back of Smoke's neck. That heat is from Arson who sits directly behind him in the third row of seating. Arson is sitting so close on the edge of his seat that Smoke can feel his breath on the back of his ear. Arson is very much aware of the discomfort he's causing because it's intentional.

Smoke turns around again and stares into Arson's eyes. They engage in a staring contest before Smoke mumbles a few words to himself and looks away. He leans to the side to move it away from Arson. He throws his arm over the headrest damn near elbowing Arson in the face. Arson's rage can be felt bleeding from the backseat.

As they come down Littleton Avenue Manson notices major foot traffic coming in and out of the townhouses of Georgia King Village. Drug customers walk in and out of the rows. Manson sits on the edge of his seat and notices packs of young thugs scattered in between the rows making drug transactions. "What's up with them?" Manson asks. "They with us or against us?"

"Nah, that's a Crip zone," Smoke replies.

Manson turns around fast enough to catch whiplash. The words can't come out of his mouth fast enough. "Crip zone?" Smoke looks at him not understanding his point. "A Crip zone in the middle of my hood? You serious?" Manson stares at him with confusion on his face. "Before I left they wouldn't even drive through here. Now you let them get comfortable enough to set up in the middle of a Blood zone?" Manson bangs the dashboard. "I don't believe this shit!"

Smoke is fired up. "Bruh, I ain't let nobody do shit. When them projects got tore down families got scattered everywhere. Crips mixed with Bloods and the murder rate skyrocketed. It's the fucking system. It's all by design."

Manson looks at Smoke with surprise. He's never known him to make so much sense. As much sense as it all makes he refuses to let him know. He looks at Smoke as if he's said the dumbest thing he's ever heard.

Smoke ignores the look on Manson's face and continues on. "I ain't taking the blame for that. I keep telling you the city don't operate like it did 15 years ago."

They bend the corner of West Market and Manson is shocked to see crowds and crowds of thugs surrounding the towers as well. He estimates about a hundred young men that he's seen in between the townhouses and the towers. Drug traffic seeps from behind the gate onto the sidewalk and on both sides of the streets. Dead set in the middle of the block two young teen-agers do their signature handshake. Manson shakes his head with frustration. "Yeah, I guess not when you leave the wrong people in command," Manson says with great sarcasm.

The heat has been taken off of Smoke as a a young teen-ager crosses right in front of them taking his own sweet time. Manson reaches over and mashes the horn with rage. The teen-ager stops in the middle of the street. He stares into the dark tints with total disrespect on his face. He begins to Crip walk right in front of them.

"Lil Bastard," Manson grunts as he reaches to the floor for the AK. He grips it in his hand as he hits the power button. "Pull up to him!" Helter swerves around the kid and stops. The teen-ager continues to Crip walk as he stares into the face of Manson with only a few feet in between them.

Manson draws the weapon into the air where the teen-ager can see and his face goes stone. He stops dancing and is petrified. Manson aims the gun and just as he's about to fire Smoke shouts out. "No, Big Bruh! He a fucking kid!" Manson snaps out of his zone and lowers the gun. He stares the young kid in the eyes. "You better learn some fucking manners." Helter cruises off.

"He's a fucking baby, Big Bruh," Smoke utters.

"I don't give a fuck. If he a baby and he banging, he can get it," Manson replies with rage. "That's the problem right there. Motherfuckers have gotten too sympathetic to the bullshit and that's why we got Crips in my hood eating while my line starving. Not to mention all the other bullshit we got going on in the city. We got a lotta cleaning up to do."

A FEW MILES AWAY

Smith and a group of young men are loaded up in the stolen Dodge Grand Caravan. They're cruising the city, 'mobbing' as they call it, just looking for anybody from the opposite side. Smith who sits in the middle row peeks up ahead at the corner of the block. His eyes light up when he sees a group of men crowding the corner around the Bodega.

"Bingo," he sings.

"We taking this?" the driver asks.

"Why wouldn't we?"

The driver slows down as Smith gets in position. He turns in his seat so that he's facing the side window. He plants the butt of the rifle in the pit of his belly and he wraps one hand on the grip and the other on the trigger. He plants his left foot against the passenger window to stabilize himself. He looks to the man standing beside him. "You get the door." He then looks to the driver. "Let's go."

The driver pulls off. The men clear the second row except for the designated door man. As they approach the corner all the men look in the direction of the approaching van. The driver waits for the perfect time to ease his foot on the brake with all the attention on them.

He slams on the brakes and one man dead center draws his gun quickly. "Whoa!" a man yells from the backseat of the van. The doorman snatches the door and it slides open horizontally. Smith opens fire. Bullets spit from the rifle with no hesitation in between.

The glass from the store window shatters and two young men collapse onto the ground. The gun yielding man fires a few rounds of his own back at the van as he backpedals away, leaving the other men to get away on their own. The gunmen takes off in flight and a couple of the men follow on his heels.

"Go, go!" Smith commands. The driver dashes through the intersection without looking either way. Smith looks back at the three bodies laying on the ground, not knowing if they're dead or just wounded. Either way he's satisfied that his attack was effective.

HOURS LATER

Manson and the crew have been riding around for hours with very little luck as far as attacks. The areas they've been hitting have been quite bare. It's like the town is walking on eggshells and everyone is quite hesitant about being on the streets for no real reason. All the prominent men are tucked out of the way or either doing their lurking too. Right now the only thing on the streets are the foot soldiers, the bottom feeders that mean very little to the team. Smoke came up with a spot that he's almost sure they can find some men of value.

The Grim Reaper sits parked in the parking lot across the street from a tall building. They been sitting here for about ten minutes watching the in and out traffic. Dope and coke fiends as well as young people pour in and out of the building by the second.

"Damn," Manson says. "Traffic crazy."

"Yeah, they got all things in there. Like a fucking drug store. Weed, percs, syrup, coke and dope, everything. I been in there a few times. Them niggas got hella guns in there too."

"I ain't worried about that," Manson says. He realizes there is only one problem as he watches the string of customers standing at the door waiting to get buzzed in. "I'm more concerned with getting past that buzzer on the door. In war everybody got guns. That ain't about shit."

Not seven minutes have passed and Manson has not only come up with a plan but he is now executing that very plan. Skelter inhales a deep breath before pressing the door buzzer. She hears the clicking of the door lock and cuts her eye to the right as a signal. As soon as the door is snatched open Arson rushes from the right side and Manson rushes from the left.

They both fight to be the first one through the doorway. Arson's determination forces him through. His rifle sounds off ferociously without hesitation. The man standing at the door is hit in the chest the very first shot and falls onto his back.

Manson's Uzi rips through the air recklessly, hitting everything in it's path. Smoke steps in as the clean up man, pegging anything that Arson and Manson have not hit. The sound of gunfire and screaming echoes in the halls as the the bullets ricochet off the walls.

"Let's go!" Manson shouts as he takes off first. Skelter takes off behind him. Smoke is on their heels. The Grim Reaper is at the curb a few feet away awaiting. Arson continues to fire until they're close to the vehicle. He then backpedals still firing a few random shots just to keep any survivors off of their heels. He gets in and Helter speeds off.

HOURS LATER

The last attack still has all of them on a high which they haven't come down off in hours. They feel like that was just the appetizer and they're in need of the Entree. They've been chasing for hours and have not found a single situation worth moving on. That is until right this moment. "Yo!" Smoke shouts. "There go one," Smoke says as he points to two men riding on a bicycle. The two men are the only two people on the whole block. "Where,,on the bike?" Manson asks. "That ain't worth it."

"Nah, Big Bruh. That's a power move. "That's the homie Sal-murder lil brother. He ain't a part of the bitch direct line but I'm sure right now he out moving with her. He come into all her beefs for whatever reason. Might as well get this one while it's here because his brother ain't gone spare none of ours."

"Say no more," Manson says as he grabs the Uzi from his lap.

"Daddy!" Skelter shouts from the second row. Manson turns around. "Can I get this one?" she asks with sad puppy dog eyes.

Her look melts him away. As bad as he wants it, he passes it off to her. "How can I tell you no?"

The two men on the bike stop at the 24 hour store in the middle of the block. They both get off the bike and the target lays the bike on the ground. They walk up to the stairs and stand in front of the window placing their orders. Helter pulls over and turns the lights out.

Skelter gets out quickly. She walks toward the store which is almost a few hundred feet away. The two men climb onto the bike and the man turns the bike around and pedals toward Skelter who he keeps his eyes on the entire approach. He watches her with general interest and not suspicion.

As they get closer to her she grips her gun tighter. With only a few feet in between her and the bike, she cuts in front of their path, placing one hand on the handle bars to stop them. She aims her gun at the man's face and squeezes the trigger. BLOCKA!

One single shot sends the man flipping off of the bike. The man on the back hops off of the bike before the bike and the other man can even touch the ground. He takes off running up the block and Skelter gets to squeezing. BLOCKA! BLOCKA! BLOCKA!

The man's body is lifted off the ground before he tumbles over. He falls flat on his face. The Grim Reaper pulls alongside of her and she dives into it. Skelter gets in with no emotion on her face, not saying a word.

Smoke watches her with amazement as Helter speeds off. As much as he hates her, right now he has no other alternative but to respect her gangster. As impressed as he is with her, still he can't allow himself to like her. Seeing her in action only confirms for him the fact that if the time ever comes he can't play games with her. He nods his head up and down with a smirk, just happy to have witnessed this because now he knows exactly what he's dealing with.

Seeing all them in action today gave him the opportunity to see how they are all built and how they operate. Right now it may seem senseless to critique them being that they are all on the same team but one thing Smoke bears witness to is the fact that this game changes everyday and you never know when the team you once played for will be the team you have to play against.

86

THE NEXT MORNING

OVER TWO HUNDRED Bloods are behind the townhouses with their attention on Mother Nature who stands on the hood of her truck so they all can see her. Two armed men stand at the exit and the entrance while one armed man stands at every alley that one could use to get inside. All that is merely for safety precautions but only a fool would attempt to attack right now with 200 men all armed and dangerous.

Mother Nature understands that her soldiers could all be feeling defeated right now. Members of their team have been getting knocked off left and right the past few days. Sure they've lost a few soldiers in war before but never to this magnitude. The last thing she wants is for them to lose hope. She realizes she must boost their faith.

"We needed this," she says with a smile. "We been real relaxed lately. Had our feet up like it can't go down any minute. Yeah we lost a few but we still ain't losing. We up as long as I'm keeping score. Now is time to get out there and turn all the way up."

Smith paces around the truck paying her no attention at all. The only thing on his mind is his next move. "The rest of the city probably counting us out because they wanna see us lose. You figure, never ever have they saw that before. They all waiting for the day but today ain't that day. Look at it like this, just when it gets to be too much for other motherfuckers, that's when it's getting to be just right for us.

So with that being said, we gonna get out there and handle this shit. We know almost everything they in which makes it that much easier. We gotta strike and keep striking, not giving them time to think or come up with a plan. Let's stop concentrating on the bottom feeder non-descript motherfuckers. They're a waste of bullets. Let's concentrate on Smoke and Manson. I want their heads," she says with a long stare of sincerity.

"Also, we got a problem," she says with a sympathetic look on her face. "The homie, Wesson, needs to be buried. He been laying in that funeral home for almost two weeks. We need to put the money together so the homie can go on about his way and rest in peace. His mother had a Go-FundMe account set up for him. I told her to take that shit down. Ours don't gotta beg.

Y'all know the homie would rob a bank to bury any one of us if he had to. Let's show him the same respect. I'm taking donations right now. Ten, twenty, or hundred dollars from everybody and his mother can go ahead and get the homie put in the ground. Let's go y'all. With no hesitation the members start digging in their pockets and making their way to her.

A COUPLE MILES AWAY

Manson and the crew are still out hunting. They've been out all night stealing a wink of sleep as they ride. Manson is driving while Helter is in the third row catching up with her zzz's. Smoke is in the passenger's seat while Arson and Skelter are seated in the second row.

Manson cruises down Orange Street and Smoke peeks over him looking into Coney Island Breakfast spot. He's trying to see how crowded it is and if it's possible for him to go in there without running into the enemy or anyone linked to the enemy. "I'm hungry as shit."

"In war we may have to go days without eating," Manson says being politically correct. The sound of his stomach growling overrides the 33 strategy of war bullshit that he's talking right now. "I will park around the corner and let her go in," Manson says as he points to Skelter sitting behind him.

Manson stops at the corner before making the left turn onto the one-way block. A man appears walking out of the block just as he's turning. A spark lights up Smoke's eyes. He quickly sits on the edge of his seat. "Oh shit," he sighs.

"What, what's up?" Manson asks. Everyone sits on alert except for Helter who is snoring away. "That's one of them?"

"Yeah and no," Smoke replies. He fumbles with the words before continuing on. "He not one of her soldiers but he with her. She be getting the work from him."

"Say no more then. So basically he's the connect that's funding the war. We knock him off and eventually her well will run dry and it will make her easier to find."

Smoke nods his head up and down and it all would make perfect sense if in fact what he told Manson was true. The truth of the matter is he is a connect who serves Mother Nature and many other people in the city but in no way is he her main source. This man is no way to even be linked to Mother Nature. The beef Smoke has with him is personal. The only problem is dude has no idea they even have a beef.

Smoke's beef is all internal. They have a woman in common and Smoke knows about him but he knows nothing about Smoke. To the man the woman is just someone he calls on the late-night but to Smoke she means a little more. He takes her very personal; personal enough that the sound of his name irks Smoke to no end. He always had the plan to wipe the man off of the map to get him out of the equation if the opportunity ever presented itself. From the looks of it right now that opportunity has just presented itself.

MINUTES LATER

The man struts casually around the corner with his bag of food in hand. His eyes are focused on the 645 Convertible BMW that sits parked on chrome rims. He admires the beauty of the car and not once pays attention to the Grim Reaper that sits parked directly in front of it. Smoke sits on the curb in between the cars, completely out of the man's sight. The man quickly approaches his car and just as he's about to pass the Toyota Smoke pops up. The man jump and stops in fear. His eyes land on the gun in Smoke's hand and immediately he throws his hands high in the air. "Yo, yo,y," he stutters.

Smoke aims at his face and squeezes. BLOC! BLOC! The man tumbles over face first and lands on his belly. Smoke dumps three shots into the back of his head and races off to the Grim Reaper. Manson pulls out of the parking space and cruises off modestly.

"That was a general's decision you made right there, I must admit," Manson says with a sparkle in his eyes. "Cut the money off and she has nothing." He nods his head up and down. "I'm proud of you." Smoke sits back enjoying the praise although his decision was not of a General, it was more of a sucker for love.

MEANWHILE

Mother Nature stands in the hallway in front of Wesson's mother and his siblings. She hands his mother the bag. That's the eight grand you need for his funeral plus a little bit more." Mother Nature's crew came up with over fifty-five hundred and she came up with the rest. If they hadn't she had already prepared herself to cover the total cost.

The woman's mouth drops in awe as the tears flood her face. Her mouth stretches wide open but no words come from it. She hugs Mother Nature tightly. She pulls away. "Thank you," she says with a face full of tears. "Thank you so much."

The woman's sobbing touches Mother Nature's heart. She holds her tighter and tighter. Seeing her in such a weak and distraught state brings the protector out of Mother Nature. She rubs her back to ease her weeping. The squeezing and rubbing sends a tingle throughout Mother Nature's body that she didn't expect.

Mother Nature backs away to contain the beast that is fighting from within. "It's nothing, we love him like our own brother. Anything else you need don't hesitate to call," she says with a sly look in her eyes.

The look in Mother Nature's eyes sends off a mixed signal that confuses Wesson's mother. Mother Nature looks her up and down, making her feel quite uncomfortable. They lock eyes and the lust that lies in Mother Nature's eyes clears up all confusion. Mother Nature bites down on her bottom lip. "And I do mean anything."

87

LATER THAT NIGHT/WEST TRENTON

AFTER A FEW more hours of driving and coming up blank Manson decided to fall back and take a breather. He felt as if they were forcing it and he knows exactly where forcing it will get you. Over the years he's learned to follow his gut. In the past anytime he went against his gut he ended up in a bad situation. Today he knows better so he does better.

Manson dropped Smoke off to his car and then dropped off Arson to the hotel. From there he, Helter and Skelter hit the highway. Ten minutes ago they arrived at Roger Gardens in Trenton, New Jersey. The war has been the only thing on his mind these past days.

He now understands what it is to miss money due to beefing. Never before did he understand because he's always been on the other side of the game, making it hard for the money guys to eat. He always preyed on the fact that the money guys couldn't go to war with him because their addiction to money would eventually cause them to step out, purely out of desperation. He's never had enough money to become addicted to it but just the little money he's made since he's been home has him thirsty for more.

A major connect awaiting him and he can't even touch the work yet. He realizes putting the dope on the street during this war could easily result in countless losses so he rather just sit on it. From the looks of it this war can possibly go on longer than he expected. He figured out a way that he can make money and continue the war at the same time.

Helter and Skelter lay out on the sofa sound asleep in the cheaply decorated but neat living-room. Manson sits in the kitchen across the table from a man whom he calls Big Bruh. Not his Big Bruh in the sense of his O.G. Just in the sense of the man being his elder and someone he respects dearly.

This man is fresh out of prison not even eight months ago. He's just served an 84 month sentence for a major gang roundup back in 2007. He along with a string of others were charged with Racketeering. Seven years ago he was known as one of the most radical and most vicious Bloods in the city who then went by the name Blue-Blood. He was named Blue because of the darkness of his skin. He's so black that he looks blue.

Now seven years older and thirty years more mature than he was before he went in, that name is something he would rather live without. Now 50 years old, he's just happy to be alive and free after all the dirt that he's done in his life. Blue-Blood was one of the smarter men who used his gang affiliation to make a profit off it. When Blue Blood was nabbed by the Feds he was one of the wealthiest of all the men who were indicted.

His money has nothing to do with the respect that Manson has for him. Manson respects his morals and his code of honor. Back when Manson was on the run for the murders in Newark he came to Trenton because of a girl he knew. Manson lived with the girl for a few months before he tried his hand at what he knew best and that was robbing.

His robbing spree of a few of Blue-Blood's workers caused the two of them to bump heads. The bumping of their heads turned out to be the best thing for Manson. Out of pure respect for Manson's gangster, Blue-Blood brought him all the way in. Blue-Blood 35 years old at the time and Manson barely 18, Blue-Blood treated him like a nephew.

He also gave Manson the key to the city and allowed him to make all the money that he wanted to. Only thing, back then Manson was never into the money. It was all about the power. Meeting Blue-Blood is one of the better things that have happened to him in life. Blue-Blood put a roof over his head for the few months that he was on the run and even kept money on his books until he was nabbed in 2007. Manson also thanks Blue-Blood for introducing him to Helter and Skelter. Without him, he would've never met two of the most loyal people he's ever had on his side.

Today Blue-Blood doesn't represent Blood like he once did but never will he denounce his affiliation. Today, he's just a grown man who has grown kids. Never foreseeing himself in a situation like this, it's hard for him to believe that it has come to this. Nobody could have ever told him he would be 50 and dead broke.

"Ay, Lil Bruh, shit just not the same these days," says Blue-Blood. "It's funny how much shit can change in just seven lousy ass years. Left here in '07 on top of the world and I come back to damn near eating out of the garbage can. Had homes in Ewing, Princeton and Hamilton before I left and I come back to a raggedy ass apartment in the projects. Used to pump out of this exact apartment and now I live here," he says with a smirk.

Manson watches him in silence as he always does when Blue-Blood speaks. He's never seen his spirits this low and beat up before.

"I showed everybody love when I was up. I come home and couldn't even get a pair of sneakers out of these lousy motherfuckers. The boots

I left the Feds with, I had to wear for five months before my daughter bought me a pair of sneakers," he says with sadness filling his eyes.

"Last month I went down to welfare just to keep some food in the refrigerator. Real talk, I started to get out there on the old me and start extorting these motherfuckers but from the looks of it ain't none of them got nothing for me to take."

Manson has heard enough. He has way too much respect for him to be sounding like a quitter. "So, you just gone lay down and die?"

He gets defensive. "When you known me to lay down and die?"

"That's what it sounds like to me," Manson lashes out.

"Ain't really much I can do. My hands tied. The few motherfuckers who can help me won't because I'm a threat. They know if I get back on board they can't eat no more. They rather see me like this than to see me up again."

"Well, I wanna see you up," Manson says as he digs into shopping bag on the floor next to him. He slides a tub of Shea Butter across the table to Blue-Blood.

Blue-Blood stares at the container with a baffled look on his face. "Shea Butter? Lil Bruh, I ain't no street merchant. That ain't gone get me up like I need to get up. Anyway a nigga got pride."

A grin spreads across Manson's face. "Shea Butter won't but a brick of pure heroin will."

"Huh?"

Manson nods his head up and down. "Yeah, that's the fake out. There's a kilo of smack inside there."

"You bullshitting me!" Blue-Blood says with joy in his eyes.

"Have I ever bullshitted you? I just landed a situation that can change our lives forever. Unlimited bricks of dope. I can have these shits coming in as fast as we can move them."

"Say word," he says but before he can say a word he speaks again. "What's the going rate though?"

Manson is silent for he has not a clue of what he should charge. He figures his best bet is to keep it real because if anyone is worthy of keeping it real with it would have to be Blue-Blood. "The people charging me sixty thousand a brick. I just wanna eat. What you think is fair to give me back? I mean the work right here, if you got somebody who can work the table we ready."

"Lil Bruh, I work the table! Fuck all that! That's the first thing I learned when I got in the dope game. Sat around with junkies and stole the game from them back in the late 70's when I was 13 years old. I tell you what, if this the right shit, I should be able to make about 800-850 bricks off this.

If I wholesale them at 165 a brick," he says as he calculates in his head like a mathematician. "That's over 140k. Give you the 60 for your people and we can split the 80 down the middle. You know I ain't no greedy motherfucker. You bringing me in, without you I ain't got nothing so it's only right I split it with you."

Manson's heart is touched. Feels good to know that after all these years in a world where everything and everybody has changed Blue-Blood has remained the same. "Well, with that being said I believe it's time for you to take back what's rightfully yours. That being your city."

"Lil Bruh, you must be sent from heaven because I been praying to God every night for a miracle. Shit, you must be God and I must be Jesus because you just resurrected me from the dead," he says with a grin. He gets excited just thinking of his getting money again.

"Awww man, awww man," he says as he paces around the table. He stops short. "Lil Bruh, you know we about to get rich, don't you? Mark my words, gimme two months and I will have Trenton back to the old days. Gimme a year and we will be on the Forbes list!"

"Now that's the Blue-Blood I know, respect and love. Spirits high!"

"Oh you ain't seen high spirits yet. I been resurrected. Now watch me come alive!"

88

THE DODGE CARAVAN pulls behind the old warehouse building which is five stories high and a whole block long. It's extremely dark and abandoned looking back here and the pouring rain makes it even more difficult to see. Smith and two of his men creep through the grass on their way to the fire escape. They latch onto the escape and climb, careful not to slip on the wet steps. Smith brings up the rear.

They finally get to the rooftop where the two men stand waiting for Smith to take the lead. He looks around the roof carefully examining what he can see through the heavy downpour of rain. He steps across the roof with each step as careful as the last. The men follow in his footsteps. Just before he gets to the edge of the roof he stops. He places one hand in the air for the men to stop as well.

He stares onto a porch across the street which is occupied with over ten men. Loud talking and laughing can be heard from the porch. Some horseplay breaks out as two men get to wrestling with each other as the other men cheer them on. Smith draws his gun first and his men follow. He aims at the porch dead center and a second later the crackling sound of gunfire rips through the sky like thunder and lighting. His two men aim and fire at the porch as well.

Caught by the element of surprise the men duck for cover, having no clue where the shots are coming from. Bullets whistle through the darkness and rain. Two men draw their guns but have no idea where to return fire so instead they take off in flight. Screams and moaning can be heard from across the street as the bullets pierce through the darkness and hit the moving targets. A few men tumble off the porch, one flips over the railing and a couple fall flat onto the porch. The other men get away, some lucky to have not been hit at all, while others have been hit but not enough to slow them down.

The shots continue on as the gunmen aim at the running targets. In seconds, three clips which equal 44 rounds have been emptied. They trot quickly across the roof and make their way carefully down the fire escape. They hop into the caravan and the driver peels off immediately.

He keeps the lights off until he pulls from behind the warehouse. The driver turns the corner and rides pass the house. He slows down as they approach the house. Satisfaction fills their hearts as they find four men laying facedown on the porch, not moving at all. Seeing this raises their spirits.

Just when they thought they were losing, they've managed to damn near even the score. In no way is this the end of the game though. They have a long night ahead of them and they plan to continue to make progress. This isn't work to them. This is fun, like the real life Grand Theft Auto. None of them care any more about taking a real life than they do taking the life of one of their video game characters. On the video game and in real life they won't stop playing until the screen reads Game Over.

89

IT'S 11 IN the morning and while most of the world is at work creating a paycheck for themselves Samirah and Tasha are lounging around in their panties watching Maury. This is Samirah's day to day routine after dropping her son off to school. This is also what Tasha has been doing all of her adult years as well. It's so much more fun for them to be here watching the craziness together.

In between commercials Tasha has been busy creating her Instagram page and every other social media page. She was forbidden to have a page while her and Big Show were a couple. Now that they are no longer together technically, she's decided to open a new page and get back out here in the world. She's already come out of her garbs and hijab. She really has no need for it since they are no longer together.

As much as she hates to believe it, she can tell by the way he treats her that he will never accept her back as his main girl. Sure he comes through for sex every couple of days but she understands that is purely out of his addiction to the pussy and not love for her. She knows that he has way too much pride to take her back after all that has happened. He would hate for the world to view him in a particular way based off what she's done and all that has happened as a result of it.

The only way she believes he would take her back is if they move far away from here and start over where no one knows them. Out of desperation she propositioned him with that the last time they were together. He denied it which leaves Tasha no hope for them as a couple. Although she loves him dearly she has no choice but to move on.

"Uh oh!" Tasha laughs. "I'm online! Bitches better guard their man! I'm on a hunt!" she laughs with her tongue hanging from her mouth. "Bitch won't be single for long because Instagram will not let me." She holds the phone up over her head. "Selfie!" she laughs. "They gone be like bitch, where you been."

Samirah is quite entertained with her. She pulls out her phone and runs over and sits on Tasha's lap. She places the phone up high over their heads. "Selfie!" she shouts before snapping a shot.

"No, bitch, not in our panties," Tasha says. "Fuck that, you trying to catch, right? Gotta set the thirst trap, bitch." They laugh together. "I'm posting it right now," Samirah says. "I'm gonna say follow my day one bitch as the caption. Watch your shit be popping with hella followers in like twenty minutes.

"What's your IG name?" Tasha asks. "Slippery when wet 69," Samirah says. "All one word." Tasha goes straight to her page and starts liking pictures as the likes and comments build up on their picture. They've forgotten all about Maury.

MEANWHILE

The day has finally come. Thanks to Mother Nature and her soldiers Wesson's body has been taken out of the cold morgue where it laid in the freezer for over two weeks and was taken to the funeral home to be prepared for the big day. Now, in the small church that's in the middle of this block is where his body lays. He's dressed more like a gentleman than the gangster that he was.

His mother had him dressed in a suit and tie, quite differently than the youth of today who are normally laid to rest in sneakers, T-shirts and gangster apparel. Although the gangsters funded the funeral, Wesson's mother asked if they could be on their best behavior here out of respect for his elders who have traveled all the way from Alabama to see him laid to rest. Mother Nature promised to keep it all under control.

At this very moment the preacher is standing over Wesson's body speaking highly of him. The words he uses to describe Wesson one would think that he's known him all his life. No one would ever believe that the preacher just saw him for the first time ten minutes ago when he stood over his coffin to speak. He speaks of all the accolades and scholastic achievements that Wesson has accumulated in his life.

He also speaks of Wesson's college dreams that seemed to shock everyone in the church. That was the very first time anyone ever heard Wesson and college mentioned in the same sentence. It was all new to everyone because his mother made it all up out of embarrassment. The last thing she wanted was for her grandparents to know that she failed as a parent and raised a thug gang-banger.

Mother Nature nor her followers could stomach all the bullshit. They all stepped out of the church minutes ago. To see one of their strongest men dressed in a monkey suit while the preacher lies on him was too much for them to bear. Almost every gangster present today stands on the outside of the church as the family members are inside listening to the lies. The people on the inside are living a lie and loving him for what they hoped he would be in life while the gangsters on the outside love him for what he really was.

Gangsters bleed the sidewalks on both sides of the streets. Not only have members of their set come to pay their respects to Wesson but members of almost every set have come as well. That is except for the enemy set. Secretly, a few of them even wish they could come to see the homie off because the truth of the matter is his gangster is well respected throughout the city. He's a true gangster who has earned the respect of even his enemies.

Several cars cruise through the small block holding traffic up as they stare at the abundance of people scouring the sidewalks. Traffic jam after traffic jam has taken place and the gangsters love the attention. Sadly, funerals for the young gangsters are like a badge of merit. They seem to take great pride in wearing R.I.P. T-shirts and standing around makeshift memorials. Once the car rides through and the passengers stare over at them, the younger wannabe gangsters take that time to show off. It's then that they start doing their signature dance and handshakes with great pride.

All the traffic of the prior traffic jam has emptied out and soon as it does another string of cars enter the block. The grill of the black, new body, Suburban leads the pack. Something about this truck screams for attention. It could be the fact that all the windows are rolled down except for the driver's window.

The very second the truck bends the corner masked gunmen pop out of each window and gunfire starts clapping consecutively. Arson and Smoke are in the back windows airing out assault rifles while Skelter is in the passenger's window squeezing two 9 millimeters into the air. They have both sides covered. Manson pops up out of the sunroof and rocks from side to side letting shots from his m16 into the air.

He fires rounds at the left side of the block then the right side and then back to left. The gangsters use the parked cars for shields. They dive onto the ground and hide underneath cars for safety. Bullets ricocheting, glass shattering, metal bending and men screaming can be heard until the truck makes it to the end of the block. Helter bends the wild left and speeds up the block, making yet another smooth getaway.

Tasha has been liking pictures for the past twenty minutes. She's made the assessment that the only time Samirah really posts are during the 1st of the month when she has a new outfit. She blows most of her welfare check on expensive clothes for herself and not necessarily for her son and the pictures are the proof. The rest of the month she posts fake deep quotes that she probably doesn't even understand herself.

Tasha skips through about thirty memes and quotes and comes across a picture of a group of men. She quickly notices Smoke and Samirah in the middle of the group. Her eyes comb the picture looking for another familiar face in the group. Her heart skips a beat as she sees a man in the back right hand corner.

She stares at the picture closer and examines it thoroughly. She begins to shiver in her panties as it all comes to back to her. The man in the picture is Bout Dat. She will never ever forget his face. She looks again just to be sure.

Samirah notices her silence as well as he body language. "What's wrong with you?"

"Nothing," she lies very quickly in a squeaky high pitched voice. She can't even cover up her discomfort. Samirah can read it from across the room but charges it off as nothing just as Tasha said it is. Tasha can't even stand the look of his face because it brings back memories of those few days they had her in their custody. She skims through the pictures and examines them closely looking for his face. She finds him in several photos.

She closes the app and leans her head back with her eyes closed. Her thoughts run wild. She's sure Smoke had to be in on it because she's never seen the other man a day in her life. The real question is if Samirah was in on it as well? Samirah looks over and flashes a meaningless smirk at Tasha. Tasha flashes one back at her in return but the question still lingers in her head.

90

LATER THAT NIGHT

MANSON LAYS BACK in the bed next to Jada, just catching up on his very much deserved rest. Jada is steaming right now because Manson is interrupting her dose of Reality television. He's been watching the news for the past two hours anticipating the details of the funeral home attack. He's heard rumors of how many were left dead but he refuses to believe the word on the street. He rather hear the facts.

Just as he doses off again he hears the words "Funeral Massacre," come out of the speakers of the flat screen. He's wide awake now and sitting on the edge of the bed as the reporter continues on. "Earlier today in the middle of a funeral, assailants opened fire, killed five and wounded more than twenty others."

Manson is full of satisfaction as the rumors are close to the actual facts. He presses the volume button so he doesn't miss a single word. He's curious to know just how much the reporters really know.

"Suspects still have not been identified. The gun battle has been reported to be a part of a rival gang war. It's reported to be retaliation in a string of murders that have been taking place throughout the city of Newark. In the past two to three weeks three dozen murders have been reported and enough injuries to fill a small hospital. The city of Newark has turned into one huge blood bath. No pun intended," the reporter says. "Here's Jake at the scene."

The screen changes and the funeral home is shown. Manson listens to the details of what he already knows and not anything different. He sits back gloating. The history that was made today he's sure will ring for years to come. This attack hasn't fully set in and he's already planning his next spectacle to outdo this one.

He rolls over to Jada with the perfect end to a perfect night on his mind. Jada recognizes the look in his eyes and automatically gets agitated. With very little foreplay, he gets on top of her, inserts himself and immediately starts stroking away. Out of fear she wraps her arms around him and pretends to be enjoying him.

Manson may be here with her physically but Smoke is indeed on her mind. She closes her eyes and imagines Smoke here in the place of Manson. That doesn't seem to work because it's all so different. His stroke, his smell and even his body feels all wrong. Their chemistry is so off-balanced that she can't even get wet.

She lays there just hoping for a speedy finish but to no avail. He slow strokes her in attempt to please her like she's never been pleased. That doesn't work because she's so emotionally connected to Smoke that even the right stroke from Manson would still feel wrong. Her body is here with Manson but her heart is with Smoke, wherever he is.

Tears of guilt well up in her eyes. Her emotions all over the place. She feels guilt in having sex with Manson. Foolishly she believes that she's betraying Smoke. She buries her face in Manson's chest to avoid him seeing the tears drip down her face. She bites onto her bottom lip so he doesn't hear a sob. She lays there as he pleases himself for he will never be able to please her sexually, emotionally or any other way. Those days are long gone.

91

SOUTHWARD/THE NEXT DAY

LUXURIOUS AUTOMOBILES ARE lined up like a car show in front of the projects. The prestigious cars coupled with the abundance of drug deals taking place makes it look like the late 80's early 90's all over.. While the rest of the city is starving these Crips seem to be feasting. While the rest of the city has become a war zone everything on this side of the border is at peace. It's like a whole different world

Crip homie, Vito Corleone, sits on the hood of his Challenger, feet up while puffing on a blunt. Another man walks up to him and peaces him with their signature shake. Before he gets there his mouth begins to run. "Yo, you heard about all the shit that's going on in the West Ward? Shit crazy, Big Bruh!" he says with excitement in his eyes. "Whole side like a graveyard, bodies everywhere. They getting like three bodies a day."

"Yeah I heard a little about it," he says with no real enthusiasm. "But you know me I don't concern myself with nothing that don't got nothing to do with us."

The man continues on. "Them motherfuckers dropping like flies."

"I can almost guarantee whatever it's about it don't involve no money. It never does with them. Slobs killing each other for nothing. Let them all die. They worthless anyway."

"I don't know what it's about but whatever it is shit crazy. Blood bitch Mother Nature versus Smoke." Vito's attention is caught. He now listens attentively. They rocked out at the lil Blood, Wesson's, funeral. Came through with choppers, chopping everything down on some straight disrespectful shit.

Whoever in that Lincoln van wilding. They shutting shit down! Nobody knows exactly who in there. The streets calling them Team 6. You know like that mysterious team of soldiers that captured Bin Laden. That Lincoln got the whole West Ward shook!"

"Team 6, huh?" Vito snickers. "Ay, well as long as that van stay in the West and don't come nowhere near the South or the East side they alright. Bring that shit anywhere near here and it will be like Desert Storm all over again."

The man smiles. "Say that!"

THE NEXT DAY

"BIG BRUH, WE gotta stay on their ass now," Smoke says with his eyes bulging from his head. "If we let up now this whole shit can turn around. That was a power-move we made yesterday but it also was the ultimate form of disrespect. We just opened the doors for whatever. All gloves are off at this point. I'm sure mother's houses, baby mother's houses and even grandmother's houses are no longer off limits right now."

Manson isn't the least bit worried. He already thought the gloves were off. In war he never wears gloves and he expects that his enemy is in the same mindset. "The gloves been off. In war you expect your enemy to go the same distance as you go if not further. The enemies' capabilities should never surprise you unless you have indeed underestimated them. And that's something I never ever do. I see every man as a threat which makes me act accordingly."

Smoke is so dead-set on trying to convince Manson of the severity of the matter that he hasn't heard a word of what Manson just spoke. "I'm sure they didn't retaliate last night because they busy trying to do something big. That shit gone bring everybody out, Big Bruh. That caper automatically made us the most hated. Which means motherfuckers gonna get with them to shut us down."

Smoke is extremely hype as he speaks, not out of fear but out of anxiety. He's in full 'GO' mode. "Mother Nature has some extended family that are not a part of her direct line but in a case like this they gonna come out for her."

"Well, in that case let's get at everybody who may even think about coming out for her," Manson replies.

"I'm already on that, Big Bruh. I made a few calls and connected some dots. I'm about to get back out here in these streets and keep striking while the iron hot!"

ONE HOUR LATER

Smoke stands at the driver's window of the tinted out Pontiac Grand Prix which is parked directly in front of Samirah's house. Inside the car are two of Smoke's soldiers. Both of the men are equipped with automatic weapons and extended clips. "Listen, for no reason whatsoever are y'all to leave this post. No getting in and out of the car until your shift is over. I don't care if you have to shit on yourself. Y'all are not to move this car. No getting in and out of the car drawing attention to yourselves. Any sight of anything that looks crazy open fire and ask questions later. Understood?" he asks as he peers back and forth into the eyes of both the men.

"Understood," they both reply like the obedient soldiers they are to him.

Smoke has set up two cars at his mother's house and has given them both the same instructions. He's assigned these jobs to his best men and has total faith that they won't let him down. Now as he creates havoc on the street he will have a clear head with no worries of the backlash landing at his loved ones doorsteps. Now with that part secured he plans to really get in the mud and get downright dirty.

93

HOURS LATER

SMOKE STEPS THROUGH the alley of the two raggedy houses. Ooo Wee follows on his heels. They stop at the steel door. As they're waiting they draw their guns. Smoke tries hard to refrain from pacing but his anxiety wins the battle. He paces two steps and the motion light comes on. "Oh shit," he whispers as he stops dead in his tracks.

He and Ooo Wee peek around nervously in the bright lights. After a few seconds the lights go off. They can hear the sound of the doors being unlocked from the other side. Both their hearts begin to pound loud enough for each other to hear. They post up on opposite sides of the door with their guns ready to blast. The heavy door creaks as it's opened. The man peeks his head out and to no surprise he steps out of the doorway. He keeps his foot on the door so it doesn't close behind him.

"How many in there altogether?" Smoke questions.

"Renegade in the booth spitting," the man whispers. "His man in the room with the producer."

"Bet," Smoke says as he steps pass the man.

"Yo, Bruh, you gotta leave all of them stinking, everybody. If niggas find out I was here I'm fucked."

"Say no more," Smoke replies. "I got you."

This man is part of Mother Nature's extended family. He has love for her but no loyalty to her. As we see love without loyalty is meaningless. It's just a word that is overused and overestimated in the world. Love is an emotion that wavers and when it does the worse is to be expected.

The man, Renegade, is an aspiring local rapper. Everything that he raps about he truly lives. He's vicious on the microphone but even more vicious with a semi-auto in his hand. He's a G under another set that's closely related to Mother Nature's set. In crucial times like this they team up and come together as one.

Mother Nature is indeed a force on her own but if Renegade brings his army onboard the tables could easily turn in her favor. The man who has set it all up is a part of Renegade's army but he grew up in Smoke's neighborhood long before he even decided to start gang-banging. For years Smoke made it possible for him to live on the block with no problems. For that reason he feels in debt to Smoke for the rest of his life.

Smoke creeps through the hallway which leads to the studio. The music coming out of the studio is eardrum bursting loud. The gangster rap that bleeds through the studio is actually the inspiration for what's about to go down. It's the perfect theme music. Renegade whispers vicious lyrics in a raspy voice over a thumping beat.

As they're approaching they listen closely to the voices inside the room. "Hold up, go back," the man says. "Right there. I wanna start from right there. I don't like how that came out.

Perfect, Smoke thinks to himself. It's obvious that Renegade is in the room and not in the booth. That makes it that much easier with all of them in one room. Smoke stops short and peeks inside the room, where he finds all three men in sight.

He takes a peek over his shoulder to make sure that Ooo Wee is in place. Smoke signals for Ooo Wee to take the lead. He passes by Smoke, gun in the air like a member of a swat team. He looks back and gives Smoke a signal that he's going in.

Ooo Wee steps in the room and before his foot can land onto the floor his gun sounds off BLOCKA! BLOCKA! BLOCKA! The shots are muffled due to the padding on the walls and the loud music which is blaring from the speakers. Renegade turns around and just as he does a bullet spirals into his forehead. He stumbles backwards and falls onto the keyboard. Renegade's partner who was leaning back in the rolling chair has now fallen out of the chair from fear.

Smoke runs over to him and dumps three in his face while Ooo Wee races over the man who is laying on the floor. Five shots sound off consecutively. Renegade lays on the keyboard, eyes open but dead with blood gushing from three holes, two in the forehead and one in the face. The other man lies dead in a fetal position.

The producer sits in his chair hands in the air, submitting. His mouth is wide open but the words can't escape it. As he thinks of what it is that he would like to say, Smoke places the gun in his wide open mouth and squeezes. BOC!

The murder quickly turns into a robbery when Smoke and Ooo Wee both start going into the dead men's pockets. They also strip them of their jewels. Smoke and Ooo Wee make their getaway as the music continues to blast loud and clear. The beat goes on!

94

UNION, NEW JERSEY

TONY PULLS INTO the strip mall parking lot and looks for a parking space. He's pissed off to find that even his assigned parking space is occupied. This is one of Tony's commercial properties that he has owned for years now. This strip mall hasn't had this much action in it in all the years that he's had it.

He continues on in search of an empty parking space. It's quite hard because the lot is packed from end to end. Trailers and utility vehicles take up almost every parking space. He finally finds a small space to slide his truck into. He gets out and steps into the storefront which the canopy reads 'On the Runway.'

Tony steps into total chaos. Camera crews, make up artists and gorgeous women walking around almost naked have the room super busy. The Vh1 camera crew operate beyond professionally as they film the group of young girls from every angle. Tony watches the scene at hand with awe of how natural the women are coming across on camera.

"Cut!" says the voice in the backdrop. All the girls relax as the crew prepares for the next set.

Tony's eyes land on the most beautiful woman in the room. The tall long legged Latin woman stands at the center of a group of people entertaining them. Dressed in a long, fitted sun dress and cheap flip flops and still she's by far the sexiest woman in the room.

Her and Tony lock eyes from across the room and she becomes quiet fidgety. She blushes before turning away from him and continuing on with her conversation with her group. Even not looking at him, her rose colored cheeks and her bashful body movement indicate that she's feeling warm and fuzzy inside just as she always does when she's around him. Tony loves the effect that he has on her. He stands there for minutes with eyes glued onto her, purposely making her uncomfortable. He steps closer to her and the group to intensify her discomfort. He's enjoying himself and her reaction to him.

"Miranda!" the Film Production Coordinator yells out from across the room. The Latin woman snatches her eyes away from Tony's and looks across the room to the coordinator. "We need you, not in this set but the next one. Get ready, please!"

The Latin woman excuses herself from the group and makes her way to the back of the room. She disappears into her office. Tony follows behind her quite discreetly, not trying to draw attention to himself. He peeks over his shoulder just as he reaches the door.

He quickly slips inside. There he finds her damn near naked. The Latin woman turns around with surprise. Her dress is draped around her ankles. Her private covered by purple lace and her hands are clasped over her breast to hide them.

"What you hiding them for? It ain't like I never saw them before," he says with lust in his eyes.

She smiles. "Close that door please, before somebody sees me." Tony closes the door and locks it. She then unveils the beautiful 36 C's with no shame. Tony doesn't even take a look at them. She runs over to him and hugs him tightly.

"You act like you're happy to see me," he says.

"I'm always happy to see you," she says before wrapping her lips around his and slamming her tongue down his throat. Tony plays it cool allowing her to do all the kissing. He palm grips her ass cheek with one hand while rubbing the other hand through her long and silky hair. He slides his hands down the back of her thong and massages her cheeks.

She pulls away quickly. "Stop, you know that's my spot," she says with horniness all over face. She backpedals away from him.

He corners her in. "Yeah and that's why I did it," he says over a dazzling and seductive smile. He backs her against the wall and begins feeling her up.

She tries to fight him off but she wants him so bad. She leans her head back in ecstasy. "Stop," she says with her mouth but her stiffened nipples banging against his lips are saying something totally different.

A knocking on the door interrupts them. Tony pulls away from her and she dashes across the room. "Here I come!" she shouts.

Tony watches as she quickly gets dressed for her set. In a minute flat she's dressed and headed to the door. "You gonna wait here for me so we can pick up where we left off?" Miranda asks.

"Nah, I have a meeting with a client in a half hour. I just came by to see your face and check up on you. If you're not too tired after all this, maybe we can catch dinner tonight," he says as he steps toward her.

They stand face to face with their hands clasped together. "I would love that," she says before kissing him passionately. She pulls back and just appreciates him for seconds before speaking again. "Babe, I can't thank you enough."

"For what?" he questions.

"For all of this. For making my dreams come true. Six years ago I left prison, not knowing what my next move would be. I had no friends and no family, just me. I was scared and didn't know what my life would become.

Now look, I'm doing what I always loved. Well, I'm too old to model but I'm teaching them everything I know. First the idea of opening up my own agency and then you come up with the idea of doing a reality television show based on it? You're a genius, babe," she says with sincerity.

Tony and Miranda have been dating for years now. Although he's not committed to her, she's very well committed to him. He puts no label on their relationship and just enjoys her while he has her. He finds that method best for him since his divorce. The next time he commits to a woman it will have to be the right woman with no doubt in his mind.

Miranda on the other hand knows in her heart that she's found the right man because no man has ever made her as happy as he does. She knows what he's been through and how that has him on the fence about committing so she doesn't pressure him. She knows that they are soulmates and in her heart she's sure that one day he will realize that she's the perfect woman for him. Until that day she will just continue to play her position and practice patience.

She becomes starry eyed just gazing into his eyes. "I'm totally grateful for all of this. Trust me I am," she says with tears welling up in her eyes. "But I have one question for you."

"Make it quick," he says in a playful manner.

"A fly gentleman like yourself, suave, and let's not forget rich."

Tony interrupts. "And let's not forget handsome either."

"Yes, and very handsome," she says while rubbing her hand over his face. "A powerful attorney," she adds. "You can have any woman that you want. Why do you even bother giving me, an ex-felon the time of day?"

"Great question," Tony replies. "Never in my career have I ever dated or even had sexual relations with a woman client of mine. Nor the wives or girlfriends to any of my clients, for that matter," he adds. "And believe me I had the opportunity with damn near all of them," he says with cockiness. "But you, I just had to have you. I guess you caught me slipping."

95

TWO DAYS LATER

THE CITY HAS been rather quiet since the funeral home massacre. There has been a few meaningless shootings here and there but nothing nearly as newsworthy as their attack. Manson isn't underestimating them the least bit. He's sure they're just laying low planning their next attack.

Manson figures after the funeral home situation his next move should be history in the making. After such a spectacle he knows he has to do something special to follow that up. At this point what he really wants is Mother Nature and Smith. Everybody else is not even worth it to him. While he's strategically planning his attack on them he decides to take this little downtime to hash out the other phase of his business.

It's pitch dark on the quiet block except for the bright lights under the canopy of the barber shop. Inside the Dominican barber shop, surprisingly there are more Blacks than Dominicans. Ten Dominican barbers stand behind the chairs cutting heads of their Black patrons. Many customers are sitting in the waiting area while others stand around in small huddles like a hangout.

Loud hip hop music blares through the speakers like a club. Huge mirrors, and flat screen televisions are spread throughout the spacious shop. A pool table and a card table, even a pull up bar occupies the back of the room. The shop looks more like a hangout than a place of actual business. Although there is haircutting business taking place, dirty business is also quite evident.

All the attention is focused on the door as the beautiful Skelter walks in. Lust fills the air as she strolls through innocent but sexily. With lightening speed she draws her gun. She stands in the center of the room with her gun in the air, scanning the room.

"Nobody move, nobody get hurt," she says as Manson steps into the shop. He walks right pass her.

"Who the owner in here?" Manson asks.

All fingers point to the barber standing at the far end. The young and flashy Dominican shrivels up in fear. He holds the straight razor in his hand frozen stiff as Manson walks up to him. He stands face to the man's chest. He carefully takes the razor from the man's hand and places it on the counter top behind him. Skelter stands in the backdrop keeping her eyes on the entire room.

"I know you're probably wondering what this is all about. Y'all ain't from here so I'm sure y'all not familiar with me but I'm Manson. You may can ask a few of your customers about me once I leave," he says with arrogance.

"I'm just coming home from a 15 year bid. I'm trying to situate some things and put some money in my pocket to feed me and my army but from what I hear a bunch of you motherfuckers are in the way," he says as he looks around the room. Everyone looks away from him, careful not to lock eyes with him.

"As of today, I will need y'all to pack it up and go back to New York, or Dominican Republic, wherever y'all from. I don't know who told y'all that it's sweet enough over here for y'all to just slide in like that and maybe it has been but things are about to change. It's operation shutdown."

Manson peeks over his shoulder at the door before giving Skelter a head nod. Everyone sits and stands on eggshells awaiting the next move. Suddenly a loud crash sounds off before the glass picture window shatters into pieces. Everyone runs for cover as the huge Chevy Tahoe backs into the room, engine racing.

The doors bust open and Smoke and Arson hop out of the backseat with their assault rifles in hand. Arson's presence makes the scene that much more intimidating. Manson scurries to the door, dragging Skelter along with him. In no time thereafter, the sound of assault rifle gunfire echoes throughout the room. People duck for cover as they shoot out the lights and all the mirrors.

The gunfire continues on until the place is destroyed. Once the gunfire ceases they climb back into the truck. Smoke hangs his head from the passenger's window, assault rifle in the air. "Business is officially over!" he says before firing a round of shots recklessly. The truck peels off, burning rubber on the marble floors.

96

THE NEXT NIGHT/9 P.M.

MANSON STEPS OUT of the Grim Reaper and walks straight to the door of yet another Dominican barber shop. He steps inside and walks through the shop like the militant general that he is. His aura demands the attention of the patrons as well as the barbers. This shop is nowhere near as lavishly decorated as the others but it's still quite packed. This is his third appearance today through the shops in the city.

Manson stops in the middle of the floor and just looks around into the faces of the people in the room. Like a flash of lightning Arson comes running into the shop with the machine gun glued to his thigh. He stops at the heels of Manson and just looks around like the madman that he is. All the movement stops and everyone watches with fear.

"Short and to the point," Manson says as he takes a step. Arson steps right behind him. "I'm Manson, the Black Charles Manson," he says with emphasis. "I don't know if your cousins from across town warned y'all already or not but I've made quite a few appearances."

Manson looks to the barber in the middle who stands near the stereo system. "Turn that down," he says pointing the stereo. "I hate raising my voice. It only gets me excited. Trust me y'all don't want me to get excited in here."

The man fumbles clumsily with the radio until it's shut off.

"I'm only giving y'all fair warning because obviously y'all don't know no better. You been getting away with it for so long that you don't know you're doing something wrong. Well, I'm here to correct your wrongs," he says with a smirk.

"Who is the owner or the manager in here? All the barbers point to the man on the end. With no other choice he raises his hand slowly. "Owner?" Manson asks.

The man shakes his head nervously. "Manager."

"Okay, good enough. Tell your boss this business is officially closed. In fact, we are closing right now. Everybody, let's go!"

People hurry to their feet. The man in the chair looks at Manson. Only half of his hair is cut. "Leave with half a hair cut or would you rather stay here with half a head?" Manson asks. The man gets up and rushes to the door behind the line of men who are exiting as well. The customers all have made their exit and now the barbers are just standing.

"Y'all too, let's go." Manson steps closer to the manager with his hand out. "Give me the keys."

The man passes the keys to Manson with no hesitation. "Okay, let's go," Manson says as he grips the back of the man's neck and forces him to the door.

All the barbers are lined up in front of the shop with confusion on their faces. Arson gets into the Grim Reaper. He rolls the window all the way down just in case he needs to get a close shot.

"Lock the gate," Manson commands the manager. The manager quickly pulls the gate down and locks it. "Give me the keys back." The man passes the keys back. "Now tell your boss I spared y'all but next time I won't. The business is shut down. Y'all can go back to New York or even over to North Newark but never back on my side. If I ever hear that this business is open and operating it will be a Dominican massacre in here. Follow me?"

The manager nods his head up and down in fear. "Now y'all go on and get away from here. Have a good night." Manson gets into the Grim Reaper and it pulls off, leaving the Dominicans on the curb. They stand there for seconds in confusion just letting it all marinate.

97

DAYS LATER

"**D**AMIEN, YOU'VE ALREADY taken one without paying for that one yet and you want to take two more?" Hamza questions. "Let's not overextend ourselves. Let's secure the money for the first one before we open a new account."

"Trust me bruh. I got plans. Don't hold me on a leash. Let me do what I have to do."

"I will never hold you on a leash. I've had a 100 percent success rate with no losses because my business runs on a COD basis."

"And I will never tarnish your success rate. Whatever I take will be paid for one way or another. These dudes will never play with me. It's guaranteed."

Hamza is uncertain about it all. "What about cash and carry accounts? I'm sure you know somebody with money."

"Honestly the people I would like to deal with are in the same situation as me. Just coming home to nothing but have access to it all. Just like you blessed me I would like to spread the love and bless others. I promise you if you can do that for me, we are on our way."

Hamza sighs. "Okay, but lets retrieve the money for these three before we go opening new accounts. Deal?"

Manson nods his head up and down. "Deal."

"I have someone who wants to speak with you," Hamza says with uncertain eyes. "I told him about you and told him I would introduce the two of you. You hear him out and if it sounds like something you're interested in, the business is between you and him. I want nothing to do with it. Okay?"

Manson doesn't reply. He's quite confused about who it is he wants him to meet and what it can possibly be about. After a few seconds of silence Hamza leads the way into his office. Manson steps into the office where he finds a Hasidic Jew. The Jew appears to be in his 60's but indeed he's only early 40's.

The man wears a yarmulkah on his head. Two long curly sideburns extend down his face. He's dressed in a dingy three piece business suit and worn out, turned over dusty shoes on his feet. At his entrance the man stares him up and down with beady eyes through his tiny wire framed spectacles. Manson stares him in the eyes coldly.

"What up?" Manson asks Hamza.

"Damien, this is my cousin Eli. Eli this is my good friend Damien," Hamza says planting his hands on both of their shoulders.

Eli extends his hand first. "How are you? I've heard so much about you."

Manson shakes his hand and gives him a nod.

"Damien, my cousin has a business proposition for you."

"I'm listening."

Hamza looks to Eli, turning the meeting over to him. "Damien, is it okay if I call you Dame?"

"No, call me Manson. Only my loved ones get away with calling me Damien and only he calls me Dame," he says as he points to Hamza with no smile.

"Okay, Manson," Eli says as he clasps his hands together. "Let me start by telling you what my profession is. "I work hand in hand with doctors all over the world. I supply them and make a good living doing it. I travel the world in search of their requests. I search high and low for organ donors."

Manson wears a confused but agitated look on his face. "I don't get it."

"You will just hear me out," he says before cracking a smile. "Hearts, kidneys, livers, I'm responsible for delivering whatever it is that they need. Somewhere in the country someone is on the waiting list for a heart transplant. A list that may be fifty people long. You got people that have it all that life has to offer but their life is on a countdown clock if they don't get the organ they're in need of. That makes them willing to pay any amount of money just to add some years to their life and continue living their luxurious lifestyles. Organs to sell on the Black Market. I'm the organ specialist."

"I'm not understanding what you're coming to me for?" he says with frustration in his eyes.

"I'm a businessman and I respect business. I never judge how a man makes a living but I do understand that your living consists of murder if it calls for it, correct?" He doesn't wait for a reply. He continues on. "Bodies on top of bodies being left dead on the street. Imagine if you could make money off of those dead bodies.

They're murdered for whatever reason, which is not my concern. My only concern are those precious organs that are left in their scumbag bodies," he smiles. "They're worth more dead than they are alive. Thrown in the dirt like dirt with no value but they're full of value to us.

You can kill two birds with one stone. Rid the world of the scumbags and make a great deal of money doing so. Anyway you would be doing a great service because most of their families don't have the money to bury them anyway." It's all starting to make sense to Manson yet he still stands quietly. "Vital organs going to waste and they don't have to."

"So, you get the organs and make a profit, what's in it for me?"

Eli smiles a huge yellow tooth smile. "I'm prepared to give you a hefty price for every organ you can get me."

Manson can't believe his ears. He's no stranger to murder but this proposition is kind of creepy to him. "What am I supposed to do cut the organs out for you?" he asks with a sarcastic smile.

Eli smiles as well. "I'll make it easy for you. How about a hundred grand for every body you bring me? Scrape their bodies off of the street and get them to me right after. Make the police officer's job easier. No one wants to do reports and investigations," he smiles. "Furthermore, with no body, there's no case. It all works out for everybody." Manson stands there just absorbing the proposition. "Take my number and think about it. There's tons of money to be made. Sleep on the idea but don't oversleep."

98

COUNTY JAIL

T'S LATE AND all the inmates are on lockdown for the night. The inmate struts along the tier tired from mopping and cleaning the kitchen. The correction officer stands at the other end of the tier with his eyes glued onto the inmate. The inmate stands in front of his cell and waves so the officer in the bubble will let him in. The buzzer sounds off and the gate opens. The inmate steps inside and Immediately begins to undress himself. The inmate on the bottom bunk looks up and sees it's him and fades back to sleep. He kneels over to take his shoes off. He's so tired that he doesn't even realize that the buzzer didn't sound off indicating that the gate was closing.

Another inmate appears out of nowhere. He has a T-shirt pulled over his face with the eyes cut out so he can see. He creeps inside, tiptoeing behind the man. Once he's close enough he lunges at the inmate who is bent over taking his shoes off. He stabs the man in the neck with the jailhouse dagger.

The man squirms to get away until the knife is jammed into his chest. The man's scream is muffled by the hand that is placed over his mouth. The other inmate wakes up and hops out of the bed in fear. He stands against the wall away from the action. His eyes stretch wide open when he sees another inmate step inside, T-shirt covering his head as well. "Don't move," the man says as a threat to the other inmate

Meanwhile the knife toting man is kneeling over the man, carving him like a turkey. He pokes and jabs the man with the knife, straight up, backhand, upward and downward. He doesn't stop poking until the man stops moving. The man lays on the floor with more holes than Swiss cheese and blood gushing from every one of them. Both men exit the cell. The correction officer purposely turns his head as the inmates exit the cell and disappear.

This hit was from Mother Nature. She used her long reach in making this happen. The correction guard was in on it as well as the guard in the bubble. Both are Blood under her set. Both young and banging but were fortunate to never have caught a case which allowed them the opportunity to work here. Even though they may not be actively banging when Mother Nature calls on them they still have to adhere to protocol.

When they took the Oath of Blood over everything, that meant everything for the rest of their lives, including this job. Mother Nature plans to touch every member of Smoke's army that may be in this jail and it will be easy because she has the guards on her side working with the many pups she have in here jailing. Smoke may not care for the men he loses in here but on paper she plans to even the score.

99

"BRUH, I'M TELLING you something ain't right," Samirah says very fidgety like. "She left here days ago without even telling me. I woke up and the bitch was gone," she says as Smoke listens attentively. "The last thing I remember talking to her about was her Instagram page she just opened up. We was taking pictures and posting and shit, then she started acting crazy."

"You went to her page?" Smoke asks.

"Yeah, she haven't posted nothing since that night. I'm telling you that bitch must know something. No way she would just up and leave like that without telling me shit. I got a funny feeling, bruh."

"Psst," Smoke sighs with no real concern. "Maybe the sucker nigga took her back and made her cut all ties off with everybody again."

"I doubt it bruh. Her pages would've been the first thing she shut down if that's the case. I'm telling you bruh, she know something."

"Yo, you tripping. I think you're overreacting."

MEANWHILE

Tasha sits in the backseat of Big Show's Bentley while Black sits in the front seat. She no longer has the privileges of riding shotgun or even alone with Big Show. He doesn't trust her anymore.

The only reason he hasn't cut her off totally is his addiction to her sex. Every time he needs a fix he has one of his men accompany him just for his own safety. He's so ashamed that he still messing around with her that he keeps it a secret from his immediate circle who know what happened. When dealing with her the men that are present are of his extended family. This is the first time that Black and Tasha have seen each other since the night Show damn near beat her to death.

As they're in hotels and motels his men sit in the car in the parking lot on guard. Riding shotgun and being alone with him are not the only privileges that have been revoked. She also cant get him on the phone exactly when she likes. She's been calling him since the night she left Samirah's house and he's just getting back to her. Right now they're sitting parked in front of her cousin's house where she's been staying.

Tasha sits on the edge of the backseat, in the middle of the two front seats, showing them her phone. She scrolls through the pictures quickly and stops at the one with Samirah, Smoke and Bout Dat in it. "That's him right there," she says as she points right in Bout Dat's face. "I will never forget that face."

Big Show snatches the phone with rage. He examines the face closely and so does Black. They look at each other with clueless faces. "Never seen him before," Black says.

"Me either. Probably because we don't play in the dirt," Big Show says. His face distorts right before Black's eyes but Tasha can't see it. If she could she would know to duck at this very second. Big Show backhands her silly. She's sent sailing backwards.

She holds her lips as it swells instantly. Blood drips from it excessively. She's dizzy from the slap and discombobulated. She's in a trance just listening to Big Show scold her. "Dumb ass bitch! I should've left yo ass in the dumpster. Sneaking around with that slut and look what that got you. Almost got your dumb ass killed. Sneaky ass bitch!" he says as he tries to get at her again.

She slides to the far end of the seat out of his reach. He then flings the phone with rage and when he does his thumb double-taps the pic. The phone smacks Tasha in the forehead. "Get the fuck outta my car before I kill yo trifling ass in here!"

"But Show," she whines.

"But my ass," he says diving over the console. "Get the fuck out!" Tasha opens the door and scrambles to get out. As she gets one foot on the ground, Big Show pulls off full speed. Tasha falls out of the car and her body rolls over to the curb. She lays there with an embarrassed look on her face as two pedestrians stare at her with compassion.

Big Show is fuming. "The dirty nigga Smoke and his man first," he says with fiery eyes. "Then the dirty bitch Samirah!"

Samirah sits on the couch with her eyes glued onto the phone. She opens it up to her Instagram page and sees new notifications. Her heart skips several beats as she sees the red heart under the picture. This is confirmation that Tasha knows and she's sure if Tasha knows then so does Big Show.

Samirah stares at the words, reading them over and over. "Oh shit," she sighs before dialing Smoke's number. "I fucking knew it!"

100

2:17 A.M.

MIRANDA LEANS BACK in the passenger's seat just enjoying the night breeze. All the windows are rolled down evenly just above eye level. Cigar smoke soars into the sky through the wide opened roof. She's gotten comfortable by kicking off her stilettos and elevating her feet.

Today was the final night of shooting for this season of her reality show. It seems as if it would never end. It's been all work for her for the past couple of months but she doesn't complain because this is the life she's dreamed of. A few years ago she had charged all of her dreams as over. Never did she believe that she would get a second chance at it all.

She's grateful to be back in the world and lives every second of the day like it's her last. She hasn't complained a single time in all the years that she's been home. She left all her complaints and sorrow inside that Florida prison. She came home not knowing her next move nor where her next meal was coming from.

She takes full responsibility for her wicked actions and has spent most of the past ten years repenting for her sins in prison and out. She has full trust in God that he has her back because ever since she's come home she's been blessed in more ways than she could imagine. She constantly fools with Tony saying to him that he's the angel that God assigned to her.

From the first time they laid eyes on each other the connection was magnetic. After the disaster she had just gone through with Sha-Rock the last thing on her mind was a man. Her concern was getting her life together. She had made a vow to herself that she wouldn't even date.

Tony, at the time, had his own dilemma. His state of affairs was quite the opposite. He was using women to get over the messy divorce with Mocha. With no emotional attachment to the many women that he had in his stable he only viewed them as a sport, never having any intentions of taking any one of them serious.

He met Miranda as he represented her and he saw something in her that he couldn't deny. Her loyalty and code of honor was something that he had never experienced with a woman. A woman that was willing to spend the rest of her life in prison just adhering to the G code was unbelievable to him. It all started as business but each time he spoke to her or saw her she left him mesmerized.

It wasn't her beauty that attracted him though. Her morale intrigued him primarily and her beauty was secondary. Nether of them can remember how their relationship ever started but they both agree that it had to be one of Tony's slick remarks that reeled her in. She's been trapped in his web ever since.

She just prays that he doesn't throw her back into the ocean like the many guppies and bottom feeders that he's come across. Her love for him is real but what they have is deeper than love. He's her best friend who has proven to her that with a friend like him she doesn't need another.

Miranda sits in the passenger's seat which is strangely on the left side of the road, nearest the oncoming traffic. Tony controls the vehicle from the right side as if it's normal and not against the law here in the States. Not only is the seating illegal but the car itself is illegal. Something about cruising around on the opposite side in a banned automobile makes him feel like an outlaw.

This car is by far Tony's favorite of his seven car collection. Although the automobile values at over three hundred grand, price isn't what makes it his favorite. He has two cars in his collection which cost more but in no way does he appreciate them nearly as much. What makes it his favorite is the fact that it's banned in the United States which means he's the only one in the country with one. Altogether there are only 499 more of them in the world, making it a rarity. At four years old, the value of the vehicle still hasn't depreciated because they have never made this model since.

He had this convertible Alfa Romeo 8C shipped from overseas last year. Alfa Romeos haven't been allowed into the country for decades yet Tony managed to pull the strings to get his in. The black 2 door sports car catches the attention of everyone. The tints do the car so much disservice hiding the red leather interior but he does himself a favor by having them. With police seeing him driving from the opposite side he is sure to attract attention that he doesn't want or need from the law. The 20 inch alloy Hartge rims sitting on low profile tires makes the car appear to glide through the darkness.

Miranda looks over to Tony with googly eyes. Her left foot is on the dashboard and her right foot is plastered against the windshield as she leans her head back and takes a pull of her cigar. She blows it out slowly, watching the smoke soar into the sky. She sings along with the lovely voice of the woman blessing Rick Ross's 'Aston Martin Music.'

"Riding to the music. This is how we do it....all night. Breezing down the freeway, just me and my baby...in our ride," she sings. "Just me and my boss, no worries at all," she says as she looks over to him with a long glare.

Tony sits back in what seems to be a world of his own. He puffs on his cigar as he keeps his eyes in his rearview mirror. About six minutes ago Tony and Miranda dropped off paperwork to one of the models that is on her show. As glamorous as she looked on the show no one would ever expect her to live in a rathole smack in the middle of the hood.

Tony makes the right turn onto 15th Avenue with his eyes still glued to the rearview. Seconds later the old body Cherokee turns right behind him. Tony wasn't sure if his paranoia was tripping or if the jeep has been following them. He first noticed it behind him about four blocks and three right turns ago.

Tony is distracted when Miranda who is turned in her seat places both of her feet onto his lap. She teases his manhood over his linen pants. Once she gets the reaction she was hoping for she plays the piano with her toes. She wiggles her toes up and down his shaft as if it's a keyboard. Tony flashes a cool grin at her before quickly diverting his attention to his side mirror. He plays it cool, not wanting her to know what he thinks is going on.

He makes a left at the corner and continues up the block. He's mindful to stay on the busy streets because he feels that may deter whatever plans they may have. Once he sees the Cherokee turn behind him, he realizes in no way is this his paranoia. He peeks over to Miranda, who is taking a drag of her cigar, eyes closed. Before she can open them, he grabs hold of the 9millimeter that he keeps stashed under his seat.

Although Tony is a successful attorney some habits never die. The only difference in today and the days of the younger Tony is the permit that he has to carry. He no longer carries a gun as a crook. Today he carries his gun as protection against the many threats that he's received in his career. He's gotten men off of murder raps that were definitely guilty and that has left a many of people angered with him. He knows exactly what he's up against which is why he never plans to be caught dead to the rear.

As the jeep gets closer to them he hopes for the better but his gangster senses tell him differently. He's sure it can either be one or two things that they're following him for. Either they're admiring the car as most do or worse. If it's the worse he has no plans of it going down without a fight.

The whole scene plays out in his mind. An all out gun battle is what he envisions. He looks over to Miranda and the thought of her in the middle of all of this makes him unloosen the grip of the gun he holds at his left side, out of her view. He thinks of his career and all the trouble he's had over the years. He knows his career can't stand another blemish. He then thinks of Miranda and what she's been through. An ex-felon with murder on her jacket could end up in a bad spot after this.

Miranda blows a smoke ring out of the window. She stares into the mirror on her side and her body tenses up. She sits up slowly as she turns toward him. "Babe, I saw that truck way back at Markida's house. I didn't say anything when I saw it turn with us. Now this the third time. I know I'm not tripping."

He looks over at her with a look of false concern. "You think?" he asks. "You probably tripping mama. Lay back, smoke your cigar and chill. You've had a long month," he says as he texts on his phone. LIL BRUH, WHERE YOU AT?

The text is returned in less than two seconds. I'M AROUND. WHY, WHAT'S UP?

Manson sits on the edge of the passenger's seat. Tony never texts him and to get a text from him in the middle of the night doesn't sit well with him. Tony's text comes back rather quickly. He reads it slowly. I'M IN NEWARK AND WAS JUST UNEXPECTEDLY INVITED TO AN ALL BLACK AFFAIR. I'M DRESSED IN ALL BLACK TOO, PRE-PARED FOR THE PARTY BUT I GOT MY OLD LADY WITH ME. I GOT A TRUCK FULL BEHIND ME, DRESSED FOR THE BLACK AFFAIR TOO. THEY INVITED ME. Manson reads it over once quite confused. Midway through the third time reading it he has it all figured out.

Manson quickly texts back to get his whereabouts. Tony sends the details to him and Manson reads them aloud. "Make a left at the corner," he commands Helter. He snatches his gun from his lap with an eager look on his face. He wonders what this is about but he will shoot first and ask questions later. For Tony to call him in need this has to be real. Tony didn't let him down and he refuses to let Tony down. Skelter and Arson sense Manson's anxiety and they grab hold of their guns as well.

Miranda is now sitting up in her seat, eyes in the mirror. She's sure she's not tripping now. The past six blocks they have been lagging behind. The traffic behind Tony has all broken off. It's now just them and the Cherokee.

The Cherokee speeds up and as it gets closer Tony grips his gun again by his side. Through the dark tinted windows he can see both the driver and the passenger have ski-masks on.

Tony watches as the traffic light changes to red long before he gets to the corner. He quickly debates whether he should stop or not. He realizes if he doesn't, all will take off from here. He decides to stop just to buy himself some time. He steers the nose of his truck to the left while leaving the back in the center. By doing that he cuts the street off, giving them no way to pull up on the side of him.

His aura is as suave and debonair as ever on the exterior but his feathers are very much ruffled. He would never let Miranda know that because he fears she will begin to panic. He can't believe that this is happening. He hasn't had a problem in his city since he was a kid and now this. He can't believe that he's really being chased around his own hometown. He's furious at the thought that they're playing him like a chump.

The Cherokee creeps up closer to his bumper. He keeps his foot off of the brake and allows the car to roll. He looks over to Miranda who sits there with a cool and calm demeanor yet her eyes signal that she's nervous. He grips her hand for reassurance. His eyes say, *I got you.*

The light changes and he steps on the gas pedal easily, trying hard not to alarm the driver of the Cherokee. With just a tapping of the gas pedal the engine roars loud enough to hear at least three blocks away. He cruises up the short block and as he nears the corner he slaps his left blinker on. He turns the corner and to no surprise the Cherokee turns right behind him. The Cherokee is steered to the left as if it's about to swerve around him until Tony steers his car, obstructing them.

With the Cherokee following almost on the opposite side of the street, Tony has view of another set of headlights. The lights become bigger in his rearview as the vehicle gets closer. Tony's text alert sounds off. As he increases speed he peeks down at his phone to read the text. BIG BRUH, I JUST GOT TO THE PARTY. I SEE YOU. GO ON INSIDE AND ENJOY YOURSELF. I GOT THE DOOR FROM HERE. Tony turns the corner casually. Miranda is happy to see that the Cherokee has not turned with them.

Before the Cherokee can even spin the corner behind Tony's car the Grim Reaper swerves around the right side of them. Just as the passenger looks over Arson is already hanging from the back window. He fires relentlessly. BOC! BOC! BOC! BOC! BOC!

Bullets are sprayed into the Cherokee. The first two strike the passenger, one in the shoulder and the other in the forearm. The third bullet rips into the driver's neck. The impact causes him to lose control of the wheel. Arson continues firing to keep them distracted so they won't have time to fire back. BOC! BOC! BOC!

The Cherokee swerves onto the sidewalk and smacks into the mailbox. He jumps out and runs over to the passenger's side where he finds the passenger leaned over the console lifelessly while the driver is ducking and trying to get out of harms way. Arson dumps another ten rounds in the Jeep before he dives back into the Grim Reaper.

Tony and Miranda hear the shots echoing in the air. She looks over to him with a look of astonishment while Tony stares straight ahead. No remorse is in his eyes because he feels none in his heart. He hates to think of how things would have gone down had he not had Manson on speed dial.

Just to think that a legal man such as himself is not even safe in the city that he grew up in. To know that no one is safe here, not even the hard working man is hard to digest. He can remember the days when the legal, working man, was off limits. He realizes that those days are now way behind him.

101

SMOKE SITS PARKED in his rental, peeking around cautiously. Jada steps onto the porch of the one family house. She's dressed in her scrubs because she's supposed to be at work right now. She already set it up telling Manson that she had to work overnight, overtime due to so many callouts.

That's the perfect alibi for her and Smoke to be able to do something they haven't been able to do in a minute and that's spend a night together in each other's arms. Manson didn't question her claim the least bit because with her working that gives him time to work as well. He can roam the streets all night hunting.

She peeks around even more cautious than Smoke. She sees a Buick with tinted windows approaching and turns her head as if she isn't paying attention to it. Surely she's watching it out of the corner of her eye though. Smoke is watching it as well, with his hand gripped tightly around his gun.

Once the car gets to the corner and continues on through the intersection Jada races down the stairs skipping a few at a time. She snatches the door open and gets inside. She knows the routine. Once she's inside she flips the lever and leans the seat way back. Smoke cruises off slowly.

MEANWHILE

The Grim Reaper pulls into the Wendy's parking lot and parks. Manson gets out of the back seat and gets into the passenger's seat of the Chevy Equinox with the Pennsylvania license plates. "Yo," the driver says, quite happy to see Manson. "What's good?"

Manson is equally as happy. He closes the door and reaches for the handshake. "It's all good?" Manson smiles.

Manson and this man met many years ago in the Feds. He's from Pittsburgh so he goes by the name Pittsburgh Pete. This man came to jail just a regular money earning dude. He was color blind and didn't represent any color but green. That is until he met Manson and fell in love with his style.

He became so obsessed with Manson that he started walking and talking like him. He even wanted to be Blood like him. Manson took him under his wing and created an animal. With Manson as his battery pack he felt invincible. He flexed the power that Manson gave him with pride.

After a few years together they were separated when the man was shipped out. Manson didn't know what to expect but was happy to hear news coming through the building that he continued on with authority in Oklahoma alone just as he did in Kansas when he was with Manson. They always kept in touch somehow or another. A few years ago when he was freed he took that authority and repositioned himself in Pittsburgh. He was always an earner but his new found power puts him many steps above where he was before he left.

"What's up though, my boy?" the dude asks with a spark in his eyes. Manson is his idol. He screws his face, gangster like. "What, you need me for something? You need me to come down and handle somebody?"

Manson laughs it off. In his mind he's thinking the man surely must have started believing his own hype. Never would he kill his spirits though. "Nah, lil bruh, I'm good."

"Oh alright. What, what you need money then? What you need?"

"Nah bruh I don't need nothing but some manpower. What your situation looking like on the heroin tip?"

"Oh, I be getting it and dumping it."

"Is it good?" Manson asks.

"Ah, so-so. Nothing to write home about. Sometimes it's up and sometimes it's down. I ain't got no rocker like I had before I went away but for the most part I can move it though." The truth of the matter is he really has nothing. He hasn't been able to get back up since he returned from prison. He's been getting by playing the middle man, brokering deals. Through an acquaintance he met in the feds he was linked to a few people in jersey who allow him to eat with them.

He takes the money from his clients in Pittsburgh, buys the work from his Jersey connections and is able to score a few dollars profit in between. "I ain't gone lie to you Big Bruh. I came back home on the bottom. I been home for two years now and I'm still on the bottom. I can't get right for shit."

"Well, let me fix that for you," Manson says as she slides the shopping bag over onto the man's lap. He opens the bag where he finds a half of a container of Shea Butter. He's confused. "That's half a key of raw dope."

"Word?" he asks with joy in his eyes.

"Can you do something with it?"

"Can I?" he asks in a high pitched voice. "I can work magic with it, especially if the number is right."

"What number works for you?"

"I mean I get it a hundred and thirty dollars a brick from my man and sell it to my people up my way for a buck forty-five. If I go through two hundred bricks a week I can score myself about three grand profit. I had a connect on the grams for like eighty-five dollars a gram but it was too much of a headache. At that number anyway. Wasn't enough profit involved."

"Okay, how about at seventy? Is that enough room for you?"

"Hell yeah! So, what's that thirty-five grand for the half? Bruh I ain't even gone lie to you, I can't even afford a half a joint. I'm just scoring a few points between the connect and my customers. The most I can buy right now on the real is about fifty grams...thirty-five hundred," he says with disappointment in his eyes. He feels like Manson needs him and he let him down.

"Who said anything about you buying? You my lil bruh. Go ahead and take it and get right. When you get right, I get right. All I ask is every three or four days bring me something through just to keep the engine rolling. Feel me?"

"Damn right I do! Thanks Big bruh!" he says with a tear in his eyes. "I'm gone make this money and make you proud of me!"

Manson smiles like a proud dad. He rubs his hand over the man's hand. "I'm already proud of you."

ONE HOUR LATER

Manson sits in the passenger's seat with a man from Philadelphia that he met while away in Otisville. This man too is another man who was quite obsessed with Manson. This man stronger than most, couldn't be broken and brought in to the gang as Manson was able to do with so many others. In jail this man's love for his religion superseded his love for any and everything else.

He was so true to his religion that Manson had no choice but to respect it. Manson is so used to seeing this man in Islamic attire that he looks strange in the latest fashion with big designer sunglasses. The only thing that hasn't changed is the dark prostration mark on his forehead and the big thick, full grown nappy beard on his face. His beard is the size of Santa Claus just jet black.

In the Feds this man was known as Angry Muslim. His anger against the world and everybody in it is the basis of his nickname. No one has ever seen him smile. He wakes up angry.

The man listens as Manson speaks and as expected his face is frowned with anger for no apparent reason. "Ay man you know me," Manson says. "I'm the same out here as I was in the prison... Extremely radical," Manson says with a smile.

"Is the war heavy though?" the man asks.

"No war is to be taken lightly. But it's okay though. I got it. There's no revolution without bloodshed."

"Bruh, say the word and I will send you a hundred big beards up here. I will pay for the whole top floor of the hotel for them to stay. You can call them out one by one as you need them. That simple, bruh. They don't know none of my guy's faces. Beards make us all look the same," he smiles.

Manson smiles at the gesture. "I appreciate that, bruh, but I'm good." Manson stares at the prostration mark on the man's forehead and isn't quite sure of how to approach the proposition. "I called you because I didn't know exactly what you was up to. I mean, but being that you got your real estate thing booming down there like you say, ain't no need for me to tell you what I got going on."

"Nah, talk to me, bruh."

Manson looks away as he slides the black plastic bag over to the man. The man opens the bag and stares at the half a brick of heroin with a spark in his eyes. "But I see that won't do you any good though. Had a great number for you and on the cuff. Pay me when you finish. Unlimited too," Manson says as he pulls the bag from the man's grip. "Them shits will keep coming and coming and coming."

Angry Muslim snatches the bag back from Manson. "Now, hold up now." He goes into deep thought. "Damn," the man says as he attempts to fight back the temptation. The anxiety overpowers him and he can't fight back any longer. "Fuck it, I'm in."

Manson smirks with sarcasm. "What happened to you deening and your real estate company booming and you being blessed and don't need the streets for nothing?" Manson pours it on thick.

"Hmph, man," he sighs looking for the perfect reply to what Manson just hit him with. After fumbling for seconds he spits out the only defense that he can muster up. This excuse is the excuse that many find fit when it comes time to justifying some bullshit. "God knows my intentions!"

102

HOURS LATER

THE CHEAP MOTEL room reeks of sex, garlic, Portuguese food, marijuana and old people. This motel is Smoke's down low spot, deep in the cut. Although the room is quite cheesy, Jada is just happy to be with him. They could've spent the night in the backseat of his car for all she cared.

Jada lays butt naked on the dingy white sheets, flat on her stomach, ass in the air, spread eagle. Smoke has attempted at his best impression of romanticism by ordering a twenty dollar pan of Portuguese chicken, rice and fries and a seven dollar bottle of Yellow tail Shiraz. Jada has never had a man attempt to romanticize her ever so she's more than impressed with the minimum. After the romance came the backbreaking sex. Now she's sound asleep.

Smoke walks around the room butt naked, limp manhood swinging. He's drained himself to the maximum. He missed her so much that he was able to give her eight orgasms and gain two for himself. They've already broken their record and the night is still very young.

Smoke stuffs his mouth with cold fries from the pan. The sound of a car pulling up catches his attention. The back brake lights of a vehicle shine brightly through the filthy curtains. Smoke walks over and cracks the curtain just enough to peek through it.

French fries fall from his mouth as he stands there not able to move. The Grim Reaper is parked close to his car. "Yo!" he shouts back to Jada. "Yo!" he shouts louder. Smoke runs over to the desk and grabs his gun from it. "Jada! Wake up!" he shouts.

She awakens startled. Once she notices his gun in hand she jumps out of the bed and stands to her feet. "What, What?" she stutters.

Smoke quickly puts his pants on without his underwear. He keeps his eyes on the brake lights of the car which are still shining brightly. Jada runs over to the window and damn near faints once she sees the Grim Reaper. "He found us," she cries. "Oh my God," she says as she steps away from the window. She places her hands over her head as she throws a tantrum of fear. "He's gonna fucking kill us," she whines.

"You better get dressed!" he says as he pulls his shirt over his head. He slides the safety off. "When they come in I'm not hesitating. Just stay close to me and I'm gone shoot our way out of here." Sounds good but he doesn't even believe it. He's sure he will not be able to out shoot them all but he damn sure is gonna try.

The backdoor opens and Arson gets out. He slams the door shut and walks toward the stairs. Smoke watches his every step as he comes up the stairs. "Here they come," he whispers to Jada who is rushing to put her clothes on. Smoke leans over to the end so he can further keep an eye on Arson. Smoke can already picture himself blowing the white boy's brains out.

Smoke's heart races as Arson gets closer. Smoke closes the curtain and steps back so his shadow can't be seen. Arson passes the window without looking in that direction. Smoke runs to the other end of the window and he sees Arson stop a couple doors away. The creaking of the door sounds off and Arson disappears. The door slams shut. The Grim Reaper cruises the lot and makes an exit.

Smoke exhales. "They left."

"He's gonna kill us," she sighs.

"Nah, the white boy staying a few doors down. We gonna have to blow the spot before they come back to get him in the morning."

"That was a close call," she says as she sits down on the bed and gets herself together. What a risky situation they are in. As hazardous as it is for them, it turns Jada on. Being that close to danger just a second ago has her adrenaline racing and her pussy watering.

She walks over to him, plants her hand on his chest. The other hand she unzips his pants. He's limp from fear. He still hasn't gotten himself together.

Jada bites down on her lip seductively. "Come on, let's go again." She juggles his manhood in her hand and gets no reaction. She gets onto her knees and pulls him through the zipper. She goes to work, pumping life into him in no time flat.

Are they addicted to each other or are they addicted to the danger rush?

103

ONE HOUR LATER

SMITH IS IN the brand spanking new triple black Cherokee which was carjacked not even an hour ago. He and four others are crammed inside, cruising the streets on a quest in search of the enemy. The Hemi engine roars ferociously under their feet and butts, rattling the ground. All five of them are very well equipped with guns and extra clips. Over three hundred rounds of ammunition is packed in this one vehicle.

Smith is in the passenger's seat with his hood drawn tight over his face with barely an opening to breathe through. He and the rest of his crew are as high as zombies right now. The driver is the only who has his eyes open and that's because he has no choice. He fights every second to keep them from shutting.

The drugs and the music has them in a zone. They have been listening to the same song on repeat for the past two hours. As Smith utters the words to the song he can't help but think of the other half to his gangster, Wesson. This song was his all time favorite song. That's the reason that Smith has made it his theme song throughout this entire war. Every murder he's caught has been inspired by this song, in the name of Wesson.

"You niggas think you feeling froggy, bitch... My niggas doggy bitch!" he shouts as he bounces around in his seat, eyes closed. "Run up on him with that 40 bitch, go retarded bitch!" he says waving the gun around recklessly. As he's rapping along the other men just bop their heads, eyes closed just feeling the music and letting it sink into their veins. The more excited he gets the more motivated they are. "Make that body flip!"

Smith visualizes Wesson and how excited he used to get singing this song and he tries to emulate him. "We dropping bodies, bitch!" he says as the vision of his best man laying in that coffin is stuck in his mind. Tears drip down in face inside of the hood where no one can see. "They say shooting is my hobby, bitch and I'm a problem kid!"

At this moment they're all so excited just looking for anybody to take their anger out on. Hopefully the anger won't be misplaced.

MEANWHILE

The Grim Reaper pulls in front of Pebbles' house. He leans back in the passenger's seat with the phone glued to his ear. The call is picked up on the third ring. Jada picks up. "Hello," she says somewhat out of breath.

Jada holds the phone to her ear as she sits straddled over Smoke. His manhood inserted deep inside her but both are afraid to move. "Nothing, I heard my phone ringing in the locker room and ran to it so I didn't miss your call," she lies.

She's so warm and wet inside that Smoke can't refrain from moving. He hits her with a few slow deep strokes. Jada leans her head back, eyes closed, just fighting back the feeling. "What you doing?" Manson asks.

Jada plants one hand in the center of Smoke's chest for balance. She makes a big arch in her back before throwing it at him quietly. "Working."

"Alright then," he says. "I was just checking up on you. Go ahead and get your work in."

"Okay, I will," she says hanging up on him without saying bye.

Manson peaces Helter and Skelter and gets out of the car, letting them go on about their way. He walks into the lobby of Pebbles' building and rings the bell. She answers with her normal amount of nasty attitude. "Who?" she barks.

"Me. Open the door."

"What you want, Manson?" she snaps.

"Open the damn door!"

The buzzer sounds off and Manson enters. He walks down the hall and stops at her door. Pebbles opens it, standing behind the door. "What you want?"

"Stop playing with me and open the door."

"No, I got company," she says staring him square in the eyes. "You can't just be popping up when you feel like it. I told you I'm gone be seeing other people since you seeing other people," she says with attitude.

Manson is more than frustrated with her little game playing. He kicks the door with all of his might causing her to stumble backwards. He walks in and closes the door. She's stark naked.

She walks away switching hard. Her enormous ass rolls vibrantly turning Manson on crazy. "Fuck you at my house for? Where your little dirty bitch at? What she out somewhere fucking and you can't find her so you come over here to fuck my shit up," she asks never turning around to look at him.

Her shitty and disrespectful attitude has him excited. He charges behind her like a raging bull. He tackles her on the bed and bends her over. He mashes her face in the bed, damn near suffocating her.

She still isn't shutting up. She mumbles words over the sheets that are in her mouth that he can't make out. She squirms to get away from him but he overpowers her. He holds her down with one hand as he fumbles with his pants with the other. Without even pulling his boxers down he aims precisely through the slit of them and inserts himself into her.

"Shut up," he says as he rams himself into her. "Shut up," he says pounding even harder. Pebbles squirms and squirms pretending to be trying to get away from him. She knows the little cat and mice game turns him on so she continues on with it. "Always fucking talking," he says as he bangs her harder with each syllable. "When you gone learn to shut the fuck up?"

Pebbles screams from pleasure. "I'm not gone ever shit the fuck up," she roars. "Who the fuck is you?" she asks. She gasps in order to catch her breath. With every slick mouthed attack she takes at him he punishes her.

"Motherfucker, you don't own this pussy no more. I'm giving it to other motherfuckers," she says knowing damn well that will do the trick to punish her severely. Her trick works and Manson pounds on her abusively just the way she likes it. She knows just how to press his buttons and she does it at her liberty.

Smith still singing the song on repeat as the Cherokee is traveling down South Orange Avenue. The car in front of them stops at the red light, forcing them to do so as well. As Smith looks up he catches the glimpse of a familiar vehicle. His eyes zoom in on the huge chrome cage of the Lincoln Van. "Yo!" he shouts to catch the attention of everybody in the van with him. He turns the radio down. "Is that them?" he asks as the van cuts across Maybaum Avenue in front of them.

"Tinted and everything," the driver says as they all watch the back of the van.

"Jump on them," Smith commands as he snatches his gun from his lap.

The driver mashes the gas pedal and swerves around the car which sits in front of them. Smith unrolls his window, preparing for battle. All his men prepare themselves as well. "Catch up quick," Smith says as he sits on the edge of his seat very hyper. The driver steps on the accelerator and in seconds they are almost bumper to bumper with the Lincoln.

"Pull on my side," Smith shouts. The driver swerves around the van quickly and there Smith is side by side the driver's side window.

Helter looks to her left and is in shock for a second or two until the sound of the 9 millimeter snaps her out of it. BLOC! BLOC! She mashes the gas pedal in just enough time for the shots to cave the back window in. Skelter leans over from the passenger's seat and fires out of the back window. BOC! BOC! BOC!

The driver of the Cherokee steers to his right in attempt to bang them off the road but Helter swerves and speeds up causing him to miss them. She has a few feet in between them. Smith continues to fire recklessly at the back of the Lincoln. Just as Skelter is about to hang out of the passenger's window she sees a police car sitting in the darkness a few feet to her right. "Oh shit," she says as she drops back into her seat. "Jake." The shots behind them cause Helter to speed up.

The sheriff officer hits his siren and takes off behind them like super-cop. He speeds up behind the Cherokee. Smith's torso hanging out of the window gun in hand is stuck in fear as the lights of the police car swirl, blinding him. With nothing else to do, he aims his gun at the windshield of the police car and fires, BLOC! BLOC! BLOC!

The passenger's side of the window shatters. The cop swerves but he continues on behind them. As the chase intensifies, the Lincoln makes the quick left and enters the Parkway, not even stopping at the toll booth. The Cherokee continues on along the empty two way street as the sheriff's car is close on their bumper. A sheriff's SUV comes out of the first cross block and joins the chase. By the time they get to the corner a string of sheriff's vehicles are in hot pursuit.

Up ahead bright lights for blocks can be seen. The driver panics, not knowing which way to go. The sound of gunfire rips behind them making the driver even more nervous. AS he approaches the corner he sees approximately twelve cop cars in front of him. Once they get to the corner they spot police cars squatting at both sides of the cross street anticipating their next move.

The driver steers to his right and jolts through the intersection at full speed. Gunfire sprays from both sides, shattering the windows and ripping through the body of the jeep. The driver continues on full throttle as the cars bust u-turns to join in behind the vehicles that are already following closely. The Cherokee is filed with fear. In fact they're all terrified.

The driver makes his way to the next intersection. Just as he's zips through it, an unmarked black jeep with no headlights on darts out at full speed. The driver of the Cherokee attempts to swerve out of the way but to no avail. The Cherokee's back bumper is struck causing it to do a 360. The Cherokee spins until it crashes into the brick building. All four doors pop open and the young men take off in a foot chase in different directions.

Smith darts through the first alley he sees. As he's running he hears gunshots. He hurdles over the first gate and launches his gun into the next yard. He continues running like a runaway slave. He runs and runs with hopes of remaining free.

104

THE NEXT NIGHT

IT'S LONELY AND deserted out. The streets are quite bare with no movement on them, yet Manson and the crew sit parked in the cut. Today they're riding in luxury in the black on black Cadillac Escalade. The Grim Reaper is out of commission today, having the windows replaced from last night's close call.

Manson has been preaching about patience the whole time they've been sitting here. With nothing going on it's been as boring as watching paint dry. Up ahead in clear view is the entrance and the exit of Mother Nature's townhouses. All of their heads are on swivel, understanding that sitting this close to the area can easily be hazardous. None of them want to be the one to admit that to Manson though. They all know better than to go against his orders.

Minutes later three men come strolling through the exit onto the street. They make their way up the block. "See what patience will get you," Manson says from the third row. "Walked right into the trap. Go!" Manson instructs.

Helter steps onto the gas and cruises up the block with the lights off. Just as they pull alongside of the men who are engaging in deep conversation, they all look over. The looks on their faces are of pure terror. Their mouths can be read as two of them say, "Oh shit," right before they take off into flight.

Skelter hangs from the passenger's side window and fires three shots. The smallest of the three men leads the pack. He dips into a dark alley where he disappears. The man in the center is struck and the impact knocks him into the garages with full force. His body ricochets off the garage and smacks into a parked car. He attempts to get up but he's been marred. Skelter fires two more shots at the running man who buckles as he's hit but he continues to hop on as fast as he can.

Manson taps Arson and Smoke on the shoulder. "Go snatch him," he commands.

Arson busts the door open and he and Smoke dash out. They grab the man from the ground and throw him in the vehicle. He's in so much pain that he puts up very little fight. Once they're inside Helter peels off.

Minutes Later, the smell of fresh blood fills the car. The smell is stomach turning to Helter, Skelter and Smoke but Manson and Arson love it. Manson sits next to the man who is bleeding like a pig from his arm, his back and his leg. He screams in agony every couple of minutes. Manson sits right next to him, gun in hand. In Manson's other hand is his phone which is glued to his ear. "I'm on my way to you. Yeah, right this minute," he says as he hangs up the phone. "Jump on 280," Manson yells to Helter.

"Smoke guide her to Canal Street," Manson says.

Smoke turns around confused. "In New York?"

"Yeah, I got work to do back here and need to concentrate," he replies as he plants his hand on the man's shoulder. "Listen, I'm gonna be perfectly honest with you. You're gonna die tonight. It's just a matter of how. You can die fast and feel almost no pain at all or you can get tortured and die slow. It all depends on the answers to the questions I'm about to ask you."

"No, please don't kill me. I will answer whatever you ask me."

"First question...where does Mother Nature live?"

The man shakes his head with tears dripping from his eyes. "I don't know," he whines.

"Wrong answer."

"I never been to her house. I swear to God."

"Ok, second and last question. Where does Smith live?"

"I don't know."

"See, I tried to speed the process up for you but apparently you want to die slow."

"No, please," he begs. "I think he lives somewhere in Ivy Hill. That's all I know."

Manson stares straight ahead ignoring the man. He begs and pleads for the twenty minutes that it takes to reach Canal Street.

"Go straight up and over the Manhattan Bridge," Manson yells out. All are in confusion as to where they're going but none of them have the heart to ask. Manson finally gets exasperated with the man's crying, begging and pleading. He hauls off and backhands the man with his gun gripped tightly in his hand. "Shut up all that fucking noise!" The man's two front teeth are knocked smooth out of his mouth. He whimpers almost silently like a sad puppy.

Manson reads the street signs once they cross the bridge into Brooklyn. "Turn left right here. Helter makes the quick left in a nick of time.

"We looking for 287," he says as he reads the addresses. "Right here, right here," he says pointing to the big warehouse.

Manson picks up his phone and dials. "I'm out front." In less than a minute the huge steel gate opens automatically. "Pull in," he instructs. Helter turns onto the sidewalk and pulls into the warehouse.

Eli stands on the side trying to peek into the dark tints. Once their inside the garage Eli presses the button and the gate closes slowly. Everyone looks around at the huge empty warehouse wondering what this is about. The man who is held captive has lost so much blood on the ride here that he's weak and can barely keep his eyes open.

Manson gets out. He and Eli meet at the hood of the car. Eli extends his hand for a handshake but instead Manson gives him a fist bump. Eli smiles with greed in his beady little eyes. "So I gather you have something for me?"

"Only if you got something for me," Manson replies coldly.

"Dame... I mean Manson, it's after midnight. No way do I have a hundred grand for you right now. You should've called me in advance."

"There's no call in advance with this shit. It's whenever, wherever. You just gotta be fucking ready. You want the business, right?"

"Yes, yes. I understand. I promise you next time I will be ready." Eli looks at the Cadillac with anxiousness. "So where is that body? In the van?"

"Hold your horses," Manson says as he walks over to the backseat of the truck. He snatches the door open and pulls the man out by the collar and slams the door. Everyone in the truck watches in a bewildered state. Eli is quite confused as well. The captive looks at Manson with pleading eyes. "What's going on? Please?" he begs.

Manson stops short in front of Eli. "I don't understand," Eli says.

"What don't you understand?"

Eli leans over and whispers into Manson's ear. "Our deal was to bring me the bodies but not live bodies. I'm an organ specialist. I'm not a murderer."

Manson draws his gun from his waistband and plants it on the back of the man's head. The man screams when he feels the gun on his head. Manson squeezes the trigger and the sound of the gunfire interrupts the scream and ends it. The man collapses onto the floor, dead and covered with blood old and new.

"No, you're no murderer. I am," Manson says staring into Eli's scared eyes. He is at a loss for words. He stares at Manson, then the gun, then the dead body and then back to Manson. He's been dealing with dead bodies for years but never has he been this close to the actual murder. "You wanted it, you got it. Hand delivered," Manson adds. "Now tomorrow I expect my money hand delivered to Hamza or else I will be back over here for another murder," he says as he walks off leaving Eli speechless.

Manson snatches the door open and holds the door before getting in. He points at Eli. "Tomorrow right?"

Eli still can't put any words together. All he can do is nod his head up and down. He steps over the body and makes his way over to the gate. He presses the button, the gate opens and Helter backs the truck out. Eli closes the gate quickly.

He walks over to the body and he's scared to death. He fears the dead man may pop up. He grabs a 2x4 from the floor just in case. As he plays back what he just witnessed, he's wondering if he may have gotten himself into something that he's not necessarily ready for.

They cruise over the Manhattan Bridge in total silence. All of them are quite confused as to what that was about but none of them question him. Manson hopes that Eli handles his end of the deal and if he does he will see the first hundred grand that he's seen in his whole life. He already has it planned out. Just ten bodies will make him a millionaire. Had he known Eli years ago he would've been a multimillionaire. He didn't but he now he does and if things go well he will catch up with all the money that he's missed. He has big plans.

NORTHERN STATE PRISON

A **MAN WRINGS** his underwear out after finishing up his shower. He entertains a few jokes being fired at him from other inmates. "Fuck outta here!" he shouts as he's making his exit. "Next day!"

He struts along the tier with the confidence of a soldier, underwear in one hand and a bag of cosmetics in the other.

A ten-year veteran correction officer sits in the booth with his full attention on the beautiful rookie officer. With his eyes on her curvaceous hips squeezed into her tight fitted uniform pants and his ears on the NFL draft that she's talking him to death about, he's completely distracted. The engagement of conversation with him is all apart of a plan. A plan that her boyfriend designed.

Her boyfriend a high-ranking Blood under Mother Nature's set orchestrated this carrying out a command from Mother Nature. He designed it strategically down to the very exact second. Every time the officer looks to the cameras she strikes another seductive pose, giving him a more clear view of her beautifully contoured body. Finally he gives up watching the cameras and gives her his undivided attention.

Just as the inmate is turning into his cell he's greeted by a sucker punch that has the impact of a mule kick. It all goes black before his eyes as he topples over. The pain of the sucker punch is taken away as the pain of a knife tearing into his gut takes over. He hurdles over, holding his stomach and attempts to defend himself by reaching out to grab the image of a man that stands before his eyes.

Still dizzy from the blow he can't compose himself. He stumbles forward as the knife is being dug into his back. The knife then pierces his side and then his neck. The man with the knife must be an octopus because the stabbing seems to be coming from every direction simultaneously. The man squeals like a pig as he's poked repeatedly.

HOURS LATER

The correction officer bangs on the door of the cell. "Count!" He looks inside expecting the inmate to wave or speak but to no avail. "Count!" he yells again, banging on the door much louder. Still the inmate doesn't respond.

The officer opens the gate and goes inside. His attention is called to the floor where he sees enough blood to make his stomach curl. He shakes his head, hoping for the better. Once he gets to the bed and pulls back the covers he finds what is to be expected. The inmate lays there dead soaking in his own blood like a pickle in a vinegar jar.

106

8:15 A.M. THE NEXT MORNING

MOTHER **N**ATURE **AND** two of her pups stand bedside here in UMDNJ hospital. The man lying in the bed is the man that escaped Team 6 last night. He made the call to have Mother Nature come see him just to pull her up on the details. He's not even one of hers so truly she cares nothing about him. He just hangs around in the way for the most part. He's good in every hood because he's no threat to anyone.

Her reason for coming here is to find out the details of Rocky, who no one has heard anything from. "Boom, we look back and bang there they go right there. It's already too late to really react because they right dead up on us. So, Rocky say go and take off. I take off right behind him but you know he slow as hell so I sprint right pass him. Lil Ez dip off like I don't know where he went."

"Who?" Mother Nature asks.

"Lil Easy. Be coming through every now and then. "Lil curly head dude with a big nose."

Mother Nature nods her head. "Nah, but anyway... Go ahead," she says with very little concern. She only concerns herself with her immediate folks.

"So boom, soon as we take off they start letting it go. Boc! Boc! Boc!" he says reliving the situation in his mind. "I turn around and Rocky rolling on the ground hit. I hear him screaming and shit.

I stop but I'm thinking like damn this nigga might already be dead. Anyway I ain't got no strap on me so it really ain't nothing I can do. We both just gone be dead. So I take off and I hear two more shots.

I get hit in the ass but I keep it pushing. I bend the corner and hide in the bushes. I see two motherfuckers get out the Caddy and carry Rocky over and put him in the car. Like I'm good. They releasing me in a minute but I'm worried about Rocky, man," he says with sadness spreading across his face.

"So he wasn't dead?" Mother Nature asks.

"I don't know. I couldn't tell from where I was at. Boom, they ride pass me and I duck back in the bushes until they gone. I hit my bitch and she bring me straight here. My shit wasn't about nothing. Bullet went in and out the ass. The doctor said luckily I had a big ass or it might have been more serious," he says cracking a joke like the comedian he is. No one finds him humorous under these circumstances though.

"This some crazy shit right here, though. I guess they kidnapping now," she says with a smile on her face. "That's the game they wanna play." Mother Nature pulls out her phone. "Anybody seen or heard from Smith? He ain't call me today. That ain't like him."

They all reply by shaking of their heads. "Last time I saw him was last night. Lil dude came through in a stolen Hemi Cherokee and they took it from him and said they was going mobbing."

"What time was that?" Mother Nature asks.

"Man that was late as hell."

Something about this sounds crazy. The only reason she can see them kidnapping Rocky is to get him to tell where she lives or maybe some of their secrets. He doesn't have any money so she's sure that can't be what it's about. He doesn't know where she lives so she's not worried about that.

She considers the possibility that maybe they call themselves holding him for a ransom and will be calling her soon. She has to get in touch with Smith to run this pas him to see what he thinks of it all. She dials him and after one ring the call is sent to voicemail. She dials right back and the same thing happens. She tries the third time and once it's sent to voicemail she begins to get nervous. She makes the quick decision to go to his house.

MEANWHILE

Smith sits on the living-room floor of his house. His hands are cuffed behind his back. He stares up at the Robbery/Homicide detective with nervousness as he scrolls through Smith's phone. He wonders who is calling back to back like that and just hopes they don't text him something crazy that can incriminate him.

Smith's mother dressed in Muslim overgarment and a niqab covering her face sits on the floor across from him. She's handcuffed as well. Through the cutouts for her eyes huge tears can be seen flooding her eyelids. Smith's older sister is present and cuffed along with them. The only people who aren't in cuffs are Smith's two little brothers and his nephew.

Just as Smith's mother and sister were leaving with the children detectives bombarded the house. The noise awakened Smith from his sleep. He thought it was just another one of his dreams but soon realized it was reality. There's no doubt in his mind one or maybe all of his men were caught last night and gave him up.

Two detectives search the cabinets in the kitchen, two are searching the living-room and five more are searching throughout the rest of the house. Smith hasn't locked eyes with his mother once in the hour that they've been here. Seeing her cry breaks his heart. He hasn't seen his mother cry since his father Big Mu-Mitt was murdered years ago. It broke his heart to see his mother cry then and it breaks his heart even more to see her crying now.

The 6 feet 8 inch tall detective comes walking into the living-room. Smith kisses his freedom goodbye as he stares at the machine gun in his hand. Two other detectives come walking behind him. Both of them have two handguns in their hands. The detective smiles. "Got eem!" he shouts with a sinister laugh.

All the detectives run over, cheering. "You got that out of his room?" the detective asks.

"Nah, the mom's room and the sister's room. His room was clean. Everybody cuffed and ready to go?"

Smith stares into his mother's eyes for the first time and he can feel the disappointment bleeding through them. Smith's sister screams loudly as the detective lifts her onto her feet by the handcuffs. Her son as well as Smith's 11 year old little brother start crying right along with her. Smith is the only one in the family with dry eyes.

The woman detective steps up. "We need to get D.Y.F.S. on the phone. Sarge, you wanna call now or wait until we get down to the precinct?"

"Let's just sort everything out at the precinct. Take everybody down. Fuck em," he says with no compassion. "Child services will come get them from the precinct and find somewhere for them to live," he says just being a wise ass as he likes to be.

Smith's older sister loses it. "No, please don't take my son. Please," she begs. At this moment everyone falls out into tears from the mother on down to the kids. Smith looks around the room with guilt in his eyes. He feels horrible that he's put them all in a situation like this. He looks at his mother and she rolls her eyes with hatred. He looks at his sister whose eyes are begging to be rescued from the madness.

"Don't take them. They're innocent. Take me. All the guns are mine."

Everyone looks at the sergeant awaiting his response. He looks around agitated like. So badly he wants to lock them all up. "Come on, Sarge," the woman begs, feeling compassion for the women and the children.

"Alright, fuck it," he growls. "Un-cuff them. Today is y'all lucky day."

Minutes later Smith is being dragged out of the house. He spots Mother Nature's jeep in the cut. They lock eyes through the front windshield. Smith is saddened because he knows how bad she needs him right now. He hates to leave her out here alone and feels like he let her down.

Mother Nature feels the same sorrow because without Smith and Wesson she feels ass naked. They've been through the most crucial situations together and they always had her back. She doesn't have the same faith and trust in anyone else in the world. As she watches Smith get slammed into the back of the car she feels like she's lost her superpowers. She watches the car pull off and her heart sinks even more.

She shakes her head. "Got damn!"

107

HOURS LATER

MANSON AND SMOKE meet up at Vailsburg park. The Grim Reaper is parked behind Smoke's car as they stand in between them almost out of sight. Smoke speaks. "So, I get with my man a few minutes ago because he was hitting my phone crazy. Remember the lil nigga that we thought got away the other night, he got hit?"

"Yeah, what about him?" Manson questions with no real enthusiasm.

"Lil nigga name Easy. He ain't bout nothing but come to find out his brother some fake ass Crip G. Like he don't get busy or none of that but he got a bag and he be feeding the homies and bailing them out and all kinds of other sucker shit. I call them type niggas G by default. Well, anyway he went to the real G's and told them what happened to his lil brother."

"Alright, so what they saying? What they want to do?" he asks very excited to finally get it on. "We may as well clean this whole city up in one sweep. Fuck it!"

Smoke sighs. He never saw himself as the most rational person in the world until dealing with Manson since he's been home. Manson thinks how Smoke used to think. Smoke's not sure if maturity has changed his mindset or just reality that Manson seems to not deal with.

"Big Bruh, we got enough on our plate right now. Let's just handle the beef at hand and the Dominicans. We can get at them Crips another time." Smoke bears witness that a Crip beef will be nowhere near as easy as the beef that they're currently in the middle of. They have more unity, more love and loyalty for one another. They also have more money which means they can make bigger bails which means there's no fear factor involved in the outlandish things they can do and bail out afterwards.

"Man, fuck all that," Manson replies with a hot head. "I'm on a fucking rampage! Niggas took shots at my two bottom chicks last night! I don't wanna hear shit from nobody! They calling you for what? What the fuck is they saying though?"

"Nothing really. They ain't calling it on. They just want a sit down with us to find out if that was meant for them or not."

"Sit down? Man, I'm too stand the fuck up to sit down with some fucking Crips. Tell them I said fuck them and they can take that how they want," he says as he walks to the Grim Reaper, leaving Smoke standing there. "Sit down," he shouts before slamming the door shut. He peels out of the parking space like a madman. He leaves Smoke standing in smoke from the pipes and the smell of burned rubber.

108

ELI SITS AT the desk in the office of Hamza's store. Stacks of hundred dollar bills are piled on the desk already as he counts through more. Manson stands on the other side of the desk watching closely and counting every bill with Eli. Once he's finished he gets up from the desk and speaks, "There it is. A hundred grand. Would you like to count it for yourself?"

"I already did," Manson replies. Hamza walks over and hands Manson an empty box to put the money in. Manson stacks the bills in the box neatly. He does a great job at pretending that the money is nothing to him but truly this is the most money he's ever seen in his entire life. He stacks it with a feeling of success embedded in him. "It's a pleasure doing business with you," Manson says.

"The pleasure is all mine," Eli replies. "I hope this isn't the end of our business arrangement.

"Oh no, "Manson says with confidence. "We're just getting started. How many of those hundred thousands you got on deck? And how long you need in between to refuel your account?" he asks. He's just testing the water to see what Eli's capacity is.

Eli smiles. "Let's just say money is no issue. As fast as you can get the product to me is as fast as I can produce the money to pay you."

"That's all I need to hear. Trust me, getting the product to you is nothing."

"So when can I expect the next shipment?" Eli asks greedily.

"Honestly, no telling. I can't put a time on it. Those things just kind of come across my desk. And when they do I'm right at you."

"Okay, I will be waiting on your call," Eli says as he reaches for a handshake. They shake hands over the business. "Well, I have business to tend to so I will be making my way out," he says as he plants a hand on Hamza's shoulder.

He stops in his tracks "Oh, I almost forgot." He grabs a box from the floor and hands it to Manson.

"What's this?" Manson asks.

"Body bags. You made such a mess the last time. In the future I will need the goods prepared before they come to me," he says with a smile before leaving the office.

Manson and Hamza stand face to face. "Glad it worked out for you," says Hamza. "No, it worked out for us," Manson replies as he hands the box over to Hamza. "That's a hundred on my tab. Twenty more grand and we can close that account." He smiles. "The engine is now rolling."

109

SMITH STEPS UP to the packed bullpen. A group of six young men have the bullpen on smash. They have the area to themselves. They've been causing friction since they stepped in here.

The gate opens and Smith steps into the bullpen. His fury is pasted on his face. He's on his way to court, wherein the judge will set a bail. He's sure his bail will be no less than a million with all the charges he has piled up against him. Even at ten percent he's looking at a hundred grand which is no different than a million to him being that he can't come up with either.

He's sure if Mother Nature could snatch him she would but in no way would he even put that type of pressure on her. All he hopes from her is to get him the best lawyer that she can afford. He already has his mind set on jailing and fighting his case like the gangster that he is.

He was taught by his father Big Mu-Mitt to take his losses the same way he takes his wins; with his head up and his chest out. He's always done that unlike whoever it was that has given up. When he finds out which one of them told on him they will feel the wrath of his fury. None of them are on the same floor with him and he's sure that has been done by design of the snitch.

Smith looks around with a vicious eye. He immediately spots a huddle of men from Smoke's camp. They stick out like sore thumbs the way they're whispering amongst each other. They have the look as if they're ready to get it started this very second.

Smith shakes the hands of the few men that he knows personally. The tension in the bullpen is thick being that everyone is well aware of the war. Inmates in every jail, prison and federal institution in state and out of state are aware of the war by now. Anywhere there are Bloods from either side together a war has presented itself.

Manson and Smoke may be winning the war on the streets but they're losing terribly throughout the prison system. In the County alone three men have been stabbed to death and over two dozen have been stabbed damn near to death. The beef has spilled over from the County on down to Southern State Prison and all the way over to the New York Federal system and all in between. Everyone peeks around expecting things to heat up any second now. With them outnumbering Smith 6 to 1 this is the perfect time for them to make a checkmate move.

Smith holds a small meaningless conversation with an old head fiend from around his way. As he's talking he pretends to not be paying the least bit of attention to his enemies. Once he's done listening to the old man praise him like a celebrity, he makes his way around the bullpen. The men from Smoke's camp keep their eyes glued onto him as he walks in their direction.

They quickly engage in a conversation, pretending to be more into it than they really are. He stops short within arms reach of all of them. He stares into their eyes one by one while snarling like a vicious pit-bull under his breath. He hates these men as if they're the actual ones who murdered Wesson. They all watch him without blinking.

"Go ahead and pop off!" he shouts loud enough for everyone to hear. "That's what the fuck y'all supposed to do, right?" He lowers his tone. "I just slaughtered like ten of y'all homies by myself and here I am."

The men are trembling in their boots. He raises his voice again. "Just like I figured, y'all ain't gone do shit. All y'all fucking hoes. I should slap the shit outta all y'all one by fucking one."

The people on the sideline are completely shocked at what they're hearing as well as seeing. Before Smith stepped in this group of men had almost everyone walking on eggshells. Here it is little old frail framed, baby faced Smith is outnumbered and they have the opportunity to not just even the score but gain some status by touching him and they won't even do it. As easy as it is for them to move out on him they all understand that their lives will be hell afterwards. That is if they're still allowed to live afterwards.

"Y'all a disgrace to Blood. Don't none of y'all bleed gangster blood. Y'all bleed pussy blood. The same blood that come out a bitch pussy for five days and the bitch still don't die. Hoes just like y'all old ass washed up G's," he says as jumps at one of the men. The man flinches with fear. After he realizes that Smith was only humiliating him, he puffs his chest up to cover up for anyone who saw him play himself.

"After I catch them too played out ass, faggot ass G's, Smoke and that washed up ass Manson and slaughter them, I'm gonna take over that hoe ass line. I don't want none of y'all bitches with me. I'm just gone do it for the fuck of it. Y'all gone either get down or lay down, pussies!" he says before spitting into two of their faces. Not a one of them makes a move.

Everyone is shocked at the spectacle that he has created. One thing they all bear witness to is the fact that he's not just gangster on the street with firearms, he's also gangster on the inside with just his heart and his bare hands. Not many can say that.

Smith feels terrible that he's left Mother Nature out there alone but he plans to make it up to her by destroying any and every enemy that he encounters in here. He has plans of leaving not a one of them standing. When it's all said and done he will have had all of them murdered. The ones he spares will have to cross over and get under him. He's no longer on the streets but the war continues.

110

THE AREA IS peaceful except for the traffic on the busy street. Smoke, Dirt and Ooo Wee sit parked in the stolen black Charger. Dirt sits behind the steering wheel as Smoke sits in the passenger's seat with the assault rifle on his lap. Ooo Wee sits in the back with a 16 shot Ruger. Their focal point is the Dominican barber shop that sits in the middle of the block, a few stores up ahead.

In their couple of week's process of shutting down the competitor, they've physically shut down over twenty businesses that have been secretly funneling drugs throughout the city. A host of other businesses have closed down on their own in fear of being shut down. This shop is one of the very few that are determined to continue on with their business.

The lights go dim inside of the barber shop. Smoke sits up in his seat and Dirt prepares for the take off. Ooo Wee slides the safety off as Smoke grips the assault rifle tightly in his hand with his full concentration on the doorway. A man steps out of the door, taking one quick glance around the surrounding area before looking behind him at the other two men who step out behind him.

Once the gate is pulled down and locked up, the men make their way to the Range Rover with the huge chrome rims. Two of the men get into the front seat while the third man snatches the back door open. Just as the doors are closing, Ooo Wee eases out of the parking space. The front doors close. "Go!" Smoke commands.

The tires squeal as the tires burn on the asphalt. Before the back door can even close, the Charger sits side by side the Rover and Ooo Wee is already out of the car, gun aimed at the driver's window. He squeezes with no hesitation, BLOCKA, BLOCKA, BLOCKA! Smoke hops out waving the AR-15. He pushes Ooo Wee to the side before unleashing. With expertise he riddles the car with gunfire.

He makes his way from the drivers side, on around to the passenger's side where he fires until the passenger keels over. He aims at the man in the backseat, who ducks low behind the seat for safety. Smoke gets closer to the backseat and dumps approximately thirty rounds before running toward the Charger. He and Ooo Wee dive into the car and Dirt peels off, doors barely shut.

TRENTON

MANSON AND **B**LUE Blood sit in his kitchen. Piles of shrink wrapped money is stacked on the table. "Lil Bruh you gave me life! You gave my whole city life.

We all thank you.

I should bring all the dope fiends to thank you one by one," he says as a joke. "A lotta mofos ain't happy though. They thought I was dead. They counted me out," he says as he's stacking the money into a duffle bag. Motherfuckers doing everything to get their hands on this work. I'm only fucking with a select few. I told them motherfuckers if you ever counted me out, you can no longer count on me. I'm taxing all them guys that shitted on me. I got these projects and The Gut over in the North on smash. Can't nobody get a dime over me!"

"I'm glad to hear that, Big Bruh." Blue Blood slides the duffle bag across the table. That's the connect money outta the way plus twenty toward your half of the money. I will get mine in the end. Give me another couple of days and I will have the rest of yours for you. Gimme 90 days and we gone be rich. Mark my words!"

MEANWHILE IN THE COUNTY JAIL

Inmate stands in the corner with a cell phone glued to his ear while another inmate stands on guard at the door watching for approaching officers. Another inmate walks into the cell with fear written all over his face. This man was sent for by Smoke who is on the other end of the phone.

"Here he goes big Bruh," says the man on the phone. He hands the phone to the approaching inmate.

He reaches for it, hands trembling. He places it to his ear. "Yeah?"

Smoke speaks loud enough for them to hear even in the background. "So you was in the bullpen when the fuckboy came in? Motherfucker touched a bunch of us and you let him walk around freely? Y'all was supposed to even the score and make his lil ass pay for what he done out here.

I been looking all over for him and couldn't find him. He end up right there within your arms reach and you ain't do shit? All in your face popping shit and y'all still didn't move out?" Smoke asks.

"Nah, Big Bruh it wasn't like that?"

"What was it like then?" Smoke asks. "You know what, don't even bother bullshitting me. I already heard how it went down. You polluting my line and you gone pay for that. Get the fuck off the phone with me."

"We was about to move out right then but," the man attempts to explain before Smoke interrupts him.

"Everything after but is bullshit. Beat it!"

The man hands the phone back looking more fearful now than when he walked in. He looks around not sure if he can leave right now. After no one says another word he makes his way out the cell. He peeks out the corner of his eyes expecting it any minute. He exhales as he's allowed to leave without friction. Although he was allowed to leave he is sure that his days are numbered. Smoke speaks into the phone again.

"Clean that up for me. Him and everybody that was in there with him."

"Got you, Big Bruh. Say no more."

112

DAYS LATER

MOTHER **N**ATURE **LAYS** in her bed in her bedroom, just staring at the ceiling. She's quite perplexed. Still no one has heard a thing about her missing soldier. It's like he just fell off of the face of the earth. If it was a kidnapping she's sure they would've made him call somebody by now.

The fact that he hasn't and he hasn't surfaced makes her quite sure that he's no longer alive. She asks herself why would they take him when they haven't taken anyone else that they have shot or even murdered? This whole ordeal is weighing heavy on her mind. To be dealing with all of this on top of Wesson's murder and Smith's arrest is just way too much for her. For the first time ever she's thought about throwing the towel in.

Bailing out isn't beneath her. Normally when things get too thick she goes out of state to her family member's home but she can't go there this time because she burned that bridge the last time she was there. Anyway, she knows that submitting will make her the talk of the city. That leaves her no other choice but to keep fighting. She's taking the loss on the streets but as long as she's winning in the prisons it's an even game to her.

MEANWHILE

The Grim Reaper speeds over the Manhattan Bridge. All the windows are rolled down except for Arson's. The excessive smell of fresh blood is stomach turning to Helter and Skelter but to Arson it's the equivalent to the smell of a perfectly seasoned pork. He takes long sniffs of the air enjoying every breath of it. The thought and the smell of murder excites him tremendously.

Smoke is no stranger to murder but sitting in the last row so close to dead bodies in the hatch gives him an eerie feeling. Killing a man is easy for him but to carry the dead bodies gives him the creeps.

Manson hasn't given it a single thought since he had the men packed into the van. The eerie feeling nor the smell is affecting him. The only thing on his mind is the fact that someone attempted to harm two of his loved ones that night. Every time he thinks of how he could've woke up in the morning to them no longer alive he gets even more furious.

In the beginning of the war he only wanted prominent figures but now that deal is off. Now no one is off limits. He plans to destroy her whole line by murdering them as he finds them. The ability to make a profit off of it is even more inspiration for him.

The two bodies in the back are of stragglers they caught just hanging around one of Mother Nature's areas. They gunned them down on sight and scraped them off the streets just as Eli explained in their original meeting. The men were packed into the bags, still alive as they took their very last breaths. This is their third trip in three days, bringing the count up to five bodies in 72 hours.

MINUTES LATER

The garage closes behind the Grim Reaper. Eli stands at the gate accompanied by a younger more clean cut Jewish man. Manson hops out energetically with his face covered with fury. He stares the younger man up and d own making him feel quite uncomfortable.

"Eli!" he shouts as he steps right pass them. Eli follows so close behind that when Manson stops and turns around, they collide. Manson peers into Eli's eyes. "Who is your friend?"

"He's no friend. That's more like a brother to me."

"Yeah, to you. I don't know him and I don't feel comfortable doing business around him. Me and you have a business arrangement. He's in my way and I don't ever want to see him again. I don't fuck with everybody."

"But Manson you have a carload of strangers every time. I never say a word."

"You better not. That's my team," he says shaking his head with crazy in his eyes. "Yeah, Team 6. It takes all of us to get the job done. You want the product right?"

Eli nods his head without a verbal reply. "Well, do me a favor and keep your mouth shut and just do as I say."

"I understand and I do apologize."

"You got my money?"

"Manson, you don't trust me," he smiles.

"This is business," Manson replies. "And its not about trusting. It's about money and I need it. I want to finish our unfinished business before starting new business. You owe me for five including these two. That's five hundred grand. May not be nothing to multimillionaire like yourself but that's enough to change my life."

"Five? I think more like four."

A stern look crosses Manson's face. "Nah. Two the first day, one the second day and two today; that's five."

"Okay, okay, calm down," he smiles. "Four or five, who is really counting?"

Manson pulls a small notepad from his back pocket. He quickly marks two slashes before showing the page to Eli. "I'm counting."

Manson gives the ok for Smoke and Arson to get the bodies from the back of the vehicle. They struggle to carry the first bag to the far corner of the warehouse. They drop it on the floor like a sack of potatoes, no compassion or regard that this was a living human being not even two hours ago. As they drop the second in the corner Eli unzips the first bag.

He gawks at the man's face which has two holes in it the size of a golf ball. A third hole is in the very center of the man's forehead. Fresh blood leaks from the bag. None of this disgusts or even makes Eli sympathize. As he stares at the bloody lifeless body all he sees is dollar signs. To him this is not about life or death it's all about the product that creates the currency that he needs to live his life. He sees every living being as potential revenue stream.

As they're coming through the Holland Tunnel, on their way home Manson feels heat coming from the backseat. The heat pierces the back of his head making him uncomfortable. He turns around and stares straight into Smoke's eyes. He's caught Smoke off-guard giving him no time to turn away. "What's up?" Manson asks.

"With what?" Smoke asks with attitude. He can't even cover up how he's feeling right now.

"With you. You alright?"

"Yeah, I'm good."

"Oh alright. If you good I'm good," he says before turning around and facing forward. He puts both feet on the dashboard as if he has no worries but truthfully he wonders what is going through Smoke's head right now. Whatever is on his mind must be quite heavy because he can feel the weight from where he is.

Indeed, Manson is correct in what he thinks. Smoke thinks of the whole ordeal of dropping dead bodies and how Manson has not once spoken to them about the details of it. He wonders if he's spoken about it to the rest of them, just not him. Whether they know the details or not he feels he should know what's going on just so he knows what he's up against.

He may have the rest of them brainwashed but Smoke has his own mind. He feels like a stunt dummy grabbing dead bodies off the street and delivering them to an unknown man. He's no fool and is quite sure this is business. He's sure that if it's business that means Manson is getting paid for it. He can't believe that he's taking the same risk if not more and hasn't been given a dime for his time or work.

Smoke is sure that no one may have the heart to question Manson but it will only be a matter of time before Manson has to tell him something. He has enough of his own stunt dummies and will never be a stunt dummy to Manson. He respects him to the fullest but in no way will he allow him to play him for a fool. He refuses to risk his freedom carrying around dead bodies for no reward whatsoever. Either Manson is going to cut him in on the business side of it or he can cut him out.

CRIP ZONE/DAYS LATER

THE **C**RIP **H**OMIES sit on the bottom step of a porch. They entertain each other with jokes and chitter chatter. Drug activity is pouring from both sides of the street. This block is like the Mecca of drugs. Every drug known to man can be bought from this very block. They have drugs that are rare in the hood such as Crystal Meth. Of course they have the essentials like marijuana but they have it in every form, including candy and brownies. It can be bought by the bag or even the pound right here.

All jokes cease for a few seconds as a black new body Chevy Suburban LTZ with dark tinted windows bends the corner. Two of the men quickly take their places in front of the G, not knowing what is coming. A third man draws his gun on the sneak tip and keeps it hidden by his leg. He positions himself wherein he can get a clean shot at the truck if need be. The G quickly looks around to make sure everybody is on point and they are. On porches across the street his team is already set up.

The Suburban creeps along the block looking like trouble. The only reason he doesn't command fire is because one, they have no open beefs and two he's not sure if the truck is the police. Both the Feds and the State Police are known to move around in the same style vehicle. He rather his men get caught with gun charges than for them to get caught slipping.

The truck stops directly across from Vito and his men. The passenger's window rolls down slowly. Manson allows his face to be seen before slowly pushing the door open. He steps out of the truck with militancy in his eyes. The black bulletproof vest he's wearing isn't even concealed. It grips his torso over the tight white T-shirt. Beads of sweat cover his forehead like a madman.

"Y'all looking for me?" he asks, staring into the faces of the men on the porch. He can tell that they're clueless as to who he is. "Manson, the Black Manson," he informs. Smoke gets out of the truck on the other side and keeps his eyes on everything. All the men stare at him very unimpressed like. "Y'all wanted me, I'm here. What's up?" he says as he steps closer to them.

The G finally speaks. "One of ours got touched the other night. We know y'all going back and forth with the broad. Just wanted to make sure that it was about her and not about ours or us."

Manson smirks. "If it was about y'all trust me y'all would know. I don't go around the target. I go right at it, dead and center. Your man was out of bounds anyway in a Blood zone. I wasn't color coding, picking and choosing, it's war. I was raised to know that if two parties are at war and it has nothing to do with you, you stay clear of both parties."

The man laughs hysterically. "Out of bounds?" he asks. "What is this Blood zone, Crip zone you speak of? What's this banging of the 1960 mindset you have? So I guess in your mind Crips are still just confined to certain areas of the city and we have not migrated all over and taken over damn near everything," he says with sarcasm in his voice.

"No, I'm very well aware of that. I have been away for 15 years if you didn't know but now I'm home."

"And you say that to say what exactly?"

"No riddles," Manson replies. "I say what I mean and mean what I say. With that being said, the answer to the original question is no, it wasn't for you or yours this time. He got in the way."

"This time?"

"Yeah, that time. Never know what the future will bring."

"Talking real crazy right now."

"No, I'm really done with talking. You fellas enjoy the rest of your night," Manson says as he steps back into the truck. Just as he's closing the door he peeks his head through the window. "But do yourself a favor and keep yours away from the places on the city map that I have marked red x's on. Anything that has a red x on it will be destroyed and so will everybody who is there." He slams the door shut. "That's just a pull up."

As Smoke is getting into the truck he sees a few men setting up. He reads the play like a player on the field. He stops and reaches for his gun as he keeps his eyes glued onto the men. They all watch him with sneaky smirks on their faces.

The G stands up and looks over the roof of the truck. With a signal of the eyes, he hold his men off. They all just indulge in a staring match with Smoke who eases into the truck, never taking his eyes off of them. Helter pulls off soon after.

Smoke sits back in deep thought. Something tells him this is just the beginning of a serious situation. He knows they could have done some damage right then but wonders why they didn't. He's baffled about why they even allowed them to leave off the block without making their move.

He's sure it wasn't fear so he has no choice but to believe they have a bigger plan. Maybe they didn't want to get their block hot, he says to himself. This is exactly what he was trying to avoid at this moment but Manson seems not to understand. One thing Smoke knows for certain is in no way will this war be anywhere near as easy as the current war they're in. This war has the potential to be bigger than the Vietnam War.

He feels now is not the right time to go at it with them but he also understands that the call is out of his hands. Manson said what he said and now it's up to them to make their move. Smoke looks behind him at the G who is on the phone right now. He's sure that call is to inform the other G's what just took place. What he's not sure of is how they will react. Time will definitely tell, though.

114

MANSON, HELTER, SKELTER and Arson stand on Samirah's porch. Smoke opens the door and holds it for Manson to enter. Once Manson is inside Smoke lets the door close in Skelter's face. She snickers loud enough for him to hear but he doesn't turn around. He continues on into Samirah's apartment.

Arson slams the door shut behind him just as Manson and the others are stepping into the kitchen. Manson take a seat at the far end of the kitchen table. "Everybody take a seat," he says as he lays the duffle bag onto the table. They all sit around the table as Manson unzips the bag and starts pulling stacks of money from it. On the table in clear view is what appears to be more money than any of them have ever seen. Well, that is except for Smoke. During his run with the Mayor he was fortunate enough to have counted through millions and millions. Even though he's been here before it still feels good to be here again. He hasn't seen real money in so many years and seeing it gives him life and hope.

Just as Manson gets to separating stacks the door opens. They all sit on the edge of their seats cautiously. Smoke stands up. "That ain't nobody but her," he says to Manson. The voice of Samirah's son eases them all. "Yo, we in here," Smoke says giving Samirah the warning. "Hold up for a minute."

Samirah disregards his instructions and continues on anyway. Her nosiness could not let her stay in there and miss getting an eye-full. Smoke steps in the doorway blocking her. "I told you we in here."

Samirah peeks over his shoulder to see what she can. "I don't give a fuck," she barks. "My son thirsty. This my fucking house," she says as she pushes him out of the way.

In passing she locks eyes with Skelter who damn near eyeballs her coldly. Samirah attempts to look away from her but she senses a coldness in Skelter's eyes that she's never seen in a woman's eyes before. The coldness causes her to back down. She goes to the refrigerator and pours her son a drink of water.

All the while she's peeking at the money pretending not to be. Manson gives Smoke the eye and Smoke speaks for him. "Come on now, yo! We trying to handle something."

"Handle it somewhere else then," she snaps. "Don't be rushing me. This my fucking house!" she slams the refrigerator door. "All y'all can fucking leave," she says as she walks toward her bedroom. She looks over her shoulder at Manson. "Not you fav!" she says with a quick smile. Manson stares at her with the same amount of hatred that he always does.

Once the door is slammed shut Manson continues on with the business. They watch in awe of the brand new, crisp looking hundred dollar bills on the top of each pile. All the piles are a hundred bills high, making one pile the total of ten grand. Manson slides five piles in front of each of them. They all wonder how much is before them and what exactly is it for.

"That's for that Brooklyn business we been handling. I thank y'all for your patience and I appreciate the fact that none of you questioned my movements," he says staring into Smoke's eyes. Smoke senses the sarcasm and looks away.

"That's fifty grand apiece for everybody. That's ten thousand for every body that we bring him. With that being said, let's end this meeting and get back on our job and stack those ten thousands up," he says followed by a sly wink. He looks to Smoke. Get them shopping bags," he says in a bossy type manner. Smoke doesn't like the way he was just commanded but still he does what he was instructed.

Everyone stacks their money into the shopping bags with appreciative looks on their faces, except Smoke. Smoke is the only one with his side eye on Manson's duffle bag. From where he's standing the bag seems to be almost full to the top. Smoke is no mathematical genius but he does understand the basics and has common sense. Common sense tells him that if Manson just passed out two hundred grand to them and the bag is still full he must not have split the money equally.

He wonders just how much Manson is getting off a body if he can break them off forty per body. His curiosity has him so far out there that he doesn't notice Manson looking at him. He snaps out of it and they lock eyes. Manson zips the bag as he continues to stare into Smoke's eyes, letting him know that he's on him. At this moment Manson sees a look in Smoke's eyes that he's seen before but never toward him. That look is jealousy and envy and Manson doesn't like it.

115

SHORT HILLS MALL

TONY OPENS THE door for Miranda to exit through Neiman Marcus. Her arms are filled with a bag from almost every store in the mall. He allows her to walk in front of him so he can admire and appreciate the view. For as long as he's had her, still he hasn't lost the flame for her. After all these years and still every time he lays eyes on her the feeling is just like the first time.

The area is packed with a few people waiting for their cars. Tony steps over to the valet attendant whose attention is so fixed on Miranda that he doesn't notice Tony standing there. He twirls the unlit cigar in his mouth while he stands there patiently with his ticket in the air for seconds before he speaks. "Whenever you're ready," he says with a grin.

The young man snaps out of it. "Sorry, sorry, Sir," he apologizes, feeling quite embarrassed.

"No need to be sorry, your eyes," Tony says as he hands the ticket over. "My woman though." Miranda turns away to conceal her blushing.

The valet attendant jogs off to retrieve Tony's car. Tony and Miranda have managed to steal the attention of everyone in the area as they stand there looking like the perfect still shot for any photographer. Tony is dressed down today, yet and still his aura makes him look like a million bucks. With his a bright white, tight fitted V-neck T-shirt, army camouflage cargo shorts and black patent leather Jordan Bred 11's on his feet he can very much blend in with any and every thug standing on the street corners.

With all the pricey timepieces that he owns, the ten dollar watch that he wears on his wrist is one of his favorites for one reason. The Casio calculator watch has stood the test of time. He bought it in the late 80's. The 27 year old cheap watch is his favorite because it reminds him of where he came from.

Whenever he looks at the watch he clearly remembers the days of him copping half ounces from the Dominicans in Washington Heights area of

New York. As they dangled the small baggie of coke with the hand held scale he had big dreams of making it big someday. Never in his wildest dreams did he think that he would make it this big. He also never imagined he would make it big on this side of the law. To others they may see a cheap, old and outdated watch but Tony sees sacrifice and humility. The watch keeps him grounded.

He looks up to the bright sun with his hand over his brow as a shield. His cigar dangles from the corner of his mouth. Miranda stands behind him, chest against his back, symbolizing that he's her protector. The shopping bags are scattered all around her feet. The huge straw floppy hat blocks the sun but any bit of it that manages to get pass the hat is caught by the oversized sunglasses that she wears. The four inch heel stilettos and the daisy dukes shorts make her already long legs appear twice as long.

The squealing of noisy brakes interrupts Tony and Miranda's mini movie and everyone turns their attention to the older model 750 BMW. Tony looks at the huge, goofy chrome rims and in his opinion feels that they are doing the car more of a disservice. He can't imagine why anyone would want to draw attention to a twelve year old BMW. He turns away from the car without giving it a second look. Through the dark tinted windows both Tony and Miranda can feel eyes burning on them.

The driver, a big, brolic young man, hops out of the driver's seat with cockiness. The attention that he feels on him causes him to increase the cockiness in his bop. He starts to sing rap verses to himself, but loud enough for the people to hear him. "I'm gone be fresh as hell if the Feds watching," he sings to the words of rapper 2 Chainz that is playing faintly in his car.

The passenger's door opens and seconds creep by before the passenger gets out. Tony cuts his eye over and when he does he gets the shock of a lifetime. He double-takes just to be sure. His heart races and his ears burn as he lays eyes on the woman who is no stranger to him.

The last time that he saw this woman was five years ago but he remembers the day clearly as if it was yesterday. The last time he saw this woman was in the courtroom. In no way was this woman a client of his that he was defending. Instead he was defending himself against this woman, trying desperately to retain his possessions. This woman is his ex-wife Mocha. For a brief second their eyes intertwine but neither one of them say a word to each other.

"I'm gone be fresh as hell if the Feds watching!" the man says loudly, interrupting their stare-off. He stands right next to Mocha and wraps his arms around her shoulder. Tony laughs on the inside at the insecure act the young man has portrayed. He discreetly looks the man up and down with a smirk on his face. He's somewhat surprised that she would even entertain a man of that caliber, after all that he's shown her in life but then again nothing she does surprises him. He hears the Mayor's words ring in his head, 'No matter how you enhance a woman's life, they always go back to their level of comfort.' He's never forgotten those words.

Mocha can read his mind. She lowers her head with shame. The very next second a cool breeze swoops around the corner as the 2 door, 2-toned Rolls-Royce, Wraith pulls into the valet area. All eyes set on the beauty of an automobile. The black paint on the bottom half is thick and creamy and the upper body is smokey grey yet showroom floor shiny. The caramel colored gut peeks bashfully through the windows. $400,000.00 of beauty and steel dominates the area.

The parking attendant runs over and grabs Miranda's bags as Mocha studies each one with envy in her eyes. The attendant quickly closes the trunk and runs over to hold the door open for her to get in. Mocha stares Miranda up and down with hatred as she passes. Her eyes lock onto Miranda's face, realizing that it's familiar.

Anger crosses her face as she figures out who Miranda is. She clearly remembers her and Tony going to see Miranda in the Florida prison. Miranda switches away sexily, putting on a show for Mocha who she feels eyeballing her. The attendant closes the door gently and races around to Tony who tips him heftily.

"Damn, son playing!" Mocha's friend shouts with no shame. Tony pretends to not hear him. "OG!" he calls out. Tony looks over to answer the call. "You painting the perfect picture. Salute!" he shouts as he places his right hand against his brow.

Tony places his left hand against his brow and with the utmost disrespect he salutes him back. Mocha reads the play and is quite embarrassed for the both of them. She shakes her head from side to side before lowering her gaze.

Tony gets in and before he pulls off the words of his favorite song rip through the sunroof. "Oh, oo-o-oh, come on, ooh yeah! Well, I tried to tell you so...yes I did. But I guess you didn't know, as I said the story goes. Baby, now I got the flow. 'Cause I knew it from the start. Baby, when you broke my heart. That I had to come again, and show you that I'm real. You lied to me...all those times that I said I love you. You lied to me...yes, I tried, yes, I tried. You lied to me...even though you know I'd die for you. You lied to me...yes, I cried, yes, I cried. Return of the Mack...it is! Return of Mack...come on! Return of the Mack...oh my God! You knew that I'll be back...here I am! Return of the Mack...once again!"

The squealing of the tires burning onto the marble overshadows the music as Tony peels off, leaving Mocha with her jaw dropped to the ground. The feeling that Tony has right now, words can't explain. The look on Mocha's face makes all the pain and the abuse that Tony took throughout the divorce period very much worth it.

116

MANSON SITS IN the passenger's seat of the Silverado pickup truck. In the driver's seat is his man Angry Muslim. "Man, that shit is fire!" he shouts. He reaches to the back seat and grabs hold of a sneaker box in a shopping bag. He drops the bag on Manson's lap. "That's sixty-eight big ones and not a dime short. I counted ten times."

"I ain't worried about that, bruh," Manson claims. "What's the response, though?"

"I just told you, fire! If you can be consistent with that grade of work I will make you a millionaire overnight," he says very hyped. "You got more?"

Manson digs into his small bag and grabs the tub of Shea Butter. He hands it to Muslim who looks at it quite perplexed. "That's the front. That's a kilo of raw heroin inside the tub. Chip away the edges and you will be able to tell the difference in the texture."

The man gets excited. He's never seen anything this smart in all his years of hustling. "Yeah, you fucking with some serious motherfuckers I see. I like this. I can ride around with twenty kilos and they will never know. They will think I'm just another Shea Butter selling Muslim merchant," he says cracking the first smile that Manson has ever seen on his face. "And I do plan to get twenty of them, too. Give me a couple months, watch and see. This the same thing though, right?"

"It's always gonna be the same thing. The nigga I'm fucking with is super heavy." Manson goes silent for a close to a minute as he thinks of the right words. "I want to run something else pass you, though."

"What's up?"

"It's a lot of money in this dope but I got hold to a plug on some other shit that's scoring me a profit like ten times faster," says Manson.

"Ten times faster than heroin?" he asks in shock. "Well, you need to bring me in on that too. Shit!"

"I'm trying to," he says flashing a smile. "Dig, I haven't told nobody about this but you. This ain't for everybody. I don't know how you gone feel about it, though."

"Man, stop beating around the bush and try my chin," he says rather anxiously.

"How many murders y'all get a year down Philly? Two hundred?"

"Two hundred? Man a couple years ago we had 360 in just four months. They reporting five or six hundred. That's all they reporting. A lot of murders go unreported."

"So you say at a low number six hundred murders a year. Imagine if a person could get fifty grand a body. How much would that be?"

The man calculates quickly. "Like 60 million."

"Okay, that may be unrealistic. Let's just say if a person can get fifty grand for just ten percent of the murders. Sixty of them."

"Shit, that's three million. Still a lot of money."

"Is it money you would want?"

"What you mean?"

"I mean, I got a plug that takes the bodies off my hands and gives me a hundred thousand for every one."

"Dead bodies?" he asks as he slides away from Manson. He looks at Manson like the devil himself.

"Yeah, dead bodies. My man sell organs on the black market."

"So, you kill the motherfuckers and take the dead bodies to him, he give you a hundred and he sell organs? You kidding me, right?"

"Have I ever kidded you? I'm willing to bring you in fifty-fifty. That's an offer I would never give anybody. You all the way outta town so it won't affect my business. Between me and you I have scored six hundred grand in like a little over two weeks."

The man watches Manson with his mouth wide open in shock. He doesn't know what to say. He always knew Manson was crazy but not this damn crazy.

"So, you with it or not?" Manson asks.

"That's some other shit right there that I never heard before. I mean, I ain't knocking your hustle but that ain't for me. I ain't selling no dead bodies. I ain't on that type time."

"You won't have to do shit. If you put the word out there niggas will bring them to you. You ain't never got to get hands on with it. I will send my team to get them."

"And you dead serious, too," he says quite shocked at it all. "That's some money I don't want right there. At the end of the day I'm Muslim."

"Yeah, a Muslim selling dope."

"Yeah and on the Day of Judgment I will have to pay for this dope and hopefully Allah will forgive me. I know for certain I won't be forgiven for selling no bodies to be stripped of their organs. You can have that," he says shaking his head. He still can't believe his ears.

"Just think it over. I'm out though. Just hit me," he says extending his hand.

The man looks at Manson's hand and thinks of the fact that those very hands pick up dead bodies and sells them. He stares at Manson's hand afraid to shake it. He looks at Manson totally different now. He's almost ready to give the dope back to him. Instead of shaking Manson's hand he fist bumps him, refusing to shake hands with the devil.

THE NEXT MORNING 4:15 A.M.

MANSON IS UP bright and early ready to get to work. One thing he knows for sure is in the dope game, the early bird gets the worm. Whenever he's sold dope in the past he was always one of the first hustlers on the block. He wanted to be there when the dope fiends got there looking for their first hit.

Today he's up early but it isn't solely for the dope fiends because the level of the game that he's playing cuts out the direct dope fiend contact. Truth of the matter is he's up early and it has nothing to do with dope. He's more enthusiastic about his other business than he is about the dope business. As he thought about it last night and realized that he grossed six hundred grand in two weeks, it's still quite hard for him to believe.

In the same two weeks he's scored about thirty grand profit with the dope. He's very grateful but in no way does that seem to add up. That's more money that he ever dreamed of having. He weighed his options carefully and realized that the dope money is good but the risk outweighs the reward at this point. He estimates the six hundred he made in six weeks will take him a year if he's lucky in the dope game. With all that in mind he's eager to get out on the streets and get to war because war equals bodies and bodies equal hundreds of thousands.

Jada watches Manson walk toward the closet but pretends to be asleep. She's such a light sleeper since Manson has been freed. Her guilt makes her a nervous wreck. Each second she fears may be her last whenever he's around.

Manson walks toward the bed and stops over her. She peeks up through one eye. As he digs into the bag she jumps up and slides over to the other end of the bed with a terrified look on her face. Manson is quite shocked at her reaction but charges it off as her being awakened out of her sleep. "Fuck wrong with you?" he asks as he drops a couple of stacks onto the nightstand on her side.

"You scared the shit out of me," she says and meaning it. She looks at the money. "What's that?"

"That's for you. Look I know I haven't done anything nice for you in a long time. Trust me even though I never tell you, I want you to know that I respect how you held it down for me all these years. You was there for me when the rest of the world turned their back on me. I want you to know I'm grateful."

Jada looks deep into his eyes and sees something that she's never seen. In all the years of them being together she's never seen him sentimental about anything. She doesn't know how to reply, especially due to the fact that she hasn't been as loyal as he may believe. She just nods her head up and down without a word slipping through her lips.

"You held it down and I told you once I got on my feet, I would take it from there. Well, I'm on my feet now and I got it from here. That lil job you got, you can call them and tell them to kiss your ass. We don't need them no more." Jada is shocked at all that he's saying. Years ago it all would've meant a big deal but today it means nothing at all because her heart is no longer with him.

"That's twenty racks right there. Get up and go pamper yourself. Get breakfast, hit the spa and go shopping. Do whatever it is that you been missing over the years," he says as he pulls stacks from one bag and put them into another bag. He puts one bag into the closet and keeps the other one with him. He's split the earnings in between the two bags.

"And burn all those fucking scrubs you got. I'm tired of seeing you walking around in them," he says cracking a genuine smile. He walks over and kisses her on the forehead. "I love you," he says before making his exit out of the room.

It's a good thing that he didn't wait on her reply because she doesn't have one for him. She can't even force the words 'I love you' to him because truly she doesn't.

Jada lays there in her emotions. Her guilt is on overload. She's also confused about the other emotions that run through her. She looks at the money and for a second thinks that she shouldn't take it. She truly feels she deserves it with all that he's put her through. She also feels that spending his money will make things that much worse if he ever found out.

MEANWHILE IN THE COUNTY JAIL

Just a few minutes shy of the crack of dawn, and while most are sleep, the sound of a beautiful voice singing graces the tier, far and near. The morning prayer is in. The call to prayer sounds off for all to hear but for the Muslims to come to pray. The man sings with his best recitation of the Arabic language.

"Yo, shut that noise up!" says a voice from the far end of the tier.

The man continues on as if he doesn't hear the disrespect.

In seconds a groggy-eyed huge young man comes storming toward the voice that he hears. The man who is singing the call to prayer continues on, eyes closed with his hands clasped over his ears. This frail old man in the prison is one of the most knowledgeable brothers here. He keeps all the Muslims in check but on the streets he has problems keeping himself in check. His love for dope supersedes his love for the religion while he's on the outside and that's why he's rarely on the outside.

The brolic young man stands over the singing man. He interrupts him again. "Didn't I tell you to shut that noise up? I'm trying to sleep. You not gonna keep waking me up every morning with that. I know that's your religion and all but you gone have to start singing that to yourself. Y'all Muslims know what time y'all supposed to pray. Ain't got to be screaming it all loud and shit," the man finishes off.

The old man stands in awe at the disrespect. Never in all his years of living has he witnessed blatant disrespect like this in any jail or prison that he's been in. In his younger and stronger years he would've punished the young man for the disrespect. Today he realizes he would only end up getting punished because the young man is three times his size.

"I didn't make this up. This has to be done," the man explains with all possible humility.

"You heard what I said," the young man says as he feels someone walking behind him.

Smith steps up in the middle of both the men. "What's up, old head? Why you stop making the call?" he asks as he pretends to not know what's going on. He doesn't look at the young man once.

"He asked me to sing it to myself so I don't wake him up," the man explains as he points to the younger man. Smith looks to the man for the very first time. They lock eyes. Smith has hatred in his eyes but the other man has something different in his.

Smith doesn't know the young man but he does know he's Blood under another set. They have no friction but Smith doesn't like how the young man moves around. The young man on the other hand knows exactly who Smith is.

"Go ahead and make the call. People waiting to pray," Smith says while staring deep into the man's eyes. The man is hesitant for a second but once realizing that the young man has taken the backseat he starts the call over.

Once the man finishes Smith speaks again. "Now go ahead and pray. Make the call everyday loud as you want to and whoever don't like it, tell them to come see me," he says looking at the young man again.

The old man replies by way of head nod before walking away. The young man stands there not knowing what to say. "You Muslim?" he asks.

"That don't matter," Smith replies. "That's oppression and that won't be tolerated on this floor no more. Not from nobody. I'm the thoroughest one on the whole floor and I don't push my weight around, oppressing and ain't nobody else gonna do it. You got me?"

Before the man can respond a high pitch shrieking sounds off in the distance. Another sounds off and another and another. In seconds the Muslims on their way to pray and anyone else who heard the screaming runs toward it. A few men crowd in front of a cell in a chaotic frenzy.

Smith makes his way over to the cell and peeks inside. There lays a man in a puddle of blood. He's been stabbed to death. After a deep stare Smith recalls the man's face. It's one of the men that he had words with in the bullpen, from Smoke's camp.

Everyone clears the area before the officers come. As Smith is walking away he's dumbfounded. He wonders if somebody from his camp made the move. Why though, he asks himself because he didn't order the hit. What he doesn't know is the hit was ordered by Smoke because the man didn't move out on Smith.

Smith counts it as one more plus for his team. He's just one that Smith didn't actually have to put hands on. Smith has no clue that there are four more that will be taken out that he won't have to lay hands on. Although the real beef is between them, the beef with the dead man and Smoke was all internal.

118

PEBBLES' **BMW SUV** pulls in front of Manson and Jada's house. As Manson is walking toward the vehicle he can already sense her attitude. He's not even in the truck yet and she's already talking. He snatches the door open and the words are in full stride. "Fuck he think I am, picking him up from another bitch house? This motherfucker done bumped his motherfucking head. He must think my name is Betty Motherfucking Spaghetti."

Manson slams the door shut and just looks at her. "What, what the fuck you want?" she asks in her normal feisty manner.

"Want you to drop me off," he says rather calmly.

"Drop you off? What your other bitch ain't got no car? What happened to her raggedy ass hooptie she had? It broke down?" she asks sarcastically.

"Will you pull the fuck off and take me down the hill?" he asks with signs of an attitude.

She pulls off burning her rage on the pavement. "And you think this shit is normal, don't you?" she asks. "Like I can't believe this shit, yo," she says to herself with a fake laugh. "Like I'm really putting up with this shit in my thirties," she continues on to herself.

"Like what the fuck is wrong with me? I'm a bad bitch! I got my own car, my own money and my own fucking condo. Like I'm bugging, fucking with a cheating ass nigga. I'm way too fucking fly for this shit. Like, any fucking nigga would die to be with me. Be turning niggas down left and right to be with a cheating ass nigga. I'm fucking tripping," she says as the tears build up in her eyes.

"I'm cheating on you," Manson asks with a serious face. "Cheating is doing shit behind your back. Everything I'm doing you know about. When I stay here you know I'm here. When I stay at your house she know I'm there. I ain't cheating on neither one of you. We all a family."

"Family?" she barks with rage. "Motherfucker I ain't no fucking Amish bitch and I ain't no motherfucking sister wife. Fuck you and that dirty hoe ass bitch! Y'all can have each other because you ain't got me!"

Manson ignores her and straight changes the subject. "Before you drop me off let's drop this off at the house," he says while tapping the duffle bag."

"No, leave whatever the fuck that is at that bitch house!"

Manson digs into the bag. He drops five stacks of money onto her lap. She tries to keep her eyes on the road but the money is screaming for her attention. "That's for you," he says. She looks over at him confused. "Over the years you made sure a motherfucker was alright and never wanting for nothing. Lawyer money and everything else and I know it hasn't been easy. I told you if I ever was freed I would get every dime back to you. That's fifty-thousand. I know over the years you've spent way more than that but that's a start to me paying you back. Drop that in your account and start replenishing your savings that I have depleted," he says with charm.

His words and his charm blow her mind to the fact that she's no longer even mad at him. "You know I didn't do any of that to hold over your head and waiting for you to pay me back. I did it because I love you and know you would've done the same and even more for me," she says with tears in the corner of her eyes.

"I know all that but I just want to show you how appreciative I am. I know I can come across like I don't give a fuck at times. Most of the times I don't but when it comes to real genuine G shit, you know how I feel about that."

Pebbles rides in silence for the first time ever. Tears drip down her face. It's not about the money because she makes her own money. It's the gesture in itself. Just when she was starting to feel like he had used her over the years and was in the midst of trying to cut him off for good, now this.

"For years you complained about everybody living it up while you busting your ass to take care of me and Rahmid," he says as he runs his hand through her silky Brazilian weave. "It's about to be our turn."

MEANWHILE

Smoke stands face to face with an associate. "Listen, bruh," the man says with excitement in his eyes. "I'm like this close," he says using his fingers, to some valuable information that I know you can use."

"Yeah?" Smoke questions.

"I might have a lead on where Mother Nature staying."

Smoke's eyes bulge. "Word?"

The man nods his head. "Word!" A smile spreads from ear to ear.

"Bruh, if you can find that out for me, anything I got you can have."

"Is that right?" the man asks as if he already has plans on what he wants as a trade.

"Yeah," Smoke confirms. "Any fucking thing!"

119

COURTYARD MARRIOTT/EAST RUTHERFORD, NEW JERSEY

MANSON AND PEBBLES just checked Arson into the hotel, with his own money of course. Now that they have a stream of revenue Manson figured Arson can now stand on his own feet. He suggested that he should get his own apartment now and out of the sleazy motel.

Arson rejected the idea and stood firmly on it. He explained that he was more than comfortable at the motel. After over two decades in prison and before that growing up in trailer homes, the cheap motel was like paradise to him. He also explained that if he got an apartment with furniture and personal items he may form an attachment.

An attachment is something that he doesn't want right now because he loves the freedom. He realizes on any given day he may have to flee the city of Newark by airplane, boat, train, bus or bicycle if the heat comes down on them. Manson totally understood Arson's stance and respected it but urged him to at least pay for better living conditions. Pebbles suggested this place because it's out of the way and in the cut.

She knows about it from her early days of stripping when she would entertain her take-out clients back when she offered sex for sale. Manson's intuition caused him to ask how she knew about the spot when in his mind he already knew. He never asked and she would never tell how she earned the money she did to hold it all down while he was gone. She will never admit to him that a great part of his lawyer fees back then she made laying on her back.

Pebbles hands a few bills to Arson who is fuming right now. He looks at the six lousy singles and gets even more angry. He can't believe he allowed them to talk him into spending close to fifty-five hundred dollars on this hotel for a month. Pebbles walks away toward the bathroom leaving Manson laughing in Arson's face.

"Lighten up, bruh, it's only money and we are about to make a lot more of it." Manson's phone rings, interrupting his laughter. It's Helter.

His heart skips a beat just as it does every time one of them calls him. "Yo?" he says quite anxiously.

"Turn to channel 5," she says through the phone. "The city going crazy. Hurry."

Manson quickly locates the remote and turns to channel 5. The first thing he sees scrolling across the screen in bold letters is, 'Invasion of the Body Snatchers.' Manson turns the volume up to hear the reporter.

"Strange reports throughout the city of Newark of a series of missing persons. It all started a few weeks ago when family members of missing persons made reports that allegedly their loved ones were gunned down on the streets but the bodies were never found afterwards. Investigations are in process but right now there are no leads. No suspects, no motives, no bodies."

Manson looks over to Arson who wears his guilt on his face. They speak telepathically. They themselves can't believe that their work in the city has made the national news. Both of them know with that fame a host of trouble can come along with it.

Arson has no fears or worries. He's just going for the ride. For him it's not about the love of the money. It's about the love for murder and supporting a man that he considers a friend.

Manson on the other hand is second guessing the whole ordeal. Just escaping the sentence that he did, he understands that just as Tony told him, if he ever stands before a judge again he's finished. As the reporter stated right now they have no leads which means now would be the perfect time to throw the towel in. He quickly thinks of the risks involved and that's doing what he dreaded; dying in prison.

Then again he thinks of the reward involved. He hasn't even touched the surface of the money that he can make with it. In just three weeks he has no money problems whatsoever. He came home from prison without a pot to piss in and now in just a few months, he's up like he's never been. In a weeks time he's already fallen in love with the money. He thinks of the risk and the reward and it's hard for him to weigh the two.

MEANWHILE

Mother Nature lays back on the bed. A beautiful, firm, and petite woman comes walking out of the bathroom wearing nothing but the towel that is wrapped around her head. Guilt rips through Mother Nature's gut as she thinks of how Wesson would feel if he were alive to see his mother here. She believes there is heaven for gangsters, she just hopes that Wesson isn't watching down on her.

Mother Nature's intentions were pure in the beginning but the more consoling she did the more lustier her thoughts became. Mother Nature's shoulder to lean on has evolved into a body to lay on. Wesson's mother so weak and distraught didn't even see the game coming and now this. Mother Nature justifies it all by telling herself that at least she's keeping it in the family. Wesson was like a son to her so she really sees nothing wrong with being with his mother. It's like keeping it all in the family. She plans to take care of her and Wesson's siblings just as she's always taken care of him. Mother Nature has thoughts of all the things she's going to do to the woman when her thoughts are interrupted by the words that come through the television speakers. "Invasion of the Body Snatchers," says the news reporter on Channel 9.

Mother Nature's attention is snatched away from the young woman and diverted to the television screen. She watches and listens carefully. The thought of all her soldiers who have come up missing has been weighing on her mind heavy. She still can't make any sense of it all, no matter how hard she tries.

Her team is looking to her for answers that she can't give them. After the first missing person she could no longer tell them with a straight face that it's nothing to worry about. Secretly they're all worried that they could easily be the next missing person. Even she knows that she's not exempt which is why she's been staying low under the radar.

After the news report Mother Nature shuts off the television as she lays there in deep thought. The woman climbs onto the bed and cuddles up next to her. Mother Nature stares at her in a daze. Her appetite for the woman has been stolen. At this point the only thing on her mind is beating the odds of being the next missing person they are reporting about.

SHORT HILLS HILTON

Jada lays face down with a pure white towel wrapped around her bottom half as the male masseuse goes to work on her. She decided to call out of work and go to have herself pampered just as Manson demanded. She checked into the hotel early this morning. She started the day off with breakfast in bed before the rest of the festivities. She's had her hair done, a Brazilian wax and a manicure and pedicure before lunch.

She's spent well over a thousand and still counting. Laying on the table right next to her is who else but Smoke. He lays there face down as the beautiful German woman works on his shoulders meticulously. No soon as Manson left the house she called Smoke and demanded that he take the day off of work as well. Together they have spent the entire first half of the day being treated like royalty, all funded by Manson.

Smoke has the pleasure of the perfect getaway without the luxury of spending a dime. He's sure all this is on Manson's dime and really he doesn't feel the slightest bit of guilt about it. Feeling like Manson has cheated him, makes him feel as if he deserves it and more. As petty and minute as it may seem Smoke sees this as pay-back, as if sneaking around with Manson's woman isn't enough pay-back. He lives with the fear of Manson finding out about him sneaking around with Jada so spending his money is quite easy.

He grunts as the woman unravels the stress from his shoulder blades. He looks over to Jada with bright eyes. "Thanks, babe. I needed this."

120

MANSON AND HIS man Pittsburgh Pete stand face to face at the gas station here on Grove Street. He's come back with all the money for Manson plus he says he has some good news for him.

"Nah, bruh," Manson says sternly. "I ain't trying to meet no new motherfuckers. I'm only fucking with people I know."

"Listen, bruh, this my old head. Him and my mother been messing around since I was a kid." Sadness covers his face. "My mother his sidepiece, his mistress," he admits with shame. He pay all her bills and the whole shit from outta state. He practically raised me. Old head always up. Rich as shit but he tight as shit, though. He's mastered the game of not giving a motherfucker nothing. But anytime I got something going on he want me to bring him in. Even though selfish, I always do though because he take good care of my moms."

"All that's great but let him come through you."

"That's the thing, bruh, he not gonna come through me. He so slick he always think somebody trying to get over on him. I need you to do this for me, bruh. He got a sample of that work and went through the roof. He said he would pay me fifteen grand just to be able to get that dope directly without me in the middle. I told him give me twenty-five and we got a deal. The motherfucker didn't even blink. It's like I'm selling you, the plug, to him. Man, let me get that twenty-five and slide that right at you on the balance I owe."

His persistence is irritating Manson but still he continues on. "He trying to cop like two keys of it, bruh, right now, cash money. That ain't about nothing. Once y'all build some trust between each other I'm sure he gone spend M's with you."

He has Manson's attention as he calculates his profit off two kilos at a minimum of twenty grand. "He ready right now?"

The man nods his head up and down. "Right now big bruh, he got the money for two of them in the car. I wouldn't bullshit you. I seen him count it out with my own eyes."

Manson thinks it over quickly. "If he buying two, cash money I will let it go for sixty-eight a joint and let you score yourself four grand in the middle."

"Bet!" Pete says with gratitude.

"If anything goes wrong it's on your back."

"Bruh, I already know how that goes. And you should already know it's death before dishonor with me and you." He waves his hand in the air, signaling the man to come over.

Manson watches as a smooth senior citizen man gets out and walks over. He's so suave that he's not walking, he's gliding. His wire frames set right at the temples of his salt and pepper faded hair. Dressed more like a golfer than a drug dealer, he has on a crisp button up shirt with a bright fluorescent sweater wrapped around his shoulders and tied around his neck. He seals the outfit off with Louis Vutton flip flops on his feet.

He stands before Manson and flashes a dazzling pearly white dentures smile as he extends his hand. They shake. "They call me the General," he says without blanking.

"They call me Manson."

"I've already heard. I've also heard so many great things about you. I can look in your eyes and feel that they are all true," he says in attempt to charming Manson. Manson doesn't budge. "I see you are quiet like myself, not a man of many words and that's great because it doesn't take long meetings to generate currency together. The longer the meeting the more bullshit and the less money involved. With that being said, I've traveled all the way from Maryland just to get my hands on the work that my son here has his hands on. What exactly do I have to do to get my hands on some of it?"

"Put your money on the wood," Manson replies.

The General looks around. "Show me the wood and I will dump it all right there."

"What you trying to do, though? What you trying to get?"

"It's not what I'm trying to get, I get what I want. As I'm sure you already know, it's a number game. If you say the magic number I can change your life overnight."

"There's no magic number. The number is the number seventy a joint."

The General looks to Pete as if he believes they're trying to work him. "See, told you. Told you, you like my pop, I won't ever try to get over on you but you don't believe me."

The General smiles. "No, I just know my boy got some shit with him sometimes," he says smiling from ear to ear. He looks to Manson. "If you can promise the same quality of work that my son here had, I can guarantee you money for three up here from Baltimore in less than four hours."

"Well, put that money on the road and hit me when y'all ready," Manson says. He shakes their hands and exits without saying another word. He's already calculating the profit as in the bank.

5 HOURS LATER/COURTYARD MARRIOTT HOTEL, EAST RUTHERFORD

Manson, Pete and the General stand around the General's accomplice as he turns the Shea Butter container upside down and dumps it onto the counter. He breaks the Shea Butter casing off with a small pocketknife and separates it from the dope. He examines the work carefully as the General awaits his response.

"Yeah, this is what we need. I can do wonders with this. Just wish there was something we could do about that number," he says biting on his bottom lip.

The General looks to Manson with hope. "The number is the number. No haggling, no negotiations. Let's not play this game."

"No games," the General says. "Your number is your number. If that's the best you can do I understand." Manson doesn't even look his way, totally ignoring him. "With that being said, let's get this started."

The General hands Manson a beautifully handcrafted, leather satchel case. Manson unzips the case and pulls out the stacks of money to count. As he's sifting through the bills the General speaks again, breaking his concentration. "Ay, a few months ago I came across a kid from Newark, a good kid. Goes by the name of Bugsy...well went by the name of Bugsy."

Manson looks up from the money with a strange look in his eyes. "You familiar with him?" the General asks.

"Why what's up?"

"Just curious that's all."

"Yeah, I knew him well," says Manson still wondering what the affiliation could be. With him knowing Bugsy he automatically figures it could be bad blood. "How you know him?

Bugsy and Manson are more than familiar. In fact, Bugsy was under Manson's line. When Manson was passing the G down it was a toss up between Bugsy and Smoke. Smoke's family ties with Manson is what got Smoke the position over Bugsy. For years Manson regretted that decision and thought that Bugsy would've done a better job than Smoke. It touched his heart to hear what happened to Bugsy. Had Bugsy been patient a little while longer Manson had big plans for him.

The General reads the expression on Manson's face. "Oh, no, nothing bad. It was all good as a matter of fact. Good kid."

"Yeah, I agree. Bugsy 2 Gunz... I gave him the name actually."

"My heart was touched hearing that news. You know, I was with him right before it all happened. I was waiting to get with him the following morning and I turn on the news and was shocked at what I saw. He carried himself like such a young gentleman I would've never known he had so much going on."

"Ay man, that's the game for you. It can all go sour for you in a second."

"By chance can you get hold of that blow he had his hands on?" the General asks with desperation.

"Nah, this what I'm doing right here," Manson says as he hands the small shopping bag over to the General. The General just watches the bag dangle in the air before looking over to his partner. His partner grabs hold of the bag.

"A pleasure doing business with you, young fella. I hope you're prepared for the magnitude of my hustle. My work ethics are impeccable. I'm an old man but I don't sleep. I have the energy and endurance of a teenager," he says with a sly wink. "I hope you can keep up with the old man."

121

DAYS LATER

THE SUBURBAN PULLS up and parks, blending right into the darkness. The block is as peaceful and serene as it should be at such a late hour in the night. They all peek around cautiously before Manson gives Arson the command. "All good."

Arson grabs the gas can from the floor in between his legs and opens the door to exit. They all watch as he crosses the street and disappears into an alley. Anxiety fills the air. This is the moment that they've all been working toward.

In the back of the two family house, Arson stands on the back porch. He pulls two bandanas from his pocket and ties them together. He stuffs the bandanas under the crack in between the door and the floor. With his foot, he sticks it as far as it can go with just enough material hanging out on his end.

He turns the gas can upside down and pours it onto the bandana and all over the porch as he backs down the steps. He strikes a match onto the matchbox, throws the burning match into the box and throws the whole box onto the porch. The burning box lands perfectly near the bandana. Arson watches with joy in his eyes as the bandanas start to crumble in the fire.

He hasn't been this close to fire in 25 years, when he was sent away for burning that family up. Just lighting a single match excites him, to see the small flame traveling is giving him a rush that he's missed. He has to peel himself from the porch because his eyes are glued to the small fire. The smell of it is euphoric to him.

He races through the alley, full speed, hands over the gas can to keep it splashing. He peeks around as he's running up the front stairs. Once on the porch he places the nozzle as far as he can underneath the door and damn near empties the gas can. What's left of the gas he pours all over the porch. He pulls a match from the matchbook and strikes it. The flame sizzles before his eyes before he tosses the match at the door. He throws the matchbook onto the porch as well. He takes off across the street and gets back inside the truck.

Smoke cuts his eye at Arson with disgust. They have been moving around together for weeks and not once have they held a conversation. The only thing they say to each other is what has to be said. Not just Arson, it is like that with him, Helter and Skelter, also. Smoke can't understand it and it makes him extremely uncomfortable. What he doesn't know is they have been instructed not to engage in any conversation outside of work related conversation.

Minutes go by and the truck is filled with anxiety. The smell of fire is in the air and it's driving Arson crazy. He fidgets in his seat uncontrollably. He rocks back an forth, rubbing his hands together.

To him only thing that's better then the smell of fire is the smell of burning bodies inside of a fire. "Yo, Manson," Arson says. Manson turns around in his seat. "You ever smelled human bodies burning or heard the screams of a man on fire?" he asks with a wicked look in his eyes.

Everyone looks at him in total shock. In all this time he's never spoken aloud for them to hear like this. He maneuvers like an autistic child, maybe because he was an autistic child. Back when he was a kid autism wasn't as widely studied as it is today, so he was charged off as crazy.

"Nah, I'm afraid not," Manson replies.

Arson doesn't say another word. He just continues to stare ahead in a daze rocking back and forth. In seconds the front door is snatched open. A small fire can be seen at the floor. A few heads can be seen gathered in the hallway. They stand there in disarray, afraid to run through the fire. Suddenly all the people disappear.

Before you know it people can be seen climbing out of the window in the alley. One by one, about six people climb through the window. All focus are on the people in the dark alley. "Nah," Smoke says. "I hope we didn't do all this for nothing."

Just as the words come out of his mouth a few of the people in the alley all gather at the window helping the person from the window. Smoke spots the red dreadlocks instantly. "Here we go!" he shouts. The out of shape Mother Nature struggles to get through the window as the man on the ground pulls her with all of his might.

Smoke snatches the 9 millimeter from his waist and prepares to get out. His heart is racing with anxiety. Manson sits on the edge of his seat anxiously. They can't believe they're right here this close. It's like a dream come true for them.

Mother Nature is finally on the ground and walking out the alley. "Up close, clean shot," Manson commands. "Them innocent people over there. I don't want none of them touched."

"Got you," Smoke says as he rolls his mask down over his face.

"Gotta hurry," Arson says. "You have approximately three and half minute span before fire engines will be roaring from everywhere." Helter, Skelter and Smoke all look at him in shock that he has it broken down to a science.

Just as Smoke opens the door and plants one foot onto the ground a police siren blares. Smoke looks over his shoulder nervously and coming around the corner is a police car with the lights strolling. He stands in shock. "Pull over!" the cop says over the loud speaker. All their hearts are pounding in their chest. Ease comes to them when they see that the police have pulled over a car.

The car and the police car are a few feet behind them double-parked. A man from the burning house runs over to the cop. He points to the burning house and the cop gets on his walkie talkie. Smoke eases back into the seat and slams the door shut. "Fuck!" Manson shouts with rage. All of them sit quite still, understanding how close of a call it was. As Manson looks across the street he notices Mother Nature staring at the truck peculiarly. She stretches her neck looking at the truck trying to figure it out. "This bitch see us," Manson whispers as if she can hear them. "Damn, we blew this one y'all."

Mother Nature keeps her eyes on the truck as she steps closer to the police car for safety. She starts to come across the street. "What to do?" Helter asks. "Go, ahead, pull out," he says as he sees her crossing the street behind them. Her eyes are glued to the license plates. Helter pulls out slowly as she turns the lights on. The cop peeks up from the car behind them but pays no real attention to them. Fire trucks come speeding around the corner.

Arson looks at his watch. "Three minutes and fifty-nine seconds. They gave us an extra twenty-nine seconds."

Mother Nature stands at the curb, eyes glued onto the truck as it cruises down the block. Before the truck can reach the corner she already has it all figured out. She's sure the people in the truck are Team 6 and this fire is their work. She looks to the police car across the street and for the first time ever she loves the police. He saved her life and she's a hundred percent certain if not for him she would've been leaving in that truck with them, against her will of course.

She feels as if the walls have caved in on her. They've found her house, her safety net. This war has now gotten deeper and she has no choice but to call for backup. She picks up her phone and gets to dialing. "Yo, big bruh, I need to see you like yesterday. Shit type crucial. Where you at? I need your help."

122

THE NEXT AFTERNOON

SMOKE STANDS AT the passenger's window of the tinted out Durango listening to every word the man in the driver seat is saying. The driver, known to the streets as Action Packed lives up to his name in every sense. He's a live wire that no one takes lightly.

He's so serious that Manson had no choice but to honor the meeting with him even though he knew exactly what it was pertaining to. Action Packed is a well respected G. His set is not affiliated with Mother Nature's but they are bridged together through the tight bond they have with each other. Action Packed and Mother Nature's history runs way back. He raised her to be the gangster that she is. She rarely calls on him unless she really needs him. In this case she really needed him.

He didn't hesitate to get on the phone with Smoke. He called barely after sunrise. When Smoke initially got the call from him his first mind was to not even hear him out. After thinking it over he realized the type of heat that Action Packed is worthy of bringing.

Smoke in no way is worried about him but he does bear witness to his strength throughout the city. He respects his gangster all across the board. He figured by not honoring the meeting he's declaring war with him. He decided to at least hear him out just to know what he really knows.

Smoke keeps his gun gripped in his pocket on the sneak tip as Action Packed talks. Despite the fact that both of them gave their word to come alone, Smoke has Ooo Wee and Dirt a block away watching the area. They have been commanded if anything appears strange to come blazing asking no questions.

"Originally she wanted me to join forces the way we normally do. I ain't gone lie," he admits. "On the strength of me and your rapport and our history I said let me talk to to the gangster and see if we can come to some type understanding."

Smoke shakes his head. "On some G shit bruh, this shit over my head. This hit came from the top. From my big bruh."

"Understood and that's why I asked if all three of us could meet. She said this whole war is some bullshit and somebody threw her name in the mix. She said y'all struck without even sitting down with her. Y'all went on word of mouth. She said she retaliated only because y'all touched one of her pride and joys. She said as far as the shit y'all trying to charge her with, she had nothing to do with it."

"That's bullshit, bruh," Smoke says trying to throw him off.

"Bruh, she won't bullshit me. She don't have no reason to. She know I ride with her right or wrong. I truly believe the Mayor dude's murder wasn't from her hands."

Smoke's mind soars away from the conversation. Damn, he thinks. She's copping out, saying she had nothing to do with it. Action Packed believes her and Smoke wonders how many others believe her. The last thing he needs is for Manson to believe her. He and Manson are just starting to get on better terms and the last thing he needs is for Manson to doubt his word right now. If Manson ever found out that this whole war was behind false pretense he's sure the next war will be him and Manson.

"Bruh on the strength of me and you can you try one more time to get all of us at the table? You and Manson and me and her and let's see if we can get to the bottom of this. Once we find out who really killed him, we will all join forces and really tear the streets up."

"I will see, bruh," Smoke claims sounding not so convincing. "Once bruh get his mind made up, it really ain't no changing that." Smoke sighs with agitation as he reaches for Action Packed's hand. He's heard him out and doesn't feel the need to stay any longer. Besides he has a strange feeling in his gut. They shake hands firmly.

"Bruh, you know every made man or woman deserves a sit-down," he says staring into Smoke's eyes.

"I feel you, bruh," Smoke says looking away from him. He takes a step back, with his eyes scanning the area.

"I have to keep it a hundred with you," Action Packed says. "If the sit-down doesn't happen I will have no choice but to ride with her. That's my people and I can't leave her out to dry."

Smoke has not a word in reply. He shrugs his hand almost helplessly. His other hand is gripped tightly on the gun. "I respect that," he says as he slowly draws his gun where Action Packed can't see. He steps one foot onto the sidewalk and spins around aiming the gun at Action Packed's head.

Action Packed's eyes stretch wide open in shock and so does his mouth. BLOC! The bullet of Smoke's gun spirals with perfection into Action

Packed's mouth. Before his head can bang into the window the bullet exits through it and caves the window in. BLOC! BLOC! Action Packed's head leans over resting onto his shoulder signaling his death. Smoke dashes off.

He gets into his car, starts it up and speeds away. As he's zipping up the block, the thoughts that race through his mind are thoughts that he may just have started another war in attempt to prevent a war between him and Manson.

123

THE COURTROOM IS packed with angry loved ones of the man who was murdered in cold blood over a year ago. They all are here to witness justice be served against the murderers. Baby Manson sits alone with obvious nervousness. Today is a special day for Baby Manson.

As a child he's been looking forward to turning 18 so he could be considered grown. No one could have ever told him he would be bringing his 18th birthday in in a courtroom. The day he becomes an adult by no coincidence at all is the same day that he could be charged like an adult and sent away for the rest of his life. As he sits here in regret he reflects on it all.

He has the bubble guts and can barely hold his bowels. He keeps peeking over his shoulder awaiting the arrival of his attorney. On the other end is his codefendant who sits next to his attorney. Behind the codefendant sits his grandmother who clenches her bible close to her bosom, praying under her breath.

Pebbles sits directly behind her son, rocking her legs. Her stomach does flip-flops as she realizes her son's life can very well end today in a sense. In the next couple of minutes their world can change as they know it. Rage covers her face as she thinks of all the money they've spent and the attorney isn't even here.

Manson sits in the back of the courtroom trying to be as less visible as possible. Rage covers his face as well. The fact that Tony is late for the court appearance that can change all of their lives makes him feel quite disrespected. As much as he respects Tony he's already made his mind up that if all doesn't go as he promised it their lives are not the only lives that will be altered. Pebbles looks over her shoulder shaking her head as if to say, 'I told you so.' Manson turns his head so as to not become further enraged.

"We can't wait any longer," the judge says quite disturbed. He nods his head at the prosecutor who stands up and makes his way toward the bench. Baby Manson looks back at his mother helplessly and once he sees the helplessness in her eyes he looks back at his father for help. He finds none. "Head to the front of the room, Mr. Bryant," the judge demands. Baby Manson turns his head quickly.

The Prosecutor begins to speak. "Your honor," the prosecutor says before he's interrupted by the swinging of the double doors. Attorney, Tony Austin steps into the courtroom confidently, capturing the attention of everyone. The ones who are familiar with him and his legacy watch him with admiration.

Tony glides across the courtroom floor like a cool summer breeze, wearing head to toe off-white. His narrow lapeled custom fit suit was inspired by Leonardo Decaprio in the Great Gatsby. His brown vest and the wood colored soles of his off white leather bucks accent each other. The slender gold tie stands out just enough without taking the attention off the boldness of the fine suit.

The judge's hatred for Tony cuts across the room like a sword. Tony flashes his hatred of the judge back at him. The prosecutor looks at Tony who stands next to Baby Manson. He nods his head at Pebbles who rolls her eyes with disgust at him. The prosecutor continues on.

"Because Murad Jackson has admitted to the above said crime and there's no evidence linking Rahmid Bryant with it we have agreed to offer the plea and Murad has agreed to accept it.

Manson sits back in amazement as he watches his money move around the courtroom, invisibly. Never before has a prosecutor been on his side and to see this just proves to him that money sure as hell does make the world go round. If he didn't know any better all this would seem official. All seems real and not staged. From the hatred that the judge and Tony have for each other, down to the prosecutor's act, it all appears naturally genuine.

What Manson doesn't understand is that with the hatred the judge and Tony have for each other, still they have put their feelings aside to make moves. Through this he's learned that as businessmen one doesn't have to like the other to make money together. It's all about the money. Although he learned it, he still has to work on that aspect.

The judge stares at Baby Manson's codefendant. "Murad Jackson, have you been coerced or did anyone threaten you or force you to take the plea?"

The young man looks around the courtroom with indecisiveness in his eyes. He looks at Baby Manson, then his grandfather who sits in the back removed from the whole scene. The old man stares at his grandson with disappointment. He looks to his grandmother who already has tears building up in her eyes. She kneels down onto the her knees and begins to pray. Seeing her like this breaks his heart. "Man, fuck that," he mumbles to himself. He then looks into the back at Manson. They stare coldly at each other.

The judge repeats the question. The young man turns his head away from Manson. "No sir."

"Did you knowingly or willingly on February 12th of 2013 conspire to murder the deceased Gerard Adams?"

The young man lowers his head. "Yes," he mumbles.

The family members of the deceased become outraged. "Murderer!"

The judge bangs the gavel. "Order!" He looks to the young man. "This court finds you guilty of murder and you face the possibility of life without parole. I hereby set your sentencing date for July 7th, 2015," he says loud and clear. He bangs the gavel. The sound of the old woman's crying shatter the walls. As the bailiffs cuff him he and his grandmother lock watery eyes.

The judge looks to Baby Manson. "The court finds you not guilty and once you are processed you will be freed." Pebbles throws her hands high in the air. "Yes," she cheers silently. The bailiff escorts Baby Manson out of the room.

Tony makes his way over to Manson who sits cool and calm. "Mr. Austin!" the judge yells. Tony looks back at him. "Thanks for presenting yourself with the proper attire in my courtroom. I had already figured I would have to hold you in contempt of court," he says with no smile at all. Tony left hand salutes the attorney as the ultimate sign of disrespect before turning away. The judge's face turns cherry red with hatred at the gesture of disrespect.

Tony and Manson shakes hands. "For a minute I thought you would be a no show."

"What and take the risk of you unleashing your pups on me?" Tony whispers in humor. "But nah, when you pay like you weigh you can afford to be a few minutes late," he says with an arrogant shrug. He leans in to whisper in Manson's ear. "Always remember this, when you feed, you lead and when you follow, you swallow."

HOURS LATER

Manson and Pebbles sit inside her truck in front of the County Jail. Manson hasn't seen Pebbles this happy in all the time that he's been home. She's even said a few sweet things to him very unlike the bitterness that normally comes out of her mouth. He doesn't feed into it because he knows she can switch up faster than a New York minute.

Tony holds the door open for Baby Manson to exit. Baby Manson steps slowly with his full attention on Tony. "Baby boy, I'm gone tell you like an old head told me. Your future lies in them nuts of yours," he says pointing toward Baby Manson's crotch.

"You're eighteen and them nuts is like brand new, barely used. You can take them nuts to the car dealer and trade them in for a brand new Rolls Royce right now. The life you live is determined by how you use them nuts. You're a handsome young man and can have it your way. You can have any woman you want. Don't be like me when I was younger and waste those nuts on women that can't help you get nowhere in life.

Baby Manson stares at Tony without blinking. "Tony continues on. "Use your nuts wisely to position yourself. Get yourself a good smart girl that's going somewhere in life with or without you. Together y'all can build some things and make yourselves a power couple. Don't waste them nuts on money grubbing, gold digging hood-rats that can't do nothing for you. Life is about positioning," he says with sternness in his eyes. "Use your nuts wisely."

Baby Manson sips the ice cold drink that Tony drops on him very gratefully. This may be the coldest drink that has ever been dropped on him. Tony just hopes that he never forgets it. Had he not forgotten it once it was dropped on him, life would have been so much easier.

Baby Manson spots his mother and father standing at the curb. Like a little kid he races over to the truck leaving Tony way behind. Pebbles gets out of the truck and meets him with a huge hug while Manson watches with his normal amount of coldness.

Manson gets out to greet Tony. They shake hands. "Thanks for everything."

"No need for thanks. It's my job," Tony replies casually.

Pebbles turns to Tony. "Yes, we thank you. I truly apologize for being a pain in your ass but you're just way too nonchalant for me. A few times I wanted to go across your head."

Tony smiles. "I'm sure you're not the only woman in the world who feels that way." Tony lifts his shirt sleeve and unintentionally shows them all what a quarter million on the wrist looks like. The saying rich is loud but wealth is quiet in this case is very true because as quiet as the watch may appear to be only the people who can understand it's language will hear it speak. Not a diamond in sight and the Flying Tourbillion by Roger Dubuis values at over 250 grand.

Pebbles can't understand the language but she can read the signs. "Beautiful watch."

"Timepiece," Tony corrects. "Watches are sold at the local drug store," he says with all arrogance intended. He fades her by turning away from her as if she's a mere peasant. Pebbles finds his cockiness quite sexy but she looks away in order for it not to be picked up by Manson. She hides it with her fake agitated expression to his comment. Pebbles finds a huge attraction to his energy and Tony can feel it. He intentionally avoids eye contact with her out of respect for Manson

Tony doesn't think twice about it. He quickly looks to Manson's son. "I'm gonna tell you like I told your father. We beat them crackers once but I doubt if it can be done again. With that being said, I pray that both of you never need me again. And that's a big statement from me because I love the dough," he says with a smile. As he's stepping away, he looks over his shoulder. "Great day gentlemen and lady," he says without even looking in her direction.

Pebbles catches an eyeful of candy and likes what she sees. For a second she allows her mind to wander and wonder what it would be like to be with a man like him; a legal man with the swag of a gangster. Just when the vision is getting good, Manson plucks the back of her head, snapping her into realty. "Fuck you looking at?"

Pebbles sighs as the truth sets in. The love of her life is a man with not even a fraction of Tony's status yet she still allows him to put her through hell. She sucks it up and deals with the reality because she knows it's the life she chose.

Tony gets into the midnight blue Aston Martin DB9 and as soon as the engine is turned over, the sound of Rick Ross's voice rips through the opened windows. "Fuck with me, you know I got it." Pebbles can't help to cut her eye in his direction one more time. They lock eyes just as Rick Ross says, "Bad bitch, I know she about it."

Tony races the engine, one foot on the gas pedal and the other on the brake. The wheels of the Aston Martin burn the pavement while squealing like a pig. He lifts his foot off the brake and the car takes off at top speed. He hits the horn twice before throwing one hand out of the sunroof with the peace sign.

Pebble's conceit has her believing that he purposely played the song for her. As she cruises off behind the Aston Martin her mind is full of thoughts. Tony has left more than a lasting impression on her. All of her life she has looked at the working, legal man as a sucker but today Tony has given her an altogether different outlook on the matter.

124

TWO WEEKS LATER

THINGS HAVE SIMMERED down in the city as far as the war with Mother Nature goes. There have been a few reporting from Smoke's sources that she pops in and out of the complex here and there but never long enough to be clocked. This whole beef has her walking on eggshells. It's like the walls have closed in on her, especially with the murder of Action Packed. Now she has really no one to rely on except for her little pups that she has no real faith in.

The jails and prisons are still heavy at war. Mother Nature is still up as far as that goes but she has no interest in the prison war. Her concern is staying alive on these streets. Her silence has Smoke and Manson in limbo. Smoke gives her a great deal of respect; probably more than she rightfully deserves. He's sure she has something up her sleeve.

Smoke has been keeping both ears to the street listening for what the people are saying about Action Packed's murder. He's heard all kind of rumors but none of them have yet been attached to him. He's still prepared for knowing that they could be on his heels without him hearing a thing. He's the most hated in this war which means the masses are stacked against him.

Business on the Black Market has been consistent. More than a few bodies a week are taken over to Brooklyn. Most of Mother Nature's soldiers are in hiding. Everyone is now afraid to be the next one to come up missing. They aren't the only ones living in fear. The news and the word on the street have many staying out of the way just to stay on the map. With all the talk of the invasion of the body snatchers, it makes it quite hard for them to come across work but still they manage.

With things being quiet, Smoke and Manson have been able to delve into their primary business which is the heroin. Smoke has been anxious to get started and continuously begged Manson. Manson on the other hand prolonged it for as long as he could. He's more interested in snatching bodies and scoring a quick profit than waiting on money to come back to him weeks later after fronting a man consignment.

Nine days ago Manson gave Smoke the purest dope that he's ever seen in his life. Sure while he was with the Mayor he's had up to 3,000 bricks, which is 150,000 bags at a time but never has he had a kilo of raw dope to himself. With the Mayor he's been held accountable for up to 400 grand at a time so owing Manson the little money for the kilo is minute to him in a sense. Having the kilo of raw heroin gives him a feeling of more control than he felt with the Mayor although he made more money with the Mayor.

Manson and Smoke agreed on a partnership. They split every dollar they make over Hamza's money. Smoke went to the table himself pretending to be a chemist. Off of the kilo he made close to 940 bricks. Going to the table himself makes him feel a sense of importance that he's never felt. While at that table he feels as if he's controlling his own destiny.

Smoke has been flooding the city with the dope putting it anywhere he can but the foundation is his complex. He also has been wholesaling to anyone that has interest in it. He loves the ten and twenty brick customers but he doesn't discriminate. He's even been breaking the bricks open and selling ten bags at a time to those who can't afford to buy a whole, fifty bag brick. In his mind every dollar counts. In total after giving Manson the sixty grand for Hamza, there will be approximately over seventy grand left for them to split.

Smoke and Dirt sit in the far end of the parking lot of the townhouses. He reaches over from the driver's seat and hands Dirt a shopping bag. "I thought I had 250 bricks left for you but that's only 227," Smoke says. "By the time you finish those I will be back up," Smoke says with a boss demeanor. He can't believe after all these years he's finally back in position. Truthfully he never thought he would see this day ever again.

Dirt skims through the bag, counting the bricks by sets of five. "Yo, you gotta tell your people they gotta turn it up the next time," he says with sorrow on his face. "It's like hit or miss. Like my P.A. people don't have a problem with it but some of my local people been complaining. I moved all I could here. I'm probably gone have to move all this outta town because the locals not gonna take it," he claims.

"Word? I don't know why. I haven't gotten not one complaint," Smoke lies with a straight face. Truthfully he's gotten well over double digits of complaints. He's in denial though and like most men in the city, he believes he can cut dope but instead he's only made a mess of it. The only reason he's been able to move it is because he has so much of it that he can afford to front a man just as much as that man can buy. Everybody loves a deal.

"Just get through that and I'll get them to turn up the next time," Smoke says.

"Alright bet," Dirt says as he opens the door. He gets out without shaking Smoke's hand. "Later, bruh!" he says before slamming the door shut. Smoke watches him walking toward his car.

Dirt has been a huge help to him in the process. In nine days he's moved over half of the 900 bricks he had. He's still an asset to him today just as he was back years ago. Smoke shakes his head though as the thought creeps through his mind that Dirt really was going to set him up.

Regardless of how much of an asset he is that won't save his life. It will only buy him more days to live. Once he's no longer an asset and can no longer be used, Smoke plans to wipe him out as he should've months ago when he realized what was going on. Dirt doesn't know the more dope he sells for Smoke the more time he buys for himself. His dope flow better never slow down for his life depends on it. If by chance his dope flow stops so does his lifeline.

125

SOUTH MOUNTAIN RESERVATION

PEBBLES SITS PARKED in the parking space staring to her right. Disgust covers her face as she stares at Jada who sits in the rented E class Mercedes, right next to her. Jada is so afraid of Pebbles that she's locked herself in the car with the windows rolled up airtight. She stares straight ahead, careful not to look in Pebbles' direction. Without looking at her she can still feel the heat from Pebbles' eyes melting through the glass of the window.

From where they both are parked, they have a clear view of what is taking place in the park. Jada's father sits on a park bench with clear evidence on his face that he doesn't want to be here. A few feet away Manson and Jada's mother walk on opposite sides of Damien Jr. Behind them is Manson's other son, Baby Manson.

Right now Manson is the happiest that he's even been in life. He dreamed of this day while in prison and today his dream has come true. Well, a part of his dream has. The other part of his dream was to have both of the women in his life in perfect harmony and enjoying this special moment with them.

When Manson told Pebbles his plan for the day she had no problem with meeting him there with their son. As much as she hates Jada, she would never take her hatred out on the child. Surprisingly, she has a soft spot in her heart for him. The fact that Jada has abandoned her son because of his situation makes her hate the girl even more. She's quite pleased that Manson is taking the initiative to step up and be in the boy's life.

A couple hours pass and just as Damien Jr. is getting warmed up to Manson and his brother, the sun is going down. He loosened up and allowed Manson and Baby Manson to walk with him alone, just as long as his grandmother was in his sight. His kids haven't been together but a few times in their life and that was in the early months, too young to be remembered. Manson watched as Baby Manson catered to Damien Jr. like a real big brother and that touched his heart on another level.

He hates that the beautiful day has to end but he's sure this is only the beginning for them as a family. Manson and Baby Manson both hug Damien Jr. as his grandmother waits for him with the door of the car wide open. Jada's father rolls his eyes at his daughter before getting into his car. She's so far removed from her parents and her son that she didn't even want to get out of the car. She blamed it on her parents and told him that once they're able to get him on their own she's all for it. Manson and Baby Manson hug for the very first time since they reunited. The boy melts in his father's arms. Manson ends the hug and his son gets into Pebbles' truck. "I'll hit you," Manson says to Pebbles who ignores him rudely.

Manson is so used to her disrespect that he doesn't think twice about it. He's so elated right now that nothing, not even her could bring him down. He gets into the passenger's seat of the car still floating on the cloud. He watches as all the cars pull off, leaving him and Jada all alone.

"Damn, I dreamed of this shit for years. I can't believe it really happened. All of us here as one big family. Not exactly how I wanted it but," he says as Jada's text alert sounds off.

Jada recognizes the code name and gets fidgety. Her and Smoke have been texting back and forth, and even spoke to each other secretly, phone in her lap on speaker, the whole time. Manson notices her discomfort. "Who that?" Jada is about to look up to the right just as she always does before she lies but she catches herself. Smoke let the cat out of the bag about her doing that when she lies and she has been mindful of it ever since. "I said who that?" he snaps.

Jada keeps her eyes straight forward fighting the urge to look up to the right. "My coworker," she lies right before he snatches the phone from her. He reads the display and the name 'Short Tanya from the Job' is spread across the screen.

"I'm telling you about something that makes me happy and you more interested in that damn phone," he says with attitude. He inhales in order not to mess up his mood. "I dug what you said about your parents and all. Your father is a hard man to deal with," he says shaking his head. "Lil Damien was comfortable and all. This not gone take long as I thought. This week I'm going to talk to your moms about giving you custody back."

Jada's neck snaps. She tries to conceal the negativity in her heart and hopes that Manson doesn't sense it. "That way you don't have to deal with them and we can all be a family as we should be," he says with a spark in his eyes. "What you think?"

Jada's text alert sounds off again. She doesn't even look down at it, just to prevent angering Manson. Jada has no reply for him. The truth of the matter is she doesn't want the son or him but in no way can she ever tell him that. "Talk to me. Tell me what you're thinking," he insists.

She sits there in a trance just imagining how miserable she would be with a son in the house that she has no love for or emotional attachment to. Couple that with a man that she has no love for or emotional connection to and she's sure she will be one miserable bitch. "Talk to me."

"I really don't know what to say," she says.

"No need to say anything. I've made the decision. I want my son home with us. End of discussion. I will talk to your moms and pops and they will have no choice but to honor what I say. I'm his father." He turns away from her, staring straight ahead. "Drive."

126

DAYS LATER/COURTYARD MARRIOTT

MANSON AND SMOKE stand in the kitchen area of Helter and Skelter's suite here near the Newark Airport. In the beginning they would travel back and forth from Trenton everyday. Manson has kept them on call in hotels since the very first time he was able to do so. Once his flow started to increase he moved them into something more comfortable. Now they hardly ever go back to Trenton unless they're with him for business with Blue-Blood.

Stacks and stacks of money are piled onto the counter top in front of Smoke who counts through a small stack of loose bills. Once he finishes counting he hands the bills over to Manson. "That's twelve-fifty right there. I gave you thirty the other day. That's sixty-six racks right there," he says pointing to the counter top. "And my man gotta give me like 34 racks. He should be done with that in no more than two days," Smoke says with great pride.

Manson is quite impressed with Smoke and he can't hide it. For the first time in a long time he flashes a smile at Smoke. He nods his head up and down. "Okay, I see you. Not even two weeks either, huh?"

Smoke gloats like a child who has made his father proud. "I told you, Big Bruh, I moves that work. Once it touches my hands it's a wrap!"

"So, we should be rich in no time then, huh?"

"Exactly," Smoke says with a smile. "And I got some other shit for us too." Manson looks up from the bag in which he's stacking the money into. "My man over Paterson got three for us right now. Said he want twenty racks apiece for him though."

Manson's facial expression changes quickly. "Hold up. You letting motherfuckers know what we got going on? Do you realize if the word get out about this we will get the fucking electric chair?"

"Nah, this ain't just anybody. This my real man. He like us."

"Like us?" Manson replies with great sarcasm. "Ain't nobody like me. I learned that a long time ago. Better stop giving motherfuckers credit they don't deserve. You better hope he ain't over there running his fucking mouth about this."

"Bruh, this one dude I ain't worried about. Me and this dude have done shit together that has never come back up."

Manson stares at him through squinted eyes. "I'm trusting your word on this. Get him on the phone and tell him the best we can do is ten apiece. Ain't nobody dictating shit to me," he says as he grabs the bag and exits the kitchen area.

Smoke quickly dials the phone and as it's ringing aloud, he holds it up to his face, staring at the screen. The man's face pops onto the screen as they FaceTime each other. "Yo," the man says very laid back like. The background shows that he's in the passenger's seat of a car.

"Yo, bruh, the best we can do is half of that," Smoke says with disappointment. "Nah, Bruh," the man replies with determination in his eyes. "Man, fuck that if I get caught with them shits, I'm going to jail for the rest of my life. You know what kind of time I will get for them shits, bruh? Y'all only trying to give a motherfucker ten racks a body? Fuck that!"

"You can't do nothing with them anyway. It ain't like you got nowhere else to move them, bruh," says Smoke.

Manson hears the conversation from the other room and he's cringing at the fact that they're talking so loosely on the phone. He stomps into the room with rage on his face. Once he sees them face to face on the screen he becomes even more terrified of the situation. He lunges at Smoke and with one swipe he snatches the phone from him. He ends the call. "What the fuck is wrong with you? Y'all talking about this shit like it's legal," he says pressing his chest against Smoke, backing him against the counter.

"Nah, Big Bruh, they can't track Facetime because it runs off Wi-Fi," he says in his defense.

Manson stares at him with disgust. "Who the fuck told you that? Them people can do whatever the fuck they want to. You keep listening to the dumb motherfucker who told you that if you want to," he says as he tosses the phone at Smoke's chest. "Put some shade on that conversation and keep your dumb ass face off that phone, dummy."

Smoke dials the numbers slowly. The man picks up on the first ring. "Yo!"

Manson speaks loud enough for the caller to hear him. "Ask him how long he had them sandwiches anyway?"

Smoke looks to Manson. "Said he got him last night."

"Ay man, tell him he got a few more hours on them before they spoil and be no good for nobody. Once that meat rot and start stinking it's a wrap. May as well take what we got for him before he stuck with him. We really don't need them. Cold-cuts five cent a pound but we willing to give him ten cents." Manson continues on with no pause. "Tell him we on our way with the cheese right now."

The dude is saying things on the other end that Smoke would never repeat. He knows what Manson will do to the man for being loose with his lips and he would hate to be in the middle of that. Smoke cuts the man off. "Be over there in a half hour,bruh!" He ends the call.

"I don't like that trying to control our price shit," Manson says. "Fuck around

go over there for three and come back with four and don't have to pay nobody shit," he says as he steps out of the room. "Let's go!"

Smoke shakes his head and sighs.

127

PATERSON/HOURS LATER/12 MIDNIGHT

MANSON AND SMOKE follow behind the man and his partner as they are led through the abandoned and deserted warehouse building. The whole ride here all Smoke could think of is his man saying something crazy to Manson and the whole situation getting out of hand. Upon introducing them they only acknowledged each other by way of head nod.

The man leads them into a small room to the side. He points to the dark corner of the room. "There they go."

Manson stares the man in the eyes as he passes him. He makes his way over to the corner where he can see three bodies thrown on top of each other. "I can't see shit!" Manson shouts as he walks away from the bodies. He passes the man with the same look in his eyes. "Y'all gone have to bring them shits out to the light," he says leading the way back to the main room of the warehouse.

The man snickers with sarcasm. Smoke looks at him with his eyes begging him to let it go.

Minutes later after the man and his partner have dragged all three of the bodies to the main room, Smoke and Manson get out of the truck. Manson walks over and studies the bodies closely. "Fucking junkies yo!" he shouts to the man. "What the fuck?"

"Nah, two of them. Not the third one."

Manson ignores him and studies the bodies even closer and is shocked to see that one of the junkies is a woman. The third one looks like a junkie but his crisp new clothes indicate that he was probably a hustler who gets high enough to look like a junkie. Blood covers all of their clothes. The younger man has an entry wound in his forehead the size of a tennis ball.

Manson uses his foot to sway the man's head to the side so he can see. Brain matter still hangs from the back of his head. The exit wound is two sizes the entry one. Manson examines the woman and finds a single bullet wound to the temple. The man has not a hole in his head or face but the excess of blood covering his whole torso indicates that he was hit several times in the chest and stomach.

Manson goes to the truck and grabs three body bags and comes right back. He tosses the bags to the man. "Bag them up and put them in the truck while I get this money right." The man bites his lip to keep his mouth shut. He watches with anger until Manson gets into the truck.

Minutes later, Manson stands at the back of the truck, hands on the raised hatch as Smoke helps the other two men throw the last body bag into the truck. Manson tosses the bag at the man. He can't hold it back anymore. "Don't throw nothing at me like I'm a dog," he says with arctic eyes.

"Or what?" Manson asks with a smirk on his face.

Smoke gets ready to step in between them.

"Ay man, let me tell you something."

"You can't tell me shit," Manson interrupts.

The man looks to Smoke. "You better tell him I ain't one of them lil niggas that be digging his ghost. I don't give a fuck. Yeah, he a G but I'm a man before I'm a Blood. G or no G, don't nobody disrespect me."

Smoke speaks with his eyes as he puts his hand on the man's chest.

Manson looks away and turns back so quickly that no one sees it coming. He snatches the man by the collar with one hand and jams his gun to the man's neck with the other. "Shut up!"

The man's partner goes to draw his gun but Smoke plants his hand over the man's hand. "Don't do that," he warns.

Arson and Skelter jump out of the truck with their guns drawn. They all surround the two men who are in shock. This is what Smoke prayed wouldn't happen. His man looks into his eyes as if to say, 'word, like that?' Smoke looks to Manson. "Big Bruh, please. This my man right here. Please, Big Bruh," he pleads.

Manson slowly unloosens the man's collar. He lowers his gun even slower. The man's pride is hurt more than anything. His lip quivers with fury. Manson backs away from him. "Watch your motherfucking mouth. All that tough shit, I ain't with. The graveyard full of tough motherfuckers like you."

The man says not a word. He just watches with steam coming from his ears. He's livid. He looks around at all the guns surrounding them and realizes it's best to keep his mouth shut.

Manson gets into the passenger's seat. Before slamming the door shut, he speaks. "I know we agreed on thirty but that's twenty-seven. I took three out since we had to travel here and come get them."

The man looks to Smoke. "I said thirty, bruh."

"Just be cool with that. They fucking fiends anyway. My connect might not even take them." The man shakes his head in despair. "It's three lousy ass grand. We can make that a hundred times over. Drop the tough guy shit and let's get this money!" Manson slams the door shut. "Agreed?"

After a few seconds of silence the man replies loud and clear. "Agreed!"

128

ONY STANDS IN the hallway of the fairly new apartment building. He holds his pointer finger inches away from the buzzer. His heart races as he debates if he should ring it or not. He stares at the tag over the buzzer which reads, 'M. Austin.' Rage fills his heart as he thinks of the fact that she's still walking around with his name after all that she put him through.

The famous word 'clarity' has brought him here. Twenty minutes after Mocha and Tony saw each other at the mall that day his business line started blowing up with calls from her. The only reason he entertained her call in the first place was just to hear what she had to say. He needed to hear her response to the picture he painted just for his own ego. Her verbal attacks was only confirmation that he had gotten even with her.

She told him that she really needs to speak with him face to face so they can give each other the clarity they never gave one another. She claims they owe that much to each other. He's quite sure what that clarity is that she speaks of. Tonight he plans to get ahead in the game by giving her a good old 'payback fuck' to let her know what she gave up. After that he plans to never answer her call again.

He places his finger on the buzzer and right before he presses he second thinks it again. Before he can talk himself out of it, he presses the buzzer. His heart pounds as he awaits an answer. Many seconds go by and he tells himself she must have fallen asleep due to the fact that he was supposed to be here hours ago.

He turns around and just as he opens the door Mocha's voice seeps through the intercom speaker. "Yes?"

He stops in his tracks. "Yo."

Mocha says not a word. The buzzer sound off loudly.

"I don't believe this shit," he mumbles under his breath. "How the fuck did I get here?" The conversation with himself stops once he gets to her door which is cracked open. He knocks gently.

"Come in," she yells from afar.

He steps in hesitantly and is slapped in the face with he and Mocha's favorite perfume which graces the air. He looks around and finds her nowhere. He closes the door shut behind him as he stares around the living-room. The room is filled with a bunch of furniture and items that he bought. As he looks around he sees their history together flash before his very eyes. Every piece of furniture sends another memory into his mind. Seeing all of the items crammed into this tiny room makes him wonder how she copes with the downsizing that she had to do being without him. He slashes that thought as he tells himself that it's the life she chose so it's not his concern.

"Where you at?" he asks.

"Come straight to the back!" she yells.

He steps through the narrow hall slowly, trying to get his thoughts together. The closer he gets to the back room the louder the smell of her perfume becomes. He stops at the door and peeks his head in. Mocha has the white satin sheet up to her neck.

She rolls over onto her side and the satin clings to her body, revealing curves and mountains almost everywhere. Her dark chocolate skin contrasts well against the milky white satin. She rests her head on her wrist with her elbow planted on the mattress. The sheet drops and her breast flop vibrantly over it. She stares into Tony's eyes with no sight of shame on her face.

"Ex-cons though? I can't lie to you, that threw me for a loop."

"You still talking about that? Later for that."

"Nah, I'm just saying. So, did that relationship start while me and you was together?"

"Is that what you called me here for? Is that the clarity you spoke about?"

She throws the covers back, exposing her beautiful nudeness. She slides to the edge of the bed, never taking her eyes out of his. She stands up boldly. Tony pretends to not even be phased by her nudity, but he is.

Truthfully he's quite impressed that all the work has held up over the years. He spent close to a hundred grand to make her look like this. She's had it all from breast jobs to fat transfers. She's maintained it well, he must admit. He becomes angered as he thinks of how he custom designed her just to have other men appreciate his creation and hard earned money.

"So, was y'all fucking while we were married?"

"Nah, you were the only one fucking outside of the house. I was too busy getting money," he says with sarcasm. "What's up, though?" he asks with cockiness.

"Like I said, we need clarity."

"We don't need nothing. I'm good. I turned the page on that chapter a long time ago. What clarity you need, though?"

"Same old cocky motherfucker you always been," she says before turning around and walking away from him. He feasts his eyes on her voluptuous rump. She makes her way over to the nightstand where her half filled glass of wine awaits her.

Tony's nonchalant exterior is only a front. As he looks her over from head to toe, he misses the feel of her firm thickness. Episodes of their best love-making play out in his mind, causing him to get an instant erection. He grabs himself without even knowing it. Mocha turns around and catches him red handed.

She takes another sip of her wine and while looking over the glass she speaks. "Let go of the cockiness," she as her eyes are locked on his hand over the crotch of his jeans. "And come over here and let's talk about this," she says with seduction in her eyes.

He's anxious to give her the 'payback sex' but he continues to play it cool. He pretends to be unimpressed with all of this. Mocha walks over to him, hips swaying hypnotically. Her stiffened nipples steals the attention from her protruding hips. She places on hand behind his head and the other on his chest while she stares into his eyes. With her mouth wide open she goes straight in for the kill.

To her surprise he turns his head, giving her his cheek. She fights with him to get his lips but he makes it impossible for her. "Stop fighting with me. You know you want it," she whispers as she gropes his manhood.

"I thought you had something you wanted to talk to me about," he says as he snatches her hand off of him. He grips her wrist tightly.

"I can't believe we are here face to face. I'm speechless," she whispers. "My pussy will have to speak for me," she says as she guides his hand over her box. Tony's tough exterior is melting. "I can say that I miss you so much. She misses you too," she says as she rubs his middle finger over her opening. "See how wet and sticky she is for you? I'm gonna be quiet and let her talk to you."

She begins kissing his lips, his cheek and his neck. She pecks all over planting wet lips all over. Tony grabs her by both arms and gently guides her to the bed. He sits her down and she lays flat on her back awaiting him.

To her surprise he turns around and makes his way to the door. "Where you going?" she asks.

Tony has a change of heart. As bad as he wanted to give her his best pay back sex he refuses to do so. After all the backstabbing she did he finds her to be not even worthy of his payback sex.

He looks over his shoulder as he stops at the door. "I'm out."

"Why? Tony, please," she says as she jumps up from the bed. She runs over and grabs his hand. "I miss you so much. Really, I didn't call you over here just for sex. I'm sure you don't want to hear this but these guys out here don't measure up to half of you. You're a hard act to follow. You made it hard for anybody after you. That was the worse mistake that I ever made in my life."

Tony stares into her eyes and he can see that she's not trying to feed his ego and she actually means what she's saying. Her eyes display defeat. After all these years it feels good to hear her admit it. A smirk spreads across his face. "But you made that mistake though. The punishment for crossing a real motherfucker is the fake motherfuckers that you end up with."

She nods her head in submission. "After all these years I can't seem to turn the page of the book. It's like I'm stuck in that chapter. Our chapter," she adds.

He leans over and kisses her on the forehead. "Enjoy the rest of your life, hun." He steps toward the door, leaving her sulking in regret. He stops at the door and turns to face her. "About that book you speak about. She desperately awaits his words. "Don't worry about turning the page. Just close the book and discard it. Start a new one with all new characters and move on with your life. Look at my character as if you killed him off. I killed yours off a long time ago," he says before turning around and walking through the hall. "New storyline, new plot and new supporting character. Life goes on."

129

MANSON IS IN Hamza's store stocking shelves and pretending to be busy. He pops into the store every so often just to keep parole from catching him slipping. Although they have never come to the job he doesn't want to get too comfortable with not showing up at all.

The little check that Hamza pays him he gives straight to parole for his fines, now that he doesn't need it to live. The store is now a front for him just as it is for Hamza. It's a meeting place. Just today alone, he's met his Philadelphia connection, the General and another three acquaintances of his.

Right from the store, he sent them on their way with a total of eleven kilos sold. Three of them was 204,000 cash money. The General bought four, spending 272,000, which is thirty-two grand profit for him. Philadelphia Muslim took two at 68,000 apiece on consignment that he can expect a return in a week. The other two were dudes he knows from the city that he fronted at 70,000 apiece, giving him a profit of 20,000. In total his profit margin for the day is 92,000 when it's all said and done. Today has been the best day that he's had thus far as a dope dealer.

Hamza finishes up with the last customer and for the first time today the store is empty. Hamza walks over to Manson with a disturbed look covering his face. Manson senses something is wrong. "What's up?" Manson asks with genuine concern.

Hamza fumbles the words in his head trying to choose the best ones. He's very careful how he speaks to Manson after their last episode. "You know the new traffic has been raising some eyebrows around here?"

"Huh?"

"One of my good friends tells me the Muslims have been inquiring about you and the traffic that comes in and out of here to see you. They even know you are an ex-gang banger, as they refer to you. A few even went as far as to say that they've never seen you pray anywhere and wonder if you're a Muslim. And if not, why do I have you working here, because this could be a job that I could be giving to one of the Muslims," he explains.

Hamza has been wanting to tell Manson about his friends meeting here but didn't know how to. His clientele has always blended in and played the part wherein Manson's customers look like thugs and drug dealers. He's sure it will take one of them to blow his operation, that has been operating successfully for years with no problems. The money that Manson is generating is plentiful and he moves the kilos as he promised he would but he's causing way too much attention as he does it.

"Man, fuck them motherfuckers. Why they worried about me? You know which one said all that? Let me go holler at them."

"No, Damien. We don't need the heat. I was afraid the change of store traffic would cause some unwanted attention. You know gang-bangers popping up and you having secret meetings on the side of the building with them. All that causes alarm."

"So, what you saying?"

"I'm just saying we have to figure out a better way to handle our business. We don't want to blow our cover down here."

Before Hamza can finish his last statement, the door chime sounds off. Smoke peeks his head in. "Big Bruh, can I speak to you out here for a minute."

Hamza shakes his head before walking away. Manson walks to the door and steps out behind Smoke. They shake hands. "Big Bruh, I got somebody who wanna talk to you. He like the head of all the Dominicans who had the shops all around. He used to be hitting my man and my man threw my name out there and asked if he could get in touch with me. I linked up with him to hear what he wanted to talk to me about. I think you need to hear this, bruh."

"Hear what, bruh? Ain't nothing them motherfuckers can do for us. We got the plug. We don't need them for nothing.."

"I know I know, just hear him out." Smoke doesn't wait for his answer before he waves the Dominican who sits in the passenger's seat of his car on. The smooth Dominican appears to be in his late thirties, early forties. He glides over very debonair like but with a shook look on his face. He stands there twirling his thumbs with nervousness.

"Go ahead," Smoke commands.

"I was telling your brother here that I can be of help to you."

"And how is that? Y'all services no longer needed around here. We got it from here."

"I know and I respect that," he claims. "I hear you got Grade A material but I test it out with my people and it can't stand up to my material I had in the city. You don't have the missing ingredient."

"What's that?" Manson asks curiously.

The man loosens up with a bright smile. "Me," he says followed by a wink. "A lot of the black people cut at the table but the work is never a solid 8,9, or 10. Lucky if it's even a 5. They're missing the main ingredient. I can get it any day of the week in abundance."

"What is the main ingredient?"

"Dominican rat poison that you can only get from my country. That's the cut we use. Add that to your material and nobody will be able to touch the work. I'm also coming to you to make a plate for myself. If you put me in charge of your table I will be sure to produce a solid 10 every time. And also for the right number I can score a few points in between my customers and you. I respect that this is your side of town and I won't make a move over here but still I need to eat."

A glow lights up Manson's face. "That's something to think about."

130

PITTSBURGH PETE CRUISES through the city on his way to Route 78. He's just got through meeting with Manson dropping off money and getting hold of more work. Manson has changed his life in no time at all. He'e been ripping through the dope a kilo per week, scoring Manson a profit of only 10,000 but scoring himself a profit of approximately ninety thousand.

When they first linked up he barely had money of his own for a few grams. In just a couple of months all that has changed. Having his own work gives him freedom that he hasn't had in the whole two years that he's been home. Also with the quality of work that Manson has, he's been able to increase his price with no complaints.

He can't believe how his life has changed drastically in such a short time. Today, in the backseat of his car is enough work to hold him for a month. That is five containers of Shea Butter in total. One of the containers is on consignment just as Manson has been giving him from the start. The other four he paid cash money for out of his own pocket.

In the beginning the money flowed so rapidly that he pissed it away with no respect for it. He's never experienced a flow like this and it has taken some time to get used to it. He's just getting his hands on real money again after all his years of incarceration so he was like a kid in a candy store throwing money away foolishly. Now that he has gotten used to it and has worked the kinks out of his system he decided that it's time to turn up and take things more seriously. He has plans to make himself Manson's most valuable player of the team sooner than later.

Just as he's making a right to hop onto the Parkway he spots a familiar car. He glances at the license plates of the approaching car just to be sure it's who he thinks it is. The Camaro slows down as it passes while the driver peeks through the dark tinted windows. He peeks through the rearview mirror and the brake light of the Camaro comes on confirming that he saw him. "Damn," he thinks to himself. This is the last man he wanted to see.

The Camaro busts a quick U-turn in the middle of the street and chases him down, hitting the horn. He continues on toward the highway as if he doesn't see him. The red light catches him and he has no choice but to stop. The Camaro swerves around and pulls onto the side of him. The window rolls down and Vito is staring at him from the driver's seat. Pete rolls his window down.

"What up?" he asks with a cheesy look on his face.

"You tell me," Vito says. "I been calling you. You changed your number on me. I ain't heard from you in almost two months. Pull over, yo!" he demands.

"I, I," he stutters as Vito zips around him and parks. As filthy as he is with five kilos of dope in the car he has no choice but to pull over for him. He pulls over and before he can park Vito is walking toward the car. He stops and Vito snatches the door open.

He gets in with his face frowned up. "What's good?"

"Shit," Pete replies, not knowing what else to say. Vito has Pete's heart in his pocket and he knows it. Pete's tough guy aura only works on those who fall for it and Vito is not one of them. Pete throws his weight around pretending to be reckless but he's selective with who he flexes on. One thing for certain he respects real gangsters and hands down Vito is one that he not only respects but fears.

"Something good. You coming through my city and not getting at me. Talk to me. Who you been seeing?" Vito and Pete met through a mutual acquaintance a couple of years ago and have been doing business ever since. Vito is the connect that has kept him alive since he's been home.

Pete's loyalty makes him feel like he's crossing him but really he's not. He owes him not a dime. Still he feels he at least owes him the truth. "Bruh, I ain't gone lie to you. I landed a great situation. That's why I haven't been to see you in all this time."

"So it's just fuck me, once you don't need me no more? I front you two and three hundred bricks at a time all this time and you find a connect and it's just fuck me?"

"Nah, bruh, it's never fuck you."

"I can't tell. Anyway, who in this city got more fire shit than me? Why haven't I heard about it?" Pete is hesitant about giving up his source and Vito can see it. "Who?" he asks putting the pressure on him.

"The Blood Homie Manson," Pete mumbles.

Vito's face distorts at the sound of Manson's name. He's been hearing it so much lately that the sound of it enrages him. "Fuck he got? Broke throwback motherfucker just coming home. He works at the Muslim store stocking books on shelves. What the fuck his broke ass got?"

Pete reluctantly grabs the small shopping bag from the backseat. He shuffles through the Islamic novelties and grabs hold of a container of

Shea Butter. He hands it to Vito who holds it in his hand looking at it cluelessly. "Fucking Shea Butter?"

"Nah, that's the front. It's raw dope inside."

Vito sits in amazement. "How much raw dope?" he asks in disbelief.

Pete really doesn't want to tell him. He's afraid if he does Vito may take it from him.

"It's a kilo in there," he admits with sadness in his eyes. He awaits the next response, gripping the shopping bag handle tightly in his hand. He would hate for Vito to know that there are four more in there.

"A kilo? You buying kilos?"

"Nah, bruh. He fronting them to me. Shits on deck and unlimited. Fire shit, bruh. That's why I ain't been getting the bricks from you. I bag it up myself and go through a key every week and a half no more than two weeks."

Vito calculates the numbers in his mind. He quickly becomes agitated as he thinks of the bricks that Pete no longer gets due to Manson stepping on his toes. The worry kicks in as he thinks of how much more money he will lose if the word gets out in the city and everybody starts to flock toward Manson. He understands that this could easily cost the Crips their control of the city.

Pete reaches for the container. Vito snatches it away from him. "I ain't gone take your work. My beef ain't with you. You my man and since you my man I'm gonna warn you. You may wanna stay outta the middle of this shit because shit about to get real crazy."

131

DAYS LATER

SMOKE AND MANSON gave the Dominican a half of a kilo to see what his capabilities are. Just two days ago he returned the work to them and like magic, customers gravitated in astronomical numbers. Once they received nothing but positive response, Manson didn't hesitate to drop two kilos on the Dominican to go to the table and add his magical mix as they nicknamed it. The Dominican they now call 'The Chef' has promised them at least 1800 bricks off of the two kilos.

His fee of $18,000.00 per kilo, he spreads out across his team of employees. He guarantees them 900 bricks per kilo but that doesn't count the extras that he manages to stretch out of it. The extra 15 or 20 bricks that he doesn't report will eventually turn into hundreds of bricks in the long run. Small profits lead to large profits.

Smoke is waiting for the dope impatiently like a father in the delivery room waiting for his child to be born. He has plans of spreading out all over the city and taking over. His wholesale brick sales and his block sales balanced, gives him and Manson close to fifty-grand profit to split after paying The Chef his fee. He hasn't been this excited about life since his days of running around with the Mayor. While sitting on the bench all these past years he would think of all the things he could've done differently so he would have been in a better position. He has no intentions of making those same mistakes this time around.

Smoke pulls into the back of the townhouses. He gets out of the car, slams the door shut and walks toward the action. He hasn't seen this much life here ever. Dope sales flow at a rapid pace. Customers pour in from every alley available.

The Mormons no longer stand at the entrance, they have moved to the center of the court. They felt standing at the entrance put a limit on the lives they could save so they've moved to a better place. Being in the center of the action they can catch every customer coming in to cop dope with hopes of distracting them from doing so. Smoke and the crew as well as everyone else has gotten so used to them walking through the city spreading the word that it's almost as if they're invisible. They don't bother anyone who doesn't want to be bothered and no one bothers them. They blend in like they grew up in these very neighborhoods and not like they just popped up a few years ago.

The young Mormon has pamphlets in both hands trying to catch everyone. "Jesus is Lord," he says. Whoever he doesn't catch, his partner catches. "Jesus is Lord," he repeats as he shoves the pamphlet into Smoke's chest.

"Come on Jonathan," Smoke says with a smile. They've been here so long the Mormons know them by name and vice versa.

"Oh, my bad, Smoke," the Mormon says emulating the slang that he's picked up over the years. It flows so naturally for him.

Smoke flies the pamphlet back at him.

An old raggedy, tall, gangly looking dope fiend comes walking in with his old raggedy dog at his side. The man and the dog have been together so long that they look alike. The German shepherd mixed with everything is just as old and frail as his owner. They both limp like cripples.

At the sight of the man a group of dealers attack him like vultures. "Doggy Mane, Doggy Mane!" they all yell in a fake southern dialect as they try to direct him to them. They have nicknamed him Doggy Man but they pronounce it mane, emulating his southern drag.

Smoke sees Doggy Mane here and takes that as a good sign. Doggy Mane is the most finicky dope fiend in all the land. Doggy Mane makes the claim to be a dope connoisseur. In all the places that Doggy Mane can buy dope, if he's here that means they have the best dope in the city. "Gimme six mane," Doggy Mane says. His deep southern accent sounds if he can be from as deep south as Mississippi. "Somebody, anybody! Six," he says, while throwing six of his seven fingers in the air. The first three fingers were chopped off years ago in a lawn mower while doing an odd job to gather some dope money.

The young dealer hands Doggy Mane the six bags he ordered and he hands him the money. Right in front of the crowd of young dealers and Smoke, Doggy Mane plucks a bag of dope and holds it up over his head, to peep the amount inside. He arches the eyebrow of his good eye as if he's impressed. He then pulls out a pocketknife and slits the bag open.

Without further ado he places the bag to his nose and devours the dope in one huge sniff. He shakes his head, eyes closed while pinching his nostrils. The dog stares up at him as he opens another bag and devours that one as well. He doesn't stop there though.

He opens another bag and another and sniffs them both as the dog watches his master with greed in his eyes. Doggy Mane busts the fifth bag open and just as they're expecting him to sniff that one, he holds his hand by his side. The dog leans over and takes a huge sniff. The dog shakes his head, eyes closed. Tears fill the dog's eyes. Everyone falls out into laughter. "Oh shit," one young boy laughs.

Doggy Mane looks at the young boy, not understanding the humor. "What? You ain't never seen a dig sniff dope before?" he asks as he busts the last bag open with his knife. "I got a sixteen bag a day habit and my bitch here got an eight bag a day habit," he explains with a straight face. "Me and this bitch been together for over 15 years. That's over 105 dog years. I eat, she eat. I sniff dope she sniff dope."

He places the bag of dope to the dog's nose and she sniffs it in totality with swipe of the nose. Both the man and the dog stare into space allowing the dope to shoot to their brain. The dog's eyes are watering like a leaky faucet. Doggy Mane gets to plucking his nostrils. "The drain there and quick too. I feel it already." He looks to his dog. "Bitch, what you think?" he asks as if he's talking to a human being.

Everyone including Smoke watches in amazement as the dog holds her head to the sky and howls. Doggy Mane looks to the crowd. "Y'all got something here. Keep it like this and y'all gone own the city," he says as he turns around and walks off with the dog glued to his side.

What Smoke just witnessed is like an epiphany. He's pleased Doggy Mane, the pickiest dope fiend in the city of Newark. He's sure if he can please him he will have no problem pleasing every other junkie in the city. Smoke looks to his crew. "It's our turn."

132

MANSON HANGS AN Islamic picture on the bare wall, centering it perfectly. Two women dressed in full Muslim garb are on the other side of the room, one kneeling and the other on a small step ladder. The one kneeling hands the tubs of Shea Butter to the other one who stacks them onto the shelves. Arson who is in disguise, wearing a small kufi on the back of his head stands on a ladder as well. With his big burly beard, he looks just like a white or Turkish Muslim. He hangs a camera in the corner of the wall, positioned at just the right angle to view the entire store.

Hamza came up with the bright idea of how to save his store from unwanted attention. He found the perfect storefront far away from his store and gave Manson the keys. Manson now has his own store to operate how he pleases. Now he feels free without having Hamza watching down his every move.

He chose to keep the same format as Hamza with hopes of running an equally smooth operation. He decided to come in from the very start in full disguise just to keep the neighboring residents off of their back and not wondering what it is that they're doing in here. It's quite evident for all to see what their business appears to be. It's been a simple task for the most part.

The hardest part wasn't getting Arson to put a kufi on his head to fake the funk as he thought it would be. To great surprise he did it without a second thought. The hardest part was getting Helter and Skelter to cover up entirely except for their eyes. He damn near had to sweet talk them to death just to do so but eventually they did.

Manson's attention is drawn to the door where he sees the most beautiful automobile that he's ever seen in his life. The white paint is so thick that it looks like a winter snowstorm outside. The chrome grill spreads across the front almost as wide as the street. The sun beams onto the chrome rims and bounces vibrantly, blinding any eye that captures it. The 4 door, Rolls Royce Ghost looks totally out of place in such a beat up neighborhood.

Two grimy looking men who look like they should never be in such a prestigious car get out of the front seats. The back doors are quite suicidal, opening from the opposite end. Manson quickly identifies a familiar face. His Muslim partner from Philadelphia is here as promised. He's dressed in regular street clothes and so are the two grimy looking men.

The fourth one, a short, stocky man is dressed in a silky thobe as pure white as the car. The hood of the thobe covers his whole head where you can't even see his face. His Gucci flip flops smack onto the pavement loudly. From several feet away Manson can sense his strength and confidence rumbling under his feet over the concrete. As powerful of a man as he is, he walks with his head hung, and eyes on the ground humbly.

This man is a close friend of Manson's friend Angry Muslim. During their time together in prison Muslim has told Manson so much about the man that he feels as if he already knows him. This man known as Castro is legendary throughout the federal prison system. Never once touching the federal prison or any other prison, yet his name rings bells like he's been in every one of them.

He's never touched the prison but many of the guys he takes care of are spread throughout the system. Those same men that he takes care of speak highly of him. A single bad word can never be uttered about him. He's loved all over the land from Atlantic City to Detroit and Arizona.

In no way is he a gangster. He's a no-nonsense businessman but has the strength of a thousand wolves and two thousand lions behind him. With an iron fist he controls the heroin and the cocaine trade in all of Atlantic City. The trades that he doesn't exactly control, he has a percentage in as a silent investor. His arms reach out into many cities and states through the drug game, just touching a little here and a little there. In Atlantic City he has his hands not just in the drug game but a many legal businesses as well. Whether the sole owner, a partner or the loan shark behind the business, Castro's hands are in almost everything in Atlantic City except the Casinos. Those are on his bucket list though.

One of the grimy men opens the door and holds it for Castro to enter like royalty. Manson's partner steps in right behind them. Castro looks around and is immediately fooled by their set up, believing they're Muslims. "As Salaamu Alaikum!" he shouts loud and clear. He is shocked that not one of them sends the greetings back to him. He takes offense but doesn't exhibit a sign.

Angry Muslim walks over to the counter where Manson is standing. He waves to Castro and Castro steps over. The two grimy men stand at the door on guard watching the outside and the inside. The bulges along their waistband are indication that they're fully loaded and trained to go at any second.

He introduces them and they shake hands firmly. "I have told both of you so much about the other one so there's really nothing for me to say."

"Are you comfortable talking right here?" Castro asks as he looks around.

"Yeah, not a problem," Manson replies.

"Okay, cool we can skip the preliminaries and get right down to business," he says with a cough over the word business. He continues on, starting with another cough. "Straight to the point....I'm in love with the material," he says with another cough over the word material. It all boils down to a number," he says as he coughs again.

The coughing is agitating Manson and makes him assume that the man is sick or just has a smoker cough. Soon he remembers Angry Muslim telling him that the man does this in conversation. The people that know him have nicknamed him Castro 'The Cough' and not because he's sick. Castro is so paranoid that he doesn't trust anyone. His reason for never catching a case is because he's extra careful. So careful that he purposely coughs every few words, foolishly believing that if someone is wearing a wire or the phone is tapped the Feds won't hear him totally because of the cough blocking out certain words.

He covers his mouth, keeping his hand there. "Say the right number and we are in business," he says with his hand over his mouth just in case Feds are watching with binoculars reading his lips.

"There's only one number that I can say and that is 68 a joint," Manson says sternly.

"There's no way possible I can pay 68."

"The number is the number."

"I'm a, COUGH...businessman and not really into the business of haggling. I'm getting beautiful material now and have been for the past, 15 years, COUGH." He continues to keep his hand over his mouth. "I'm at 63 right now and I know we all have to eat which is why I'm willing to meet you halfway. I can't pay a dime over 65, COUGH...but if you can meet me at 65 I'm prepared to take," he peeks around to make sure no one is eavesdropping. He places his hands over his mouth and coughs and muffles, "Fifteen right now." He finishes it off with a series of coughs.

Manson is annoyed by the man because he feels as if his flexing but underneath it all a deal of this magnitude does sound good. He's sure Hamza will be very impressed with him with a deal like this on his hands. After he gets over the hype of the deal he starts to calculate. As heavy as it may sound at 65 his profit is only $75,000.00 on a $975,000.00 deal. Just a few bucks short of a million and he will make less than a hundred grand for himself. Although 75,000 is one hell of a score, when he thinks of the big scheme of things he has to question the value of it.

As Manson is debating the deal his thoughts are interrupted by a few key words that come through the speaker of the flat screen television on the wall across from them. Body Snatchers have added two more counties to their roster," the news reporter says loud and clear. Helter, Skelter and Arson all stop what they're doing and fix their eyes and ears onto the television. All four of the other men watch because they see the affect that the report has on Manson and the crew.

"Reports of missing bodies have been made in Hudson and Bergen Counties. Over five bodies have been reported missing from Paterson and a half of a dozen from Jersey City," the reporter continues on. "Authorities are not sure if the missing persons are linked in anyway or just random acts."

Manson and the crew keeps their ears and eyes glued as the reporter states the obvious. Manson's partner is trying to get eye contact with Manson to read his eyes. As he listened on his mind went back to the day that Manson propositioned him. He clearly remembers the wage Manson offered and calculates Manson's earnings at 1.1 if in fact the bodies are his work.

Judging by the look on all of their faces Angry Muslim is sure that is their work being talked about on the television. Manson and Smoke have tapped into other resources and have stretched out into other cities. The man gets nervous and feels like any minute now Feds will be running up in the store. "Hey y'all, what we gone do?" he asks as he looks to Castro then Manson.

Manson hates to make a deal of such magnitude for such a small profit margin for himself. Eli has him spoiled. He can score fifty off of one body after splitting the proceeds with his team. As he looks at the television he realizes that they will soon have to fall back from snatching bodies because the heat will be all over them.

For all he knows right now someone may be throwing his name to the police. With that in mind he realizes that he must not lose focus. Heroin is the primary focus and the only reason he came across the Eli was because of him and Hamza's heroin dealings. As hard as it may be to keep his focus on the dope he knows he has to. Seventy-five grand is seventy-five grand no matter how it comes.

Castro coughs loud and places his hand over his mouth. "Fifteen a month, every month, COUGH...I promise you that."

Manson shrugs his shoulders. "Sixty-five it is but has to be fifteen and not one under."

Castro gives one of the men at the door a head nod and he exits the store. Helter, Skelter and Arson get back busy with what they were doing before the news report. Signs of heavy thought wears on all of their faces. Each of them entertain whatever thought that report has caused. Even if they never admit it to Manson they all understand the graveness of their actions and what the end result could easily be.

In three minutes flat the man comes back into the store carrying a MCM briefcase bag. He walks over and hands the bag over to Castro. The man at the door stands right in front of it, facing the outside. Without permission he locks the door. He watches with his hand close to his gun, looking for anything that may appear suspicious. Manson leads Castro to the back room.

After feeding the money into the money machine Manson finds the money not short a single dollar of $975,000.00. It wasn't a single dollar over either and that sort of angered Manson. Coming with exactly 975 grand meant he was sure that Manson would honor the price that he stated. One thing Manson hates is for someone to think they can make him do something that he doesn't want to do.

Castro enters the room followed by Manson. In Castro's hand is two shopping bags filled with containers of Shea Butter. His empty briefcase is in the other. Manson grabs a few items from the shelves, a book, an incense holder, and other novelties. He drops them in the bags just for the sake of the front.

An elderly woman somewhere in her late 70's comes walking into store interrupting them. The little old woman, dressed in a long church woman skirt, French coffee stockings and thick sole orthopedic shoes obviously has walked into the wrong store because she looks like the model Jehovah Witness. The big wig on her head is twisted terribly, exposing her missing edges underneath it. Either she read the word religious on the sign wrong or she's mistaken this place for the bingo hall.

"Hello Ma'am, may I help you?" Manson asks very politely.

"She's with me," Castro intervenes. The old woman steps over to Castro and he hands her the shopping bags. She takes them from him and makes her way back over to the door. The man holds the door for her to exit. "My transporter."

"God bless!" the woman shouts before stepping out of the store. Manson can't help but to laugh out loud. Today he's seen it all; a good wholesome church woman transporting dope and wishing them all blessings. He shakes his head at the thought of it.

Castro switches the briefcase to his left hand and reaches for Manson's hand with his right. They shake hands. "It's been my pleasure meeting you as well as doing business with you. I hope to make many millions with you," he says quite humbly. "See you next month sometimes."

He nods his head and walks toward the door. The man at the door gently takes the briefcase from him and steps out the door first. He looks both ways before giving them the signal.

Manson's partner flashes a wink before turning around. "Thanks, bruh. I will get my P.C. on the next one," he whispers with a smile. He exits.

Manson watches the old woman get into the old Buick Electra which has to be a 1977 at the latest. The old cream colored license plates are a clear indication of how long she has had the car. She slowly seats herself in the driver's seat and ten minutes later she pulls off, both hands on the wheel at about seven miles an hour. Manson and the crew all laugh at the sight of it. As old, sweet and innocent as the woman appears no one would ever suspect her to be hauling millions of dollars of dope.

133

ONE MONTH LATER

I'S **10:30** AT night and the back of the townhouses is packed like it's daytime. It's crowded like a small stadium. The tenants, young, old and babies are out enjoying the day. Business has been so good back here that Smoke decided to throw a cookout. With the tenants being his biggest customers he figures he's taken so much from the them that it's only right that he gives back to them and their children.

Four grills are burning around the courts. People are lined up waiting for a taste of the meat that has the whole area smelling delicious. Fiends work the grills as the hustlers continue to deal the dope. Although it's a celebration, business still must go on.

In just one month Smoke's daily brick count is well over 100 bricks a day. The rapid incline of sales has everything to do with The Chef and his magical mix. Each batch has gotten better and better. Not only has it picked up out here, but Smoke's brick sales have picked up all over the city and whatever other city that he has access to. In a matter of weeks he has become a man of importance again.

Smoke and his crew not only invited all the dope fiends they knew to the cookout but they invited everybody they know from chicks to old people. They even sent the word to the Mormons to invite all the Mormons that travel the city. Right now, a total of a dozen Mormons float around passing out literature and stuffing their faces with food. They're comfortable as if they're home.

One Mormon stands on a crate, holding a bullhorn to his mouth. He preaches as if the people have come here to hear him speak the word. "And now behold, my brethren, ye know that these commandments were given to our father, Lehi, wherefore, ye have known them before and ye have come unto great condemnation, for ye have done these things which ye ought not to have done!" he shouts loud and clear enough for anyone that may want to hear him.

The sad part is not a soul is listening to him. The people are busy buying dope, shooting dope, sniffing dope or eating. He's wasting his breath but seems to have more than enough of it. He continues on energetically.

In the background the voices of the dealers can be heard. As low as they are against the bullhorn anyone in search of dope can hear it clearly. "Block Party! Block Party!" the dealers yell.

Just three weeks ago Manson and Smoke agreed to change the name of their dope. Manson wanted to name it as such as a dedication to the Mayor. Smoke's reason was purely about the money. With the reputation the Block Party name holds, he's sure that will bring the fiends from near and far; and it has.

The loud screeching of tires interrupts it all. Everyone looks to the entrance where the candy apple red 4-door, M6 BMW with heavy tints cuts through the lot with great expertise. This piece of beautiful eye candy belongs to Smoke. Candy apple red with the pure white leather seats is enough to fulfill any car lover's sweet tooth. He copped the new toy just a few days ago.

Smoke has the whole city in an uproar over the beautiful automobile. Ever since he got the car his business has increased. He will never forget the day the Mayor told him, he's a walking billboard. The prestigious vehicle has branded him, making everyone want to get their hands on the dope.

They all figure if he can cop a hundred thousand dollar car, cash money, then he's the man they need to be with. What they don't know is sure he cashed the car out, but it was nowhere near a hundred thousand dollars. As beautiful as the car is on the outside, under the hood it's literally a piece of junk. It's a salvage vehicle that he can't even get the title for. The car has flood damage and probably won't last him a year.

He paid a third of the sticker price at the auction. He paid a fiend they know as Body and Fender to get it for him. Body and Fender is the local mechanic. Body and Fender is the baddest mechanic in the business and could make millions if he could kick his dope habit.

Body and Fender also has a dealer's license. His other hustle is allowing people to go the dealer's auction with him so they can buy cars for cheap. Smoke paid Body and Fender ten bricks to take him to the auction and get the car of his choice. In total he spent thirty grand and ten bricks of dope to look like a power figure in the neighborhood.

Body and Fender informed Smoke that the car won't last a year but still he bought it. He's confident that he won't even need a year with it. He's using it for marketing purposes. Six months in this car and with the

Block Party stamp and he believes he should be able to then cop a Ferrari or two cash money, and he plans to. He also plans to enjoy the women that gravitate to the car. All around the board it's a win-win situation for him.

Smoke zips through the parking lot, swerving around the packs of people that are standing around. He grips the steering wheel with both hands bopping in his seat shouting along with the words of Drake. "I'm here for a good time not a long time, you know I... I haven't had a good time in a long time, you know I... I'm waaaay up, I feel blesssed, waaaay up, I feel blessed!"

Smoke parks in the vacant parking space right next to the Buick Lucerne. Dirt gets out of the Buick and gets into the back seat. Ooo Wee is in the passenger's seat. Dirt shakes their hands quickly and with no hesitation Smoke drops a shopping bag on his lap. "How much is this, Big Bruh?" Dirt asks.

"Like 970 bricks."

"Good!" Dirt shouts. "I got 'em waiting on me. They loving this shit. Motherfuckers saying they haven't had nothing like this since the old Block Party. You like the new Mayor, Rest in Peace!"

Smoke blushes crazily. "Yeah, rest in peace," he mumbles.

"Here," Dirt says. "That's a hundred and ten dollars short of a hundred and fifty- thousand. I will give it to you on the next one."

Smoke looks at him with his lips poked to the side. "Nigga, I ain't sweating no punk ass hundred dollars," he says as he points to the radio. "We waaaay up," he sings bopping from side to side.

Dirt smiles. "I'm out, y'all." He opens the door and before he slams it shut Smoke speaks.

"Hit me when you get to your destination. Let me know you got there safe."

"No doubt," he replies before closing the door and walking to his car. He pulls off immediately.

Just as Smoke and Ooo Wee get out a voice sounds off near the alley a few hundred feet away from them. "Yo, Big Bruh!" the youngen says with evident distress on his face. "Hurry!"

Smoke automatically thinks the worse. He fumbles for his gun underneath his waistband as he's running over. By the time he gets there a few of his men are standing crowded in the alley. He can't see what they are standing over. He finally makes it closer to them. "What up?"

The huddle opens up and there he sees Doggy Mane laid stretched out. His dog stands over him protective like. "This nigga dead," says one of the young men.

"What the fuck happened?" Smoke asks.

"I don't know. He just copped like eight bags and did six of them right in front of me and gave two to the dog. That was like ten minutes ago. He must have fell out right after."

The dog hovers over the man, whimpering sadly. Smoke kneels down closer to the man and nudges the dog with his elbow but the dog is solid in her stance, protective of her master. Smoke places his hand on the man's chest, then leans closer with his ear to his nose. "This nigga dead as shit. Damn," he says in shock.

"That's that Block Party for you," Ooo Wee says with no compassion. "We killing motherfuckers. Damn!" he says laughing and causing the others to laugh. Not a one of them shows the least bit of compassion.

Smoke stands up, looking around to see who may be watching. Standing at the edge of the alley are a few nosey tenants and a Mormon. "He okay?" the nosey old woman asks.

"Yeah, he good. Just gotta get him some water," Smoke lies.

Smoke whispers to his men. "Yo, get him up from here before everybody see him. Put him in the basement of 215." As Doggy Mane lays there Smoke doesn't see him as a human being. He sees him as a profit. He plans to double back later to get the man and take him to Manson to score his ten grand profit.

Three of Smoke's men grab the man and the dog goes crazy. She growls viciously and snaps at them as they try to get closer to her master. Smoke kicks the dog with all of his might, breaking two ribs on contact. "Fuck outta here, mutt!"

The dog whines and runs off whimpering. She stands at the edge of the alley with the rest of the people watching her master be dragged away. She cries and whimpers before howling at the moon in distress. After 105 dog years, her and her Master have been separated. A sad day in a dog's life.

MINUTES LATER

SMOKE ZIPS THROUGH the street blasting Big Sean's 'Blessed' as he's on his way to drop off the money Dirt just gave him. His mind is on getting the body over to Manson so they can make their way over to Brooklyn. Smoke pulls into the parking space right in front of Samirah's house and slams the gear into park. He hops out and jogs to the house.

"Be right back," Smoke says. He exits the car and races up the steps with Dirt's money and the money he's accrued from the block today. In total the bag holds close to three hundred grand. He disappears into the house and Ooo Wee quickly presses eject to the CD and hides it in the console. He's been forced to listen to this song ever since Smoke got the car and he's now fed up with it.

Smoke walks through the living-room into the kitchen. He stops at the trash can in the corner. He snatches the bag of garbage out of the can and drops the bag of money into the can. He places the garbage bag on top of the bag of money.

He then makes his way toward Samirah's bedroom. He goes to the closet and fumbles inside the shoe box. He grabs a total of twenty-five bricks for the sale that he has waiting for him back at the townhouses. He drops the dope into a shopping bag and makes his way out of the apartment.

Smoke locks the door and skips down a half-a-flight of stairs. Just as both feet touch the ground, his phone rings. He stops mid-stride to answer it. In the second that he looks down at the display, a tinted out Durango bends the corner wildly.

The flash that zips across his eyes snatches his attention from the phone. As he looks up the first thing he sees is a masked gunman raised up out of the roof. The gunman fires as the Durango approaches. BLOC! BLOC! BLOC! BLOC! Smoke stands in surprise for two seconds before another set of shots sound off from the back driver's window. BLOCKA! BLOCKA! BLOCKA!

Smoke gets low. As he fumbles for his gun a tinted out Cherokee approaches on his side of the street. Loyalty or stupidity leads Ooo Wee out of the car to bail Smoke out. He stands at the opened door and fires four inaccurate shots at the Durango. His aid gives Smoke time to get hold of his own gun.

Shots come at him from both sides. He aims at the Durango and fires twice then quickly aims at the Cherokee and fires three shots to keep them at bay. Three doors of the Durango pop open and the gunmen fire as they approach him. A series of shots from the Cherokee and Ooo Wee is left toppling over, face first.

Smoke backpedals away, firing nonstop. Just as he spins around to take off in flight, he turns right into a speeding bullet that crashes into his collar bone. He continues on, running with shots sounding off rapidly behind him. His speed is taken away from him when he's struck in the back of his thigh. The sound of the shots are getting closer as he nears the gate.

It takes all of his strength to hop onto the gate and climb it. He drags the wounded leg like dead weight. Once he reaches the top of the gate, he hears a single shot. He jumps onto the ground and right before he lands a slug crashes into the back of his skull.

The impact snaps his neck forward before his body follows. He falls onto his knees with pain. Fear for his life lifts him from the ground and he drags himself along. As he cuts across to the next alley spots appear before his eyes followed by darkness. In less than three steps he stumbles and falls. Lights out....

135

HOURS LATER/UMDNJ HOSPITAL

MANY THUGS WITH sad faces sit outside of the hospital lobby. Manson and Jada step pass them and into the lobby which is packed with more of Smoke's friends. Judging by the people, the sadness and the tears, one would think Smoke was a good guy and not the slimeball that he is. The love and support for him is in the air.

Manson has left Helter, Skelter and Arson in the car parked in the Pathmark parking lot across the street. He doesn't know what eyes are in the room and he doesn't want those eyes to get a close view of his team. The less people that can identify his team the better. As he steps into the room all eyes are on him. All of Smoke's associates are in an uproar with anger covering their faces. They pace back and forth causing a great deal of tension for the regular common folk in the room.

Manson and Jada were home when he received the news. Jada insisted that he let her go with him. Foolishly Manson believes that she's here to support him but really she's here for the love of her life. It's killing her to keep a straight face and not show her true feelings.

Two of Smoke's soldiers run over to Manson. They step to him with admiration. "Big Bruh, just give me the word where this came from and I will round everybody up and go handle this ASAP," he whispers.

"Just slow down," Manson replies. "Don't nobody move until I give the command," he says as he blows pass the two young men.

Samirah comes out of nowhere and bum-rushes Manson. She dives into his arms, hugging him tightly. "I don't believe this shit, Fav," she sobs. Manson doesn't even reciprocate the hug. His hatred for her can be seen from across the room.

He shoves her off him as politely as he can. "What the fuck happened?"

"I don't know but when I got home, my whole block was taped off. Ooo Wee was dead on the spot. They said bruh bruh died twice in the ambulance."

"Nobody on your block saw nothing?"

"Yeah, my nosey ass neighbor said it was a Cherokee and a Durango. I'm scared as hell to go home. All that shit in there. I'm scared that they probably gonna raid the house. What if whoever done this comes back tonight?" Big Show and Tasha have crossed her mind. She wonders if they're the ones behind this. She knows Smoke has a great deal of enemies but she isn't counting them out. "What should I do?"

"Just let me think."

Jada stands behind Manson not even paying attention to Manson and Samirah's conversation. She scowls around the room, spotting every girl that she knows Smoke to have dealt with. Seeing them crying over the true love of her life sends her into a jealous frenzy that she can't even show. Because of the fact that Manson is in the picture she knows that it's selfish for her to expect him to commit to her but that doesn't stop her from expecting it.

Smoke's mother walks up with teary eyes. Manson wraps his arms around her. She can't even speak. "What they say, Auntie Em?"

"They're getting him ready for surgery now. They said there's no time to waste. He can't even breathe on his own. He's lost so much blood," she says with tears dripping down her face. "Everybody here been nothing but rude to me except for one cop. No one can see him because he's handcuffed to the bed but the cop has been nice enough to tell me everything step by step."

"How is it looking for him, though?" Manson asks.

"They say it's fifty-fifty. Let's just keep our fingers crossed."

Jada crosses her fingers at her side. It will take them to cross their fingers and their toes because out in the city and in this very hospital lobby there are many people crossing their fingers that he doesn't make it out alive.

TWO NIGHTS LATER/HILTON HOTEL, NEWARK AIRPORT

THE HOTEL LOBBY is packed with Haitian men. Altogether there is a total of over fifty men, young and old with long, thick, matted dreadlocks. The Haitian clerk at the counter eyeballs them all trying to find a familiar face because she believes they have to be members of her favorite soccer team back home.

Two men stand at the counter before the clerk. "We need twenty-five rooms.

All on the top floor?" she asks. She assumes they must be about to throw a wild party and the top floor would be the best place for them.

Just as she's checking the availability Manson comes stepping through the automatic doors. He steps up to the counter next to the man in the middle. They shake hands and exchange smiles without saying a single word to each other.

Manson looks to the clerk behind the counter. "How much will that be?"

"With tax," she says hesitating as she punches the calculator. "That will be $4,075.00 with taxes. Manson pulls a hefty wad of money from his pocket and gets to counting. He piles the stacks onto the counter. "Sorry Sir, I will need a credit card to put on file."

Manson piles another stack onto the counter. "That's another thousand right there for you. We don't have a credit card."

"Okay, one minute, sir," she says gathering all the bills. "Let me talk to my manager." She leaves and in not even a minute she comes back with a handful of keys.

The man gathers the keys and the receipt. He then passes the keys out to the men and they start making their way to the elevator. Manson and the man step out of the lobby.

They shake hands again, this time more meaningful. They then step away from the building and stop in the middle of the parking lot. "So, what's up?" the man asks.

This man here is one of the few great men that Manson met while in the Feds. He goes by the name of Zoe Blood and he's from Florida. He's a member of the infamous Haitian Zoes. He and Manson linked up in ADX Florence in Colorado. He's one of the most vicious men that Manson met in all of his years in prison.

Listening to Manson's many war stories made him develop an obsession for the whole Blood lifestyle. He grew so fond of it that he joined the Blood gang underneath Manson. All the men that he's come here with are Manson's army from the Florida sector. Once Manson got the news of Smoke's situation he got on the phone with his Florida sector and his California sector.

He has sectors all over the country but he chose his top two because he has no time to waste with this. He ordered the Zoe and his Haitian Bloods to get on the highway immediately. He wired Zoe Blood five grand for travel expenses and they put over twenty cars on the highway. Manson has his California Bloods on standby just in case the Zoes can't handle the job but that he highly doubts.

"You know who did it?"

"Yeah, I know exactly who did it. It's an ongoing war that has been going on for months."

"Well, let's finally get it over with," Zoe Blood says with determination in his bloodshot red eyes.

Manson goes into his pocket again and hands Zoe Blood everything in it. "Feed them and get whatever they need. No need to worry about arsenal, I got more than enough. I will call on them as I need them."

137

THE NEXT DAY

SMOKE IS A fighter in every sense because just when everybody counted him out, he pulled through. Twelve hours ago he awakened cuffed to the bed and quite confused. It wasn't until his nurse told him the few details that she knew of that he began to remember all that had taken place.

He flips over to get off his butt which is sore from all the laying around. His butt is not the only thing sore. His chest, back and leg are all filed with pain. He lays there plugged to a few machines. The young, beautiful nurse comes in just as he opens both eyes. "How you feeling?" she asks.

"In major pain," he replies. "I need Percocet," he says.

"I already know," she replies. She hands him a cup of water and two Percocets. She peaks over her shoulder to make sure no one is watching before she drops ten more in his hand. She gives him an unprescribed bonus of five Oxycontin as well. Smoke dumps the majority of the pills in his hand quickly and washes them down with the water. "Let me change your bandages. I will be back in two minutes." She exits the room and before he can close his eyes good he feels the presence of someone at the door again.

His heart stops beating when he lays eyes on his two least favorite people in the whole world. Coming through the doorway are the two agents that The Mayor nicknamed Federal Agents, Dumber and Dumbest. "Hey Smoke," Agent Dumbest says with a smile. "How you feeling?"

Agent Dumbest holds the evidence bag in his hand which is Smoke's gun, the twenty-five bricks and a wad of cash. Smoke shakes his head in defeat. Agent Dumbest speaks again. "Smoke, why you don't call us no more? We used to stay in touch but ever since your cousin, your Big Bruh, the Black Manson," he sings with sarcasm, came home we don't even have a line on you anymore. You changed your phone number and everything."

Agent Dumber takes over, giving Smoke no time to reply. "We've been hearing about you but we haven't heard from you. So many beefs in the street that ended in murder but we don't get into your business. We just let you do whatever you want to do. That's what friends do for each other," he says with a sarcastic smile. "But I'm not going to lie to you we were curious as to what your boy Bout Dat could've possibly done for you to do that to him. We know how close you two were."

Smoke can't believe his ears. His heart skips a beat. His mouth opens but no words come out. "What, what, I, I did to him?"

"Smoke, stop it. You know we know everything. We know about Wu and Splat and even the Dominicans. We let all that slide because we thought we were friends. Friends don't treat each other like that though, Smoke. Even though you treat us like strangers we will still honor our friendship,." he says as he steps closer to Smoke. He pulls a key from his pocket and unlocks the handcuffs. He holds the cuffs in the air. "As a token of our friendship."

Smoke watches him with uncertainty. He's so focused on them that he doesn't even notice the nurse who has stepped into the room. She sees the Feds and backs out without being seen. Agent Dumbest hands Smoke the evidence bag and hands him a card. "That's our number just in case you have forgotten it. Call us," he says before turning around and walking out of the room. Agent Dumber flashes a wicked smile before following.

Smoke stares at the evidence bag and his free hands and none of it has really sunk in yet. He hears a tapping on the door and quickly he tucks the bag underneath his pillow. The nurse walks in with fresh bandages. "I'm back," she sings. As she changes his bandages she notices he's no longer handcuffed to the bed but she continues on as if she doesn't see a thing.

HOURS LATER

The Camaro pulls up to the hospital and double parks as Smoke's nurse comes strutting toward the car. The driver, Vito leans over from the driver's seat and forces the passenger's door open. The nurse gets inside and greets him with a warm smile before exhaling a huge sigh. She leans over and they peck each other's lips. She leans her head back coupled with another sigh.

"Long day?" he asks.

"Beyond. Long two days. You know I pulled damn near a triple."

"Getting that money. That's what we do."

"Damn right we do," she says with a smile. "But yo, you will never guess what the fuck I saw today," she says, pausing to build the hype. "My patient, Smoke or Chalk, whatever you call him."

"Yeah, that motherfucker," he says with hatred in his voice. "What about him?"

"I walk into the room and the Feds in there so I back out without being seen. Now you know he a prisoner and cuffed to the bed but when they leave, he has no cuffs on. I've never seen nothing like that, ever. Usually when they cuffed to the bed once they get better they're off to the County. Even the cop that was watching the door, he wasn't even there after they left."

Vito listens with his mouth wide open. "Like free?" he asks, not believing his ears.

"As a bird," she sings. "But please don't tell nobody I told you this. I don't need no trouble with the Feds or my job."

"I got you, babe. No worries. Between me and you."

138

OTHER NATURE IS deep in the cut of her townhouses. She leans against the wall as three of her soldiers all equipped with firearms, surround her in a tight circle. They pass the blunt around to each other, just smoking and talking bullshit. A young boy comes running toward Mother Nature with a wad of money in his hand. He hands the money to her. "That's twelve hundred," he says before dashing off across the courts.

As she's counting through the money a U-Haul truck cruises through the entrance. She pays no attention to the truck. She just continues on, counting. It's when the second U-Haul truck comes in that she looks up from the money.

The second truck makes a left and the first one has made a right. Halfway around the court, they both stop almost parallel to each other. Just as the trucks capture everyone's attention it's already too late. The Haitian Bloods spill from the back of the trucks, assault rifles and semiautomatics already firing.

Forty Dreads spread out around the area like a scene from a war movie. Machine gunfire sounds off consecutively without a second in between. The element of surprise has caught everybody off guard. Instead of trying to fire in their defense, they run for their lives.

The young men attempt to get away but the Haitians hawk them down one by one. Gunfire rips through the air like the 21 gun salute. Mother Nature's men see the gun yielding dreads running all over the place and instead of firing to protect her or even themselves they all take off in opposite directions. Mother Nature stands in total shock, not able to move. Fear has her paralyzed.

She peeks around the building using it as a shield. Her heart is pounding like a drum. She has never ever seen anything like this in her life. It's all happening so fast. She watches as her soldiers are gunned down like deers being hunted. She's even more terrified as she watches her men being dragged into the U-Haul trucks, some alive and some dead.

She finally gets the heart to move to save herself from being a captive. As she turns around and takes a step she's faced with her biggest nightmare of the past couple of months. Manson stands eye to eye with her. He snatches her by the collar and shoves the M16 into her mouth. She gulps with fear.

"Finally we meet," Manson says with a smile of satisfaction spreading across his face slowly." "I'm Manson, the Black Charles Manson. Now let's go," he says shoving her. She gives in submissively. To her this is her worse nightmare but to him it's a dream come true.

139

TWO HOURS LATER

ELI STANDS IN the back of the warehouse dressed in pajamas and slippers. Manson still hyped up from the action, paces around frantically. He's pacing Eli into hypnosis. Helter and Skelter sit back in the Suburban waiting patiently.

Manson stops short when his phone rings. He picks up. "Yo! Okay!" He looks to Eli. "Bust the gate. He here."

Eli rushes over and hits the button. The gate opens slowly, and the grill of the U-Haul is in plain view. Once the gate is barely up high enough, Arson pulls into the warehouse. Eli hits the button, closing the gate just as Arson is hopping out of the truck.

Manson places a skid onto the forks of the forklift that is parked behind them. Once it's stacked securely, he climbs onto it and drives it across the warehouse. "Bust the back," he commands Arson as he passes him. Eli stands behind Arson, not having a clue of what to expect. Arson lifts the gate and what lies before Eli's eyes is quite overwhelming.

Blood spills down the lift of the truck by the gallon. Bloody bodies are stacked on top of each other with no regard. Manson hops off of the forklift and he and Arson quickly start dragging the bodies from the truck and dropping them onto the skid. Eli has never seen anything as gruesome as this. Heads with holes in them the size of softballs, brain matter splattered over the faces, and enough blood covering them to fill up a swimming pool. The smell alone in the truck is enough to turn one's stomach, let alone the sight.

Once 12 bodies are stacked onto the skid Manson hops on it and speeds across the warehouse. He positions the skid precisely in the corner before dropping it. He backs out of the corner, swings a turn and speeds back across the room. He hops off and he and Arson start stacking the bodies across the forks with no skid while Eli watches in amazement. He's never seen this many dead bodies at one time.

Manson speeds across the warehouse with this batch and dumps them near the others. He comes back and dumps the last three bodies onto the forks. By now him and Arson are both drenched in fresh blood. He drives across the warehouse as Eli follows the forklift. Once Eli gets there, he examines the bodies quickly, trying to get an exact count of them. Manson uses the forks to separate the bodies for him to see.

"What we got, 23?" Eli asks.

"Yep," Manson smiles thinking of the score.

"Uh, what's that 2.3?" A grimaced look spreads across his face. "Wasn't quite expecting this."

"Me either, but you said as fast as I could get them to you, you could get me the money. So, get me the money."

"Okay, no worries, calm down. Just give me a day or two and you will have every dollar." Eli notices something peculiar as he stares at the bodies. "I can't give you full price for that one," he says pointing. "It has no head on it."

"Don't worry about that one. That one was on me," he says as he walks away. He peeks over his shoulder. "Wasn't business, it was personal. Call me when you got the bag. Until then, nothing else comes over. We are on strike until the 2.2 presents itself. Later!"

140

THE NEXT DAY

SMOKE SITS ON the edge of the bed in pain as Samirah helps him to get dressed. She puts his shirt over his head and gently pulls his arms through the arm openings. He's being released from the hospital right now and in no way should be. He's nowhere near recovery but his lack of medical insurance has them damn near kicking him out of the hospital.

Samirah was shocked to get his call today talking about him being released and he made her promise not to tell anyone. When she got here her first question to him was about the handcuffs that she heard he was in. He lied to her explaining it was only for questioning and she bought the lie.

"Sis, if anybody ever ask you about this, just say you bailed me out of the County. Anybody," he emphasizes. "Even Big Bruh. I hate niggas all in my business. Feel me?"

"You already, bruh bruh," she says staring into his eyes with sincerity.

Smoke sits back on the bed, waiting for his discharge papers. His mind is heavy.

"So, you a hundred percent sure this was Mother Nature's work?" Samirah asks.

"If not her, it came from Action Packed's people. No doubt about that."

"You know, I was thinking about Big Show. I tried to hit Tasha up just to see how she would be acting. Bitch changed her number and everything. We can't count them out either bruh. I just have to get out of that house. I don't even feel safe in there no more after this. I'm scared as shit for me and my son."

MEANWHILE

Maurice from the Federation skims through the newspaper quite angered. "Damn, been reading the paper everyday looking to see if he killed over," Maurice says as he lays the paper onto the table. "They haven't posted nothing since the original article."

"And if the grease-ball don't die, we back at his ass again," says Sal. "The shit don't stop until he stop breathing."

With Smoke's mind on Mother Nature and Action Packed, not once has he thought about the many people that he has crossed over the months. Nor has he even thought about Wu who he murdered over the dope months ago. He may have forgotten all about it but there are others who haven't. Some beefs never die.

Maurice and Sal being the two sneaky old heads that they are, knew the perfect time to go in and make their move. With all eyes on Mother Nature that leaves no eyes on them. The level of patience they have exhibited is what separates the men that they are from the boys. Smoke should just hope that their patience hasn't run out and they come right back at him because their patience could easily rock him to sleep this time, forever.

Just as Samirah is bent over tying Smoke's sneakers, the words coming out of the television capture his attention. "A Massacre has taken place inside of a low income housing complex yesterday in Newark," says the reporter. Those keywords from the reporter has Smoke's full attention as well as Samirah's.

"Detectives believe the heinous crime is a result of an act of revenge of some sort. Several men were packed into U-Haul trucks after being gunned down. At this time an ongoing investigation is taking place to see if this has any connection to the Invasion of the Body Snatchers series of missing persons." Smoke sits erect. His aura attracts Samirah's attention. "What up, bruh bruh? You alright?"

Smoke ignores her, eyes still on the t.v. screen. "The Body Snatchers is the name linked to the string of missing person's reports that have shaken up the city as well as Trenton and cities inside of Hudson County. With the help of a few sources detectives now know the group behind the missing persons as Team 6. Still no information regarding the individuals who make up Team 6, no motive nor the whereabouts of the missing persons."

Smoke watches the screen, mouth stretched wide open. He's surprised at all that the news reporters know. If the reporters know that much he's sure the police know much more. He's sure they are smart enough not to share everything they know. He just wonders what else they know and who their sources are. For the first time during all of this, Smoke actually considers the trouble that could come along with this. Hearing the exact details of their criminal behavior makes him feel like the walls are closing in on them.

141

THREE DAYS LATER

SMOKE OPENS THE door for Manson to enter. Manson switches his small overnight bag from his right hand to his left hand just so they can shake formally. Manson pulls Smoke toward him and hugs him tightly. Smoke is shocked at the genuine love that he feels coming from Manson.

Manson pulls away from him. "You good?"

"Of course," he replies as convincingly as he can. Smoke closes the door and limps away. Manson follows behind him watching his limp with compassion in his eyes.

"Auntie Em in there?" Manson asks, pointing to the room.

"Nah," Smoke replies walking pass her room to his room. He finally gets to the room where he steps inside and takes a seat on the foot of his bed.

"So, when they take you to the County?" Manson asks.

"Man they took me outta the hospital like a day or two after. I been in the County ever since," he lies. "Judge set the bail and I got Samirah on the phone with the bail bondsman ASAP."

"What niggas in there talking about? You didn't run into none of them from the other side?"

"Nah, they had me in medical. So I didn't see nobody. I haven't heard from nobody either." Smoke says pretending that he knows nothing about what he heard on the news. Manson is so secretive with him that it bothers him. He just wants to know if he will speak on it or not.

"What you thinking, though?"

"I'm thinking that shit come with the game. You already know the shit, bruh. But I have to get better so I can get back out here and get at my business. Plus this shit cost me bread. I spent money on bail," he lies. "And I'm missing money everyday. "Put too much work in out there to go days without work. I ain't trying to start from scratch all over again."

"You just worry about getting better. The business gonna be there. I got that part taken care of. As far as losing money, don't worry about that at all. Here," he says as he drops the bag into Smoke's lap. Smoke unzips the bag and is shocked that it's filled with money bottom to top. "That's 220."

Smoke looks up, mouth wide open. "What's this for?"

"Took 22 over to the spot and cashed out. That's your cut?"

"Twenty-two? Got damn, that's half of an army." Smoke is impressed by Manson's honesty with him as well as the loyalty. The fact that he's paying him for work that he didn't even put in means a great deal.

"Yeah, Mother Nature's army. Told you it wasn't s hard as you been making it all these years," Manson says sarcastically.

Smoke is annoyed by the comment but is able to overlook it as he thinks of the fact that he holds damn near a quarter of a million in his hands. Each day just seems to get better and better. As twisted as it may sound, he truly does feel blessed. He's always heard the saying, 'after hardship comes ease.' In his mind he believes that all his years of suffering and being dead broke was to bring him to this day of ease.

He feels like he's totally deserving of all the fortune that has come his way because he's been more than patient. As bad as he's been doing over the years he never complained, he just took it on the chin and charged it to the game. He bears witness to the fact that in the game, one day you're up and the next day you're down. Now that it has come back around, he feels like God is blessing him for his patience; whatever God that is that he worships. He's not a man of religion so he will never understand that what he calls a blessing from God could very well be a gift from the devil.

Manson continues on. "We took over her land like the Americans did the Indians. Wiped them all out and replaced them. Before it's all said and done we will do the same thing to the whole city. We will own the city again like we did before I went away. Watch what I tell you."

142

HOURS LATER/3:39 A.M.

MANSON CREEPS THROUGH the pitch dark cemetery. He uses his iPhone as a flashlight to find his way, even though he's come here enough times that he could probably find the gravesite in the dark. Smoke limps slowly behind Manson and Arson is behind him. Smoke carries the leather bowling ball bag in his hand, held away from his body. The hairs stand up on the back of his neck and his ears jump with nervousness. The whole scenery is more than enough to creep him out.

Manson stops short. He stares at the tombstone and a strange energy fills his body. He allows the chemistry to connect for a few seconds before kneeling over and placing his hand on the tombstone. He inhales before speaking.

"Peace, Big Bruh! It's been a minute but I been out here grinding. If anybody understand the grind, I know you do," he says banging his fist against the tombstone with a smile. "Things really coming together for me out here. I know you used to tell me to stop thanking you but I can't. I thank you for stepping up and saving my life. I know you didn't do it for brownie points but still I cant thank you enough. I wish there was some way that I could repay you for all that you done for me but I can't. So forever I will be in debt to you.

But as far as my word to you, I'm here to honor that today. I told you that I would get to the bottom of things and find out who was behind the situation. I did," he says with pride. "I also said when I found them I would have their head on a plate for you. And, I do," he says looking back at Smoke.

He gives the signal and Smoke steps up closer. He kneels down with the bag in his hand. Holding the bag a few inches from the ground he unzips it and turns it over, allowing Mother Nature's head to roll onto the tombstone.

Smoke swallows the puke that is filling up his mouth. He refuses to allow them to see him as weak. He fights back the panic attack as he attempts to take his eyes off of Mother Nature's head but he can't. Also, he can't stop thinking of the fact that Mother Nature has been murdered for something that she had nothing to do with.

If Manson ever found out that he lied on Mother Nature just to save his own life, he's sure the next big war would be in between him and Manson. Now that Mother Nature is out of the picture he hopes that he's heard the last of his negligence in the matter. Now that the debt has been repaid to the Mayor, hopefully everybody can now live happily ever after; Except for Mother Nature, that is.

"And I'm out," Manson says with great pride. He bangs his fist against the tombstone before standing up.

He stares at the tombstone for seconds before placing his right hand over his eyebrow. "Salute, Big Bruh!" Manson spins around and notices Smoke standing there in a daze. He nudges Smoke with his elbow to snap him to. "Salute strength," he commands.

Smoke places his trembling hand over his brow. He salutes, staring at the tombstone. He tries to conceal his guilt as Manson watches him. As soon as Manson's attention is off of him he turns around head hanging low.

Manson starts to creep through the cemetery. Today is one of the proudest moments of his life. Never has he felt a happiness like this. To have honored his word to the man that he idolizes is a feeling that he never knew existed. He wouldn't care if his life ended right this very moment because he feels he has completed his purpose in life.

143

DAYS LATER

MANSON SITS ACROSS the desk from Tony in Tony's office. Sitting on the end of the desk is Mei Ling, the deceased Mayor's girlfriend. She sits in there innocent and in suspense of what this meeting is all about. On the other end of the desk sits Blondie, the other woman that was in the Mayor's life until his death. Blondie sits there in vanity of herself. She stares into the small mirror in her hand, applying her lipstick, flinging her hair and falling more in love with herself.

"I know you both are wondering why I called y'all her today so without anymore delay I will turn the floor over to my friend here," Tony says as he points over to Manson.

Manson stands up. "Neither of you know me but I feel as if I know both of you personally. The Mayor was a dear friend of mine and if not for him I wouldn't be standing here today. There's no way I can repay him so the only way I can think of cleaning my slate with him is by doing something for the people I know he loved," he says with sincerity. Blondie blushes from ear to ear, fluttering her long eye lashes while Mei Ling stares at her with disgust.

Manson digs into the book-bag that lies on the desk. He grabs two stacks of bills and hands a stack to each of them. They stare at the money with confusion. "That's twenty-thousand. Through conversation I understand that twenty-thousand was the monthly allowance for the both of you. I know neither of your financial situations at the time and it's really none of my business. By giving you this money I feel that I am fulfilling my obligation to my brother. All you simply have to do is report here to my man Tony on the first of the month, every month and he will have twenty grand for you."

Mei Ling interrupts. "No, I can't take this from you," she says handing the money back to him.

He refuses to take it. "It's not from me. Look at it as it has come from him. I will not take no for an answer."

Tony sits back quite impressed with Manson. This has to be the biggest act of homage that he has ever seen paid to anyone. Right now he respects Manson more than ever. He does wonder though if Manson is committing to something that he may not be able to stick to. He doesn't know Manson's financial situation but he does understand that forty grand a month is a big nut for even someone you love; let alone someone you barely know. Regardless if he can keep it up or not, Tony is impressed with the gesture in itself.

Both women thank him gratefully and the meeting ends. Blondie leaves first, switching away sexily. Once she's made her exit, Mei Ling leaves right behind her. Manson feels as if he's done a great thing. His heart feels light and just happy to be able to help the man that helped him.

"That was big of you," Tony says.

"I'm just doing the right thing, and speaking of the right thing," he says as he picks up the book-bag. He hands the bag to Tony. "For you," he says.

"For me? What's that?"

"That's for all the hours you spent on my case."

"Nah, the Mayor paid for that."

"You spent many hours on my case even after his death. Nothing in life is free. That's two hundred grand. Take it please, I insist."

"I can't take that money."

"I can't take no for an answer. I hate owing someone. Even though you think I don't owe you, I can't sleep at night until I have repaid my debt. Look at my eyes," he says pointing to the big bags underneath them. "I'm tired. Let me get some sleep," he says with a sarcastic smile.

Tony no longer rejects the bag. He takes it and places it on his desk in front of him. "What's going on? You come in here throwing big money around. You hit the Megamillion or something."

"I don't gamble," he says with a straight face. "I only deal with sure shots. I'm up right now, way up," he boasts. "Like 2.7 up and counting."

Tony is shocked and his expression doesn't hide it. "Manson we have talked about this already. I don't care to know your business but anyway you're up like that in such a little time that can no way be good," he says with genuine concern. Truthfully he is quite curious to know what he's doing that has scored him such a profit. He hasn't heard of those type numbers in the streets in years.

"I'm not gonna bullshit you. This money is as filthy as it comes. Blood money is an understatement. But I beg you if you know any way that I can clean this money I will follow your lead. I know in this game nothing lasts forever. I would love to walk away in the sunset and live happily ever after but I don't even know where to start."

"You have close to three million dollars, you start by stopping what you're doing as of yesterday."

"And do what, live off the money, go broke and have to start over again? Doesn't make much sense to me. If you can point me in the right direction, you got my word that I will stop that very moment. Until then I will continue on with my sure shot. Like, right now I'm doing it like bruh," Manson boasts.

Tony shakes his head from side to side. "In all my years of representing dealers at this level, I've never seen anyone do it like bruh." Tony cracks a smile. "You my man and I can't let you get beside yourself like that."

Tony shoots Manson back down to size but he doesn't take offense. He smiles as well. "Okay, so what I'm feeling myself. On the real though, I need your help."

Tony nods his head, fighting the urge to intervene. He's promised himself that he wouldn't involve himself in his client's personal business ever again but that 2.7 that Manson speaks of has him second guessing his decision. He can think of a million ways to clean three million dollars.

As Manson stares into his eyes asking to be helped, Tony has to bite his tongue just to keep his mouth shut. All the prior years he managed to keep himself out of clients affairs for none of them had any real affairs to involve himself in. Tony quickly thinks back to the night when he called on Manson.

Manson came to his aid without asking the details. Still to this day he hasn't questioned him about it. It's never even come up. He called on Manson and Manson delivered. Tony hates to get involved in Manson's affairs but how can he tell him no when he feels that he owes him?

144

THE BLACK ON black Lincoln Navigator cruises into the parking lot of the townhouses and not a bit of the action stops because everyone is familiar with it. Smoke watches from the backseat as drug sales flourish at a pace that he's never seen. He looks around at the many strange faces and feels like a tourist in his own complex.

Helter pulls into a vacant parking spot. Manson looks over to Smoke and can see the aggravation on his face. "Come on, I want you to meet my man." Manson gets out and Smoke follows reluctantly. Manson waves Zoe Blood on as he approaches him.

Manson and Zoe Blood greet each other with love. "Zoe, this my lil bruh, I told you about. Smoke, this Zoe."

They stare at each other for seconds through ice cold eyes. Zoe breaks the ice barrier by cracking a grin. "I heard so much about you, feels like we already met. All this nigga talked about in the bing was you," he says with a bigger grin.

This is a shock to Smoke's ears. He just wonders exactly what all the talk about him was about. Knowing all that has happened, he's sure it couldn't be anything good. Manson senses the bitterness in Smoke and quickly diverts. "How shit going?" he asks Zoe. Looks like y'all right at home."

"Ay man, the game the same from state to state, just different players with different team jerseys on. When you a hustler you can fit in anywhere there's a hustle," he says with his grin spreading.

Smoke's temples pulsate as he's watching Zoe. Manson keeps Zoe's attention just to prevent him from seeing the look in Smoke's eyes. He's sure Zoe has picked up on it. "I'm out of here. Just wanted to introduce y'all two," Manson says as he's reaching for Zoe's hand. "Be back through later."

Manson spins off and wraps his arm around Smoke's shoulder and spins him as well. As they're walking away he whispers to Smoke. "Fuck is that all about?"

The words are burning in Smoke's throat and he can't contain them. He refuses to pretend like he's okay with this. "Bruh, I can't front, I ain't feeling this shit. This me back here. I put my blood sweat and tears into this.

I was out here in the cold when no money was coming through this motherfucker. Now these ugly dirty motherfuckers out here reaping the benefits of my work. Bruh, they gotta go. I don't give a fuck about them over there in Mother Nature's spot. They can have that shit, just send all their asses over there. Fuck that bruh, this shit ain't right."

"Bruh, don't look at it like that," Manson says. "You gotta look at the bigger picture. Let them have this shit, just for the time being anyway. Don't worry about this little ass spot. You got the rest of the city to eat off. Fuck that, you got the whole state," he rephrases.

"No more standing out here on front line. You a General, you bigger than this anyway," Manson says as he opens the backdoor of the Navigator. He gets in, leaving Smoke on the outside. Smoke takes one more look at the area and fury seeps into his soul.

He feels as if his home has been invaded or better yet the land he discovered has been taken away from him. He listened to Manson's encouragement speech but only sees it as the Vaseline wipe down before getting fucked. More than anything right now, he feels like he's been used.

He also finds it quite strange that he's never heard a word about this man until the other day. In his eyes Manson just pulled him out of nowhere with not even a warning. He looks around and feels some type of way seeing the strange faces. He's starting to feel as if this could have all been a part of Manson's plan from the very start.

It's ironic to him how fast he got them here after Smoke got shot. For a brief second his mind entertains the thought that maybe he got shot so that they could be here. A strange feeling comes over him. A feeling of distrust.

Manson has threatened him that he would wipe out the whole line and import homies from across the country to take their places. Strangely that threat has played out right before his eyes. The Haitians have invaded his area and there's no sign of a familiar face. Manson has instructed all the originals to leave.

He's set them up here and in Mother Nature's spot. He's sure he has plans for other spots as well. Manson has done what he always threatened he would do and now has Smoke wondering what other plans he may have.

145

SMOKE SITS PARKED in the cut on the fairly decent residential block with a thousand bricks in his lap. Just as he becomes more impatient, his attention is caught by a speeding Coke can which bends the corner and approaches his direction. The Hemi engine growls viciously. The Coke can slows down and parks across from him.

Smoke looks at the Challenger somewhat in awe. It's red and silver just like the famous Coke brand. The word Coke is printed boldly on both sides in stickers. The logo extends from the roof on down to the hood. The gas tank is chromed out and made to look like the opening tab of a can. The windows are tinted darkly. The car looks like it should be on a NAS-CAR racetrack sponsored by the Coca Cola company and not here on a ghetto street.

The door opens and Dirt steps out. Dirt is blushing from ear to ear. He hasn't felt this good in many years. He quickly bites down onto his bottom lip to contain his blushing. He struts with pride.

Smoke on the other hand tries hard to erase the jealousy from his face but the look won't go anywhere. He manages to muster up a twisted side grin just as Dirt steps over the yellow line in the street. Dirt hops into the passenger's seat and as soon as he and Smoke lock eyes again, he can no longer fight back the feeling. He cheeses from ear to ear, awaiting the praise.

Smoke doesn't want to seem like a hater so he fumbles for something to say. "I was expecting Dale Earnhardt Jr. to jump outta that motherfuck-er. Whose is that?" he asks, hoping that it's not his.

"That's me, Big Bruh. Just got it out of the shop this morning. I bought it last week though."

"Last week? Damn, we keeping secrets now? In the shop for what?" he asks thinking that maybe the car was a salvage like his BMW? "Body and Fender got it from the auction for you?"

"Nah, hell no!" Dirt shouts. The disgraceful look on Dirt's face has Smoke angry. It's as if he's too good to drive a car from the auction. "I got that straight from the lot."

"As is? How many miles?" Smoke asks, hoping that maybe the mileage is high. He needs something to make him feel better about it all.

"Nah, she was butt naked when I got her. I got all the stickers and logos put on myself. That's why it been in the shop all week," he explains. "She only got like 18,000 miles on her. She a baby," he says with a smile.

"What kind of note you got?"

"Note? I don't do those, Bruh. I buy the whole car," he says arrogantly. "Bruh, I been fucked down for a minute but I know what to do with that bread when I get it. I been killing the streets all this morning. Nothing out here fucking with me," he brags.

Smoke becomes more angered as it feels as Dirt is rubbing it in his face as well. With Dirt being his most valuable player he knew Dirt had to be scoring a few bucks for himself but he also figured Dirt was spending it as he went along. Now popping up with this car shows that he has not. The slimeball in Smoke allows himself to wonder just how much money he's holding onto.

"But later for that, bruh, I got some news for you. I just seen my nephew ten minutes ago to collect some money he had for me and he told me some crazy shit."

Smoke is all ears. Dirt shakes his head with sadness. "He said your name came up in the meeting last night. About that Action Packed shit."

"What about it? What they talking about? What they want to do?" Smoke asks. He sits erect in his seat in go mode.

"Nah, they ain't really saying much of nothing. They named like you and two other names and was like as of right now it's a toss up. I told him to keep his ears open and be sure to keep me posted."

"Well, I may as well get the party started and start rocking to the beat."

"Nah, nah, bruh, let's just hold tight for a minute," Dirt says. His mind is on the money and he knows if they start beefing the money will go on the back burner.

"I ain't never sat around and waited for motherfuckers to set up on me. You think your nephew will have a problem working it for us?"

"I will look into it, bruh and see where he stand."

"Yeah, you do that. You know my motto though, you either with me or against me. Ain't no grey area!"

146

LATER THAT NIGHT/TWENTY GRAND LOUNGE

THE BAR IS packed from wall to wall. The people here aren't the bourgeois crowd but more like the bottom feeders of the city. All the people here are the people who refuse to get raped at the bar by overpriced drinks. With shots costing two dollars everyone in the bar is pissy drunk or close to it. The bar is filled with gang-bangers and the women who love them.

Samirah who has been in here for hours is drunk out of her mind. She's been bumming drinks since she's got here. She's not bumming drinks because she has to, she's bumming them because she wants to. Smoke makes sure that her pockets are full every day since he got back into position. She's just so used to swindling and getting over that she can't help herself.

Her bumming stopped once a man who has been sweet on her for years walked into the bar. Once he saw her he took over as her sponsor for the night. He has no problem buying the drinks for her because he figures the drunker she gets the better his chances are of taking her home with him tonight. He's only spent twenty dollars so far and she's already slurring in speech and groping his manhood under the bar. Her swindle is backfiring on her just as most of her swindles do. Her hand on his manhood and his hand down her jeans, finger popping her makes him sure the twenty dollar investment will be well worth it in the end.

Samirah is too drunk to even get horny. The finger popping isn't even phasing her in the least. The only thing she desires right now is more alcohol. She takes another swig of the glass of Hennessy. As she throws her head back to gulp the last drop she notices a familiar face stepping into the bar. She squints her eyes, blocking out the blurriness, to make sure that it's him. Automatic rage sinks in as she confirms that it's the man she met at the massage parlor.

Without even realizing it she slams the empty glass onto the bar. The man next to her speaks. "You alright?"

"Yeah, I'm good," she lies. She keeps her eyes on the man as he makes his way deep into the corner and disappears in the crowd.

Fury sobers her up quickly. She told herself she would just let it go but seeing him in here tonight makes that quite hard. She wants revenge. She looks around with hopes that someone she knows is in here to handle him for her but to no avail.

There's only one person that she's sure she can count on and that's her brother. With him being wounded and trying to recover she really hates to call on him. If there was anybody else that she could call right now she would but there isn't. She digs down the front of her jeans and grabs the man's hand from her box. She snatches his finger out of her. He looks at her, noticing her change of mood.

"Be right back," she says. She covers her face just so the man can't see her just in case he's looking her way. She walks to the entrance of the bar, not staggering a bit. The only thing she's drunk off right now is anger.

She steps out of the bar and to the side where no one is. She immediately starts dialing. Smoke picks up on the second ring as he always does for her. He worries about his mother and Samirah so much that whenever they call his heart gets to beating fast. "Yo?" he asks anxiously as if he's expecting bad news.

"Bruh, bruh," she whines in her best little girl impersonation. She knows how overprotective he is over her and she knows how much he hates to hear her sad. "Where the fuck you at bruh?" she asks. She's changed her sad little girl voice to a voice of rage.

"I'm at the Telly, what's up?" he asks on edge.

"I'm here at the Twenty Grand just minding my business," she whines in her sad voice again. "And this nigga gone come up to me trying to holler. I said I'm good. This nigga start tripping and calling me all kind of bitches and hoes!" she says switching to her angered voice. "I don't know him from nowhere but he must know us because he was like bitch, I will slap the shit out of you and wait for you to call your brother."

Smoke can't believe his ears. "What?" he asks in surprise.

"Yeah, pointing in my face and the whole shit. I wish I was a nigga I would've fucked him up in here," she says. "All in bitches face talking tough," she fake cries.

"Where he at?"

"He still in the bar. I came outside to get away from him. I didn't know what he was gone do to me in there."

"Man, fuck that! Sit tight, I'm on my way! Keep your eyes on that nigga and don't let him leave. If he try to leave start popping shit to stall him. I will be there in 15 minutes!"

MEANWHILE

The Lincoln Navigator exits the ramp of the Manhattan Bridge in route to Eli. Two bodies lay peacefully in the back of the truck. Both are men from Trenton that went against Blue-Blood's plans. He had them both gunned down and tucked away waiting for Manson to get there. Manson paid him twenty-thousand upon arrival, hoping that will inspire him to bring more bodies to him.

Just as the Navigator creeps through the intersection a New York police car passes by them slowly. "Fucking pigs on the left," Manson says from the backseat. Helter tries hard to keep her eyes on the road but gets the uncontrollable urge to cut her eye. Just as she does her and the female officer lock eyes. Helter looks away, eyes on the road.

She peeks through the side mirror where she sees the cop car busting a wild U-turn in the middle of traffic. "They on it," she warns as she keeps her eyes glued onto the face of the driver through the windshield. The driver speeds up to catch up with them and in seconds they are almost bumper to bumper.

The sound of a bullet being slammed into the chamber echoes from Arson's direction. Manson looks over and sees a focused look in Arson's eyes as he grips the gun tightly in hand. "Easy bruh," Manson says. He looks up ahead at Helter. "Watch your speed. They probably just running the plate to make sure it's clean. Hopefully," he says as he leans over and grabs the assault rifle from the floor. He lays it gently on his lap.

Skelter peeks over her shoulder and sees the guns drawn so she follows their lead. Now the three of them are loaded and ready for warfare. Silence fills the air except for the thumping of four nervous hearts. They all premeditate the scene. In their heads, they shoot their way out of the jam in a back and forth gun battle. In all of their minds, they stand as the victorious ones. They all know in this game it can go any way in any given second and they just hope and pray that it goes their way.

The police car stays within a foot of their bumper as they creep through the intersection and cruise through the narrow block. "What to do?" Helter asks with desperation.

"Just drive regular," Manson replies.

"Make the turn coming up or nah?" she asks.

"Yeah. Don't drive and get lost. They will really pull us over then." He turns his head slightly to the left so he can peek at the car out of the corner of his eye. Arson stares straight ahead with war in his eyes. He breathes hard enough through his nostrils to fill the whole truck with air. His nostrils flare like a raging bull each time he exhales. He breathes hot, loud and long breaths.

Helter slaps the left blinker on many feet away from the corner. Her heart pounds in her chest as she slowly approaches it. With as perfect a turn as she can make, the vehicle bends the corner. The police car approaches the corner and speeds through the intersection. Helter exhales gratefully. "All good," she sighs. The whole truck becomes at ease.

TWENTY GRAND LOUNGE

The man wears a defeated look on his face as he steps out of the bar, looking for Samirah. There's no sign of her anywhere. He was sure she was pussy in the bag but now he feels like a sucker that she has taken him for drinks and broke away from him. He steps back into the bar just as another man is stepping out.

Around the corner on the small and dark one way block there sits a triple black Cadillac CTS with the engine running. In the Cadillac, Smoke is in the driver's seat, Dirt is in the backseat and Samirah sits in the front seat. The only thing on her mind is the revenge that she's finally about to get. The fact that he cared nothing about her life is enough to make her care nothing about his. She could have easily obtained a STD or even worse so she has no sympathy nor compassion for what is about to take place. "There he go, right there," she says as her eyes are glued onto the corner. The running engine captures the man's attention. He double takes but continues on, paying very little attention to it. He makes his way to his car which is parked in the middle of the block.

Smoke looks back to Dirt. "Snatch him and bring him in."

"Man, I can off him right here. It's dark as shit out here."

"Nah, just do as I say," Smoke says, already thinking about the profit.

Dirt gets out and starts taking big steps behind the man. He pulls his cap lower and lower with every step. The man peeks behind and sees Dirt following. His body language indicates that he senses danger. He cuts into the street and continues on his path. He looks over his right shoulder and notices Dirt has gotten closer.

He's so focused on Dirt that the sound of the Cadillac's engine racing doesn't get his attention until it's too late. Smoke taps his leg just enough to knock him off balance. Before the man knows it Dirt has him by the collar, gun in face. Fear causes the man to attempt to put up a fight.

He reaches for Dirt's gun arm with desperation. Dirt manages to nudge him off with his elbow before BOC! BOC! The two shots to the leg take his balance away from him. The man lets out a scream to get anyone's attention. Dirt manhandles him and forces him into the backseat of the Cadillac.

He shoves the man across the seat and gets in behind him. He slams the door shut and Smoke pulls off. "Hold, hold, what's up?" the man stutters with fear. He looks around in a puzzled state.

Samirah turns around with a smile already painted on her face. "Oh, you don't know what's up?"

Smoke stops short at the corner. The man's life flashes before his eyes as he realizes where he knows Samirah from. Just as the memories of his whole life flash they stop at the hotel the night of the event. His jaw drops with no words to say.

With great speed Smoke turns around and rests his gun on the man's forehead. With not another second in between he squeezes the trigger. BLOCKA! The man's neck snaps back and his head bangs into the back window before bouncing onto the headrest. His body flops over falling over onto Dirt's shoulder. Samirah watches with wide open eyes. She shocked at what she just witnessed but still she feels no remorse. Satisfaction is all she feels.

BROOKLYN/ONE HOUR LATER

Manson and Eli are in Eli's office. Stacks of hundred dollar bills are spread across his desk. Manson counts along with Eli as he flicks through the thick stack in his hand. Eli counts it twice just to make sure he hasn't given an extra one away.

"There you go, six hundred thousand," he says pointing to the money. Manson starts dumping this week's earnings into his bag. "Hey, my people have been complaining about the quality of the work." His face shows his fear of Manson's reaction but still he must say it. "The organs are damn near decayed. The hearts are barely pumping. The lungs black and polluted and the kidneys are diseased. The people are walking dead. Zombies," he says with disgust. "No more drug addicts if you can help it."

"I only brought you three drug addicts in all," Manson says in reply.

"No, they've all been drug addicts from the youngest to the oldest. Those people have no clue of what they're doing to their bodies consuming what they believe to be simple drugs. Let's see if we can get a better quality of material before the people no longer want to deal with us."

Manson's phone rings. He quickly answers. "Alright bet." He hangs the phone up "My people out front. He just caught something on a whim."

Manson and Eli make way to the warehouse. Eli presses the gate opener. The gate opens slowly and the blue halogen lights of the Cadillac shine brightly against the wall. The Cadillac enters the warehouse and Eli closes the gate.

The passenger's door opens and Smoke gets out limping in pain from his gunshot wounds. "Big Bruh, I'm gone need help with him," he says as he opens the back door.

Manson's has one question on his mind at this time. If Smoke is in the passenger's seat who is in the driver's seat? Smoke knows how sacred this place is to Manson. Time after time again, he's told Smoke to never tell anyone the whereabouts or even the details of this situation. Just as he's about to call Smoke over to the side and chastise him the driver's door opens.

Samirah gets out with excitement in her eyes. "Hey Fav," she sings. "Fav, y'all is crazy. All this time y'all is the body snatchers who been all over the news." "Team 6, huh," she says with a great big smile. "Y'all is crazy."

Manson utters not a word in response. He looks over to Smoke who has helplessness in his eyes. "I had no choice, Big Bruh. My man helped me put him in the car but I dropped him off. I needed Sis to drive."

Manson walks off, leaving the words in her mouth. He goes the backseat where he finds the victim still leaking. "Arson!" he yells as he grabs the dead man by the feet and gets to pulling him out of the car. Samirah stands in amazement, just wondering what her cut of the profit will be. At the end of the day none of this is personal. It's all business.

TWO DAYS LATER

MANSON SITS IN the car dealership before the Jewish car dealer here on Route 46. On the table in front of him he has over stacks and stacks of crisp bills. He's not talking much because he doesn't feel the need to. His money is speaking up for him loud and clear. Smoke sits on the other end of the desk with his money saying a few words as well.

He was referred to the dealer by Eli. Eli vouched for him giving him the opportunity to do whatever it is he wants to and get whatever it is that he wants. The crook of a Jew is willing to take any amount of money, under the table, without reporting a dime of it to the government. That gives Manson free range to get whatever it is that his heart desires.

"The BMW is ready to roll off the lot right this moment," the Jew says. "The other two I can have ready in no more than two days." He looks over to Smoke. "Yours is special order so it will take at least a month to customize."

Disappointment covers Smoke's face. After seeing Dirt the other day he decided he couldn't allow himself to be outdone. He considers Dirt 'the help' and in no way will he be out-shined by him. He plans to set the city on fire with his new toy. His lack of patience makes him ready to forget all about the car he wants and settle for the next best thing. He's sure he will regret it if he does so he decided to just wait it out.

Manson on the other hand is not doing it for the people. He's doing it solely for himself. For many years he's sat on the sideline while everybody else played. Never being in a position to play hardball, he just accepted what his hands called for. Now that his hands call for more he plans to do more.

While sitting in those prisons and seeing the pictures that his comrades would show off, he realized that he had shortchanged himself and never really lived. Now that he has a second chance at it he plans to catch up and do all the living that he's never done.

30 MINUTES LATER

Manson pulls in front of Jada's house in Smoke's rented Cadillac CTS. He dials her phone before he even parks. "Yo, come outside." He ends the call before she can even reply.

In minutes she comes downstairs with skepticism on her face. Her heart pounds rapidly as she sets eyes on the Cadillac. She's familiar with it because she has rode in it a few times since Smoke has rented it. They have even had a few quickies in the backseat. Her face is covered with guilt when she spots Manson's face through the windshield.

He gets out and meets her at the curb. Just as he does a milky white 5 Series BMW Gran Turismo with the eggshell white interior pulls up behind the Cadillac. Jada keeps her eyes on the car as Smoke gets out of it. She fidgets with nervousness at the sight of Smoke. Although Smoke doesn't even look in her direction the chemistry can be felt by anyone but Manson. They both avoid contact with each other out of pure guilt.

Manson holds his hands out for the key and Smoke hands it to him. He looks to Jada who is quite confused with it all. Smoke makes his way to his car without saying a word. Manson hands her the keys. "This for you mama."

Jada's eyes stretch wide open with joy. "Huh?"

"No huh, you heard me," Manson says with a smile. "I told you it's our turn," he says as he hands her the keys.

Jada loses her composure right before his eyes. She rushes him and bear hugs him, damn near knocking him down. "Thank you!" Manson feels great joy in knowing that he has pleased her but he keeps it under wraps. He displays his normal lack of emotion as she hugs him tightly.

An ice cold draft is coming from the Cadillac that is screaming for Jada's attention. She's drawn in by it and when she looks in that direction she sees Smoke turned around in his seat staring at her. His draft causes her to freeze. Her whole aura changes as the feeling of guilt creeps in. She unloosens her grip and slowly backs away from Manson. He notices the change instantly. "What's up?" he asks.

She looks upward to the right, looking for the lie to feed him. She peeks over at Smoke who rolls his eyes with jealousy. "Nothing, nothing at all."

148

SAMIRAH IS ON the phone listening to the caller on the other end as she looks onto the newspaper that she holds in her hands. "Thank you! Thank you!" she cheers. "So, all I have to do is go down there and switch my Section 8 over?" she asks.

"References? I already put my references down," she claims. "No, that's my mother. Felisha, oh that's my best friend." She listens as the woman speaks. "Oh, my landlord? This landlord where I live right now?" she asks as disappointment crosses her face.

She may have run into a problem because her landlord can't stand her. Many times he's tried to put her out but New Jersey laws make it hard for a tenant to be kicked out in the cold. Her and her landlord have been to court at least a dozen times. She's sure her landlord would never put in a good word of referral for her.

She can't blow her chances of getting this apartment. It's perfect for her. It's out of the hood and in the cut which is what she needs right now with all that's going on. The thought that Big Show will kick her door in any minute has been tormenting her. Now the murder of the dude from the massage parlor haunts her at night, and has her in fear that maybe someone knows that she was behind his murder.

She just needs to get out of this apartment and into one far away where no one knows where she is. She already has plans of bringing no one to her new spot outside of Smoke, Manson and her mother. Her son's father won't even have the privilege of knowing where they are. He will have to meet them at a neutral spot on his weekend to get his son.

"Can I get a referral from him?" she asks slowly as she thinks of a lie. "I have to tell you the truth," she says, speaking in a fake intelligent voice. The voice is nowhere near convincing. Anyone who hears her speak can tell that she's as uneducated as they come.

"Me and my landlord don't really get along. He's a slumlord and gets mad because I be needing stuff fixed. He ain't nothing but an umbilical liar," she says using umbilical instead of habitual. She continues on as if she has said nothing wrong. "Please, I just have to have this apartment.

My son room got bedbugs and he can't even sleep in his room," she lies, hoping for pity.

"Okay, thank you! I appreciate it so much. I will call Housing Authority first thing in the morning and have them call you. Again, thank you!" she says just as Smoke is stepping into the apartment. She jumps for joy afer the call is ended.

Smoke looks at her wondering what the happiness is about. "I got the apartment, bruh, bruh. It's way in the cut and nobody gone know where we at. Nobody," she adds. "Then I can finally get some fucking sleep."

149

DAYS LATER

TONY HAS THOUGHT long and hard about what Manson said to him the other day. Although he's promised himself that he would not get involved in client's personal lives, that's a huge task for him. After getting himself out of the mess the Mayor had him in, he vowed to keep it all business from that day on but he constantly finds himself attaching himself to his clients on a personal level. His problem is always wanting to help and be looked at as a good stand up guy. Sometimes in doing that he places himself in some crazy situations.

The bright fire engine red Bentley Continental GTC comes roaring into the parking lot. The engine roars ferociously for such a smooth looking luxury car. The black convertible top and leather interior tones down the bright red just a little and makes it less blinding. Two hundred thousand dollars worth of beauty glides through the lot.

This sparkling eye candy is Manson's gift to himself. He just picked it up not even two hours ago. This is his first big boy car so in no way is he used to the attention that it brings. While on the highway people pulled up to it giving him the thumbs up and snapping pictures with their camera phones.

The attention has him uncomfortable and second guessing his decision of buying it. He's sure the attention can cause him a world of problems if the wrong eyebrows are raised. For that reason he plans to never bring the car near the city. Manson has stayed low and under the radar all of his life and can't believe that he has gotten caught up in the hype of the new 'show off era.' Sitting behind the steering wheel of his own Bentley is not a dream of his but it sure does feel good. Now if he could just put his paranoia to the side for a moment, he could enjoy and appreciate that moment.

The rumbling of the engine leads Tony and his guest to the window. They watch as Manson gets out of the car and walks toward the entrance. Tony gawks at the beauty that is parked before his eyes. He has a loss of words because he never took Manson as the luxury car type.

Seeing this only makes Tony even more curious to know what Manson has going on. It also makes him doubtful about why he's even called him here. He doesn't need the heat nor the backlash of whatever it is that Manson is indulging in. "I don't know about this, man," Tony's guests says. "The man you want me to meet comes to the meeting in a fire truck. That's a little too loud for my liking."

"Mine too," Tony admits. "He must have just got that. I've always taken him for low-key."

"Nothing low-key about that. Maybe we need to rethink this."

"Take it easy," Tony says. "He's a little rough around the edges but he's solid. He's a man of integrity and honor. Just trust me. Have I ever steered you wrong?"

The tapping on Tony's office door interrupts them. "Come in!" Tony shouts.

The door opens and Manson peeks his head inside before stepping in. "What up?" he asks. His eyes are glued onto Tony. He doesn't even acknowledge Tony's guest. Tony meets him in the middle of the room and they shake hands. He turns Manson toward the other man. Manson looks the man up and down and notices he has a style quite similar to Tony's. He's dressed in casual attire but still fly. His style is similar to Tony's but he has only half of Tony's pizazz. His mannerisms don't come across as natural and appear to be forced. Manson sees him as a mini Tony in training.

Tony introduces them and they greet each other coldly. Manson can sense the man's discomfort in meeting him. "D.B., this here is a good friend of mine, Michael Barnes. We go back to the sandbox. And Mike, I've already told you all about him."

Michael nods at Manson with a warm smile. "Let's sit," Tony says as he takes a seat at his desk. Manson and Mike sit side by side, both mindful not to let their shoulders touch. "D.B., I thought long and hard about our conversation and as always I would like to help. I have a situation here," he says pointing to Michael, that can possibly open up many doors for you. I mean, I've come up with a few ideas for you to get started on changing some things over."

Manson freezes in paranoia. He doesn't feel comfortable with Tony talking so freely in front of a stranger. "Don't worry. This man is like me. Anything we talk about in here I'm sure will stay in here. Correct?" he asks Michael.

"Absolutely," he confirms.

"D.B., my man here is the next Mayor of the city. Manson's eyes bulge as he gives the man a closer look. Tony laughs. "No, no, no," he says with laughter. "Not that kind of Mayor. He will be the next Mayor of the city on the legal side. Well, at least we are working toward that. I'm confident that he's the best man for the job. I'm not just saying that because he's my good friend. I'm saying that because he loves and understands the mechanics of this city. He's all about the youth and genuinely cares about our people.

I will be helping with his campaign. I brought you here to see if we can possibly bring you on board." Tony awaits a reply.

"I'm no politician. Bring me on board to do what?"

Tony inhales deeply and exhales slowly. "Well, as you know money makes the world go round. As great of a man for this job that me and a host of other people may think he is, without the proper exposure we don't have a chance. This man is a brand and he needs marketing and exposure. As I said I will be helping with his campaign and not just standing with him holding signs either. I believe in him so much that I will be contributing money to his campaign.

My money will not be enough though. We will be collecting from various sources because this can get rather costly. The Italian candidate that we are running against, of course has us beat financially. We would like to bring you in as one of the financial investors of this campaign."

Manson sits with confusion on his face. All of this is foreign to him. A criminal such as himself being asked to join forces with a man who once he gets into office, will have the agenda of putting him and men like him in jail forever? This sounds quite absurd and disrespectful to him.

"Bruh, since you told your man all about me and since everything stays in this room," he says with a brief pause. "I'm gonna say it just like this. "I'm on the opposite side of the track. I'm from the dirt. How does me putting my money into a campaign help me? I put my bread up and he gets into office and then he puts me out of business by hiring more cops to not only stop my flow but send me away forever as well."

Tony nods his head while waving his index high in the air. "To the contrary. If my man here gets into office we all win. And those worries you have won't even exist because you will be *in*."

"In?"

"Yes, *in*. As long as you keep the murder rate in this city down you will be able to make all the money you can count. Being *in* gets you first hand knowledge of everything that is going to take place in the city long before it takes place. You will know when trouble is coming your way and how to get out of harms way.

Also, on the legitimate side of things the doors of opportunity will be open for you. Whether it be real estate that you would like to get your hands on for dirt cheap or business permits pulled for store fronts or whatever," he says staring into Manson's eyes. "You will have the key to the city to do whatever it is you like. If my man here gets in and becomes the controller of the city," he says before tapping Manson's chest. He then taps his own chest. "Then we control the city."

"But if he doesn't get in?"

"Then we continue on with what we all were doing before this. It's all a risk. Nothing in business is guaranteed. You take risks every single day. Risks that could send you away forever. This risk here will never send you away. The only thing you could possibly lose is a few dollars, not your freedom. On the flip-side, if we win, the money possibilities are endless. Just look at it as a flip. In a flip, when you go to score anything can happen. In this flip we can either win or lose but everybody makes it home that night."

It all makes sense to Manson. He's already thinking of the possibilities, both legitimate and illegitimate and his mind is racing. "What type of investment are we talking about? What will it cost me to get *in*?"

Manson watches both of them as he waits for his answer. Tony takes a deep breath as Michael looks away. "Two hundred and fifty grand will get you *in*."

Manson can't believe his ears. How can Tony even fix his mouth to ask for a quarter of a million dollars. Before Manson can say a word of negativity, Tony speaks again. Again, look at it as a flip. We already spoke about numbers between me and you. Tony flashes a sly wink. What I'm asking for won't even cause you to flinch if it doesn't work out for us. On the other hand if it does work out for us the number you spoke to me about will increase ten fold. Think about it and let me know if you are out or in."

The money truly isn't an issue for Manson. His finances have progressed wonderfully since their last meeting a few weeks ago. With his Brooklyn business and his heroin business combined his stash has increased by more than three times the amount Tony is asking for.

Manson sits for seconds staring at Michael, attempting to get a read on him. Michael stares into Manson's eyes without blinking. Manson's energy radar doesn't pick up the slightest static. Something makes him believe in him. More importantly, he believes in Tony.

"Nothing to think about," Manson replies confidently. I don't know him to believe in him but I believe in you. I'm in."

THREE HOURS LATER

Traffic moves out of the way as the bright Bentley speeds down Route 78 through the darkness at about 120 miles per hour. Inside, Manson sits in the passenger's seat holding onto the edge of his seat. He's scared for his life but the speed is giving him such an adrenaline rush. "Yo, yo, easy now," he says as he watches the speed gauge increase by another forty miles an hour.

"I got this, Pop," Baby Manson says as he zips in and out of the traffic like a speed demon. "I been driving since I was 11, Pop," he says with no shame.

On the streets he's known as a monster behind the wheel. Although he's vicious with a pistol, he's strongest point is his driving. In the street wars he and his team have been in he's always the designated driver. They all trust him to get them out of the stickiest situations.

"Pop, if you ever need a driver, holler at me," he says while totally forgetting who he's talking to. He's so caught up in the hype. He swerves into the right lane, sliding right in between two cars. He zooms past the car in the left lane and zips right in front of it, cutting it off with no regard. "I will get you out of any situation. Whole police force and state boys," he brags.

Manson is saddened at what he hears from his son. It hurts him that his son thinks that is regular life. He takes the total blame for his son being misguided. "Nah, nah, slow it down. Neither one of us got license. We don't need no trouble from the Jake." Baby Manson continues on so caught up in the hype that he increases the speed instead of decreasing it. "Yo, I said slow it down." The aggression in Manson's voice makes him start breaking down the speed.

"Pop, this shit fast as shit," he says not realizing who he's actually talking to. Once he peeks over and sees the look on Manson's face he apologizes for his language. "Pop, you gotta let me hold this one day."

"I got you as soon as you get your license," Manson replies.

"I'm serious though, Pop. I ain't playing."

"I don't play. Get your license and I might give it to you. This ain't nothing but material, a possession. We don't get attached to items. They come and they go."

Baby Manson gets off of the highway and is caught by a red light. He looks over at his pops very proudly. His emotions are at an all time high right now. Just spending quality time with his father while he drops the facts of life on him is like a dream come true for him. He always envied the guys who had this all of their life. He blames the way he is on the fact that he never had it.

This is a dream come true for Manson as well. They've been together since early this morning. They started off the day with breakfast at IHOP. Manson then left his son in the car while he met with Tony and his guest.

From there they went to the mall wherein Manson tried to make up for all the years that he's missed in his son's life. The whole backseat is filled with sneakers and clothes.

"Pop, thanks for all the clothes."

"It's nothing. I owe you that and some. It's been a long time. I told you if you get back in school and get your GED I would do what you need me to do. I promise you I will catch up with all I owe as long as you promise to stay off them streets like I asked you to." The streets are all he knows. He can't imagine living the life of a square. He doesn't even know what he would do for entertainment if not for the streets. As bad as he wants to promise his father that he won't, he can't because just like his father he's a man of his word.

Baby Manson nods his head and looks away. "I'm serious," says Manson. "It's my fault that you even got caught up in this. If I was home you would've never had to experience none of that. I'm here now though and we can erase all that shit and start from scratch."

Manson places his hand on his son's shoulder and melts him away. Baby Manson stares straight ahead, eyes wide open. He's afraid to blink because the tears will surely start to fall from his eyes. Manson sits in the passengers seat feeling quite sentimental himself.

For the next few minutes they ride in silence. Baby Manson parks in front of Damien Jr's home. Manson takes the lead, getting out first and his son follows. Manson goes to the trunk and both of them fill their arms with the many bags of clothes that Manson has bought for his other boy.

He leads the way to the house feeling like something that he's never felt like before and that's a proud father. This is just the beginning though. He plans to be referred to as one as the best fathers in the world. May be far fetched but that doesn't mean he will stop shooting for the title.

150

THE NEXT NIGHT

MANSON AND THE crew sit uncomfortably in the Buick Enclave. Helter of course is in the driver's seat and Arson is in the passenger's seat. Skelter and Manson sit in the back. Helter parks a few doors away from Samirah's house and looks back at Manson who sits behind the passenger's seat.

Just as she's fully parked, a raggedy Chevy Lumina cruises pass them and double parks right in front of Samirah's house. The driver mashes the horn like a madman. You can sense pure rage within the horn blowing. In less than a minute Samirah is standing on the porch with her son.

She grabs his hand, pulls him down the stairs and drags him to the car. She snatches the door open. Anger is evident in her body language. She kisses her son before putting him into the backseat. She slams the door with all of her might. As she walks away, the driver, her son's father yells a few words of disrespect.

"Fuck you!" she shouts loud enough for all the neighbors to hear. "Broke bastard!" she shouts. He shouts a few more words that are muffled. "Eat my ass!" she shouts as she bends over and slaps her ass.

She continues on up the stairs and slams the door. The Lumina speeds off. Once the car disappears into the darkness Manson sits on the edge of the seat. He pulls his cap low over his eyes, before taking a deep breath.

He opens the door slowly and notices Skelter's anxiousness. He shakes his head as he plants his hand on her knee. "Calm down, I got this?" He gets out and Skelter follows behind him. With each of Manson's steps uncertainty is evident. The closer he gets to the house, the slower he walks.

Manson peeks around as he rings the doorbell. Skelter stands in the alley, peeking over the porch bannister. As he's waiting his eyes never stop watching his surroundings. Samirah peeks through the peephole and snatches the door open once she spots Manson's face. "Fav!" she shouts in her normal playful demeanor before the door is fully opened.

Manson forces his way into the hallway, with his leather glove covered hand clasped over her mouth. Skelter rushes inside and closes the door behind herself. Manson gives her the head nod and she takes off into the apartment before him. Manson has Samirah off of her feet, hand over her mouth walking into the apartment. She attempts to kick and fight her way out of his grip. She bites down on to his hand but never penetrating through the leather.

Skelter busts into the bedroom and heads straight for the closet. She quickly locates the money, guns and dope just as Manson said she would. She dashes out of the bedroom into the living-room. Samirah fights for her life while Manson just holds her down.

Manson looks up and spots the bags in Skelter's hand and he forces Samirah onto her back. He plants his knee in her chest so she can't get up. He takes his hand from over her mouth. Samirah's mouth opens wide but not a scream comes out. The bright flash blinds her before the sizzling bullet rips through her scalp. The silencer on the 9 millimeter muffles the sound to almost none at all. Samirah's head drops back lifelessly. He looks down at her and sadness creeps into his heart. Her wide opened eyes stare up at him making him second guess his decision. He hated to have to do this but he felt as if he had no choice.

Although, they're taking the work and money, this is no robbery. His only reason for robbing the place is to make it appear to be a robbery and to also remove the work before the cops get here. He's sure this amount of money and dope will lead to an investigation that he doesn't need at this time.

This has everything to do with the hatred that he holds for Samirah. That hatred wasn't always there though. The hate came into play once he found out that she was linked to the Mayor's case and the informant slid in through her. He always knew she had a big mouth and loved gossip which is why he never let her into his business.

One thing he's certain of is that her mouth is still as big. She can't help herself and because he knows that he refuses to allow the same thing to happen again. Her murder was part revenge for what she done and part suspicion of what trouble her mouth may cause in the future. With Smoke bringing her in on their Brooklyn business he's sure she won't be able to keep that a secret. Right now he's not sure who knows who Team 6 really consists of.

His first mind was to murder her the same night before she could run her mouth to a single soul but if he knew he would have to murder Smoke as well. The timing wasn't right for that so he declined his decision. The reason he has taken so long in handling this is because he has fought back and forth with himself about carrying it out. The past few nights he hasn't been able to sleep a wink in fear of her knowing the details.

Finally the back and forth battle had to end. He understood that he had to do this whether he wanted to or not. Today was the absolute last day that he had to do it with Samirah about to move in a couple days. In a conversation with Smoke he let the cat out of the bag about Samirah moving. Manson pretended that he didn't even hear it by not responding to it. He knew he had to make a move quick or things could get tricky. For her to get murdered at a new apartment would make it all the more unbelievable that it came from an enemy.

Manson places his two fingers gently onto her eyelids and closes them shut. He leans closer to her and plants a kiss on her forehead. He and Skelter exit the apartment and step onto the porch as if nothing has happened. He makes sure the door is locked before he leaves.

Manson gets into the car and for the first time ever they can see regret all over his face. He seats himself and Helter cruises off. No one says a word. Manson leans his head back as the sorrow creeps into his heart and overflows.

His mind is occupied with thoughts of them running around as kids. She's always idolized him for as far back as he could remember. Truthfully, she looked up to him more than she ever did Smoke. When she says the word 'Fav' he always knew it was genuine but it meant nothing to him because the hatred for her actions had erased any sign of love that he had for her.

Manson bears witness that true leaders don't make tough decisions because they want to. Those decisions are made because they have to. This was one of those tough decisions. Right now as sad as he may be he has to charge it to the game. Anytime in life that he's had to do something that he didn't want to do but had to be done, he gets over it by charging it to the game. He's sure charging this one to the game won't be as easy as any other situation that he had to charge but he has no choice. What's done is done. He's also positive that Smoke will never be able to charge this to the game.

151

THE NEXT MORNING

SMOKE SPEEDS THROUGH the block like a madman. The cherry red sirens blaze the block near Samirah's house. Smoke is terrified. His mother called him close to an hour ago, crying hysterically. He couldn't make out a word of what she was saying to him. He was tucked away in his hiding spot when she called. He ran damn near every red light to get here.

The excess of police have him worried about going to the house. He's sure Samirah has been nabbed for the drugs, money and guns. All he can think of is being nabbed as well. He slams the gear into park. "This shit ain't looking right," he says to himself.

Smoke looks up at the many cops that surround the house. He debates with himself if he should go or not. He can't let his little sister take the weight so he has no choice but to turn himself in. "Damn," he says as he thinks of all that is about to take place once he turns himself in. With his two prior gun charges the guns that were there could get him trigger lock and possibly get him labeled a career criminal. "Some bullshit," he utters. He takes a deep breath before getting out of the car.

As he's walking he peeks over the crowd of nosey neighbors that are surrounding Samirah's house. The closer he gets to the house, the more he rethinks it all. Suddenly, he's stopped at the yellow tape by a police officer. "You can't come in here."

"What? I live on this block. What's going on?" He waits for the cop to give him some clarity on the matter.

"It's a murder scene. Nobody can cross the tape."

Those words stop Smoke's breathing. It all becomes one big blur to him right now. The flashing red lights up ahead hypnotize him. He feels like he's caught up in the matrix. His shoes feel like they have weights on them making it hard for him to take another step. In a trance like state he crosses the street.

As soon as the cop takes his attention off of him he lowers himself under the tape and walks toward the house. His heart is pounding so hard that he can barely breathe. He spots his mother standing in front of the house with a few people surrounding her. They all seem to be consoling her.

His thoughts, his heartbeat all seem to be at a standstill. He just continues walking in his trance. As he's crossing the street his mother spots him. He walks over to her slowly. The people around her are some people from her church, the pastor, the deacon and his wife. They all watch with a hatred for him on their faces.

Smoke stops, still in his trance, just staring into his mother's teary eyes. This can't be true, he thinks to himself. His heart is numb. None of this is registering in his mind. His mother hauls off and slaps him dizzy, awakening him out of his trance. "My baby, they killed my baby," she cries. Her words pierce through his soul.

He feels as if his life has come to an abrupt end. Still in somewhat of a state of unconsciousness he just stands there. "It's all your fault," she cries as she punches and kicks him. Smoke stands there with no words as the punches have no effect on him because his body and mind are numb from the news.

The church members grab her and pull her off him while he puts up not a fight. She has attracted the attention of the people who are standing close to them. "They killed her. That should've been you. It was you they wanted!"

Smoke notices the cop in the street now paying attention to the scene that his mother is causing. "Ma, stop," he says with tears building up in his eyes, too. He reaches for her which makes her start fighting all again. She stops mid-fight and grabs hold of her chest. She hyperventilates. Smoke has seen her like this before and both times were heart attacks.

Sympathy covers his face. As he reaches out to hug her the pastor intervenes. "Son, son, just walk away and let her calm down."

"Emma, are you okay?" the deacon's wife asks as she wraps her arms around her.

She nods her head up and down trying to speak. When she finally does she looks over to Smoke with a hatred in her eyes that he's never seen before. "You get the hell away from me, you devil," she cries. "It should've been you. It should've been you," she sobs.

Smoke notices two police coming over toward the commotion and he backpedals away sneakily. He watches as the police officer approaches his mother. He peeks over his shoulder before fast trotting. His pace evolves into jogging. Where he's going, he has not a clue. His whole world has just seemed to come to an end. The words his mother spat, "It should've been you," replays over and over. At this very moment he totally agrees with her, he wishes it was him.

Police swarm the back of the townhouses. The Haitians lay back in the cut, not even visible. The two Mormons stand right at the yellow tape that surrounds the abandoned house. The Coroners van pulls up and the medical examiner gets out. He takes his sweet old time just casually strolling along. The cop lifts the yellow tape for him to cross.

He steps into the apartment and makes his way down the steps to the basement. He slapped with the pungent odor of death that's in the air. It doesn't bother him the least bit because he has grown accustomed to it over the years. The closer he gets to the bottom of the stairs the more atrocious the smell becomes.

He stops short and pulls a cheap cigar from his pocket. He's not much of a smoker but he keeps a cigar handy for times like this. The strong smell of the cigar suppresses the smell of death, making it easier to stomach. He lights the cigar and puffs on it as he makes his way over to the body.

Laying in the corner of the basement is Doggy Mane. Right next to him dead as well is his faithful bitch. Seeing her master lay here for days dead to the world eventually got the best of her. It wasn't a broken heart alone that killed her. Had she had dope she could've probably coped with his death but she didn't. The lack of dope had her involuntarily kicking her dope habit. She died from a broken heart mixed with dope sickness.

Two young men from the Humane Society step down the stairs. As the medical examiner is examining Doggy Mane, the two young men throw the dog into a bag and carry her away. After 105 dog years, Doggy Mane and his faithful bitch have now separated. R.I.P. Doggy Mane and his faithful bitch.

152

LATER THAT NIGHT

"**D**ON'T FUCK THIS up, bruh. No mistakes. Everything gotta count," Smoke says from the driver's seat.

"Got you, bruh, say no more," Dirt replies with his hand gripped tight around his gun.

Bright lights illuminate the dark and peaceful block. The huge chrome grill of the approaching car sparkles through the darkness. Smoke and Dirt's hearts pound to the same beat. "Here we go, baby, finally," Smoke says.

They've been stalking this crib for hours tonight hoping that Big Show would eventually present himself and he has. Smoke is here avenging his sister's death. He's not a hundred percent sure if her murder was revenge for his act of kidnapping Tasha but he's not counting anyone out. He's coming for anybody that he believes could be behind it.

Smoke's eyes are glued to the Bentley as it cruises by. He catches a glimpse of a female passenger. "Good, the hoe bitch in the car with him. Two birds, one stone," he says as he watches the car in the side mirror. The car is turned into the driveway. "Now."

Dirt gets out of the car quickly. He creeps along the curb. His all black attire has him camouflaged in the darkness. His heart races with anticipation as he sees the interior light come on. Unexpectedly the passenger's door opens and Tasha makes her way to the gate. He picks up his pace and just as she's opening the gate he takes a few giant steps toward her.

The gunshots start ringing long before he gets there. BOC! BOC! Like a deer in headlights Big Show stares through the window. The bright light gives Dirt a clear aim. He aims precisely and squeezes. BOC!

The window caves in right before the car goes in reverse. Dirt stands at the window and squeezes agains and again. BOC! BOC! He watches as Big Show's body is thrown into the passenger's seat. The car rolls back slowly and Dirt trots behind it. BOC! BOC!

Tasha's scream pierces the airwaves. Dirt runs over to her where she stands against the gate petrified. Her eyes widen and her mouth opens. Just before she can scream again he squeezes the trigger. BOC!

Her body collapses onto the ground with no sign of life left in it. As she lays on the ground, face up. Dirt gets a perfect view of her face and realizes that she's not Tasha. With no remorse at all, he takes off in flight. Two birds with one stone but one of the birds wasn't the right bird.

153

FIVE DAYS LATER

SMOKE PARKS IN front of Cotton Funeral Home. After turning the car off he tucks one gun in the front of his waistband and another along his right hip. He peeks around attentively. He's totally out of bounds even being here on the Crip side of town.

He attempted to get his mom to hold the funeral on his side of town but she won't even hear him out. She hasn't said a word to him since that night. He's still not allowed in her house. The only bridge of communication that he's had with her is through Manson, who she has no attitude with whatsoever. That in itself makes him angry and jealous at the same time. Maybe it's the $15,000.00 Manson gave her to cover the funeral cost that made her have no issue with him.

Smoke had not a dime to contribute to the funeral because the majority of his money was in the house. Smoke lost $190,000.00 in cash, of his own money and 1,100 bricks of dope that he owes Manson for. He was always told to never keep the money with the guns and the work but when things are moving so fast one can easy lose track. His total savings was up to over $500,000.00.

Using fifty-thousand here and a hundred thousand there to cover Manson's money so he would never have to wait, never really gave him time to build a stash. His money was always working. Just a couple weeks ago before the purchase of the car, in which he's still waiting for, his total net worth was a few dollars short of 700,000. In all his years of living he's never dreamed of having that much money.

In his best days when he was working with the Mayor, at the height he never saw more than 240,000 of his own money. Now he's back to the drawing board. He's not flat broke but his money is on the streets tied up in the flip. Once his team is finished he will have money again. Truthfully the money isn't even a thought to him right now because no matter how much of it he has he could never buy his sister's life back.

The newspaper has her murder charged as a possible robbery. In Smoke's gut, he feels the murder may have been an act of revenge against him coupled with a robbery. He has no clue of who could be behind this because he can think of close to a hundred people that would want revenge against him. Why now, is what he keeps asking himself.

All these years of his sister being here and him doing dirt in the city, no trouble has ever come to her doorstep. That makes him think that maybe it wasn't revenge and just what the paper said, a robbery. For the second time in his life he was up financially, by selling dope all over the city. He never thought he would ever be a target of robbery.

Him being a bad guy all of his life, always against the money earners in the city, makes it hard for him to believe that this brief dope run has taken him out of the bad guy bracket and put him in a place where the bad guys are now out to get him for his money. The tables have turned and he understands that is the game but what he won't do is charge off the murder of his sister. Somebody has to pay for this. He doesn't know who is behind it so he has made a pact to his sister that anybody that he thinks can be behind it will have to pay for it.

He hasn't prayed to God since he was about 10 years old but every night since her death he has been on his knees in prayer. He hasn't been really praying to God though. He's been talking to Samirah. He's apologized to her and begged for her forgiveness until his face is drenched in tears. Over and over he begs her to just give him a sign of who did that to her. Still he hasn't gotten a sign from her. He can't help but to think of the fact that just a few more days and this wouldn't have happened. She would've been tucked in the cut where no one could find her.

He lifts the Sprite soda bottle which is filled with the prettiest shade of purple liquid. He throws his head back and devours the codeine syrup in one consistent guzzle. He licks the flavor from his lips before tucking his gun away. Being high is the only way that he's been able to cope with his life and Samirah's death.

He approaches the funeral parlor with dark shades on to cover his swollen tear filled eyes. The sidewalk is crowded on both sides of the street. Seems as if everybody in the city is here to see her off. Smoke knows some are here out of love, others are here out of hate, and there are those who are just here as a social gathering for gossiping purposes.

He's sure his sister's death will be trending on Instagram with all the posting of pictures and "rest in peace Samirah" hashtags. The truth of the matter is he doesn't even want to be here but no way he could not show up. The people watch as Smoke approaches. No one says a word to him because they fear what his reaction may be. He walks pass them all as if he's a stranger, knowing no one at all.

He steps into the funeral home and all eyes are on him. Maybe it's his guilt but he feels looks of disgust all coming his way. He avoids them all as he makes his way to the coffin. The closer he gets the better view he has of his sister.

His heart gets heavy as he gets a clear view of her face. His heart pounds and his eyes water underneath the shades. He feels like he's about to break into pieces right now but he can't let the people see him like this. Just as he's about to step within ten feet of the coffin he hears, "Get out of here!"

The sound of his mother's voice breaks the peace. Smoke looks over to her with surprise. "Get him out of here!" Smoke stops in his tracks, not knowing what to do. The whole room watches like they're at a movie just minus the popcorn. He's embarrassed and wishes he could disappear right now. "Go now!" she says in a demonic voice. She stumbles back a few steps holding her chest as she does every other time she gets excited.

A few people come to her aid while Smoke watches her with tears now dripping from underneath the dark shades, shamelessly. Manson appears out of nowhere. He wraps his arm around Smoke and escorts him out. "Come on, bruh. Let her calm down."

Manson has to almost drag Smoke out. This is the last time he will ever see his sister and he refuses to miss the opportunity. Once they get outside the people notice the conflict in his demeanor and keep their eyes glued onto him. Manson with his arm still wrapped around Smoke's shoulder leads him across the street. They dip into a bare space on the corner, away from the people.

"Some bullshit, bruh. My lil sister leaving and I can't even say my goodbyes," he says with tears slipping into his mouth. He lowers his head, not able to face Manson.

"Easy, bruh, Auntie Em just feeling it right now. We gonna get you in there to see her."

"Bruh, somebody gotta pay for this shit. You know how much my sister and my mother mean to me. It's like I lost both of them in one day."

"I know," Manson says nodding his head up and down.

"I'm about to wild, yo!" he says as he turns around and punches the wall. Niggas think shit sweet. I'm about to turn the fuck up, bruh, I'm telling you! I know somebody standing out here know something," he says looking around through the many crowds of people. "I should just tear this whole shit up!"

"And embarrass your mother even more? You talking crazy right now."

Smoke can't contain the tears. They drip from his eyes rapidly as he lets it all go. He paces a few circles in deep thought. "Bruh, why it feel like you ain't with me, bruh? Like this happened days ago and we haven't made a move on nothing yet. Whole city supposed to be on fire right now."

"Ain't with you?" Manson asks with a false sense of genuine concern on his face. "That's my family in that box, too. I just don't see the sense in getting out there taking indirect shots and miss the motherfucker responsible."

"Man, fuck all these motherfuckers! In my eyes they all responsible."

"You dealing with emotions right now and I get it but we have to hit this from a different angle. The streets talk, bruh, you know that. Nigga responsible will surface."

Manson's calm demeanor is pissing Smoke off right now. "Bruh, I swear to God when I find out who did this, I'm wiping out everybody he love, from grandmothers on down to babies. Fuck that!"

Manson's guilt presents itself for the first time. Sympathy for the pain that he's caused Smoke and his aunt has him feeling sorrow. He's even questioned his act and wonders if he really had to make the move. He's sure this will haunt him forever but for all the reasons known, he feels she had to go.

As a man Manson doesn't feel right. At this moment he feels like a coward in hiding and that doesn't sit well with him. His pride speaks out of turn. "Bruh, in my heart I knew this day would come, not exactly this but some kind of disaster. I always urged you to keep her out of your business and out of the way. She was the weakest link." Manson manages to shut his pride up before he says something that causes alarm. In between his silence his pride speaks out again. "And the weakest link gets popped first."

Smoke looks to him with surprise. The coldness in Manson's words and his aura are shocking to Smoke. Manson can feel the tension building between them and he breaks it by walking off. Smoke watches with hatred that he's not even attempting to hide.

To charge his sister's death off due to her being the weakest link as if that justifies it is hard for him to accept. Nor was he ever expecting those words to come out of Manson's mouth. The fact that they did confirms what he already thought. Manson never cared for his sister and that's why he's feeling like Manson isn't with him on this, because truly he isn't.

SMOKE LAYS IN the bed, eyes fixed on the ceiling in deep thought. His heart is heavy and he feels like a part of him is missing and it is. Without his sister he questions if he even wants to live. The fact that he's the reason that she's no longer living causes guilt that he's sure will never go away.

Even if he could ever get over the guilt he's sure his mother will never allow him to. Right now he's not even sure if his mother will ever speak to him again in life. Also, not knowing exactly who her murderer is makes it all the worse. He questions, what if Big Show wasn't the one behind her murder and how about the real murderer is walking around totally in the shade.

Smoke sniffs the snot that drips from his nose as he cries silently. Jada cuddles closer to him to try to console him. She knows how bad he needs her right now. She wishes she never had to leave his side but her time here is almost up. "You gonna be alright?" she ask as she hugs him tighter.

Smoke is so hurt that he can't even lie. "Nah, I'm not. Me and that girl like twins and the fact that she not here no more is crazy to me. Like, I can't even believe it. My mother told me she wish it was me instead of her. I understand her pain but damn," he sniffs. "Like my mind all over the place right now," he says as he clasps his hand over his eyes to cover the tears. "I can't believe that this motherfucker acting like this ain't nothing. Like he don't give a fuck about my sister, his own fucking cousin." Jada looks away, not able to face him. "I swear it feel like he don't give a fuck."

Jada shakes her head with sadness on her face. The look in her eyes causes him alarm. "Why you looking like that? What's on your mind?" he asks.

"Nothing," she says as she gets up and starts to get dressed. Smoke gets out of the bed and turns her around to face him. He knows her just as well as Manson does. Right now he can sense that she wants to say something. "Why the fuck you looking like that for?"

She hesitates before answering him. She hates to be the one to tell him this but she feels she has to. "That's because he's not acting," she whispers.

"What?"

"He's not acting. He couldn't stand Samirah," she mumbles as she looks away. "He feels like she's the reason that all that took place years ago. He always said to me if she never let the informant in none of that would've happened."

"Man, fuck that informant! Fuck the Mayor! Fuck all that! How the fuck this nigga take stranger's side over family?" Smoke paces with steam coming from his nostrils. "This motherfucker gone make me knock his shit off sooner than later." He paces a few more circles. "Yo, you think he hated her enough to do that to her?"

Jada stares at him with no reply. She loves Smoke dearly but she will never be the one to put something like that in his head, even if she believed it to be true. "Nah, I know he didn't like her but I don't think he would do something like that to her."

Smoke stands in deep thought. "The way he was acting at the funeral all nonchalant, I don't know. And what if he the one that had me shot, trying to get me the fuck outta here?" he says staring at the wall behind her. The puzzle seems to be coming together right before his eyes.

"It's funny how he had them Haitian niggas on deck soon as I got shot. Like he just knew I was gone be the fuck up outta here. I have to look a little deeper into this shit. He mad about motherfuckers he don't even know dying and Mirah murdered and he not giving a fuck," he rambles on. "All this shit sound crazy to me. Something about this shit not right."

155

THE NEXT DAY

SMOKE CRUISES THROUGH the dark, narrow block with his focus on the raggedy house to his right. A few teenage boys crowd the bottom of the stoop. Smoke peeks through the dark tinted windows as he passes at a speed that doesn't alarm them. His heart pounds rapidly as he spots his prey, front and center.

He watches in his rearview mirror to make sure no one has made a move. The boys continue on and that's an indication that they barely paid attention to him driving by. He finds a parking space at the far end of the block and eases into it. He picks his phone up and dials quickly. Dirt picks up on the other end. "Yo?"

"Yeah," Smoke grunts. "All good."

"Bet," Dirt replies before ending the call.

Dirt bends the corner on foot, snapback low over his eyes and hand tucked in his pocket. He peeks around every few steps just observing his surroundings. Smoke is turned around in his seat, chest filled with anticipation. He watches through the back window as Dirt approaches the boys with a moderate step.

The taller of the three boys is Baby Manson. After thinking long and hard Smoke is more believing that Manson has maybe taken the shot at him as well as murdered Samirah. It's not proven yet but when it is the war will begin. For right now he just wants to get even; an eye for an eye and a tooth for a tooth.

In his heart he feels that Manson has taken one of his so it's only right that he takes one of Manson's. He could have went at Helter, Skelter or even Pebbles but he wants something that he's sure Manson loves. The scales will be even and they both can play the game of deception that Manson started playing first. Smoke feels he has done nothing but be loyal to Manson all of his life but his loyalty never seemed to matter to him. He's not ready to start an all out war with Manson at this moment so he will be sleepwalking him from this point on. When the perfect time presents itself he will execute his attack against Manson.

Smoke sent Dirt on this mission without explaining the details. Dirt has no clue of the disaster that he's putting himself in. If he did he probably would think twice. Smoke can't afford to let him know just in case he runs his mouth and it gets back to Manson. For all Dirt knows these are just some teenagers who have to be dealt with for whatever reason.

As Dirt gets closer to the boys he looks over his shoulder to his left as if he's focused on something. The men stop all movement with their eyes on the stranger. Peeking through his side-eye, Dirt turns toward them quickly, gun already aimed. He fires at the huddle. BOC! BOC!

The huddle opens up, all men fleeing in different directions. Dirt aims at the youngster who seems to be raging at him like a mad bull. He fires as he backs up to gain distance in between them. BOC! BOC! The boy is struck in the shoulder sending him stumbling a few steps backwards.

Dirt gets a glimpse of shiny chrome in his peripheral and when he looks up there's Baby Manson standing on the steps with his gun aimed at Dirt's head.

BLOCKA! BLOCKA! BLOCKA!

Dirt ducks low and fires a desperation shot just to save his life. BOC! Baby Manson steps up the stairs backwards to get a better aim and to also get out of the way of exchanging fire. He aims at Dirt who is low to the ground attempting to get away. He runs around the car and uses it for a shield. He lifts his head up and fires but as soon as he lifts up Baby Manson fires two of his own. BLOCKA! BLOCKA!

Smoke watches in the distance with great disappointment. Even from the distance this doesn't look good. The sound of back and forth gunfire has him nervous for Dirt. So badly he wants to go bail Dirt out but he can't take the risk of Baby Manson seeing him.

Smoke watches as Dirt runs in the middle of the street at full speed. Baby Manson has stepped off the porch and onto the street. He's firing consecutively. Smoke reacts quickly.

He gets out of the parking space and reverses at full speed, meeting Dirt halfway. Dirt snatches the door open and dives into the backseat. Smoke speeds off with the door swinging wide open. The shots ring off in the distance.

Dirt is out of breath and panting. "Yo, that tall bastard was strapped!"

"You had the drop on them, though! How the fuck you let some kids back you the fuck up? I knew I should've handled this shit myself! This shit don't end here."

156

T HE BEAUTIFUL, 2015 matte red convertible Corvette Z06, with the plum colored gut is the center of attention in the Home Depot parking lot. The only miles the car has on the dashboard are the ones that it took to get here from Pittsburgh, Pennsylvania. In the driver's seat is Manson's man, Pittsburgh Pete and in the passenger's seat is Vito the Crip. Vito applied some pressure for this meeting. Pete stayed out of it for as long as he could. He eventually reached out to Manson letting him know that Vito wanted to meet with him.

Manson was quite hesitant at first but once the urgency was expressed his curiosity was piqued. Pete doesn't know the details of this meeting and asked if things are to go disastrous that he not be held accountable for bridging the meeting. He knows how radical both parties can be and would rather stay neutral if possible. If he had no choice but to choose a side it would be with Manson.

Vito met Pete here. It appears that he has come alone but that isn't the case. He has a car-full of his Crip soldiers sitting at the other end of the parking lot watching it all. Pete sits on eggshells not knowing how all of this will take place. If there was any way he could remove himself from the equation right now, he would.

The Suburban with Manson and the crew inside zips into the parking lot and comes straight over to Pete's car. Pete gets out of the car, leaving Vito inside. "Let me holler at him first," he says awaiting a reply.

"Go ahead and do you," Vito says calmly. His hand is gripped on his gun all the while.

Pete gets out and as he's walking toward the truck the back door opens up. He gets in and slides in as Manson slides to the middle. Arson slides over closer to the window to make room for them. The backdoor is shut.

They shake hands firmly. "What up, Big Bruh?"

"You," Manson replies. "Damn, that thing looking good," he says regarding the car. "Looks like somebody eating."

Pete is so nervous that he can't even find the words to thank Manson. He just smiles and nods his head. He looks around at the semiautomatics in clear view on everyone's lap. The first thing that comes to mind is pandemonium. "Big Bruh, again, the only reason I got involved is he practically begged me to. I don't know what's on his mind but however it goes, you already know," he says as he lifts his shirt revealing his gun on his waist. "We can leave his ass right here."

"Depending on what he talking that just might be what it is," Manson says without blinking an eye. He tucks his gun in the back of his waistband and nudges Pete to get out. Pete forces the door open and they both exit.

Before the door is closed Vito gets out. Heavy tension is in the air as Manson and Vito stare into each other's eyes with very few feet in between them. Once they get face to face Vito eases the tension by putting his right hand onto his brow and saluting Manson. Manson sends him a head-nod in return. Manson gets right to the point. "What's the deal?"

"Short and sweet...I been hearing a lotta things about you. First let me commend you for coming home after all that time and reinventing yourself. Not many are able to do that. My reason for reaching out is two-fold. I don't know if you know or not but we been controlling the city for the past few years."

"Nah, I been out of the loop," Manson replies with sarcasm.

Vito smiles it off and continues on. "Well, grade A dope, coke, whatever a motherfucker need basically they had to come through us. I'm surprised your people never told you that. But anyhow I been hearing great things about this dope you're supposed to have and I'm wondering is it open to us as well or is this a Blood only situation? I'm a businessman and if it makes dollars it makes sense. With the quality of work that I hear you have and me and my army as the machine behind it, the opportunities are endless.

Manson listens with surprise. He really didn't know what to expect from this meeting. Manson is so old school and stuck in his ways that he still can't fathom Bloods and Crips doing business together and hanging out with each other. As a Blood he hates Crips but as a businessman he understands why it makes sense to do business with them.

"I'm gone keep it totally G with you because that's the only way I know how to do," Manson says. "I ain't really into mixing it up like that. I'm old school. Been like this all my life. I take this banging serious. I'm official from here all the way back to the West Side. This ain't no East Coast thing to me but as a businessman I understand the potential of green involved in it all. I say all that to say if the deal makes sense I can put my personal views to the side and do business with you. But business is all that it can ever be in between us."

"Bruh, first of all any deal I do make sense. Second, I'm not in search of new friends my damn self so I can totally respect that. All I needed was the green light. Give me a few days to tie some loose ends and I will hit bruh," he says planting his hand on Pete's shoulder and get him to hit you."

"Bet," Manson says before spinning around and stepping away.

"Hold up a second," Vito says. Manson stops and turns around. "Told you it was two fold." He licks his lips as he chooses his words mentally.

"What's up?" Manson asks quite agitated like.

"I don't know how to tell you this but I feel the need to. Sometimes we be so high in the sky that our ears don't be to the street. I mean, I'm in the sky but always got one ear on the ground. I know you been away and so much has happened since you left. I don't know what you know and what you don't know but what I do know is every story I ever heard about you was solid all around the board," he says before taking a breather.

"In my heart I believe if you knew certain things certain motherfuckers wouldn't be around you."

"What you getting at? The whole beating around the bush bullshit is killing me."

"Bottom line, you got niggas in your camp that the streets unanimously agree that he ain't real right. This ain't no he say she say either because I don't do that. I deal with facts only. Two years ago my man was supposed to meet with main man and main man never showed up but the Jake did. Jake nabbed my man with a hundred bricks and a pistol. That pistol was my man third one. Got him trigger lock.

Last summer main man busted a move with some Bloods I know personally. After the perfect getaway they busting down the bread on the homicide and main man get a call and leave in a fake rush. Not five minutes later the people come kicking the doors down. Here and there lil funny shit been popping up but niggas keep it quiet like they scared to expose main man. I mean I never did no crime with him and never plan to so I said fuck it. The only reason I'm speaking up about it now is because I respect your G and don't want you sleepwalking in the dark."

"Who the fuck is main man?" Manson asks with attitude.

Vito continues on without answering. "Few weeks ago main man laid up in the hospital cuffed to the bed." Manson's antennas go up and his ears open wide. He's boiling inside at the fact that Vito feels comfortable enough to slander his family. He stands on edge. "I know somebody personally who work down there and they come in the room and the people there talking to him. They leave, my folks come in and the cuffs is gone."

Manson has heard enough. "What the fuck is you saying, though?"

"I'm just saying what other niggas is afraid to say to you."

"Listen man, where I'm from you don't destroy a man's character without proof. Also where I'm from defamation of character usually leads in death if the accusations are not accurate."

"Bruh, I'm from the same place."

"Also," Manson adds. "I'm confused as to why you feel comfortable slandering my kin folk to me."

"Bruh, slander is making false statements."

Manson flexes his temples without saying a word for seconds. "Being that you brought it here, we gone take it there. As a man you should be willing to stand by what all you said, right?"

"Absolutely."

"Okay, so when we all sit at the big table I would like you to present those same events accompanied with whatever proof or witnesses you have. If not I will consider it slander and defamation of character and from that point we will rock to the beat from there," he says with viciousness in his eyes.

Vito smirks at Manon's threat as if he's not the least bit bothered by it. "Name the date, the time and the meeting place and I'm there."

157

DAYS LATER

MANSON SITS BEHIND the counter of his store. He takes a peek at his watch as if the last time he looked wasn't less than a minute ago. He hides his rage by the huge smirk covering his face. He looks through the big window with discouragement.

They may think that Manson is all alone but surely he is not. Arson and Helter and Skelter are in the back room watching them on camera and ready for war if war presents itself. Manson has them out of sight for two reasons. One reason is to give them the impression that he has no fear or worry about being outnumbered by the other side. The other reason is, he doesn't want them to see the faces of his team. The less they know, the better.

Vito, and four other Crips are present; one of them being Vito's Big Homie. Vito sits on a stool, scrolling through his phone while the two others hold a meaningless conversation. Vito's Big Bruh walks around the store curiously. Just to kill boredom he grabs books from the shelf and skims through them page by page.

Crips make Manson's blood boil. He can't stand the sight or even the smell of them. He's second guessing if inviting them here was a good idea. Judging by how infuriated Smoke was when Manson told him the details of what was said, Manson is not sure if a bloodbath will take place right here in the store.

As ruthless as he's heard Vito and his crew to be his ego tells him that they would never disrespect his store so he's really not worried about them. He's more worried about how Smoke will react when all is put on the table and is said to his face. He's sure Smoke will jump off the ledge just as he did the day he told him what was said.

Vito looks up from his phone. "Bruh, how long we gone wait for him? We been here for over an hour now."

Manson gets pissed but he doesn't show it. His anger is geared toward Vito's cockiness to the matter. Manson can't believe that Smoke wasn't the first one here to defend his honor. Smoke has messed up a few times but never has he left Manson hanging.

Manson stood up in Smoke's defense the other day. Today he's questioning himself and Smoke. The fact that Smoke hasn't showed up is not a good sign to him. The fact that he has left Manson looking stupid once again is not a good sign for Smoke.

"Bruh, we can set this meeting up again if y'all want," Vito says standing up. "But I brought my Big Bruh here for the other thing we talked about." The other man walks over to Vito, eyes on Manson. "Can we get down to business?"

Manson's ego and pride makes him hesitant of doing business with them. As much as he hates the thought of it, he considered the financial gain involved. He hates it to be true but understands that Crips are the central nervous system of the city. With that being understood he realizes how much more money he can make by dealing with them. There's a whole world of money out there he's missing but through them he can get it.

Manson stretches his arms over his head as he stands up. He rotates his neck to pop out the kinks. "What is it that y'all need from me?"

Vito's Big Bruh laughs sarcastically. "Need? We don't *need* nothing from you. What we want is to open up a pipeline with you. We ready to play ball just need to know the score?"

"One sixty a brick," Manson replies.

The man laughs in Manson's face disrespectfully. "Bricks are for kids. Anyway if I was buying bricks it wouldn't be for a buck sixty. I sell them for cheaper than that. I need the raw. We got half a million to spend. What can you do for us? Rather what can we do for each other?"

"Seventy-two grand a joint," Manson replies. "No haggling, no negotiating."

Vito interrupts. "That's crazy. I heard you at sixty-eight with motherfuckers who ain't got no money."

Manson is taken aback. He's sure Pete has told them his price because no one else could have. The other four grand tax is his way of making himself feel better for even doing business with the other side. It took everything in him to even be in this place with them.

Maybe now they will feel disrespected by the number and leave him alone. He would rather that any day. The only reason that he's considered this is due to what he learned from the Judge, the prosecutor and Tony. Had he not witnessed that with his own eyes they would never be here in the same room together talking business.

"What can we do to get the number we heard you at?"

Manson can bullshit them but the upright man that he chooses not to. "I'm sure y'all give tax breaks for the men of your hue just to keep them ahead of the rest of the world, right? Well, I have to take care of my like minded ones as well. It's the game."

Vito nor the man like what they're hearing but they respect it. "If you can meet us at 70, we got money for seven of them. We got ten thousand dollars change left over after that. Maybe that can go toward another one, leaving us owing you a sixty-thousand dollar balance. That one on the cuff will help us over the hump of paying more than the average Joe.

I understand the color difference but me I'm color blind when it comes to business. Maybe one day in the future you will be there but until then, we will play the game your way." Manson would hate to admit that he's very much impressed with the mannerisms and the business mindset of both of them. It's no longer a wonder to him how they control the city. The man continues on. "All I ask is that you do no business with any other Crips."

"Oh, that you will never have to worry about."

Minutes later, the meeting is wrapped up and as soon as Vito and his team are out of the store Manson calls Smoke once again. "He listens with rage as the phone rings over and over. He's starting to worry about Smoke.

Smoke's phone rings quite loudly. The only other noise in the room is the sound of wet and sloppy dick slurping. Jada is on her knees, kneeling before Smoke. Smoke stands there balanced on one leg while the other foot is on the edge of the bed. He looks over to the nightstand where the phone is and sees 'Big Bruh' spread across the display.

His groove is somewhat interrupted. He's sure that Manson is pissed with him for standing him up and he knows he has some real explaining to do. What excuse he will make he's not sure of. He will deal with that when the time comes.

For now he has other things to deal with. He sends Manson's call to voicemail and gets right back into his groove. He places one hand under Jada's chin and the other on the crown of her head. He slow fucks her mouth until Manson, the meeting or even his phone calls are no longer in his mind.

158

SMOKE GETS OUT of the Ford Taurus just as Manson is getting out of the Suburban. Manson's first time hearing from Smoke was an hour ago. He got so frustrated with Smoke not picking up that he stopped calling. He's very curious to hear what answer Smoke has for him.

Smoke extends his hand for a handshake but Manson doesn't reciprocate it. He just stares into Smoke's eyes. Smoke pretends that he doesn't know why Manson is being this way toward him. "What up, Big Bruh?"

"What up? What you mean what up? What the fuck happened to our meeting yesterday? I called you off the hook. I know you saw it."

"Nah, bruh, my bad. I lost my phone and had to get a new one," he says holding his phone up. The new case on his phone is supposed to be confirmation. "Luckily they was able to switch all my contacts."

"But what about our meeting? You stood me up."

"Bruh, no disrespect to you but fuck that meeting. It's shoot on sight wherever I see them motherfuckers. I ain't got time to be playing around with them."

"So, basically you said fuck me and the meeting? I put myself on the line and that's how you do me? You never know how that shit could've went. Me and the other side meeting and you didn't even give a fuck enough about me to make sure I'm good?"

"Nah bruh never that. I just got mad shit on my mind. I'm out here on these streets trying to find out where that hit on Mirah came from," he says as he keeps a close eye on Manson. He wants to see his reaction and his body language. Manson, a seasoned master of deception, doesn't even flinch. Smoke continues on. "It wasn't fuck you. It was fuck them."

"But what about your reputation? It's fuck that too? You didn't give a fuck enough to come and clear your name?"

"Bruh, since when we start giving a fuck what people think? Anyway, the people talked about Jesus Christ in his day. Fuck all that shit. Niggas gone talk. I'm chasing this money and other more important shit. I got your sixty-thousand stacks profit for you in the car from that last batch. Plus, I got two in the trunk ready to be shipped to Brooklyn," he says before flashing a winking eye.

"Let's get out of here and go cash the fuck in," he says trying to hype Manson up as he does his little soldiers. "The other shit ain't about nothing. Shoot on sight, you hear me? I know shit gone get heavy once I bust my move but fuck it. I know this is what you been wanting from the beginning anyway. The time is now. We got our money right and can now afford to go to war with them. Let's get it."

Manson nods his head up and down but all this sounds type weird to him. Smoke is not giving a fuck about his name and his reputation and now all of a sudden he's ready to go to war. Something is strange about all of this to him. As much as Smoke may say that he doesn't care what the people say it's a lie.

The two bodies in the trunk are proof that it's a lie. The two men are initially responsible for spreading the rumors about him from the very beginning. These two are just the beginning. One by one he plans to knock off anyone that he's heard has said an ill word about him.

"So, we going to Brooklyn or not?" Smoke asks.

"Of course we are and after that we need to set up another meeting with them. I don't like the things they saying, regardless if you're cool with it or not. That war we can set off right at the meeting. Like you said, it's time."

159

THE NEXT MORNING

MANSON WALKS INTO Tony's office with a duffle bag in his hand. Tony smiles with satisfaction, already figuring what's in the bag. "D.B., my man!" he says as he gives Manson a thug hug. "What's up? For what do I deserve the pleasure of your presence this lovely morning?"

"I thought long and hard and I want in," Manson replies.

"That's music to my ears," Tony says. Manson hands the bag over to Tony without hesitation. "How much is this?"

"You said two hundred and fifty would get me in, right? There it is. Bring me in."

A smile spreads across Tony's face. "D.B. I'm telling you this is the best investment you can ever make. Once our guy gets in we will be royalty in this city. There won't be anything we can't do. Thank you," he says as he reaches for Manson's hand.

Manson locks hands with Tony. Tony can see the thoughts running through his mind. "Don't worry. We will get in. You look like your mind is running a mile a minute."

"Nah, I ain't worried about that. I trust you and just like you said the other day, it's a risk. I get that and I'm not worried about it. I'm just happy that you think enough of me to bring me in on such a great possibility."

"Then, what's on your mind then?"

"I know you hate when I bring up Bruh and that case but I have a question for you."

Tony's face saddens instantly. "What's up?"

"I just need a few details. Like, I know how the federal informant got in but is that the only way?"

"What do you mean?"

"Like, did anybody else work on that case?"

"D.B., honestly I couldn't tell you. I was in so deep with him that on several occasions my career was on the line. It's by the grace of God that

I'm still able to practice law. They had me labeled as a drug dealer and not an attorney. My love and loyalty to him made me disregard everything.

Once he was murdered I had to back away from the case. For a minute I forgot I was an attorney and I wanted to get out on the streets and avenge his death my damn self. I took a couple of months off to get my mind right. It was then that I was able to separate the business and the personal. I was hurt but I had to pull back all the way. After the funeral when they closed the coffin, I had to close the personal ties. I never once looked at the paperwork to figure any of it out. It was better for me that way."

Manson can see the tears building up in Tony's eyes. "I understand all that but right now I'm in between a rock and a hard spot. From what I hear, somebody in my camp supposedly is hot. I never really listen to rumors but I just need clarity. Even if it's not on this case, I'm wondering is there any case that he may be tied to. I just need to know before we go any further."

"Who is the person at question?"

"My little cousin, Smoke. Is there anyway you can check that out for me?"

Tony inhales a deep breath. "Damn," he sighs. He shakes his head from side to side.

"Sorry to get you back in the mix of this but I can't keep moving around with him with those thoughts in my head."

"I totally understand," he says as he sinks into deeper thought. "Let me make a call and see what I can find out. Just give me a couple of days. Until then stay cool and don't do nothing crazy."

"Got you."

160

DAYS LATER/PETER LUGERS STEAKHOUSE/PHILADELPHIA

THE SMOOTH, CHARMING Attorney, Tony Austin, sits at the table with a steak the equivalent size of a Fred Flintstone Brontosaurus steak in front of him. He entertains the steak while being entertained by his beautiful, long time friend and ex-lover. Their conflict of occupations have them meeting on the low just as they always have. With Tony being an attorney that the Federal Government hates she's forced to keep her love for him hidden from the world.

"So, you pop up again in my life, for what?" she asks with evident sarcasm in her voice. "What is it that you need from me this time?"

"We are friends right? Why do I have to need something from you? Why can't I just want your company?"

I haven't heard from you in years. Why now?"

"Knock it off. You know why you haven't heard from me. That was your choice."

"Yes, my choice because you weren't ready to give me what I needed. I gave you two choices and you chose the one that worked for you."

"I didn't choose what worked for me. I chose what worked for us."

"Let me decide what works for me. You keep worrying about what works for you. Who are you to tell me what works for me?"

"You have a dream life with a millionaire husband who worships the ground you walk on. As I told you back then, I could never be the cause of you losing all of that."

"I had it all with no happiness. I was willing to give it all up to be happy with you."

"You know all I had going on at the time. I had just got out of a messy divorce and was just trying to find my way in life."

"We could have found our way together. What you were looking for was right here you under your nose but you were too cocky and arrogant to see it."

Tony flashes a sinister smile. "My cocky arrogance is what you like most about me. Say that ain't so?"

Her stern aura changes. She blushes from ear to ear. "You know that's what I love the most about you. So, why didn't you just tell me what I needed to hear?"

"I couldn't tell you to leave him and that's what you wanted to hear me say. I could never tell you to leave. That was a decision that you had to make on your own."

"Well, I made it three years ago on my own."

"So, how come I never got the memo?"

"Tony, cut the bullshit. What is it that you need from me?"

"Well, since you continue to ask. The Mayor file, can you get that for me?"

"Tony, are you still on that? Let the scumbag rest in peace. I know you consider him a friend but you almost blew your career messing around with him. And mine," she adds.

"You know I can't let you talk about a friend like that. I still guard him and our friendship, the same way I would guard me and your friendship."

"I don't want to be involved in this. It's too risky."

"Life is risky. Me and you sitting here at this table, a Federal Attorney and a Federal Agent, that's risky." He grabs her hand over the table. "So, can you get that file for me?"

She stares into his eyes. "Maybe. But let's say that I can. What's in it for me? I need to know if the risk outweighs the reward, so I can decide what's best for me." She takes a breather before speaking. "What's it worth to you? What are you willing to put on the table?"

"I know nothing is free so what do I need to put on the table?"

"By doing this I will be putting my career, my livelihood on the line. There's no more multimillionaire husband there to catch me if I fall. It's just little old me now. If I do this for you, I will need to know that I'm secure."

Tony is shocked at her words. "After all we had, we dealing with money now?"

"Fuck your money. I need more. Before I do this I need you to put something that means something to you on the table."

"What would that be?"

"Your heart. If you can guarantee me that I will put everything I have on the line. If I lose it all I will be good, knowing that regardless of what, it's me and you to the end."

Tony grabs his chest and pretends that he's snatching his heart out of his chest. He slams his hand onto the table. "Is that all you need for collateral? There it is, you got it."

She grabs his hand and pretends that she's taken his heart out of his hand. "The deal is sealed. Give me a day or two to get hold of it. After that just promise me that we will work on us. I waited my turn patiently."

"The wait is over. I promise."

161

TWO DAYS LATER

DIRT STEPS OUT of Jordan's breakfast spot on South Orange Avenue. Both hands are filled with bags. At 12 noon they're just getting breakfast. He steps past the group of men who are crowding the sidewalk. They're feeling quite territorial and staring him up and down. He stares back into their faces individually. He peeks over his shoulder at the men just as he steps around the corner where Smoke is awaiting him. He snatches the door open, bag in hand and just as he does, tires squealing on the asphalt catches his attention.

He turns to his left where he sees a Cherokee Laredo spin the corner. A Glock 40 with an extended clip hangs from the passenger's window. BLOCKA! BLOCKA! BLOCKA! The back driver's side window shatters into many pieces. Dirt hits the ground, ducking for cover. A gunman raises up, hanging his torso over the ledge of the passenger's window of the Cherokee. He aims over the roof of the car and fires more shots. BLOCKA! BLOCKA!

Smoke leans over in the driver's seat to get out of the way of the shots. He fumbles with his own gun. The window is rolled down with just barely enough space for him to stick his gun through which makes it hard for him to get a clean shot. He still fires anyway. BOC! BOC!

The gunman courageously pushes the door open and gets out of the Cherokee and just as he does Smoke realizes that the gunman is Baby Manson. Baby Manson and Smoke lock eyes through the slightly parted window. They both are frozen for seconds before shots sound off from both of their guns. Neither of them hit their target, just the sound of steel ripping into the steel of the body of the vehicles. Baby Manson takes two shots as the driver of the Cherokee speeds off.

Dirt grabs the headrest and pulls himself inside. "Yo, hurry the fuck up!" Smoke shouts. Dirt slams the door shut and Smoke speeds off in pursuit of the Cherokee.

"Yo, what the fuck?" Dirt says as he finally gets his gun from his waistband.

"That was the young motherfuckers from across town!" Smoke shouts.

Smoke keeps his eyes on the Cherokee which is now bending the corner. He mashes the gas pedal with determination. In his heart he's almost sure that Baby Manson recognized him. He believes they must have remembered the car or Dirt's face from the night of the shooting and maybe on a whim they spotted them today.

He's positive that Baby Manson is clueless to the fact that he was behind the tinted windows that day. If by chance he recognized him it wasn't until now. Either he recognized him and froze with fear or he just plain out froze from fear. He can't take the risk of Baby Manson telling Manson what they did the other day so he has no choice but to hawk him down and finish him off.

The Cherokee bends the corner wildly. A Newark Police car is approaching on the way to the scene of the crime and spots the reckless driving Cherokee. The Cherokee zooms straight pass the cop car at about 90 miles an hour.

The police lights flash on as the police car makes a U-turn in the middle of the street. The police car follows behind the Cherokee with the speed building up. The police officer in the passenger's seat gets on the radio and makes the call over the airwaves. In less than a minute police cars are swarming the street in every direction.

"Oh shit!" Baby Manson says frantically. "The whole fucking force on us!"

Smoke bends the corner in search of the Cherokee and sees no sign of it. What he does see is police cars everywhere. "Fuck!" he shouts. His heart damn near stops beating as he thinks of what is to come.

His gut tells him that Baby Manson saw his face and with that being said he already knows what the outcome will be. The war between him and Manson that he was avoiding but knew would eventually happen has just begun. He looks over to Dirt who has no clue of what they just got themselves into. "Shit, just got real."

MINUTES LATER/EAST ORANGE, NEW JERSEY

The Cherokee is turned over on the sidewalk on the corner of the residential block. East Orange police cars as well as Newark police cars surround the Cherokee. The driver of the Cherokee is laid on his stomach in handcuffs in the middle of the street. After the crash he never made it across the street before he was caught.

Up, several hundred feet away, Baby Manson is being dragged through an alley by a cop. Tears fall from his eyes. The tears have nothing to do with his fear of the law or his fear of jail. Those tears have everything to do with the fear of his father.

162

DAYS LATER

SMOKE PULLS OVER at the corner of Jada and Manson's block. He pulls out his phone and gets to dialing. Jada picks up anxiously. "Yeah?"

"Where you at?" he asks.

"I just got the room. About to jump in the shower. Where are you?"

"Like fifteen minutes away. Just leave the door open and I will be there by the time you get out of the shower."

"Okay but I don't have all night. I have to be leaving here in less than two hours."

"I got you. Go ahead and take your shower and I'm right at you." Smoke ends the call with the quickness. He looks over to Dirt. "Showtime."

Smoke pulls up to Manson and Jada's house and parks a few houses away from it. He gets out and Dirt follows behind him. Smoke peeks around before he dips into the narrow alley. His slow pace turns into a fast trot, as fast as he can walk with his not so healed wounds.

Once they get to the back porch, Smoke gives Dirt the signal to lead the way. Dirt runs up the small flight of stairs. He fumbles with the locks for a few seconds before his magic is worked. The door is opened for them to enter. Breaking and entering is another one of his many street trades.

Smoke steps in behind him and closes the door. Smoke leads the way up to the second floor. Dirt works his magic faster this time than he did downstairs. In less then two minutes they're in the apartment searching high and low.

Smoke searches while keeping an eye on Dirt so that he doesn't miss a single thing. Every valuable they find he wants to know about it. Smoke runs straight for the bedroom closet. He pulls the many shoe boxes from the shelf and to no surprise at all he finds two duffle bags.

He unzips the bag and there lies stacks and stacks of new, crisp bills. Dirt stands over his shoulder, eyes on the money. "Got damn! We just hit the fucking lottery!"

Smoke drops to the floor and crawls underneath the bed where he finds another bag that he's sure is full of money. He unzips it and, exactly, it is. They tear the whole house apart in less than twenty minutes. They search high and low and once they're sure they haven't missed anything, Smoke leads the way out of the apartment.

FIVE MINUTES LATER

Smoke's phone rings again for the twentieth time. He's frustrated to the max with so much going on at once and Dirt hasn't shut up yet. "Yo, I'm willing to bet that's like at least close to a million in all them bags together. Yo, ain't no looking back from here. It's really our turn."

As much money as they recovered, Smoke still isn't fully satisfied. He was hoping to find a few kilos of dope as well. This move right here was all or nothing for him. He's sure Manson knows all about him being behind Dirt taking the shots at his son. One thing Smoke knows is Manson will never show his hand.

"Yo, so you sure this shit ain't gone link back to us?" Dirt asks with evident nervousness.

"How the fuck could it?" Smoke replies hastily.

"What about that shit with his son?"

Smoke just informed Dirt of everything on their way to Manson's house for the robbery. It was then that his nervousness crept in. Smoke eased the nervousness by telling him that there would be enough money in the house for them to pick up and start over somewhere else. Dirt was all for that.

"I'm still not sure about that. But something tells me he saw my face. It was impossible not to."

"How the Big Homie acting, though? Did he mention anything about his son to you?"

"You never can tell with that motherfucker. He's one of the sneakiest bastards walking the earth. He will smile right in your face and you will never know the difference." The truth of the matter is Smoke doesn't know how Manson is acting because he hasn't been around Manson. He's been avoiding all of Manson's calls. He will never tell Dirt or anyone else that, though.

"Sneakier than you?" Dirts asks as a joke to ease the moment.

Smoke doesn't find the joke the least bit humorous. "Yo, we need to put this money and them guns in the trunk. The last thing we need is to get pulled over on a humbug and lose it all."

"Hell yeah! Be on that show the dumbest criminals!" Dirt says accompanied by laughter.

"Yo, the next move is on that bitch, Pebbles, his other baby mother house. I know it's a couple million in there. We go in there, tie her ass up and push her once we get the bag."

"Damn, you on a mission, bruh."

"I'm on some real fuck everybody shit. I told you whoever ain't with me is against me."

"Well, I'm glad I'm with you," Dirt says with a smile.

Smoke pulls over and parks in the first vacant parking lot. He throws two duffle bags onto Dirt's lap and hits the trunk button. Dirt hops out and the trunk raises open automatically as he's walking toward it. Smoke gets out with two bags in his hand as well. They meet at the trunk. "Yo push them all the way to the back to make room for these. Put them guns toward the back," Smoke instructs.

Dirt slides the top half of his body into the trunk as he makes room for the bags. Smoke peeks around twice as he lifts his gun from underneath his shirt. He places the barrel of the gun near the back of Dirt's head. He looks around again for safety measures. That's the furthest it can go?" Smoke asks.

"Yeah," Dirt replies as he turns around to face Smoke. His eyes stretch wide open terrified. BOC! Dirt's body drops into the trunk. Smoke peels his body out of the trunk and discards of it like garbage. He slams the trunk shut and takes off for the driver's seat. He speeds off recklessly.

163

TWO HOURS LATER

J ADA'S **BMW** TURNS onto her block. She's highly irked for many reasons. One of those reasons is Manson is in the passenger's seat. Of all the days that he wants to come home early this had to be one of them.

Not even twenty minutes after Smoke got to the Hotel and Manson was calling her and quizzing her of her whereabouts. She's not sure if he was truly tired or if his gut instinct picked up on her being up to no good but he demanded that she come pick him up. He claimed that him and the crew had a long day and he was sending them all on their way home and he was stuck without a ride. She tried to buy herself some time with a few excuses but it didn't work. He demanded she pick him up from the store within twenty minutes.

Her and Smoke managed to get a quickie in before she left. There was no time for a round two or even a shower. She just prays that he doesn't try to get some when they get in. In silence, she's been praying on it the entire ride.

Jada parks in front of the house. She turns the interior light on before leaning over to slide her feet into her flips flops. Manson looks over and what he sees enrages him. Her thong peeks over her low waistband jeans. The tag of her panties is on the outside.

He yanks her thong into a wedgie. "Owww," she screams in a high pitched voice.

The look in his eyes terrifies her. "Fucking panties on backwards," he snarls. "What?" she asks as if she didn't hear him. He doesn't repeat himself, he just stares at her as if he's trying to read her. "You never made a mistake and put your boxers on backwards? Damn, a simple mistake," she says as she gets out and slams the door shut. She prays that he brought that and doesn't further investigate it.

She rushes up the stairs trying to get a lead on him. Her plan is to sneak into the bathroom and take a quick wipe down just in case he wants to check her out. She's trotting while he drags along sluggishly up the stairs. She opens the apartment door and before she can even step in she notices that the living room is wrecked.

All the chairs are turned over and so is the television. Paintings have been stripped off the walls and thrown onto the floor. Manson steps in and the look on her face confuses him. He looks in and his heart begins to race.

He reaches for his gun as he steps into the apartment. He tiptoes, hoping to catch someone here. His gun making it into each room before him, he aims high and low. Jada steps through the apartment behind him with her heart pounding with fear.

He sees the back door open and takes off for it. He steps onto the back porch, looking down the stairs. Not a peep can be heard. He steps back into the bedroom which is by far the messiest room of them all.

He sees the wide open closet with everything from the shelves laying on the floor. In his heart he already knows so he's afraid to look on the shelf. He takes a peek and there are no duffle bags. He drops onto the floor and peeks under the bed and realizes there are no bags there either.

His heart sinks as he thinks of the 1.4 million dollars that is not here anymore. Rage replaces the sorrow as he thinks of the fact that somebody made away with it. The violation he feels right now is something that he never felt before. He can't imagine who would have the balls to disrespect him like this. He leans back against the door thinking long and hard about who could have done this.

164

DAYS LATER

"**S**O, YOU NOT gone bail my baby out?" Pebbles ask from the driver's seat of the her new truck. The silver metallic Range Rover Sport with the none other than a blood red leather interior is a gift to her from Manson. He traded her BMW in to the Jew and gave him the balance of the total cost of the Rover.

Manson stands on the outside with his head hanging in the truck listening to her as she gets more feisty by the second. "You just gone let my baby sit in jail and you got the money to get him out?"

"Yeah," Manson replies with a straight face.

"Why though?"

"Why? You really asking me this? We just spent a lot of money getting his little dumb ass out of trouble and what he do? He get right back into some more dumb shit."

"You didn't even hear him out. He says he really has something to tell you about this. Says he has an answer for all of this."

"What's his answer? Why he gotta tell me and not you?"

"Because of his fake ass gangster code he got, that's why," she snaps. "I tried to get it out of him."

"He not telling you because there's nothing to tell. He's just playing mind games to get us to feeling sorry for him and bail him out."

"If you're not gonna bail him out, I am. Call your attorney friend and tell him I'm on my way to him."

"I'm not gonna calling him and embarrass myself. We just stood before that judge. A lot of strings and favors were pulled to get him out of that shit he was in."

"Well, if you're not gonna call him, I'm just gonna go there."

"Pebbles, don't make me call him and tell him not to deal with you. I will. Furthermore, you don't have no property or proof of income to pay that ransom bail he has. You got proof of income?" He pauses for a few seconds. "I thought not."

"He need to sit down there and think about some things right now. No more youth-house. He wanna play a grown man game? Now he in there with grown men. Maybe now he will learn his lesson."

A bit of compassion crosses his face. "I love him just like you do but he hard-headed. He gone have to fight this case from the inside because I'm not bailing him or even getting him a lawyer. He will fight the case with a public defender. If he loses, he will get no more than five years. Maybe that's what he needs to get his mind right." Tears creep into the corners of Pebbles' eyes. "He needs to learn his lesson."

"You never learned your lesson but still I never gave up on you. Look, after fifteen years you're right back in the game and guess what? I'm still by your fucking side to the end."

Manson is speechless. She has a true blue point right there. All he can do is turn around and walk away from the truck. He places his hands in the air, palms up while shrugging his shoulders. "Hey, tough love!"

165

SUMMIT, NEW JERSEY

TONY SITS INSIDE of Fiorino's Italian Restaurant. Across from him is a much younger woman who sits feeling quite out of place. "I know you're wondering who I am and why I invited you here, correct?"

"Yes," she says while lowering her eyes bashfully.

"As you know I'm an attorney and my reason for tracking you down is not just because you're beautiful," he says trying to charm away the tension. She blushes just as he expected her to. "But to inquire about one of my prior clients." He pauses because he hates to even relive this.

"Several years ago you and your partner were assigned to a call for a man in East Orange. A shooting victim," he says peering into her eyes. "Yeah, I know you get a hundred of those a day but this was no regular man. This man was one of the highest profile drug dealers in the city. Everyone knows him by the Mayor." Tony watches as the woman's face turns to stone right before his eyes.

She starts fidgeting uncontrollably. She gets up from the table clumsily. "I have to go."

"Wait, please," Tony says as she stands up. "What's the matter? Are you familiar?" He grabs her hand to comfort her.

"Yes, I'm familiar. I want no parts of this."

"Parts of what?"

"This whole fiasco. I put this behind me years ago. I had to take a leave of absence behind that. Still that wasn't enough. I finally had to leave that job just to get peace of mind."

Tony is lost. This appears deeper than he actually thought. He can't let her leave him in limbo like this. "But what are you talking about?"

"What happened that day I never repeated to anyone, not even my boyfriend at the time because I feared what would happen if I did."

"What could possibly happen to you? You arrived to the scene and he was dead when you got there. It's not your fault. It was God's will."

"It wasn't God's will. I had him back alive," she utters. "He was supposed to live and because of me he didn't. I have to live with that forever," she says with tears building up in her eyes. "That's the reason why I gave the job up. I was hired to save lives not take them," she says lowering her gaze and staring onto the floor.

"Then what happened? Why wasn't his life saved?"

"I'm leaving," she says as she turns around. "Sorry, I can't help you."

Tony chases behind her. "Please wait." He grabs her hand gently and pulls her toward him. "I need answers. That wasn't just an ordinary client to me. He was like my brother. I can't go on without knowing."

"Look, I don't want any trouble. Just let me go please."

"Trouble with who? Are you afraid of the people in the street?"

"I was but I got over that fear. I thought they would avenge me for not saving his life. But my fear is bigger than that."

"What can be bigger than that?"

"Listen, I don't want trouble. I've put all that behind me now."

"It's not behind you, you're facing it."

"Look, I have three daughters who I raise with no help. I can't be taken out of their lives nor can I allow them to be taken away from me."

"I promise you that will never happen."

"How can you promise that? They threatened to make my life hell and take my kids if I uttered a word of this to anyone."

"Who are they that you are speaking about?"

"The law," she whispers. "The Feds," she sobs. "Can you please just keep me out of this?"

"You're out of it. No one knows me and you are here and I will never speak about what you tell me. If anybody attempts to take your kids away I will fight for them like they are mine. I'm the best attorney in the world," he says arrogantly. "Please for my own sanity, just tell me?"

She stands in silence for many seconds. "I had him alive. I did my job and brought him back. He was breathing, eyes open and alert. Until they came in flashing their badges and told me to back off. So I did. I didn't know what else to do. They wanted him dead."

Tony hugs her while she sobs away like a baby. "I'm sorry but the guilt is not yours. Had nothing to do with you. That beef was personal. Thank you for helping me to regain my sanity and giving me the closure I needed to move on." He hugs her tighter. "Thank you."

166

DAYS LATER/ESSEX COUNTY JAIL

BABY MANSON STANDS at the phone booth with the phone glued to his ear. As the phone rings he prays that his father answers. He knows better than to call his father's phone from jail but he leaves him no other choice. Pebbles got so tired of telling him that Manson has nothing to say to him right now that she gave him the number and told him to call until he finally picks up.

He calls on the three-way with his mother, or the three-way with anybody who will allow it and he calls directly every chance he gets. Regardless of who he calls with or how he calls Manson refuses to pick up. He's sure he's pissing his father off giving everyone his number to call but he's desperate. His hope simmers slowly the more rings he hears.

The call goes to voicemail and he immediately starts to dial again. Seeing Smoke's face behind those tints was like a nightmare to him. All of his life he looked up to Smoke. He admired Smoke even more than his own father.

While Manson was away all he had to look up to was Smoke. Hearing Smoke's name ring bells in the street made him feel proud. To know that his idol was behind the shooting that day breaks his heart. He wonders if the attack was for him or for one of the other dudes.

He doesn't know what to do or even what to believe at this point, which is why he needs to get in touch with his father so he can give him some clarity. Also, he needs to explain his side of the story and how he wasn't looking for trouble but somehow trouble found him. Baby Manson's heart sinks in his chest as the call goes to voicemail once again. He bangs the receiver on the hook and stomps off like a baby throwing a temper tantrum.

MEANWHILE

Tony paces circles around his desk while Manson is seated awaiting the details. Manson turns his phone off out of frustration of his son calling back to back. He tucks his phone into his pocket while he awaits the news that Tony has for him. Tony has a mouthful to say but is choosing his words carefully. He understands that what he's about to tell Manson can result in a catastrophe. He just hopes that he isn't dragged into it in any way, form or fashion. That is if he hasn't already dragged himself into it.

He fears exactly what Manson has told Smoke about their dealings. His name has been in the clear for years and the last thing he needs is to have it rekindled in some gang-banging affiliation. He's sure the money he took from Manson could not only end his career but get him sent to prison as well.

"Well, I did my research and I found out some things."

Manson's ears and eyes are wide open. He can tell by Tony's demeanor that the news is bad. "Give it to me."

"Well, the bottom line is this. I got hold of your cousin's paperwork and this is what I found," he says as he points to a code on the top. "5K1," he says pointing to it.

Being in the Feds all those years has him totally aware of what the code means. "He's a fucking rat?"

"I dug up the paperwork to the case and I see no proof of him telling. No statements or indications. The 5k1 indicates that he did cooperate but there's nothing stating how he cooperated."

"Well, how could that be? He got the stamp for something!"

Tony swallows the lump in his throat. "This is all off record, my mouth to your ears. I done further research after discovering all of this and what I come up with is this." He lays the paper on his desk. "I believe they used your cousin to murder him."

"Huh?"

"They had nothing on him and wanted him so bad they would have him murdered just to satisfy their hate for him. I believe they gave your cousin the option to murder him to free himself and everybody else that was dragged into the situation. No one did a day in prison. Everybody's slate was wiped clean and the file was buried. No investigation of the murder, no nothing. My source told me that in the ambulance he was brought back to life and was breathing on his own until the Feds came in and ordered them to back away from him to let him die."

Manson's thoughts are racing. His cousin has cooperation on his jacket. The same cousin that knows his every move. The feeling of betrayal sets in as he thinks of how Smoke lied to him all this time. It all makes sense to him now why Smoke never went to war over the murder. He feels suckered as he thinks of the Mother Nature beef and how he was fighting a war for a cause that didn't even exist.

"Lil Bruh, I have to ask you this. Does he know anything about the money you gave me?"

Manson looks at Tony like he has three heads. "Bruh, I don't run my mouth. What happens between us stays between us. I ain't one of them niggas, bruh." Manson bangs his hand on the desk almost knocking it off the legs. "I don't believe this shit!"

"Believe it. This is all part of the game. The new game. The old rule book is no longer. Everything goes. Dog eat dog and every man is out to save himself. The 5k1 saves him. He has diplomatic immunity. He can do whatever he chooses for the most part and they won't even touch him. The only thing left for you to do at this point is to try to save yourself."

167

ESSEX COUNTY JAIL

MANSON STANDS IN front of the glass with the phone close to his ear. On the opposite side of the glass is Baby Manson. The only reason that Manson is here today is because Baby Manson told Pebbles that he needs to see his father concerning Smoke. With Smoke in hot water with Manson he just had to know what else his name is attached to.

"Pop, we wasn't doing nothing, just on the block chilling. Then all of a sudden some dude come around the corner and start blazing for no reason. I grab the thing from my man because he was scared to use it," Baby Manson lies. He can't tell his father that he was strapped.

"The nigga send a few my way and I go right back at him." Manson can see the passion and the love for the game in his son's eyes as he tells the story. He watches his son brokenheartedly as he tells the details animatedly. "Bang, bang, bang," Baby Manson says as he stares over Manson's head in a daze as if he's reliving it. "He takes off running and I hawk him down. I got a clear shot but I couldn't hit him for nothing. I was too anxious.

The getaway car backs up and he dives in to it. They pull off but I get the plate number and lock it in my mind. A couple of days later while we was just riding around we see the shooter going into a restaurant. We squat for him to come out. He spins the corner and we come behind him. I can't lie I knew you would be heated with me but I was still pissed that he tried to take my life. I jump out and I'm going...bang, bang, bang. The driver sends a few at me. Through the window I get a clear view of the driver." Baby Manson's face becomes long and saddened.

"Who was it? You recognized him?"

"Yeah," he says with a brief pause. "It was Uncle Smoke."

Manson can't believe his ears. Baby Manson continues on with the details. He sent two at me and sent two back at him. I wasn't even trying to hit him because I thought maybe he didn't know it was me. I was just trying to back him up but I wanted him to see my face. I wanted him to recognize me."

290

Baby Manson can see the fire in his father's eyes and he fears what may happen next. "Pop, I know for sure it was a mistake. He couldn't have known it was me."

"There was no mistake," Manson replies with certainty. "I'm sure those shots were meant for you."

Baby Manson is confused. He can't believe that a dude that helped raise him would try to murder him. All this is too much for him to wrap his head around.

"Listen son, just sit tight for a couple days and I will get you out of here. I will get the attorney on this ASAP. I got the money to snatch you now but it's not gone be that easy because the bail is so high. I will need signatures to match the amount of paper that I'm putting up. Just hold it down. This ain't the youth-house. A whole different world. Just lay low and in a few days I will get you out of this mess."

Baby Manson can sense worry in his father's eyes. "Pop, I'm good. Jail is jail and the same rules apply. I can do this shit standing on my head. I ain't worried about jail. I was more worried about you cutting me off. Now that I know that ain't happening. The rest of this is a cake walk that I can do with my feet up."

Manson stares at his son quite impressed. For the first time ever he doesn't see his son as the baby that he watched come out of the womb. He sees a certified gangster, Baby Manson. As much as he hates the fact and the circumstances, he respects his son's G. Manson hangs the phone up and salutes his son before making his exit.

168

LATER THAT DAY

MANSON WALKS CASTRO and his men toward the door. Castro shakes Manson's hand and bows his head humbly. "Peace, brother."

"Peace," Manson replies with much respect for him. Why wouldn't he respect him when he's just spent close to a million and a half in cash. Castro claimed that he would be buying 15 kilos of the heroin every month. Today he just bought 20. Manson takes great pride in knowing that Castro's business has increased by thirty percent in the few months that they've been doing business.

Castro's men step out before him just as they always do. Once they're all on the outside, Manson slams the door behind them and locks it securely. He flips the sign around so that it reads 'Closed.'

Manson watches as they cruise away in the low key Dodge van. Once they're out of sight, he pulls out his phone and begins dialing. He hasn't seen Smoke in a couple of weeks and that is clear indication of Smoke's guilt. He's sure that Smoke knows he's on to him by now and will never step anywhere near him. Manson has to make him believe everything is okay just so he will find comfort.

Manson has been as patient as he can with the whole situation and gets pissed every time he thinks of the fact of Smoke sending him to voicemail. His rage leads him to call every few days. The money Smoke owes him is nothing to him. He charges it off as even due to the money that he took from Samirah's house. It's the disrespect that angers him.

He's sure that Smoke originally starting laying low because he kept pressuring him about meeting with the Crips. Now it has gotten much bigger. His disappearing act makes Manson point directly at him as the culprit for breaking into his house as well. As hard as it will be for Manson to pretend that he doesn't know, he has no choice. If he ever gets Smoke on the phone, he has to make him believe that everything is good between them just so he can see Smoke face to face. If Smoke gets an indication that he's mad Manson is sure he will never meet up with him.

To Manson's surprise the phone is picked up on the fourth ring. "What?" Smoke barks hastily. Smoke's demeanor takes Manson by surprise. Smoke has never spoken to him in this manner.

"What up?" Manson asks in the most pleasant voice that he can muster up.

"You tell me," Smoke barks even hastier.

"Where you been, bruh? I been calling you and looking for you everywhere."

"I been around. Anyway, what you looking for me for, that bread?"

"Nah, bruh. I'm more concerned with your well being. I just wanted to make sure you good," Manson says with rage bleeding through his veins. "Money ain't about nothing, bruh." Smoke's attitude is driving him crazy, yet he doesn't want him to sense it. He has to keep his cool if he expects to reel Smoke in.

"I'm always good," he says with sarcasm. "And about that bread, I'm gone get at you with that in a minute. Just be patient."

Manson inhales just to calm himself down. His blood is boiling. "Lil Bruh, you need to get with me so we can kick it face to face like brothers and G's."

"Brothers?" Smoke asks with sarcasm. "We haven't been brothers since we were kids. You treat me like a fucking stranger. Take stranger's side over your own fucking blood. Now you talking about I ain't right because some shit some fucking crabs told you? All the work I put in throughout this city? Yeah, I slipped up in some ways but I'm a certified G and you know it!"

"You're right, bruh, absolutely right."

"Fuck that you right shit! All I wanted was to be respected by you. That's it but instead you make me look like an asshole every chance you get! I spent my whole life trying to impress you but nothing I do impresses you."

"I always been impressed by you. I just wanted you to always keep your best foot forward and never get comfortable. You all I really got out here. Bruh, let's link face to face."

"Hell no! So you can try to kill me? If nobody else in the world know you, I do. We ain't meeting nowhere so you can kill me just like you killed my sister. Your own fucking blood!"

"Killed your sister? I love your sister. That's my sister, too. Bruh, you emotional and talking crazy right now. Why can't we just meet up?"

"Because I don't fucking trust you! You took some fucking crabs word over mine, your own fucking blood."

"Bruh, I got the word. I know the truth. It's all been cleared up. I totally understand. I just want you to know that I rather you did that than done the other thing. Where you at? I'm coming to you."

"No, the fuck you ain't. Come to me and one of us gone die. I don't believe shit your sneaky ass saying. You wanna kill me for what? Because you want to hold me responsible for what happened to your idol? You love a stranger over your brother and will kill me over him? Family don't mean shit to you!"

"That's not true. Just get with me so we can get off these phones talking crazy like this. Where can I meet you?"

"We ain't meeting nowhere."

Manson becomes desperate and has to dig into his bag of tricks. "Anyway, I want to talk to you about putting that G back on your chest."

"Nigga, fuck your G! That shit don't mean nothing no more out in these streets. My name hold more weight than yours. You just a washed up motherfucker and if it wasn't for me niggas would've been pushed your shit back."

Manson is livid, yet he remains as cool and calm as he can. "Bruh, let's meet."

"Didn't the fuck I say that we ain't meeting nowhere? And understand when we do run into each other, we ain't brothers and we ain't friends. I'm giving you the heads up like the G that I am, regardless of what you think of me. If you see anybody who even look like me you better start firing because I'm coming for you.

Do understand that I'm not gone stop until I'm standing over you and sure your ass is dead. I was the most loyal motherfucker in the world to you. I could've been got your head knocked off but I spared you out of love and loyalty. That loyalty ain't in the picture no more. From this point on treat me as the enemy because that is what you are to me. On my sister, I'm gonna get our revenge! Just remember that you drew family blood first. Nothing or no one is sacred. The gloves are off."

The call goes dead and Manson stares at the phone while the threats echo in his head over and over. The puzzled look that he displays is replaced with a smirk that covers his whole face.

169

SMITH, LAYS BACK in his room with his feet kicked up. He may look like he's relaxing but indeed he's always working. As he sits here in what seems to be peace he's thinking of mischief that he can cause. Ever since he got to jail he's been causing mayhem but after receiving the news of the death of Mother Nature and the disaster that was caused in his hood, he turned it up more than ten notches. Like a one man army he's master-minded the deaths of so many behind these jail bars and every other jail that he has a connect in.

They may have destroyed his bloodline out on the streets but as long as he's alive that line will always be alive. Since Mother Nature is no longer here, he's taken it upon himself to give himself the G. He's informed everybody that from this day on the G status belongs to him and they either fall in line or be dealt with. There were a few dudes who were next in life for the status but he took it upon himself to skip over them. Many have whispered amongst those they trust but very few have the heart to say anything aloud. He now sits at the top of the throne. He's also made a few men from Smoke and Manson's set fall in line under him as well. It was either get under them or lose their life. He likes to refer to it as them converting. He jokingly says that he's turned them all to believers so they converted and now worship him.

A man who appears to be in his 40's stands at Smith's door. His demeanor is quite humbling. "Big bruh," he says careful to not alarm Smith by raising his voice. A man almost double Smith's age yet he calls him his Big bruh. Smith finds nothing strange about it and accepts it deservingly.

"What up?"

"Got some good news for you."

"Come in," says Smith.

The man steps into the room quite honored. "Guess who just touched?"

"Who?" Smith asks.

"Baby Manson."

"Baby Manson?"

"Yeah, Manson's son."

Smith stands to his feet eagerly. "What, where?"

"Yep, I just got the word. He downstairs though on 3-1."

Smith hops around energetically while slamming his fist into the palm of his hand. "Yo, get in touch with Officer Barnes and see if he can get him moved up here with us, ASAP. Tell him I got him."

"No doubt, Big Bruh. I'm on that right now for you."

Smith's eyes light up demonically. All the moves that he's made thus far he's sure are quite meaningless to Manson because they were mere pawns. To touch Baby Manson would be comparable to taking a man's Queen on the chessboard. "Checkmate," he says with a smile.

170

T**HE BACK OF** the townhouses is packed with vehicles parked all over the place in no particular order. The drug activity is close to none due to the late hour. A few sales sprinkle in here and there but in another hour and half the sales will be at their peak just like any other day. All the sales are directed to the Haitian young man who serves the customers as he keeps his attention on Manson and the meeting that is taking place.

What started off as 40 Haitian Bloods has evolved into almost double. Once Zoe Blood found his way around the city and a level of comfort he decided to spread his wings, with Manson's permission of course. One by one, even two by two he sent for more of his men from Florida. Now there are more than 70 of them spread out in between these townhouses and the townhouses they took over that belonged to Mother Nature. Slowly but surely he plans to send for more of his men and just wait for Manson's command to take over the whole city.

Outside of the Haitian Bloods there are over two dozen strange faces present at this meeting. Those unknown men are of Manson's California Sect. Manson made the call less than two days ago and twenty-seven of his Californians made the trip straight from Leuders Park in Compton. They just arrived approximately three hours ago and all are ready to go to work.

Manson stands at the head of the meeting, not saying a word. In his hand he holds a stack of papers. He hands half the stack to Arson who stands on his left and the other half to Skelter who stands to his right. They each take a paper and hand the stack to the person next to them.

In minutes all are staring at the paper in their hand. On the paper is a poster size picture of Smoke's face. It's a picture of his mugshot with his height and weight description on the side. Manson allows them all to lock and load the photo into their memory bank.

"He's my family but in no way are you to take it easy on him. He's armed and dangerous and he knows that I'm coming. He's a one man army but I'm not sure who he has with him. What I am certain of is that he will not go down without a fight. There's no room for slipping when it comes to him so kill him wherever you see him."

Manson ends the meeting by walking away and getting into the passenger's seat of the Black Tahoe. Arson, Helter and Skelter follow his lead and hop into the truck behind him. Soon thereafter everyone has packed into the fleet of cars. The Tahoe leads the way out onto the streets and one by one each car exits behind them. They bleed onto the streets going in their own direction. They all use different routes but the finish line is the same for all of them with one goal in common.

171

TWO WEEKS LATER

THIRTEEN DAYS OF riding with no sleep. The cars have been on the road every second of the past days, just alternating drivers. They have searched high and low and still no sign of Smoke. Manson has no idea of where he could be hiding or if he's even hiding.

Manson knows firsthand that Smoke can get low and sink way underneath the radar. Manson never thought he would see this day when the two of them would be going head up. He spared him all these years in the name of love but if he knew this day would come he would've been pressed the button a long time ago. Smoke's comment about him drawing family blood first continues to replay in his head.

Manson feels type invincible so he has no worry about himself. He's sure Smoke isn't bluffing being that he has already gunned for his son. Because of that Manson has both Jada and Pebbles laying low in hotels a few miles away from each other. There is no doubt in his mind that him or his army will eventually catch up with Smoke. There's also no doubt in his mind that Smoke is going to take a few bodies with him.

Manson may have been hard on Smoke for obvious reasons but never has he honestly underestimated Smoke's gangster. He may have never admitted it to Smoke but he respected his gangster to the fullest. Just at times Smoke would disappoint him. But now at this day and time Manson realizes that he respects Smoke's gangsterism more than he even knew.

Now with them on opposite sides he is forced to look at it for what it is and that is Smoke is to be handled and dealt with a certain way. He's taught Smoke well and now he worries that Smoke will use his own tactics against him. Manson knows he's smart and crafty which is why in no way will he sleep on him. He needs this handled immediately just so he can breathe easy.

Manson waits at the gate of Eli's warehouse as it raises slowly. In the back of the truck there lies the bodies of five young men. Two of the men are from Trenton who got caught up in a small turf war in Blue-Blood's projects. The other three men are Smoke's associates.

While in the midst of their travels Manson stumbled across them. He's not sure if the men even know of the beef that he and Smoke have on their hands. He decided to get them out of the way just in case. More than anything the profit was the deciding factor.

Manson pulls the all black Cadillac truck into the warehouse and as the gate is closing he hops out. He gives Eli a fist bump and passes right by him walking toward the back. Eli has never seen him so hype. He's usually laid back.

Manson's adrenaline has been racing for days now. He's on a war high. He slams the skid onto the forklift and then hops into the seat. He speeds across the warehouse and slams on the brakes at the back of the truck.

Arson gets out to aid him. Eli stands in suspense. He never knows what to exactly expect when it comes to Manson. Arson lifts the hatch and together they start dragging the bodies and dumping them onto the skid.

Eli is shocked at the quality of the work. Sure there's blood and bullet holes everywhere but they are nowhere near as gruesome looking as most of the other shipments. They dump the last body onto the skid and Arson slams the hatch shut. Manson steers the forklift over to the lighted area of the warehouse as Eli walks side by side the forklift, still examining the bodies.

Blood leaks from the bodies, leaving a bloody trail from the truck to the corner of the warehouse. Manson parks the lift in the corner and hops off of it. "I hope you got all my money. These five right here, the two from yesterday and I didn't forget about the two from last week," he says with all seriousness on his face.

"Damien, I mean Manson, why must we work ourselves up over money? Money comes and it goes. You scrutinize me over every dollar as if I haven't changed your life for the better, financially. Haven't I granted you more financial freedom than you have ever known?" He smiles. The smile quickly fades away. "And what two from last week?"

"Eli, don't play with me. I told you to have all the money when I got here. I got people to pay. Break me off," he demands.

Eli shakes his head as he steps away. He can never get away with a single dollar with Manson but that doesn't stop him from trying again. Manson paces around with his mind racing as he waits for Eli to return.

He has to get back on the streets to make more money. All the money that he's making now is just replacing the money that he's sure Smoke broke into the house and stole. The thought of that alone makes him beyond furious. He really hopes that he's the one that catches Smoke because he wants to kill him with his own hands. That is the only way he will be totally satisfied.

Eli enters the room and Manson's eyes are glued to the bag. Eli hands the bag over to him. Manson gently snatches the bag from him. "How much is in here, Eli?"

"Nine hundred as I owe," Eli says before he's interrupted by the sound of the door behind him crashing down. Both Manson and Eli turn toward the back door where they see three Swat team members dressed in full riot gear and gas masks on their faces.

"Freeze, FBI!" The third Fed throws a tear gas bomb which clouds the area quickly.

Both Manson and Eli take off in the opposite directions when the sound of the front door caving in echoes loudly. Nearly twenty Swat Team members soar through the doorway in single file. Once all are inside they scatter around the warehouse. Thick, smoky tear gas fills the entire warehouse in seconds.

Arson hops out of the passenger's seat of the Tahoe, AK-47 in hand. He refuses to get up caught up like this and get taken down without a fight. Like a reckless maniac he unleashes fire. Eli screams at the first sound of gunfire. He raises his hands in submission before diving onto the floor.

Rapid gunfire sounds off from every direction and after the first two rounds Arson lays flat on his stomach, dead to the world. As Manson attempts to run through the thick smoke he snatches his gun from his waist. He can't see through the smoke to get an aim at anyone. He coughs hysterically as the smoke fills his lungs.

He stumbles blindly right into the arms of a Fed. "Don't move," the Fed says placing his gun to Manson's temple. Manson puts up very little fight as his gun is pried from his hand.

172

DAYS LATER

SMOKE SITS IN the G5 Jet, in the window seat, staring out into the thick clouds. He's in deep thought. He stares to the front of the jet where Agents Dumber, Dumbest and another unknown Fed sit. The unknown Fed and Agent Dumber are both sound asleep. Agent Dumbest sits in the front reading from the newspaper. Smoke watches as he gets up and walks toward him.

Dumbest stops at Smoke's seat. He hands him the newspaper. Smoke accepts it hesitantly. The headline gives him the chills.

FEDERAL AGENTS CRACK THE INVASION OF THE BODY SNATCHER'S CASE.

On Wednesday Federal Agents were tipped by a confidential informant that they had information regarding Team 6, who has been responsible for not only 99 percent of the murders that have taken place over the past year but the disappearance of those bodies. The informant informed them that every other day loads of dead bodies are brought to a Brooklyn warehouse belonging to 58 year old Eli Schwartz.

An all out gun battle opened up in the warehouse on the day of the arrests, resulting in the murder of Damien Bryant, known to the street as the Black Charles Manson and his accomplice, 50 year old White Supremacist, Adam Beckham from Oklahoma. When federal officials bombarded the warehouse Beckham opened fire and his life was taken seconds later.

Schwartz a Jewish business man was responsible for supplying organs to doctors in the country and out of the country on the Black Market. Informant states that bodies were gathered from Trenton up to Northern Jersey and parts of Pennsylvania. Damien Bryant, a.k.a. The Black Charles Manson was the ring leader who had the responsibility of obtaining the bodies. Six men have already been linked to Manson in the Organ Scandal.

Eli Schwartz has already given up five of the doctors who he states paid him close to a million dollars per body. He cooperated in hopes of a lighter sentence. Also arrested in ties with this investigation is Schwartz's first cousin, 40 year old Ezekiel Dweck known in the Islamic Community as Hamza Mohammed. Dweck, also Jewish, played the role of a Muslim store owner but was really a heroin dealer who was responsible for pouring into the streets countless kilos of heroin per week, disguised in Shea Butter containers.

Dweck's heroin business stretched through twenty-nine of the fifty-two states. Dweck used Manson and his status in the Blood gang to funnel the heroin through the streets of Newark. Manson imported Bloods from California and Florida and hired them as enforcers and murder for hires. In total Federal officials have rounded up nearly two hundred men. Many more are being sought. The investigation continues.

Smoke feels like a living piece of shit right now. His status in the streets was legendary until this ordeal. Now he will go down as a dishonorable rat. His legacy has been destroyed. His name will never be spoken of in honor again.

Back when he murdered the Mayor it was his choice to either testify on the Mayor or murder him. Of course he chose the latter. By murdering him, he felt that he kept his name in good standing.

Smoke foolishly thought he did the favor for them and they would wipe his slate clean and he could go on about his business. It wasn't until months later when they arrived at his doorstep that he understood differently. They told him they had a job for him. Their threats of bringing up the old case made him do exactly what they needed of him. The jobs didn't stop there. They came back again and again. It was as if they were never going to be done with him.

Once Manson came home Smoke stayed clear from them, even denied their calls. The last thing he wanted was for his cousin to find out that he crossed over. He knew that would get him an early grave. Once Manson got wind of it all he knew things between them would never be the same. He also knew his days were numbered from that very second because it wouldn't be long before everything was revealed.

In the beginning when Smoke declared war against Manson it was more like committing suicide. He didn't want to live with the fact that the streets would know him as a stool pigeon-rat. He also didn't want to live without his sister. He contemplated his own suicide but as many times as he pulled that trigger in the past he didn't have the heart to pull it on himself.

He knew making threats to Manson was the easiest way to get taken out of his misery. A few days later after thinking it all over he decided that he didn't want to die because he had way too much living to do. He also knew the war that he declared with Manson could never be taken back. He knew for certain that the Haitian Bloods as well as any other Blood that Manson had in his network would be out hunting for his head.

It was then that he made the phone call to the agents. He told them he had two big cases for them but once he rolled over he would never be able to walk the streets of Newark or anywhere near New Jersey ever again. Smoke slaughtered everybody who knew to ever be associated with Manson, not in the murder sense but in the sense of telling on them. He told on every Blood that Manson made a move with and even Vito and his OG. He didn't want to take the risk of them hunting for his head later.

Smoke told everything without leaving out a single detail. The only thing he didn't tell is that in which he didn't know. There was very little that he didn't know such as the out of town plugs that Manson had buying the dope. Another detail that he had no knowledge of are the real names of Helter and Skelter.

He gave them the nicknames but he had no real information on them not even where they are originally from. Smoke is sure that Helter, Skelter and whatever others that he didn't know from out of town would be the ones that Manson would use to hunt him down. The shame of his cowardly act coupled with his paranoia of being tracked down made him certain that he needed to be relocated. He explained to them that he needed to solidify himself a lucrative situation wherever they relocated him to just so he never, ever had to come back to Newark for as long as he lives.

Smoke can't believe that he has sunk so low. He sulks in self-hatred for a few seconds before he finds justification for his actions. He thinks of his sister that is no longer here and he thinks of the loyalty that he has also displayed toward Manson. He thinks of how Manson never showed him the love that he feels he deserved.

In minutes his self hatred session is over and he has found all the justification he needs to live on without regret. Little by little he makes himself believe that what he did is no strike against his gangster because Manson deserved it. Even though he doesn't believe it himself, this will be what he rides on for the rest of his life. He sighs deeply. His hand is grasped onto tightly. He looks over to his right and there Jada sits with a warmness in her eyes that makes him feel better. She grips his hand tighter for support.

Without words, through her eyes she makes him feel like a man when he really feels like a mouse. With the whole world now against him, he's sure one day he will be good, just as long as he has her by his side.

HUNDREDS OF MILES AWAY

Tony paces around his desk with his eyes glued onto the newspaper article. His heart rips through his chest as he reads the details slowly, careful not to miss anything that could possibly tie him into this case. He's full of regret for even dealing with Manson from the very beginning. The thoughts of that late night keep creeping into his mind. He hears the gunshots over and over in his head. He reads the last line over and over. "Many more being sought. The investigation continues." At this point all he can do is pray that he is not of the many more being sought.

Tony stops in front of Dre, who sits at his desk. He lays the article in front of Dre for him to read. By pure coincidence Dre just happened to be here at the time of Tony finding all this out. After being fed up with Tony ignoring his calls, Dre decided to come to the office and demand that Tony introduce him and Manson.

Dre hasn't been anywhere near here since the day he jumped into the Hudson River and escaped the feds. Dre reads the article, careful not to miss a single word. When he's done he looks up to Tony with his mouth stretched wide open. It's as if it was meant for him to see this with his own eyes. He takes it all as a sign for him to stay away from the game.

"Now will you thank me for not introducing you to him? You complain, saying you're down because you don't have the money you're used to. I see it differently, though. In my eyes each day you're alive and free, you're *up*. Rather wake up broke than to wake up in prison. Each day you have your freedom, you have the chance to turn it all around."

Dre is speechless. He listens to Tony with his undivided attention. "Thanks, bruh."

The Dominican that Smoke and Manson refers to as 'The Chef' sits at the head of the table as the overseer. He's surrounded by two older Dominican men, three older Dominican women and two young women. Hospital masks cover all of their faces to prevent the intake of the raw dope. Every one of them have a mound of dope in front of them and a smaller mound of the Dominican rat poison.

The Chef keeps his eyes on this table as well as the table in the dining room. From where he's seated he can view both at the same time. He doesn't trust any of them when it comes to this dope. He can't take the risk of someone stealing and costing him his life. The table full of young Dominican girls have one responsibility and that is bundling up the packets of dope and taping them into a 50 packet brick.

In total there are three kilos of the dope that haven't even been opened yet. On the kitchen table they have two kilos spread out in the mounds. On the dining room table amongst the seven women there are approximately 500,000 bags (10,000 bricks) of Block Party, packaged, stamped and ready to hit the street.

The Chef has learned long ago that in this game patience is the virtue. The saying get down or lay down never made much sense to him until running across Manson and Smoke. He totally understood that this is their town and he should play by their rules if he wanted to continue eating. He exerted patience and now look; he's the last man standing.

The smoke has cleared and here he is with about 15 kilos of the purest dope he's ever had in his career. With Manson and Smoke in custody and nobody to give the dope to, he sees it all as a come-up. He's played his position and it all paid off. Now he can take the city back over, with them out of his hair. He hadn't planned it to go like this but he has no problem that it has.

In a perfect world he would sell all the heroin and take over the city once again but in a perfect world guys like Smoke wouldn't exist. The sound of the front and back door being knocked off the hinges at the same time destroys his hopes of every thing going perfectly from here. The Chef stands up as if he's looking for an escape. The words that are shouted loudly, "FBI!" is confirmation that a perfect world doesn't exist.

TWO HOURS LATER/HOUSTON TEXAS

The federal agents lead the way of the jet. Smoke and Jada step out hand in hand. Smoke grips a duffle bag in his other hand. In the bag he has four hundred thousand dollars of his own money and the 1.4 million that he stole during the break in at Jada and Manson's house. He still hasn't told her that he was behind the caper. Not that she would even care if he did.

Two black tinted out Suburbans sit a few feet away from them. Agent Dumber opens the back door for Smoke and Jada to enter. Jade slides in first and Smoke slides in behind her. Agent Dumber slams the door shut and gets into the front seat. Agents Dumbest and the other agent walk to the Suburban in front. The Suburban in front pulls off first. Before the driver follows behind he turns around in his seat. The young white man smiles from ear to ear. "Hey, Smoke. How are you?"

Smoke squints his eyes just to make sure that he's seeing correctly. He's as familiar with this man as he is familiar with anyone from his team. Day in and day out they have been around each other for years and never would he have expected this. The man in the driver's seat is one of the Mormons.

He can't believe that all the while he's been thinking them to be innocent and just out there spreading the word but really they were Federal Agents. He thinks of all the Mormons who travel throughout the city day in and day out with no one paying the least bit of attention to them. All the while they are taking notes. Now he understands how Dumber and Dumbest knew about all the murders.

The Mormon's smile disappears. "I know its hard to believe, ain't it?" he asks before laughing demonically. He quickly mashes the gas pedal and catches up with the other Suburban. Smoke sits back caught up in thought and understanding that the game is no longer fair.

MINUTES LATER

The Suburbans are parked side by side in front of a newly constructed building. The Feds get out and Jada and Smoke follow. Once they are out of the truck the first thing Smoke takes notice to is the blood red Maserati Gran Tourismo that he bought from the dealer. Never getting the chance to drive it, he demanded that it be shipped wherever they relocated him to. That and a few other things were all apart of the situation that he designed for himself in return for cooperating.

The driver's side door of his Maserati opens and another familiar face presents itself. "Smoke, my man!" the Mormon shouts. Next to the Maserati is Manson's convertible Bentley. That door opens and another Mormon that Smoke has seen roaming throughout the city, gets out. Both Mormon's give Agent Dumber the keys.

Dumber tosses the keys to Smoke who catches them in midair. He's quite shocked. "His and hers!" Agent Dumbest says with a smile. "You and your lady there can now ride in luxury. You deserve it," he says as she steps toward the entrance of the building. "I know you may be feeling bad but don't be so hard on yourself. You've done us a favor as well as done yourself a favor."

Smoke looks up at the overhead sign as he steps under it. He reads it aloud. 'Barbie's Doll House.' Once he steps inside his eyes are laid upon the most beautiful bar that he's ever seen. Wall to wall mirrors, brand new hardwood floors, expensive curtains and platinum trimming grace the room. The smell of new everything lingers in the air.

"You like it?" Agent Dumbest asks.

"It's cool!" Smoke replies. He's uncertain about why they have brought him here.

"Glad you like it because it's yours."

"Huh?"

"Yeah, it's yours."

"We open for business tomorrow. Can you imagine the magnitude of the drug deals that transpire inside of a strip bar? Naked women breed money. This will be the central nervous system of all the crime in all of Texas. You can make yourself a living and at the same time you can help us."

Despair covers Smoke's face. Just when he thought he was done with them or they were done with him, the saga continues. After the case he just helped them crack and that's still not enough for them. They still want more. He thought he would be able to kick his feet back and live happily ever after with Jada but they have other plans for him.

Agent Dumbest speaks. "Get ready to put your game face on. We have a lot of work to do."

THE END

ACKNOWLEDGEMENTS

BACK AGAIN AFTER a brief layoff. First, I would like to thank God for the mercy that he has bestowed upon me. Never in a million years did I ever imagine I would be an author. Still to this day it's quite shocking to me. I think of all that I have been through in life and at the time I would question; why me? Now as a writer, I understand why me. All that I have been through has been material for the 13 years, 12 novels that I have written. I thank God for sparing my life on those streets and leading me out of the darkness. As a believer I want for my brother what I want for myself so I ask God to extend that same mercy on other good men who are looking for a way out, ameen!

Second, I have to thank my readers for your patience and your consistent support. My readers mean the world to me and it's you that inspire me to keep the pen blazing. Do understand that I am never, not writing, just may be caught up in the business aspect of it all. There's always work to do when you're doing it from an independent standpoint. Independence is all I know and wouldn't have it any other way.

I also want to thank my family and support system, my mother, my wife, my brother, my sister, my daughters, my aunts, my uncles, a host of cousins and friends. A fighter is only as strong as his cornermen. Having y'all behind me keeps my battery pack charged. As long as y'all believe in me I have no choice but to believe in myself.

To my wife, one of the biggest challenges was writing these books with a newborn baby on my lap but I did it. I thank you for the gift for she has made me a better man. Through her I learned more patience and another level of endurance. I love you!

13 years ago my brother and I built this publishing house with the intent of having something to pass down to our children. It's been a constant grind over the years but knowing the goal makes it all worth it. When I'm dead and gone I just want to have left behind a legacy that our children can continue to build upon. Fajr, Aziz, Nahla and Surah, all the ideas and plans we have for this company will take us two lifetimes to conquer. It's halftime for us. We are working our hardest but when that buzzer sounds

off it's up to y'all to jump in the game and lead the team to the championships. Always remember, regardless of what True 2 Life Forever!

Also have to thank the whole True 2 Life team from the reviewers to the graphics team and editors. I thank you all for putting up with my whip-popping. My goal is always perfection or close to it.

In closing, I would like to give a special thanks to all my readers behind those walls. As y'all should already know by now, y'all are the ink in my pen. Every word written is written with y'all in mind. Y'all been supporting me from day one and I want y'all to know that I am totally grateful. I can't respond to each letter but please know that none of what you have written to me was in vain. I appreciate it all.

Do understand that the goal in me writing this book was two fold. Of course I wrote it for your enjoyment and to ease your mind of the mental pressure you may be under but I also wrote it to give you a clear view of what today looks like on those streets. Let me add that I meant no disrespect to my own religion nor any other religion with what I have written in this book. I clearly just wanted to shine the light on what others see in a day like today.

We live in a time wherein religion seems to no longer be sacred. We live in a time where religion seems to be a mere form of a hustle. Religion is no longer guarded. It's mixed right on in with the dirt that one intends to do. Some may even see it as a gang or cult. Overall, the value of religion has seemed to depreciate. Today it's money rules over everything.

Whether you have been away for twenty years or one year, in this book you will get a glimpse of that game that you left behind. Understand that I write fiction but this is as close to fact as you will ever get. In that game there's no more loyalty or trust. It's a dog eat dog world and only the grimiest survive.

Through the Block Party series I have taken you through every aspect of the game and depending on what year you left the streets, you can pick up the book of that year and see what has changed since you left. Love, loyalty and honor no longer exists. There's no more G code. Everything goes!

From you reading this book I hope I have deterred you from even thinking about going back to the streets once you return home. Let me clear up any misconception you may have; there is nothing left for you out there. Whatever you didn't get, you won't get. The graveyards are filling up at a rapid pace and so are the Federal institutions.

Those streets, forget about them. Use the remaining time you may have to build a solid plan for the rest of your life. Although I'm quite grateful for how y'all have supported my career, I don't wish jail on anyone. I would rather your support from a freedom standpoint.

In closing I would like to salute all the standup, honorable men and women that are left in the world. That species of a human being is almost extinct. Always remember, true winners lose the same way they win, with their heads up and their chest out.

True 2 Life Salute!

STREET KNOWLEDGE BOOKSTORE BRINGS TO YOU AN EXCLUSIVE INTERVIEW WITH AL-SAADIQ BANKS

SKP: What's good Al?
ASB: Peace! Peace!

SKP: Man it's been a minute since you last dropped Young Gunz. Can you fill us in on what Al Saadiq Banks been doing?
ASB: Yeah, it's been a minute. I been concentrating on film and adapting my books into screenplay.

SKP: How much of your writing played a part of your growing up in New Jersey? And did your living in NJ feel as if you were locked in a box to where you couldn't get out?
ASB: All of my writing is based on me growing up in Newark, every aspect of my writing. Actually I never felt trapped wherein I couldn't get out. My mind doesn't work like that. Even as a kid I always saw myself as soaring to the next level. Never knew I would be a writer or really what I would do but I knew I would do something. Writing is just one of the many things that I have touched on in life. Before writing I was a boxer who had a pro boxing contract on the table. I also have an Engineering degree from College that I attended while indulging in a bunch of negativity on those streets. I'm also an art major wherein I graduated from a high school of the Arts. So, I say all that to say I have always taken education quite serious despite the lifestyle that I had chosen for myself. In my heart I was destined to get out, just wasn't sure how so I tried my hand at everything.

SKP: How much prison time did you serve for those who don't know? And when did you actually put the pen to the pad?

ASB: I thank God that I have never touched the prison. I had a couple of bumps and bruises but I have never done any time. I jailed on those streets, experiencing everything that comes with it. I was shot up in August of 1993 and August of 1994. I have been tied up over that money and I tied up for retaliation over that money. I did my time out there on the streets. I started writing back in 2002, just basically venting and letting it all out.

SKP: Let me ask this question because your fans and other authors have been wanting to know the answer to this question. Why haven't you signed anyone to your company?

ASB: I've never signed anyone to my company because I haven't gotten to where I want to be as of yet. Signing authors is a big responsibility that I watch others take lightly. I would never want to play with a person's career, understanding that their livelihood is in my hands. I'm definitely thinking of signing talent in the near future being that I finally have all the channels wide open. I also feel that I finally understand the business enough to publish others successfully.

SKP: What gets Al Saadiq Banks in a writing mode?
ASB: I'm always in writing mode. Finding the time to write is my struggle. If I could I would sit around and write all day long.

SKP: What do you think about today's urban writers? And do you have a favorite?

ASB: Honestly, I don't really do the industry like that so I don't really know what's out there as far as the quality of work nor the quality of the people producing the work. I kind of just do me and stay out of the way. The writers out there who I respect has nothing to do with their books and everything to do with their code of honor. I'm a man of principles. I don't care how many best sellers you have or how many platinum selling albums or how much money you got. None of that means anything to me. I judge a man by his principles and code of honor. As far as fiction, I have never really read a fiction book in totality. Fiction really isn't my twist. I enjoy books of conspiracy theory and self-motivational and business books. I also have stayed away from fiction fearing the fact that if I start I will begin to look at it as competition and want to outdo every book I read. I believe that may affect my craft by competing and not writing from my heart.

SKP: What's the difference between authors of 10 years ago, and now?

ASB: The only difference I can see in the authors of ten years ago and today is the fact that ten years ago we got out there and rubbed shoulders with our readers, trying to build a base. Today social media is the closest they will get to their readers.

SKP: What make your books so special?

ASB: I really can't answer what makes my books so special. All I know is I give every book my two hundred percent and I will never just give my readers anything for a buck. I've lived the life so that allows me to go in deeper than those who have not. Those elements together I believe helped me to build my base of readers.

SKP: What troubles you the most about the book game?

ASB: Politics of the game and distribution have always been the obstacles of the game for me. It's tough for an independent out here in this business because of the channels that are closed off for us. It's like the only way you can jump over certain hurdles is if you sign with the major publishing houses. It has gotten better over the years though with the internet though. The middleman is not as relevant as he used to be.

SKP: So tell your fans about the new book OUTLAW CHICK, and would this be a series?

ASB: No, Outlaw Chick is not a part of a series. It's a standalone project. It's different from my other books for a few reasons. It's a fast paced, action packed, Bonnie and Clyde story. I usually allow my stories to simmer and build up but I've learned over the years that the attention span of the young reader is decreasing. Some don't have time for the foreplay, they just want to rock out. In this book I rocked out from the start, hoping to attract a younger demographic and actually be able to hold their attention. Is it a Block Party? NO! LOL It's a total different vibe but if you enjoy my writing style you can appreciate it just as much as any one of my other projects. By adding in the female character as his accomplice my goal was to entice the female reader to want to read as well.

SKP: Another thing your fans want to know is why haven't you come out with the TRAUMA UNIT book?

ASB: This is the first time I heard about a book about the Trauma Unit. It never even crossed my mind. It's like the Trauma Unit was never planned. They just sort of popped up in the books. I don't know if you read Strapped or not but the unit was broke up in that book.

SKP: Block Party, No Exit, Sincerely Yours, Caught'Em Slippin, just to name a few is considered classic books. What will make OUTLAW CHICK add to that collection of classics?

ASB: I just write from my heart. I don't write with the intent that this one will be a classic and this one won't. The readers decide that. All I can do is my absolute best and hope the reader feels me.

SKP: What is it that AL Saadiq Banks have in line as far as projects?

ASB: Block Party 5 is due to release in a few months. Trust me, this book is everything that you are looking for! This Block Party 5 is one my favorite Block Party's just minus the Mayor. All the jewels and big money is there as well as some very thought provoking aspects. I am totally confident that this book will shut down the game for a minute. Also the Strapped film series as well as the Block Party movie is on the way. We are taking baby steps into this but we are working.

SKP: Well bruh, keep up the good work. Any last comments or shout outs?

ASB: I thank you for the interview and I would like to thank every dude behind the wall that has supported my career over the years. Understand that every time I sit down to pen a novel I do so with you in mind. I write to take a few hours of pressure off a dude's mind while he doing that time. I understand how close I was to being in that same position and because of that I don't take this gift for granted. I do this for US! As much as I appreciate your support, I would rather have you supporting my writing from the free side of the world. Also any stand-up solid dude that has the opportunity to read this interview, I beg you to salute the real solid stand-up dudes around you. It ain't many of us left so the ones who are, need to know that they are appreciated. The dishonorable have taken over the world and get praised and that may make one question if he chose the right path. Do understand that real dudes see you and appreciate you. Salute!

BOOK ORDER FORM

Purchase Information

Name: _____

Address: _____ City: _____

State: _____ Zip Code: _____

$14.95 - No Exit _____
$14.95 - Block Party _____
$14.95 - Sincerely Yours _____
$14.95 - Caught 'Em Slippin' _____
$14.95 - Block Party 2 _____
$14.95 - Block Party 3 _____
$14.95 - Strapped _____
$14.95 - Back 2 Bizness (Block Party 4) _____
$4.99 - Block Party (Comic) _____
$14.95 – Young Gunz _____
$14.95 - Outlaw Chick _____
$14.95 – Block Party 5k1.1 Book 1 _____
$14.95 – Block Party 5k1.1 Book 2 _____

Book Total: _____

Add $5.75 for shipping of up to 3 books.
Add $1.00 for each additional book. Free shipping for orders of 6 or more books.

Total included: _____

Make Checks/Money Orders payable to:
True 2 Life Publications - PO Box 8722 – Newark, NJ 07108

Made in the USA
Lexington, KY
30 July 2016